D0969022

The Western Hall of Fame

THE WESTERN HALL OF FAME

An Anthology of Classic
Western Stories Selected by
the Western Writers of America

Edited by
**BILL PRONZINI AND
MARTIN H. GREENBERG**

William Morrow and Company, Inc.
New York   1984

Wes

Wes,

C. 1

57794

CONTENTS

INTRODUCTION

A good Western story, as a past president of the Western Writers of America, Noel Loomis, once wrote, is one in which "an honest and competent attempt is made to portray the West with fidelity, in good taste and in an interesting manner . . . not sweet, not sordid, but as real as caked salt on a horse's withers." True enough. But how does one define that rara avis, the *great* Western story?

There is no easy answer to this question. But a partial one, perhaps, is that it is a story that truly captures the essence and scope of Western life; that makes the reader think and feel and ponder, in addition to entertaining him, and that lingers in his memory. And perhaps the degree of such a story's greatness can be measured in terms of the number of discerning readers who appreciate and respond to these qualities.

No more discerning body of readers exists anywhere, certainly, than those men and women who write Western fiction and nonfiction—the members of the Western Writers of America. Founded in 1952, WWA is an organization of professional authors, publishers, editors, agents, filmmakers, and affiliates (historical institutes, librarians, aficionados) dedicated to raising the standard and the standing of Western literature. Its active members past and present have produced many thousands of novels, short stories, articles, biographies, histories, films, and even successful Broadway plays. Most live in the West and know intimately its land, its people, its history, and, of course, its fiction.

With these facts in mind, we approached WWA's officers with the idea for *The Western Hall of Fame* and received their permission to use the WWA imprimatur and to send each member of the organization a letter ballot. That letter read in part:

> Dear WWA Member:
>
> The purpose of this letter is to invite you to participate in an exciting anthology project co-sponsored by the Western Writers of America, to be called *The Western Hall of Fame*. The book, which will be published by William Morrow & Company in early 1984, will consist of the best Western stories of all time as selected by a vote of those of you who write in the field.
>
> Please list below your five favorite stories and their authors, in order of preference. They may be of any type, from any period, by writers living or deceased; the only restriction is that they should be under 15,000 words in length. (You may also make additional selections on the back of this sheet, if you wish.)

We received a substantial number of ballots in response to this request, along with enthusiastic support of the project. The stories you are about to read are those that received the highest number of the votes cast.

For the record, the top five selections were (first-place votes, followed by total votes, in parentheses):

"Pasó por Aquí," Eugene Manlove Rhodes (9,16)
"Lost Sister," Dorothy M. Johnson (7,15)
"Stage to Lordsburg," Ernest Haycox (6,15)
"A Man Called Horse," Dorothy M. Johnson (4,13)
"The Blue Hotel," Stephen Crane (4,12)

It should be noted that "Pasó por Aquí," Eugene Manlove Rhodes' masterpiece of characterization and realism, is quite a bit longer than 15,000 words. Omitting it because of its length, however, would have been unconscionable. If it is not the greatest of all Western short fiction, it unquestionably ranks among the top five. Without it, *The Western Hall of Fame* would not be the book it is.

For similar reasons, we have included a pair of stories each by two other acknowledged giants of Western fiction, Ernest Haycox and Dorothy M. Johnson. Both "Stage to Lordsburg" (on which the classic film *Stagecoach* is based) and "A Day in Town" by Haycox, and both "Lost Sister" and "A Man Called Horse" by Johnson, received numerous votes and are of equal quality. To have eliminated one story by each would have been unfair to both writers.

As we had hoped when we embarked on this project, the balloting was more or less evenly divided between the older Western story ("Pasó por Aquí," "The Blue Hotel," "The Outcasts of Poker Flat," "The Notorious Jumping Frog of Calaveras County," "Tappan's Burro," "An Afternoon Miracle," "Wine on the Desert") and the contemporary Western story (the two each by Haycox and Johnson, "Outlaw Trail," "Stubby Pringle's Christmas," "Blood on the Sun," "The Winter of His Life," "The Indian Well," "Isley's Stranger"). Nor could we have asked for a better balance of story types, themes, settings, and periods of Western history.

Equally diverse is the lineup of authors. Although not noted for their Western stories per se, Mark Twain and Stephen Crane were among the pioneers of the form and wrote some of its best fiction. Three other literary writers, Bret Harte, O. Henry, and Walter Van Tilburg Clark, *are* noted for their Western fiction—Harte and Henry for their short stories, Clark most prominently for that brilliant novel of the dark side of human emotions, *The Ox-Bow Incident*. Zane Grey and Max Brand (Frederick Faust) were the most prolific and popular writers on Old West themes in the early years of the century, Grey with such novels as *Riders of the*

Purple Sage and *Arizona Ames,* Brand with his many fine pulp tales and novels (*The Untamed, Destry Rides Again*). Eugene Manlove Rhodes published several other works of high literary merit, among them *The Proud Sheriff* and *Stepsons of Light.* Such novels as *The Adventurers* and such collections as *Murder on the Frontier* and *Rough Justice* have been read by millions of Ernest Haycox fans.

Jack Schaefer's *Shane* is considered one of the four or five best traditional Western novels ever written, and his short stories have received almost as much critical acclaim. Dorothy M. Johnson's short stories have also been widely lauded, and several—"The Hanging Tree," "The Man Who Shot Liberty Valance," "A Man Called Horse"—have been made into successful films. S. Omar Barker has been called "the poet laureate of the Old West"; hundreds of his rhymes have appeared over the past fifty years, along with many fine short stories. Thomas Thompson has won two Best Short Story Spur Awards from the Western Writers of America, and has contributed a number of outstanding novels to the literature of the Old West. Lewis B. Patten was likewise a highly popular novelist, with such excellent books as *A Killing in Kiowa* to his credit. And Clay Fisher (also known as Will Henry and Henry Wilson Allen) is unquestionably one of today's finest writers of Western historical fiction, having been the recipient of no less than four Spur Awards, including two Best Novel Spurs for *From Where the Sun Now Stands* and *Gates of the Mountains.*

These seventeen stories, then, thanks to the expertise and accommodation of the members of WWA who voted for them, are indeed the "best of the West" and richly deserve their enshrinement in this version of the Western Hall of Fame.

—BILL PRONZINI and MARTIN H. GREENBERG

March 1983

The Western
Hall of Fame

THE BLUE HOTEL

Stephen Crane

I

The Palace Hotel at Fort Romper was painted a light blue, a shade that is on the legs of a kind of heron, causing the bird to declare its position against any background. The Palace Hotel, then, was always screaming and howling in a way that made the dazzling winter landscape of Nebraska seem only a gray swampish hush. It stood alone on the prairie, and when the snow was falling, the town two hundred yards away was not visible. But when the traveler alighted at the railway station, he was obliged to pass the Palace Hotel before he could come upon the company of low clapboard houses which composed Fort Romper, and it was not to be thought that any traveler could pass the Palace Hotel without looking at it. Pat Scully, the proprietor, had proved himself a master of strategy when he chose his paints. It is true that on clear days, when the great transcontinental expresses, long lines of swaying Pullmans, swept through Fort Romper, passengers were overcome at the sight, and the cult that knows the brown reds and the subdivisions of the dark greens of the East expressed shame, pity, horror, in a laugh. But to the citizens of this prairie town and to the people who would naturally stop there, Pat Scully had performed a feat. With this opulence and splendor, these creeds, classes, egotisms, that streamed through Romper on the rails day after day, they had no color in common.

As if the displayed delights of such a blue hotel were not sufficiently enticing, it was Scully's habit to go every morning and evening to meet the leisurely trains that stopped at Romper and work his seductions upon any man that he might see wavering, gripsack in hand.

One morning, when a snow-crusted engine dragged its long string of freight cars and its one passenger coach to the station, Scully performed the marvel of catching three men. One was a shaky and quick-eyed Swede, with a great shining cheap valise; one was a tall bronzed cowboy, who was on his way to a ranch near the Dakota line; one was a little silent man from the East, who didn't look it and didn't announce it. Scully practically made them prisoners. He was so nimble and merry and kindly that each probably felt it would be the height of brutality to try to escape. They trudged off over the creaking board sidewalks in the wake of the eager little Irishman. He wore a heavy fur cap squeezed tightly down on his head. It caused his two red ears to stick out stiffly, as if they were made of tin.

At last, Scully, elaborately, with boisterous hospitality, conducted them through the portals of the blue hotel. The room which they entered was small. It seemed to be merely a proper temple for an enormous stove, which, in the center, was humming with godlike violence. At various points on its surface, the iron had become luminous and glowed yellow from the heat. Beside the stove Scully's son Johnnie was playing high-five with an old farmer who had whiskers both gray and sandy. They were quarreling. Frequently the old farmer turned his face toward a box of sawdust—colored brown from tobacco juice—that was behind the stove, and spat with an air of great impatience and irritation. With a loud flourish of words, Scully destroyed the game of cards and bustled his son upstairs with part of the baggage of the new guests. He himself conducted them to three basins of the coldest water in the world. The cowboy and the Easterner burnished themselves fiery red with this water, until it seemed to be some kind of metal polish. The Swede, however, merely dipped his fingers gingerly and with trepidation. It was notable that throughout this series of small ceremonies, the three travelers were made to feel that Scully was very benevolent. He was conferring great favors upon them. He handed the towel from one to another with an air of philanthropic impulse.

Afterward they went to the first room, and, sitting about the stove, listened to Scully's officious clamor at his daughters, who were preparing the midday meal. They reflected in the silence of experienced men who tread carefully amid new people. Nevertheless, the old farmer, stationary, invincible in his chair near the warmest part of the stove, turned his face from the sawdust box frequently and addressed a glowing commonplace to the strangers. Usually he was answered in short but adequate sentences by either the cowboy or the Easterner. The Swede said nothing. He seemed to be occupied in making furtive estimates of each man in the room. One might have thought that he had the sense of silly suspicion which comes to guilt. He resembled a badly frightened man.

Later, at dinner, he spoke a little, addressing his conversation entirely to Scully. He volunteered that he had come from New York where for ten years he had worked as a tailor. These facts seemed to strike Scully as fascinating, and afterward he volunteered that he had lived at Romper for fourteen years. The Swede asked about the crops and the price of labor. He seemed barely to listen to Scully's extended replies. His eyes continued to rove from man to man.

Finally, with a laugh and a wink, he said that some of these Western communities were very dangerous, and after his statement he straightened his legs under the table, tilted his head and laughed again, loudly. It was plain that the demonstration had no meaning to the others. They looked at him wondering and in silence.

II

As the men trooped heavily back into the front room, the two little windows presented views of a turmoiling sea of snow. The huge arms of the wind were making attempts— mighty, circular, futile—to embrace the flakes as they sped. A gatepost like a still man with a blanched face stood aghast amid this profligate fury. In a hearty voice Scully announced the presence of a blizzard. The guests of the blue hotel, lighting their pipes, assented with grunts of lazy masculine contentment. No island of the sea could be exempt in the degree of this little room with its humming stove. Johnnie, son of Scully, in a tone which defined his opinion of his ability as a cardplayer, challenged the old farmer of both gray and sandy whiskers to a game of high-five. The farmer agreed with a contemptuous and bitter scoff. They sat close to the stove, and squared their knees under a wide board. The cowboy and the Easterner watched the game with interest. The Swede remained near the window, aloof, but with a countenance that showed signs of an inexplicable excitement.

The play of Johnnie and the graybeard was suddenly ended by another quarrel. The old man arose while casting a look of heated scorn at his adversary. He slowly buttoned his coat, and then stalked with fabulous dignity from the room. In the discreet silence of all the other men, the Swede laughed. His laughter rang somehow childish. Men by this time had begun to look at him askance, as if they wished to inquire what ailed him.

A new game was formed jocosely. The cowboy volunteered to become the partner of Johnnie, and they all then turned to ask the Swede to throw in his lot with the little Easterner. He asked some questions about the game, and, learning that it wore many names, and that he had played it when it was under an alias, he accepted the invitation. He strode toward the men nervously, as if he expected to be assaulted. Finally, seated, he gazed from face to face and laughed shrilly. This laugh was so strange that the Easterner looked up quickly, the cowboy sat intent and with his mouth open, and Johnnie paused, holding the cards with still fingers.

Afterward there was a short silence. Then Johnnie said, "Well, let's get at it. Come on, now!" They pulled their chairs forward until their knees were bunched under the board. They began to play, and their interest in the game caused the others to forget the manner of the Swede.

The cowboy was a board whacker. Each time that he held superior cards he whanged them, one by one, with exceeding force, down upon the improvised table, and took the tricks with a glowing air of prowess and pride that sent thrills of indignation into the hearts of his opponents. A game with a board-whacker in it is sure to become intense. The countenances of the Easterner and the Swede were miserable whenever the cowboy thundered down his aces and kings, while Johnnie, his eyes gleaming with joy, chuckled and chuckled.

Because of the absorbing play none considered the strange ways of the Swede. They paid strict heed to the game. Finally, during a lull caused by a new deal, the Swede suddenly addressed Johnnie. "I suppose there have been a good many men killed in this room." The jaws of the others dropped and they looked at him.

"What in hell are you talking about?" said Johnnie.

The Swede laughed again his blatant laugh, full of a kind of false courage and defiance. "Oh, you know what I mean all right," he answered.

"I'm a liar if I do!" Johnnie protested. The card game was halted, and the men stared at the Swede. Johnnie evidently felt that as the son of the proprietor he should make a direct inquiry. "Now, what might you be drivin' at, mister?" he asked. The Swede winked at him. It was a wink full of cunning. His fingers shook on the edge of the board. "Oh, maybe you think I have been to nowheres. Maybe you think I'm a tenderfoot?"

"I don't know nothin' about you," answered Johnnie, "and I don't give a damn where you've been. All I got to say is that I don't know what you're driving at. There hain't never been nobody killed in this room."

The cowboy, who had been steadily gazing at the Swede, then spoke. "What's wrong with you, mister?"

Apparently it seemed to the Swede that he was formidably menaced. He shivered and turned white near the corners of his mouth. He sent an appealing glance in the direction of the little Easterner. During these moments he did not forget to wear his air of advanced pot-valor. "They say they don't know what I mean," he remarked mockingly to the Easterner.

The latter answered after prolonged and cautious reflection. "I don't understand you," he said impassively.

The Swede made a movement then which announced that he thought he had encountered treachery from the only quarter where he had expected sympathy, if not help. "Oh, I see you are all against me. I see—"

The cowboy was in a state of deep stupefaction. "Say," he cried, as he tumbled the deck violently down upon the board, "say, what are you gittin' at, hey?"

The Swede sprang up with the celerity of a man escaping from a snake on the floor. "I don't want to fight!" he shouted. "I don't want to fight!"

The cowboy stretched his long legs indolently and deliberately. His hands were in his pockets. He spat into the sawdust box. "Well, who the hell thought you did?" he inquired.

The Swede backed rapidly toward a corner of the room. His hands were out protectingly in front of his chest, but he was making an obvious struggle to control his fright. "Gentlemen," he quavered, "I suppose I am going to be killed before I can leave this house! I suppose I am going to be killed before I can leave this house!" In his eyes was the dying swan look. Through the windows could be seen the snow turning blue in the shadow of dusk. The wind tore at the house, and some loose thing beat regularly against the clapboards like a spirit tapping.

A door opened, and Scully himself entered. He paused in surprise as he noted the tragic attitude of the Swede. Then he said, "What's the matter here?"

The Swede answered him swiftly and eagerly, "These men are going to kill me."

"Kill you!" ejaculated Scully. "Kill you! What are you talkin'?"

The Swede made the gesture of a martyr.

Scully wheeled sternly upon his son. "What is this, Johnnie?"

The lad had grown sullen. "Damned if I know," he answered. "I can't make no sense to it." He began to shuffle the cards, fluttering them together with an angry snap. "He says a good many men have been killed in this room, or something like that. And he says he's goin' to be killed here too. I don't know what ails him. He's crazy, I shouldn't wonder."

Scully then looked for explanation to the cowboy, but the cowboy simply shrugged his shoulders.

"Kill you?" said Scully again to the Swede. "Kill you? Man, you're off your nut."

"Oh, I know," burst out the Swede. "I know what will happen. Yes, I'm crazy—yes. Yes, of course, I'm crazy—yes. But I know one thing—" There was a sort of sweat of misery and terror upon his face. "I know I won't get out of here alive."

The cowboy drew a deep breath, as if his mind was passing into the last sages of dissolution. "Well, I'm dog-goned," he whispered to himself

Scully wheeled suddenly and faced his son. "You've been troublin' this man!"

Johnnie's voice was loud with its burden of grievance. "Why, good Gawd, I ain't done nothin' to 'im."

The Swede broke in. "Gentlemen, do not disturb yourselves. I will leave this house. I will go away, because"—he accused them dramatically with his glance—"because I do not want to be killed."

Scully was furious with his son. "Will you tell me what is the matter, you young devil? What's the matter, anyhow? Speak out!"

"Blame it!" cried Johnnie in despair, "don't I tell you I don't know? He—he says we want to kill him, and that's all I know. I can't tell what ails him."

The Swede continued to repeat. "Never mind, Mr. Scully; never mind, I will leave this house. I will go away, because I do not wish to be killed. Yes, of course, I am crazy—yes. But I know one thing! I will go away. I will leave this house. Never mind, Mr. Scully; never mind. I will go away."

"You will not go 'way," said Scully. "You will not go 'way until I hear the reason of this business. If anybody has troubled you, I will take care of him. This is my house. You are under my roof, and I will not allow any peaceable man to be troubled here." He cast a terrible eye upon Johnnie, the cowboy and the Easterner.

"Never mind, Mr. Scully, never mind. I will go away. I do not wish to be killed." The Swede moved toward the door which opened upon the stairs. It was evidently his intention to go at once for his baggage.

"No, no," shouted Scully peremptorily; but the white-faced man slid by him and disappeared. "Now," said Scully severely, "what does this mean?"

Johnnie and the cowboy cried together, "Why, we didn't do nothin' to 'im!"

Scully's eyes were cold. "No," he said, "you didn't?"

Johnnie swore a deep oath. "Why, this is the wildest

loon I ever see. We didn't do nothin' at all. We were just sittin' here playin' cards, and he—"

The father suddenly spoke to the Easterner. "Mr. Blane," he asked, "what has these boys been doin'?"

The Easterner reflected again. "I didn't see anything wrong at all," he said at last slowly.

Scully began to howl. "But what does it mane?" He stared ferociously at his son. "I have a mind to lather you for this, me boy."

Johnnie was frantic. "Well, what have I done?" he bawled at his father.

III

"I think you are tongue-tied," said Scully finally to his son, the cowboy and the Easterner, and at the end of this scornful sentence, he left the room.

Upstairs the Swede was swiftly fastening the straps of his great valise. Once his back happened to be half turned toward the door, and, hearing a noise there, he wheeled and sprang up, uttering a loud cry. Scully's wrinkled visage showed grimly in the light of the small lamp he carried. This yellow effulgence, streaming upward, colored only his prominent features, and left his eyes, for instance, in mysterious shadow. He resembled a murderer.

"Man! man!" he exclaimed, "have you gone daffy?"

"Oh, no! Oh, no!" rejoined the other. "There are people in this world who know pretty nearly as much as you do—understand?"

For a moment they stood gazing at each other. Upon the Swede's deathly pale cheeks were two spots brightly crimson and sharply edged, as if they had been carefully painted. Scully placed the light on the table and sat himself on the edge of the bed. He spoke ruminatively. "By cracky, I never heard of such a thing in my life. It's a complete muddle. I can't, for the soul of me, think how you ever got this idea into your head." Presently he lifted his eyes and asked, "And did you sure think they were going to kill you?"

The Swede scanned the old man as if he wished to see into his mind. "I did," he said at last. He obviously suspected that this answer might precipitate an outbreak. As he pulled on a strap his whole arm shook, the elbow wavering like a bit of paper.

Scully banged his hand impressively on the footboard of the bed. "Why, man, we're goin' to have a line of ilictric streetcars in this town next spring."

" 'A line of electric streetcars,' " repeated the Swede stupidly.

"And," said Scully, "there's a new railroad goin' to be built down from Broken Arm to here. Not to mention the four churches and the smashin' big brick schoolhouse. Then there's the big factory, too. Why, in two years Romper'll be a met-tro-*pol*-is."

Having finished the preparation of his baggage, the Swede straightened himself. "Mr. Scully," he said, with sudden hardihood, "how much do I owe you?"

"You don't owe me anythin'," said the old man, angrily.

"Yes, I do," retorted the Swede. He took seventy-five cents from his pocket and tendered it to Scully; but the latter snapped his fingers in disdainful refusal. However, it happened that they both stood gazing in a strange fashion at three silver pieces on the Swede's open palm.

"I'll not take your money," said Scully at last. "Not after what's been goin' on here." Then a plan seemed to strike him. "Here," he cried, picking up his lamp and moving toward the door. "Here! Come with me a minute."

"No," said the Swede, in overwhelming alarm.

"Yes," urged the old man. "Come on! I want you to come and see a picter—just across the hall—in my room."

The Swede must have concluded that his hour was come. His jaw dropped and his teeth showed like a dead man's. He ultimately followed Scully across the corridor, but he had the step of one hung in chains.

Scully flashed the light high on the wall of his own

chamber. There was revealed a ridiculous photograph of a little girl. She was leaning against a balustrade of gorgeous decoration, and the formidable bang to her hair was prominent. The figure was as graceful as an upright sled stake, and, withal, it was of the hue of lead. "There," said Scully, tenderly, "that's the picter of my little girl that died. Her name was Carrie. She had the purtiest hair you ever saw. I was that fond of her, she—"

Turning then, he saw that the Swede was not contemplating the picture at all, but, instead, was keeping keen watch on the gloom in the rear.

"Look, man!" cried Scully, heartily "That's the picter of my little gal that died. Her name was Carrie. And then here's the picter of my oldest boy, Michael. He's a lawyer in Lincoln, an' doin' well. I gave that boy a grand eddication, and I'm glad for it now. He's a fine boy. Look at 'im now. Ain't he bold as blazes, him there in Lincoln, an honored an' respicted gintelman! An honored and respected gentleman," concluded Scully with a flourish. And, so saying, he smote the Swede jovially on the back.

The Swede faintly smiled.

"Now," said the old man, "there's only one more thing." He dropped suddenly to the floor and thrust his hand beneath the bed. The Swede could hear his muffled voice. "I'd keep it under me piller if it wasn't for that boy Johnnie. Then there's the old woman—Where is it now? I never put it twice in the same place. Ah, now come out with you!"

Presently he backed clumsily from under the bed, dragging with him an old coat rolled into a bundle. "I've fetched him," he muttered. Kneeling on the floor, he unrolled the coat and extracted from its heart a large yellow brown whisky bottle.

His first maneuver was to hold the bottle up to the light. Reassured, apparently, that nobody had been tampering with it, he thrust it with a generous movement toward the Swede.

The weak-kneed Swede was about to eagerly clutch this

element of strength, but he suddenly jerked his hand away and cast a look of horror upon Scully.

"Drink," said the old man affectionately. He had risen to his feet, and now stood facing the Swede.

There was a silence. Then again Scully said, "Drink!"

The Swede laughed wildly. He grabbed the bottle, put it to his mouth, and as his lips curled absurdly around the opening and his throat worked, he kept his glance, burning with hatred, upon the old man's face.

IV

After the departure of Scully the three men, with the cardboard still upon their knees, preserved for a long time an astounded silence. Then Johnnie said, "That's the dad-dangedest Swede I ever see."

"He ain't no Swede," said the cowboy scornfully.

"Well, what is he then?" cried Johnnie. "What is he then?"

"It's my opinion," replied the cowboy deliberately, "he's some kind of a Dutchman." It was a venerable custom of the country to entitle as Swedes all light-haired men who spoke with a heavy tongue. In consequence the idea of the cowboy was not without its daring. "Yes, sir," he repeated. "It's my opinion this feller is some kind of a Dutchman."

"Well, he says he's a Swede, anyhow," muttered Johnnie, sulkily. He turned to the Easterner. "What do you think, Mr. Blane?"

"Oh, I don't know," replied the Easterner.

"Well, what do you think makes him act that way?" asked the cowboy.

"Why, he's frightened." The Easterner knocked his pipe against a rim of the stove. "He's clear frightened out of his boots."

"What at?" cried Johnnie and the cowboy together.

The Easterner reflected over his answer.

"What at?" cried the others again.

"Oh, I don't know, but it seems to me this man has been reading dime novels, and he thinks he's right out in the middle of it—the shootin' and stabbin' and all."

"But," said the cowboy, deeply scandalized, "this ain't Wyoming, ner none of them places. This is Nebrasker."

"Yes," added Johnnie, "an' why don't he wait till he gits *out West?*"

The traveled Easterner laughed. "It isn't different there even—not in these days. But he thinks he's right in the middle of hell."

Johnnie and the cowboy mused long.

"It's awful funny," remarked Johnnie at last.

"Yes," said the cowboy. "This is a queer game. I hope we don't git snowed in, because then we'd have to stand this here man bein' around with us all the time. That wouldn't be no good."

"I wish pop would throw him out," said Johnnie.

Presently they heard a loud stamping on the stairs, accompanied by ringing jokes in the voice of old Scully, and laughter, evidently from the Swede. The men around the stove stared vacantly at each other. "Gosh!" said the cowboy. The door flew open, and old Scully, flushed and anecdotal, came into the room. He was jabbering at the Swede, who followed him, laughing bravely. It was the entry of two roisterers from a banquet hall.

"Come now," said Scully sharply to the three seated men, "move up and give us a chance at the stove." The cowboy and the Easterner obediently sidled their chairs to make room for the newcomers. Johnnie, however, simply arranged himself in a more indolent attitude, and then remained motionless.

"Come! Git over there," said Scully.

"Plenty of room on the other side of the stove," said Johnnie.

"Do you think we want to sit in the draught?" roared the father.

But the Swede here interposed with a grandeur of confidence. "No, no. Let the boy sit where he likes," he cried in a bullying voice to the father.

"All right! All right!" said Scully, deferentially. The cowboy and the Easterner exchanged glances of wonder.

The five chairs were formed in a crescent about one side of the stove. The Swede began to talk; he talked arrogantly, profanely, angrily. Johnnie, the cowboy and the Easterner maintained a morose silence, while old Scully appeared to be receptive and eager, breaking in constantly with sympathetic ejaculations.

Finally the Swede announced that he was thirsty. He moved in his chair, and said that he would go for a drink of water.

"I'll git it for you," cried Scully at once.

"No," said the Swede, contemptuously. "I'll get it for myself." He arose and stalked with the air of an owner off into the executive parts of the hotel.

As soon as the Swede was out of hearing, Scully sprang to his feet and whispered intensely to the others. "Upstairs he thought I was tryin' to poison 'im."

"Say," said Johnnie, "this makes me sick. Why don't you throw 'im out in the snow?"

"Why, he's all right now," declared Scully. "It was only that he was from the East, and he thought this was a tough place. That's all. He's all right now."

The cowboy looked with admiration upon the Easterner. "You were straight," he said. "You were on to that there Dutchman."

"Well," said Johnnie to his father, "he may be all right now, but I don't see it. Other time he was scared, but now he's too fresh."

Scully's speech was always a combination of Irish brogue and idiom, Western twang and idiom, and scraps of curiously formal diction taken from the storybooks and newspapers. He now hurled a strange mass of language at the head of his son. "What do I keep? What do I keep? What do I keep?" he demanded, in a voice of thunder. He slapped his knee impresisvely, to indicate that he himself was going to make reply, and that all should heed. "I keep a hotel," he shouted. "A hotel, do you mind? A guest under my roof has sacred privileges. He is to be intimidated by none. Not one word shall he hear that would prijudice him in favor of goin' away. I'll not have it. There's no place in this here town where they can say they iver took in a guest of mine because he was afraid to stay here." He wheeled suddenly upon the cowboy and the Easterner. "Am I right?"

"Yes, Mr. Scully," said the cowboy, "I think you're right."

"Yes, Mr. Scully," said the Easterner, "I think you're right."

V

At six o'clock supper, the Swede fizzed like a fire wheel. He sometimes seemed on the point of bursting into riotous song, and in all his madness he was encouraged by old Scully. The Easterner was encased in reserve; the cowboy sat in wide-mouthed amazement, forgetting to eat, while Johnnie wrathily demolished great plates of food. The daughters of the house, when they were obliged to replenish the biscuits, approached as warily as Indians, and, having succeeded in their purpose, fled with ill-concealed trepidation. The Swede domineered the whole feast, and he gave it the appearance of a cruel bacchanal. He seemed to have grown suddenly taller; he gazed, brutally disdainful, into every face. His voice rang through the room. Once when he jabbed out harpoon-fashion with his fork to pinion a biscuit, the weapon nearly impaled the hand of the Easterner, which had been stretched quietly out for the same biscuit.

After supper, as the men filed toward the other room, the Swede smote Scully ruthlessly on the shoulder. "Well, old boy, that was a good, square meal." Johnnie looked hopefully at his father; he knew that shoulder was tender from an old fall; and, indeed, it appeared for a moment as if Scully was going to flame out over the matter, but in the end he smiled a sickly smile and remained silent. The others understood from his manner that he was admitting his responsibility for the Swede's new viewpoint.

Johnnie, however, addressed his parent in an aside. "Why don't you license somebody to kick you downstairs?" Scully scowled darkly by way of reply.

When they were gathered about the stove, the Swede insisted on another game of high-five. Scully gently deprecated the plan at first, but the Swede turned a wolfish glare upon him. The old man subsided, and the Swede canvassed the others. In his tone there was always a great threat. The cowboy and the Easterner both remarked indifferently that they would play. Scully said that he would presently have to go to meet the 6:58 train, and so the Swede turned menacingly upon Johnnie. For a moment their glances crossed like blades, and then Johnnie smiled and said, "Yes, I'll play."

They formed a square, with the little board on their knees. The Easterner and the Swede were again partners. As the play went on, it was noticeable that the cowboy was not board whacking as usual. Meanwhile, Scully, near the lamp, had put on his spectacles and, with an appearance curiously like an old priest, was reading a newspaper. In time he went out to meet the 6:58 train, and, despite his precautions, a gust of polar wind whirled into the room as he opened the door. Besides scattering the cards, it chilled the players to the marrow. The Swede cursed frightfully. When Scully returned, his entrance disturbed a cozy and friendly scene. The Swede again cursed. But presently they were once more intent, their heads bent forward and their hands moving swiftly. The Swede had adopted the fashion of board-whacking.

Scully took up his paper and for a long time remained immersed in matters which were extraordinarily remote from him. The lamp burned badly, and once he stopped to adjust the wick. The newspaper, as he turned from page to page, rustled with a slow and comfortable sound. Then suddenly he heard three terrible words. "You are cheatin'!"

Such scenes often prove that there can be little of dramatic import in environment. Any room can present a tragic front, any room can be comic. This little den was now hideous as a torture chamber. The new faces of the men themselves had changed it upon the instant the Swede held a huge fist in front of Johnnie's face, while the latter looked steadily over it into the blazing orbs of his accuser. The Easterner had grown pallid; the cowboy's jaw had dropped in that expression of bovine amazement which was one of his important mannerisms. After the three words, the first sound in the room was made by Scully's paper as it floated forgotten to his feet. His spectacles had also fallen from his nose, but by a clutch he had saved them in air. His hand, grasping the spectacles, now remained poised awkwardly and near his shoulder. He stared at the cardplayers.

Probably the silence was while a second elapsed. Then, if the floor had been suddenly twitched out from under the men, they could not have moved quicker. The five had projected themselves headlong toward a common point. It happened that Johnnie, in rising to hurl himself upon the Swede, had stumbled slightly because of his curiously instinctive care for the cards and the board. The loss of the moment allowed time for the arrival of Scully, and also allowed the cowboy time to give the Swede a great push which sent him staggering back. The men found tongue together, and hoarse shouts of rage, appeal or fear burst from every throat. The cowboy pushed and jostled feverishly at the Swede, and the Easterner and Scully clung wildly to Johnnie; but through the smoky air, above the swaying bodies of the peace-compellers, the eyes of the two warriors ever sought each other in glances of challenge that were at once hot and steely.

Of course the board had been overturned, and now the whole company of cards was scattered over the floor, where the boots of the men trampled the fat and painted kings and queens as they gazed with their silly eyes at the war that was waging above them.

Scully's voice was dominating the yells. "Stop now! Stop, I say! Stop, now—"

Johnnie, as he struggled to burst through the rank formed by Scully and the Easterner, was crying, "Well, he says I cheated! He says I cheated! I won't allow no man to say I cheated! If he says I cheated, he's a————!"

The cowboy was telling the Swede, "Quit, now! Quit, d'ye hear—"

The screams of the Swede never ceased. "He did cheat! I saw him! I saw him—"

As for the Easterner, he was importuning in a voice that was not heeded. "Wait a moment, can't you? Oh, wait a moment. What's the good of a fight over a game of cards? Wait a moment—"

In this tumult no complete sentences were clear. "Cheat"—"quit"—"he says"—these fragments pierced the uproar and rang out sharply. It was remarkable that, whereas Scully undoubtedly made the most noise, he was the least heard of any of the riotous band.

Then suddenly there was a great cessation. It was as if each man had paused for breath; and although the room was still lighted with the anger of men, it could be seen that there was no danger of immediate conflict, and at once Johnnie, shouldering his way forward, almost succeeded in confronting the Swede. "What did you say I cheated for? What did you say I cheated for? I don't cheat, and I won't let no man say I do!"

The Swede said, "I saw you! I saw you!"

"Well," cried Johnnie. "I'll fight any man what says I cheat!"

"No, you won't," said the cowboy. "Not here."

"Ah, be still, can't you?" said Scully, coming between them.

The quiet was sufficient to allow the Easterner's voice to be heard. He was repeating. "Oh, wait a moment, can't you? What's the good of a fight over a game of cards? Wait a moment!"

Johnnie, his red face appearing above his father's shoulder, hailed the Swede again. "Did you say I cheated?"

The Swede showed his teeth. "Yes."

"Then," said Johnnie, "we must fight."

"Yes, fight," roared the Swede. He was like a demoniac. "Yes, fight! I'll show you what kind of a man I am! I'll show you who you want to fight! Maybe you think I can't fight! Maybe you think I can't! I'll show you, you skin, you cardsharp. Yes, you cheated! You cheated! You cheated!"

"Well, let's go at it, then, mister," said Johnnie coolly.

The cowboy's brow was beaded with sweat from his efforts in intercepting all sorts of raids. He turned in despair to Scully. "What are you goin' to do now?"

A change had come over the Celtic visage of the old man. He now seemed all eagerness, his eyes glowed.

"We'll let them fight," he answered, stalwartly. "I can't put up with it any longer. I've stood this damned Swede till I'm sick. We'll let them fight."

VI

The men prepared to go out of doors. The Easterner was so nervous that he had great difficulty in getting his arms into the sleeves of his new leather coat. As the cowboy drew his fur cap down over his ears, his hands trembled. In fact, Johnnie and old Scully were the only ones who displayed no agitation. These preliminaries were conducted without words.

Scully threw open the door. "Well, come on," he said. Instantly a terrific wind caused the flame of the lamp to struggle at its wick, while a puff of black smoke sprang from the chimney top. The stove was in mid-current of the blast, and its voice swelled to equal the roar of the storm. Some of the scarred and bedabbled cards were caught up from the floor and dashed helplessly against the farther wall. The men lowered their heads and plunged into the tempest as into a sea.

No snow was falling, but great whirls and clouds of flakes, swept up from the ground by the frantic winds, were streaming southward with the speed of bullets. The covered land was blue with the sheen of an unearthly satin, and there was no other hue save where, at the low black railway station—which seemed incredibly distant—one light gleamed like a tiny jewel. As the men floundered into a thigh-deep drift, it was known that the Swede was bawling out something. Scully went to him, put a hand on his shoulder and projected an ear. "What's that you say?" he shouted.

"I say," bawled the Swede again, "I won't stand much show against this gang. I know you'll all pitch on me."

Scully smote him reproachfully on the arm. "Tut, man!" he yelled. The wind tore the words from Scully's lips and scattered them far alee.

"You are all a gang of—" boomed the Swede, but the storm also seized the remainder of this sentence.

Immediately turning their backs upon the wind, the men had swung around a corner to the sheltered side of the hotel. It was the function of the little house to preserve here, amid this great devastation of snow, an irregular V-shape of heavily encrusted grass, which crackled beneath the feet. One could imagine the great drifts piled against the windward side. When the party reached the comparative peace of this spot, it was found that the Swede was still bellowing.

"Oh, I know what kind of a thing this is! I know you'll all pitch on me. I can't lick you all!"

Scully turned upon him panther fashion. "You'll not have to whip all of us. You'll have to whip my son Johnnie. An' the man what troubles you durin' that time will have me to deal with."

The arrangements were swiftly made. The two men faced each other, obedient to the harsh commands of Scully, whose face, in the subtly luminous gloom, could be seen set in the austere impersonal lines that are pictured on the countenances of the Roman veterans. The Easterner's teeth were chattering, and he was hopping up and down like a mechanical toy. The cowboy stood rocklike.

The contestants had not stripped off any clothing. Each was in his ordinary attire. Their fists were up, and they eyed each other in a calm that had the elements of leonine cruelty in it.

During this pause, the Easterner's mind, like a film, took lasting impressions of three men—the iron-nerved master of the ceremony; the Swede, pale, motionless, terrible; and Johnnie, serene yet ferocious, brutish yet heroic. The entire prelude had in it a tragedy greater than the tragedy of action, and this aspect was accentuated by the long, mellow cry of the blizzard as it sped the tumbling and wailing flakes into the black abyss of the south.

"Now!" said Scully.

The two combatants leaped forward and crashed together like bullocks. There was heard the cushioned sound of blows, and of a curse squeezing out from between the tight teeth of one.

As for the spectators, the Easterner's pent-up breath exploded from him with a pop of relief, absolute relief from the tension of the preliminaries. The cowboy bounded into the air with a yowl. Scully was immovable as from supreme amazement and fear at the fury of the fight which he himself had permitted and arranged.

For a time the encounter in the darkness was such a perplexity of flying arms that it presented no more detail than would a swiftly revolving wheel. Occasionally, a face, as if illuminated by a flash of light, would shine out, ghastly and marked with pink spots. A moment later, the men might have been known as shadows if it were not for the involuntary utterance of oaths that came from them in whispers.

Suddenly a holocaust of warlike desire caught the cowboy, and he bolted forward with the speed of a bronco. "Go it, Johnnie! Go it! Kill him! Kill him!"

Scully confronted him. "Kape back," he said, and by his glance the cowboy could tell that this man was Johnnie's father.

To the Easterner there was a monotony of unchangeable fighting that was an abomination. This confused mingling was eternal to his sense, which was concentrated in a longing for the end, the priceless end. Once the fighters lurched near him, and as he scrambled hastily backward he heard them breathe like men on the rack.

"Kill him, Johnnie! Kill him! Kill him! Kill him!" The cowboy's face was contorted like one of those agony masks in museums.

"Keep still," said Scully icily.

Then there was a sudden loud grunt, incomplete, cut short, and Johnnie's body swung away from the Swede and fell with sickening heaviness to the grass. The cowboy was barely in time to prevent the mad Swede from flinging himself upon his prone adversary. "No, you don't," said the cowboy, interposing an arm. "Wait a second."

Scully was at his son's side. "Johnnie! Johnnie, me boy!" His voice had a quality of melancholy tenderness. "Johnnie! Can you go on with it?" he looked anxiously down into the bloody, pulpy face of his son.

There was a moment of silence, and then Johnnie answered in his ordinary voice. "Yes, I—it—yes."

Assisted by his father he struggled to his feet. "Wait a bit now till you git your wind," said the old man.

A few paces away the cowboy was lecturing the Swede. "No, you don't! Wait a second!"

The Easterner was plucking at Scully's sleeve. "Oh, this is enough," he pleaded. "This is enough! Let it go as it stands. This is enough!"

"Bill," said Scully, "git out of the road." The cowboy stepped aside. "Now." The combatants were actuated by a new caution as they advanced toward collision. They glared at each other, and then the Swede aimed a lightning blow that carried with it his entire weight. Johnnie was evidently half stupid from weakness, but he miraculously dodged, and his fist sent the overbalanced Swede sprawling.

The cowboy, Scully and the Easterner burst into a cheer that was like a chorus of triumphant soldiery, but before its conclusion the Swede had scuffed agilely to his feet and come in berserk abandon at his foe. There was another perplexity of flying arms, and Johnnie's body again swung away and fell, even as a bundle might fall from a roof. The Swede instantly staggered to a little wind-waved tree and leaned upon it, breathing like an engine, while his savage and flame-lit eyes roamed from face to face as the men bent over Johnnie. There was a splendor of isolation in his situation at this time which the Easterner felt once when, lifting his eyes from the man on the ground, he beheld that mysterious and lonely figure, waiting.

"Are you any good yet, Johnnie?" asked Scully in a broken voice.

The son gasped and opened his eyes languidly. After a moment he answered, "No—I ain't—any good—any—more." Then from shame and bodily ill, he began to weep, the tears furrowing down through the bloodstains on his face. "He was too—too—heavy for me."

Scully straightened and addressed the waiting figure. "Stranger," he said, evenly, "it's all up with our side." Then his voice changed into that vibrant huskiness which is commonly the tone of the most simple and deadly announcements. "Johnnie is whipped."

Without replying, the victor moved off on the route to the front door of the hotel.

The cowboy was formulating new and unspellable blasphemies. The Easterner was startled to find that they were out in a wind that seemed to come direct from the shadowed arctic floes. He heard again the wail of the snow as it was flung to its grave in the south. He knew now that all this time the cold had been sinking into him deeper and deeper, and he wondered that he had not perished. He felt indifferent to the condition of the vanquished man.

"Johnnie, can you walk?" asked Scully.

"Did I hurt—hurt him any?" asked the son.

"Can you walk, boy? Can you walk?"

Johnnie's voice was suddenly strong. There was a robust impatience in it. "I asked you whether I hurt him any!"

"Yes, yes, Johnnie," answered the cowboy, consolingly, "he's hurt a good deal."

They raised him from the ground, and as soon as he was on his feet, he went tottering off, rebuffing all attempts at assistance. When the party rounded the corner, they were fairly blinded by the pelting of the snow. It burned their faces like fire. The cowboy carried Johnnie through the drift to the door. As they entered, some cards rose from the floor and beat against the wall.

The Easterner rushed to the stove. He was so profoundly chilled that he almost dared to embrace the glowing iron. The Swede was not in the room. Johnnie sank into a chair and, folding his arms on his knees, buried his face in them. Scully, warming one foot and then the other at the rim of the stove, muttered to himself with Celtic mournfulness. The cowboy had removed his fur cap, and with a dazed and rueful air he was running one hand through his tousled locks. From overhead they could hear the creaking of boards as the Swede tramped here and there in his room.

The sad quiet was broken by the sudden flinging open of a door that led toward the kitchen. It was instantly followed by an onrush of women. They precipitated themselves upon Johnnie amid a chorus of lamentation. Before they carried their prey off to the kitchen, there to be bathed and harangued with that mixture of sympathy and abuse which is a feat of their sex, the mother straightened herself and fixed old Scully with an eye of stern reproach. "Shame be upon you, Patrick Scully!" she cried. "Your own son, too. Shame be upon you!"

"There, now! Be quiet, now!" said the old man weakly to this slogan, sniffed disdainfully in the direction of those trembling accomplices, the cowboy and the Easterner.

Presently they bore Johnnie away, and left the three men to dismal reflection.

VII

"I'd like to fight this here Dutchman myself," said the cowboy, breaking a long silence.

Scully wagged his head sadly. "No, that wouldn't do. It wouldn't be right. It wouldn't be right."

"Well, why wouldn't it?" argued the cowboy. "I don't see no harm in it."

"No," answered Scully, with mournful heroism. "It wouldn't be right. It was Johnnie's fight, and now we mustn't whip the man just because he whipped Johnnie."

"Yes, that's true enough," said the cowboy, "but—he better not get fresh with me, because I couldn't stand no more of it."

"You'll not say a word to him," commanded Scully, and even then they heard the tread of the Swede on the stairs. His entrance was made theatric. He swept the door back with a bang and swaggered to the middle of the room. No one looked at him. "Well," he cried, insolently, at Scully, "I s'pose you'll tell me now how much I owe you?"

The old man remained stolid. "You don't owe me nothin'."

"Huh!" said the Swede, "huh! Don't owe 'im nothin'."

The cowboy addressed the Swede. "Stranger, I don't see how you come to be so gay around here."

Old Scully was instantly alert. "Stop!" he shouted, holding his hand forth, fingers upward. "Bill, you shut up!"

The cowboy spat carelessly into the sawdust box. "I didn't say a word, did I?" he asked.

"Mr. Scully," called the Swede, "how much do I owe you?" It was seen that he was attired for departure, and that he had his valise in his hand.

"You don't owe me nothin'," repeated Scully in the same imperturbable way.

"Huh!" said the Swede. "I guess you're right. I guess if it was any way at all, you'd owe me somethin'. That's what I guess." He turned to the cowboy. " 'Kill him! Kill him! Kill him!' " he mimicked, and then guffawed victoriously. " 'Kill him!' " He was convulsed with ironical humor.

But he might have been jeering the dead. The three men were immovable and silent, staring with glassy eyes at the stove.

The Swede opened the door and passed into the storm, giving one derisive glance backward at the still group.

As soon as the door was closed, Scully and the cowboy leaped to their feet and began to curse. They trampled to and fro, waving their arms and smashing into the air with their fists. "Oh, but that was a hard minute!" wailed Scully. "That was a hard minute! Him there leerin' and scoffin'! One bang at his nose was worth forty dollars to me that minute! How did you stand it, Bill?"

"How did I stand it?" cried the cowboy in a quivering voice. "How did I stand it? Oh!"

The old man burst into sudden brogue. "I'd loike to take that Swade," he wailed, "and hould 'im down on a shtone flure and bate 'im to a jelly wid a shtick!"

The cowboy groaned in sympathy. "I'd like to git him by the neck and ha-ammer him"—he brought his hand down on a chair with a noise like a pistol shot—"hammer that there Dutchman until he couldn't tell himself from a dead coyote!"

"I'd bate 'im until he—"

"I'd show *him* some things—"

And then together they raised a yearning, fantastic cry —"Oh-o-oh! if we only could—"

"Yes!"

"Yes!"

"And then I'd—"

"O-o-oh!"

VIII

The Swede, tightly gripping his valise, tacked across the face of the storm as if he carried sails. He was following a line of little naked, grasping trees which, he knew, must mark the way of the road. His face, fresh from the pounding of Johnnie's fists, felt more pleasure than pain in the wind and the driving snow. A number of square shapes loomed upon him finally, and he knew them as the houses of the main body of the town. He found a street and made travel along it, leaning heavily upon the wind whenever, at a corner, a terrific blast caught him.

He might have been in a deserted village. We picture the world as thick with conquering and elate humanity, but here, with the bugles of the tempest pealing, it was hard to imagine a peopled earth. One viewed the existence of man then as a marvel, and conceded a glamour of wonder to these lice which were caused to cling to a whirling, fire-smitten, ice-locked, disease-stricken, space-lost bulb. The conceit of man was explained by this storm to be the very engine of life. One was a coxcomb not to die in it. However, the Swede found a saloon.

In front of it an indomitable red light was burning, and the snowflakes were made blood color as they flew through the circumscribed territory of the lamp's shining. The Swede pushed open the door of the saloon and entered. A sanded expanse was before him, and at the end of it four men sat about a table drinking. Down one side of the room extended a radiant bar, and its guardian was leaning upon his elbows listening to the talk of the men at the table. The Swede dropped his valise upon the floor and, smiling fraternally upon the barkeeper, said, "Gimme some whisky, will you?" The man placed a bottle, a whisky glass, and a glass of ice-thick water upon the bar. The Swede poured himself an abnormal portion of whisky and drank it in three gulps. "Pretty bad night," remarked the bartender indifferently.

He was making the pretension of blindness which is usually a distinction of his class; but it could have been seen that he was furtively studying the half-erased bloodstains on the face of the Swede. "Bad night," he said again.

"Oh, it's good enough for me," replied the Swede hardily as he poured himself some more whisky. The barkeeper took his coin and maneuvered it through its reception by a highly nickeled cash-machine. A bell rang; a card labeled "20 cts." had appeared.

"No," continued the Swede, "this isn't too bad weather. It's good enough for me."

"So?" murmured the barkeeper languidly.

The copious drams made the Swede's eyes swim, and he breathed a trifle heavier. "Yes, I like this weather. I like it. It suits me." It was apparently his design to impart a deep significance to these words.

"So?" murmured the bartender again. He turned to gaze dreamily at the scroll-like birds and birdlike scrolls which had been drawn with soap upon the mirrors in back of the bar.

"Well, I guess I'll take another drink," said the Swede presently. "Have something?"

"No, thanks; I'm not drinkin'," answered the bartender. Afterward he asked, "How did you hurt your face?"

The Swede immediately began to boast loudly. "Why, in a fight. I thumped the soul out of a man down here at Scully's hotel."

The interest of the four men at the table was at last aroused.

"Who was it?" said one.

"Johnnie Scully," blustered the Swede. "Son of the man what runs it. He will be pretty near dead for some weeks, I can tell you. I made a nice thing of him, I did. He couldn't get up. They carried him in the house. Have a drink?"

Instantly the men in some subtle way encased themselves in reserve. "No, thanks," said one. The group was of curious formation. Two were prominent local business men; one was the district attorney, and one was a professional gambler of the kind known as "square." But a scrutiny of the group would not have enabled an observer to pick the gambler from the men of more reputable pursuits. He was, in fact, a man so delicate in manner when among people of fair class, and so judicious in his choice of victims, that in the strictly masculine part of the town's life he had come to be explicitly trusted and admired. People called him a thoroughbred. The fear and contempt with which his craft was regarded were undoubtedly the reasons why his quiet dignity shone conspicuous above the quiet dignity of men who might be merely hatters, billiard markers or grocery clerks. Beyond an occasionally unwary traveler who came by rail, this gambler was supposed to prey solely upon reckless and senile farmers, who, when flush with good crops, drove into town in all the pride and confidence of an absolutely invulnerable stupidity. Hearing at times in circuitous fashion of the despoilment of such a farmer, the important men of Romper invariably laughed in contempt of the victim, and if they thought of the wolf at all, it was with a kind of pride at the knowledge that he would never dare think of attacking their wisdom and courage. Besides, it was popular that this gambler had a real wife and two real children in a neat cottage in a suburb, where he led an exemplary home life; and when any one even suggested a discrepancy in his character, the crowd immediately vociferated descriptions of this virtuous family circle. Then men who led exemplary home lives, and men who did not lead exemplary home lives, all subsided in a bunch, remarking that there was nothing more to be said.

However, when a restriction was placed upon him—as, for instance, when a strong clique of members of the new Polywog Club refused to permit him, even as a spectator, to appear in the rooms of the organization—the candor and gentleness with which he accepted the judgment disarmed many of his foes and made his friends more desperately partisan. He invariably distinguished between himself and a respectable Romper man so quickly and frankly that his manner actually appeared to be a continual broadcast compliment.

And one must not forget to declare the fundamental fact of his entire position in Romper. It is irrefutable that in all affairs outside his business, in all matters that occur eternally and commonly between man and man, this thieving cardplayer was so generous, so just, so moral, that in a contest he could have put to flight the consciences of nine tenths of the citizens of Romper.

And so it happened that he was seated in this saloon with the two prominent local merchants and the district attorney.

The Swede continued to drink raw whisky, meanwhile babbling at the barkeeper and trying to induce him to indulge in potations. "Come on. Have a drink. Come on. What —no? Well, have a little one, then. By gawd, I've whipped a man tonight, and I want to celebrate. I whipped him good, too, Gentlemen," the Swede cried to the men at the table. "Have a drink?"

"Ssh!" said the barkeeper.

The group at the table, although furtively attentive, had been pretending to be deep in talk, but now a man lifted his eyes toward the Swede and said shortly. "Thanks. We don't want any more."

At this reply the Swede ruffled out his chest like a rooster. "Well," he exploded, "it seems I can't get anybody to drink with me in this town. Seems so, don't it? Well!"

"Ssh!" said the barkeeper.

"Say," snarled the Swede, "don't you try to shut me up. I won't have it. I'm a gentleman, and I want people to drink with me. And I want 'em to drink with me now. *Now*—do you understand?" He rapped the bar with his knuckles.

Years of experience had calloused the bartender. He merely grew sulky. "I hear you," he answered.

"Well," cried the Swede, "listen hard then. See those men over there? Well, they're going to drink with me, and don't you forget it. Now you watch."

"Hi!" yelled the barkeeper, "this won't do!"

"Why won't it?" demanded the Swede. He stalked over to the table, and by chance laid his hand upon the shoulder of the gambler. "How about this?" he asked wrathfully. "I asked you to drink with me."

The gambler simply twisted his head and spoke over his shoulder. "My friend, I don't know you."

"Oh, hell!" answered the Swede, "Come and have a drink."

"Now, my boy," advised the gambler kindly, "take your hand off my shoulder and go 'way and mind your own business." He was a little, slim man, and it seemed strange to hear him use this tone of heroic patronage to the burly Swede. The other men at the table said nothing.

"What! You won't drink with me, you little dude? I'll make you, then! I'll make you!" The Swede had grasped the gambler frenziedly at the throat, and was dragging him from his chair. The other men sprang up. The barkeeper dashed around the corner of his bar. There was a great tumult, and then was seen a long blade in the hand of the gambler. It shot forward, and a human body, this citadel of virtue, wisdom, power, was pierced as easily as if it had been a melon. The Swede fell with a cry of supreme astonishment.

The prominent merchants and the district attorney must have at once tumbled out of the place backward. The bartender found himself hanging limply to the arm of a chair and gazing into the eyes of a murderer.

"Henry," said the latter as he wiped his knife on one of the towels that hung beneath the bar rail, "you tell 'em where to find me. I'll be home, waiting for 'em." Then he vanished. A moment afterward the barkeeper was in the street, dinning through the storm for help and, moreover, companionship.

The corpse of the Swede, alone in the saloon, had its eyes fixed upon a dreadful legend that dwelt atop of the cash-machine: "This registers the amount of your purchase."

IX

Months later the cowboy was frying pork over the stove of a little ranch near the Dakota line when there was a quick thud of hoofs outside, and presently the Easterner entered with the letters and the papers.

"Well," said the Easterner at once, "the chap that killed the Swede has got three years. Wasn't much, was it?"

"He has? Three years?" The cowboy poised his pan of pork while he ruminated upon the news. "Three years. That ain't much."

"No. It was a light sentence," replied the Easterner as he unbuckled his spurs. 'Seems there was a good deal of sympathy for him in Romper."

"If the bartender had been any good," observed the cowboy thoughtfully, "he would have gone in and cracked that there Dutchman on the head with a bottle in the beginnin' of it and stopped all this here murderin'."

"Yes, a thousand things might have happened," said the Easterner tartly.

The cowboy returned his pan of pork to the fire, but his philosophy continued. "It's funny, ain't it? If he hadn't said Johnnie was cheatin', he'd be alive this minute. He was an awful fool. Game played for fun, too. Not for money. I believe he was crazy."

"I feel sorry for that gambler," said the Easterner.

"Oh, so do I," said the cowboy. "He don't deserve none of it for killin' who he did."

"The Swede might not have been killed if everything had been square."

"Might not have been killed?" exclaimed the cowboy. "Everythin' square? Why, when he said that Johnnie was cheatin' and acted like such a jackass? And then in the saloon he fairly walked up to git hurt?" With these arguments the cowboy browbeat the Easterner and reduced him to rage.

"You're a fool!" cried the Easterner, viciously. "You're

a bigger jackass than the Swede by a million majority. Now let me tell you one thing. Let me tell you something. Listen! Johnnie *was* cheating!"

" 'Johnnie,' " said the cowboy, blankly. There was a minute of silence, and then he said, robustly, "Why, no. The game was only for fun."

"Fun or not," said the Easterner, "Johnnie was cheating. I saw him. I know it. I saw him. And I refused to stand up and be a man. I let the Swede fight it out alone. And you —you were simply puffing around the place and wanting to fight. And then old Scully himself! We are all in it! This poor gambler isn't even a noun. He is kind of an adverb. Every sin is the result of a collaboration. We, five of us, have collaborated in the murder of this Swede. Usually there are from a dozen to forty women really involved in every murder, but in this case it seems to be only men—you, I, Johnnie, old Scully and that fool of an unfortunate gambler came merely as a culmination, the apex of a human movement, and gets all the punishment."

The cowboy, injured and rebellious, cried out blindly into this fog of mysterious theory, "Well, I didn't do anythin', did I?"

THE NOTORIOUS JUMPING FROG OF CALAVERAS COUNTY

Mark Twain

In compliance with the request of a friend of mine, who wrote me from the East, I called on good-natured, garrulous old Simon Wheeler, and inquired after my friend's friend, Leonidas W. Smiley, as requested to do, and I hereunto append the result. I have a lurking suspicion that *Leonidas W.* Smiley is a myth; that my friend never knew such a personage; and that he only conjectured that if I asked old Wheeler about him, it would remind him of his infamous *Jim* Smiley, and he would go to work and bore me to death with some exasperating reminiscence of him as long and as tedious as it should be useless to me. If that was the design, it succeeded.

I found Simon Wheeler dozing comfortably by the bar-room stove of the dilapidated tavern in the decayed mining camp of Angel's, and I noticed that he was fat and bald-headed, and had an expression of winning gentleness and simplicity upon his tranquil countenance. He roused up, and gave me good day. I told him that a friend of mine had commissioned me to make some inquiries about a cherished companion of his boyhood named *Leonidas W.* Smiley— *Rev. Leonidas W.* Smiley, a young minister of the Gospel, who he had heard was at one time a resident of Angel's Camp. I added that if Mr. Wheeler could tell me anything about this Rev. Leonidas W. Smiley, I would feel under many obligations to him.

Simon Wheeler backed me into a corner and blockaded me there with his chair, and then sat down and reeled off the monotonous narrative which follows this paragraph. He never smiled, he never frowned, he never changed his voice from the gentle-flowing key to which he tuned his initial sentence, he never betrayed the slightest suspicion of enthusiasm; but all through the interminable narrative there ran a vein of impressive earnestness and sincerity, which showed me plainly that, so far from his imagining that there was anything ridiculous or funny about his story, he regarded it as a really important matter, and admired its two heroes as men of transcendent genius in *finesse.* I let him go on in his own way, and never interrupted him once.

"Rev. Leonidas W. H'm, Reverend Le—well, there was a feller here once by the name of *Jim* Smiley, in the winter of '49—or maybe it was the spring of '50—I don't recollect exactly, somehow, though what makes me think it was one or the other is because I remember the big flume warn't finished when he first come to the camp; but anyway, he was the curiousest man about always betting on anything that turned up you ever see, if he could get anybody to bet on the other side; and if he couldn't he'd change sides. Any way that suited the other man would suit *him*—any way just so's he got a bet, *he* was satisfied. But still he was lucky, uncommon lucky; he most always come out winner. He was always ready and laying for a chance; there couldn't be no solit'ry thing mentioned but that feller'd offer to bet on it, and take any side you please, as I was just telling you. If there was a horse-race, you'd find him flush or you'd find him busted at the end of it; if there was a dog-fight, he'd bet on it; if there was a cat-fight, he'd bet on it; if there was a chicken-fight, he'd bet on it; why, if there was two birds setting on a fence, he would bet you which one would fly first; or if there was a camp-meeting, he would be there reg'lar to bet on Parson Walker, which he judged to be the best exhorter about here, and so he was too, and a good man. If he even see a straddle-bug start to go anywheres, he would bet you how long it would take him to get to—to wherever he was going to, and if you took him up, he would foller that straddle-bug to Mexico but what he would find out where he was bound for and how long he was on the road. Lots of the boys here has seen that Smiley, and can tell you about him. Why, it never made no difference to *him*—he'd bet on *any* thing—the dangdest feller. Parson Walker's wife laid very sick once, for a good while, and it seemed as if they warn't going to save her; but one morning he come in, and Smiley up and asked him how she was, and he said she was considerable better —thank the Lord for his infinite mercy—and coming on so smart that with the blessing of Prov'dence she'd get well yet; and Smiley, before he thought, says, 'Well, I'll resk two-and-a-half she don't anyway.'

"Thish-yer Smiley had a mare—the boys called her the fifteen-minute nag, but that was only in fun, you know, because of course she was faster than that—and he used to win money on that horse, for all she was so slow and always had the asthma, or the distemper, or the consumption, or something of that kind. They used to give her two or three hundred yards' start, and then pass her under way; but always at the fag end of the race she'd get excited and desperate like, and come cavorting and straddling up, and scattering her legs around limber, sometimes in the air, and sometimes out to one side among the fences, and kicking up m-o-r-e dust and raising m-o-r-e racket with her coughing and sneezing and blowing her nose—and *always* fetch up at the stand just about a neck ahead, as near as you could cipher it down.

"And he had a little small bull-pup, that to look at him you'd think he warn't worth a cent but to set around and look ornery and lay for a chance to steal something. But as soon as money was up on him he was a different dog; his under-jaw'd begin to stick out like the fo'castle of a steam-boat, and his teeth would uncover and shine like the furnaces. And a dog might tackle him and bully-rag him, and bite him, and throw him over his shoulder two or three times, and Andrew Jackson—which was the name of the pup—Andrew Jackson would never let on but what *he* was satisfied, and hadn't expected nothing else—and the bets being doubled and doubled on the other side all the time, till the money was all up; and then all of a sudden he would grab that other dog jest by the j'int of his hind leg and freeze to it—not chaw, you understand, but only just grip and hang on till they throwed up the sponge, if it was a year. Smiley always come out winner on that pup, till he harnessed a dog once that didn't have no hind legs, be-cause they'd been sawed off in a circular saw, and when the thing had gone along far enough, and the money was all up, and he come to make a snatch for his pet holt, he see in a minute how he'd been imposed on, and how the other dog had him in the door, so to speak, and he 'peared surprised, and then he looked sorter discouraged-like, and didn't try no more to win the fight, and so he got shucked out bad. He give Smiley a look, as much as to say his heart was broke, and it was *his* fault, for putting up a dog that hadn't no hind legs for him to take holt of, which was his main dependence in a fight, and then he limped off a piece and laid down and died. It was a good pup, was that An-drew Jackson, and would have made a name for hisself if he'd lived, for the stuff was in him and he had genius—I know it, because he hadn't no opportunities to speak of, and it don't stand to reason that a dog could make such a fight as he could under them circumstances if he hadn't no talent. It always makes me feel sorry when I think of that last fight of his'n, and the way it turned out.

"Well, thish-yer Smiley had rat-tarriers, and chicken cocks, and tomcats and all them kind of things, till you couldn't rest, and you couldn't fetch nothing for him to bet on but he'd match you. He ketched a frog one day, and took him home, and said he cal'lated to educate him; and so he never done nothing for three months but set in his back yard and learn that frog to jump. And you bet you he *did* learn him, too. He'd give him a little punch behind, and the next minute you'd see that frog whirling in the air like a dough-nut—see him turn one summerset, or maybe a couple, if he got a good start, and come down flat-footed and all right, like a cat. He got him up so in the matter of ketching flies, and kep' him in practice so constant, that he'd nail a fly every time as fur as he could see him. Smiley said all a frog wanted was education, and he could do 'most anything—and I believe him. Why, I've seen him set Dan'l Webster down here on this floor—Dan'l Webster was the name of the frog—and sing out, 'Flies, Dan'l, flies!' and quicker'n you could wink he'd spring straight up and snake a fly off'n the counter there, and flop down on the floor ag'in as solid as a gob of mud, and fall to scratching the side of his head with his hind foot as indifferent as if he hadn't no idea he'd been doin' any more'n any frog might do. You never see a frog so modest and straighfor'ard as he was, for all he was so gifted. And when it come to fair and square jumping on a dead level, he could get over more ground at one straddle than any animal of his breed you ever see. Jumping on a dead level was his strong suit, you understand; and when it come to that, Smiley would ante up money on him as long as he had a red. Smiley was monstrous proud of his frog, and well he might be, for fellers that had traveled and been everywheres all said he laid over any frog that ever *they* see.

"Well, Smiley kep' the beast in a little lattice box, and he used to fetch him down-town sometimes and lay for a bet. One day a feller—a stranger in the camp, he was—come acrost him with his box, and says:

" 'What might it be that you've got in the box?'

"And Smiley says, sorter indifferent-like, 'It might be a

parrot, or it might be a canary, maybe, but it ain't—it's only just a frog.'

"And the feller took it, and looked at it careful, and turned it round this way and that, and says, 'H'm—so 'tis. Well, what's *he* good for?'

" 'Well,' Smiley says, easy and careless, 'he's good enough for *one* thing, I should judge—he can outjump any frog in Calaveras County.'

"The feller took the box again, and took another long, particular look, and give it back to Smiley, and says, very deliberate, 'Well,' he says, 'I don't see no p'ints about that frog that's any better'n any other frog.'

" 'Maybe you don't,' Smiley says. 'Maybe you understand frogs and maybe you don't understand 'em; maybe you've had experience, and maybe you ain't only a amature, as it were. Anyways, I've got *my* opinion, and I'll resk forty dollars that he can outjump any frog in Calaveras County.'

"And the feller studied a minute, and then says, kinder sad-like, 'Well, I'm only a stranger here, and I ain't got no frog; but if I had a frog, I'd bet you.'

"And then Smiley says, 'That's all right—that's all right —if you'll hold my box a minute, I'll go and get you a frog.' And so the feller took the box, and put up his forty dollars along with Smiley's, and set down to wait.

"So he set there a good while thinking and thinking to himself, and then he got the frog out and prized his mouth open and took a teaspoon and filled him full of quail-shot— filled him pretty near up to his chin—and set him on the floor. Smiley he went to the swamp and slopped around in the mud for a long time, and finally he ketched a frog, and fetched him in, and give him to this feller, and says:

" 'Now, if you're ready, set him alongside of Dan'l, with his fore paws just even with Dan'l's, and I'll give the word.' Then he says, 'One—two—three—*git!*' and him and the feller touched up the frogs from behind, and the new frog hopped off lively, but Dan'l give a heave, and hysted up his shoulders—so—like a Frenchman, but it warn't no use—he couldn't budge; he was planted as solid as a church, and he couldn't no more stir than if he was anchored out. Smiley was a good deal surprised, and he was disgusted too, but he didn't have no idea what the matter was, of course.

"The feller took the money and started away; and when he was going out at the door, he sorter jerked his thumb over his shoulder—so—at Dan'l, and says again, very deliberate, 'Well,' he says, '*I* don't see no p'ints about that frog that's any better'n any other frog.'

"Smiley he stood scratching his head and looking down at Dan'l a long time, and at last he says, 'I do wonder what in the nation that frog throw'd off for—I wonder if there ain't something the matter with him—he 'pears to look mighty baggy, somehow.' And he ketched Dan'l by the nap of the neck, and hefted him, and says, 'Why blame my cats if he don't weigh five pound!' and turned him upside down and he belched out a double handful of shot. And then he see how it was, and he was the maddest man—he set the frog down and took out after that feller, but he never ketched him. And—"

Here Simon Wheeler heard his name called from the front yard, and got up to see what was wanted. And turning to me as he moved away, he said: "Just set where you are, stranger, and rest easy—I ain't going to be gone a second."

But, by your leave, I did not think that a continuation of the history of the enterprising vagabond *Jim* Smiley would be likely to afford me much information concerning the Rev. *Leonidas W.* Smiley, and so I started away.

At the door I met the sociable Wheeler returning and, he buttonholed me and recommenced:

"Well, thish-yer Smiley had a yaller one-eyed cow that didn't have no tail, only just a short stump like a bannanner, and—"

However, lacking both time and inclination, I did not wait to hear about the afflicted cow, but took my leave.

THE OUTCASTS OF POKER FLAT

Bret Harte

As Mr. John Oakhurst, gambler, stepped into the main street of Poker Flat on the morning of the twenty-third of November, 1850, he was conscious of a change in its moral atmosphere since the preceding night. Two or three men, conversing earnestly together, ceased as he approached, and exchanged significant glances. There was a Sabbath lull in the air, which, in a settlement unused to Sabbath influences, looked ominous.

Mr. Oakhurst's calm, handsome face betrayed small concern in these indications. Whether he was conscious of any predisposing cause was another question. "I reckon they're after somebody," he reflected; "likely it's me." He returned to his pocket the handkerchief with which he had been whipping away the red dust of Poker Flat from his neat boots, and quietly discharged his mind of any further conjecture.

In point of fact, Poker Flat was "after somebody." It had lately suffered the loss of several thousand dollars, two valuable horses, and a prominent citizen. It was experiencing a spasm of virtuous reaction, quite as lawless and ungovernable as any of the acts that had provoked it. A secret committee had determined to rid the town of all improper persons. This was done permanently in regard of two men who were then hanging from the boughs of a sycamore in the gulch, and temporarily in the banishment of certain other objectionable characters. I regret to say that some of these were ladies. It is but due to the sex, however, to state that their impropriety was professional, and it was only in such easily established standards of evil that Poker Flat ventured to sit in judgment.

Mr. Oakhurst was right in supposing that he was included in this category. A few of the committee had urged hanging him as a possible example and a sure method of reimbursing themselves from his pockets of the sums he had won from them. "It's agin justice," said Jim Wheeler, "to let this yer young man from Roaring Camp—an entire stranger —carry away our money." But a crude sentiment of equity residing in the breasts of those who had been fortunate enough to win from Mr. Oakhurst overruled this narrower local prejudice.

Mr. Oakhurst received his sentence with philosophic calmness, none the less coolly that he was aware of the hesitation of his judges. He was too much of a gambler not to accept fate. With him life was at best an uncertain game, and he recognized the usual percentage in favor of the dealer.

A body of armed men accompanied the deported wickedness of Poker Flat to the outskirts of the settlement. Besides Mr. Oakhurst, who was known to be a coolly desperate man, and for whose intimidation the armed escort was intended, the expatriated party consisted of a young woman familiarly known as "The Duchess"; another who had won the title of "Mother Shipton"; and "Uncle Billy," a suspected sluice-robber and confirmed drunkard.

The cavalcade provoked no comments from the spectators, nor was any word uttered by the escort. Only when the gulch which marked the uttermost limit of Poker Flat was reached, the leader spoke briefly and to the point. The exiles were forbidden to return at the peril of their lives.

As the escort disappeared, their pent-up feelings found vent in a few hysterical tears from the Duchess, some bad language from Mother Shipton, and a Parthian volley of expletives from Uncle Billy. The philosophic Oakhurst alone remained silent. He listened calmly to Mother Shipton's desire to cut somebody's heart out, to the repeated statements of the Duchess that she would die in the road, and to the alarming oaths that seemed to be bumped out of Uncle Billy as he rode forward.

With the easy good humor characteristic of his class, he insisted upon exchanging his own riding-horse, "Five-Spot," for the sorry mule which the Duchess rode. But even this act did not draw the party into any closer sympathy. The young woman readjusted her somewhat draggled plumes with a feeble, faded coquetry; Mother Shipton eyed the possessor of "Five-Spot" with malevolence, and Uncle Billy included the whole party in one sweeping anathema.

The road to Sandy Bar—a camp that, not having as yet experienced the regenerating influences of Poker Flat, consequently seemed to offer some invitation to the emigrants —lay over a steep mountain range. It was distant a day's severe travel. In that advanced season the party soon passed out of the moist, temperate regions of the foothills into the dry, cold, bracing air of the Sierras. The trail was narrow and difficult. At noon the Duchess, rolling out of her saddle upon the ground, declared her intention of going no farther, and the party halted.

The spot was singularly wild and impressive. A wooded amphitheater, surrounded on three sides by precipitous cliffs of naked granite, sloped gently toward the crest of another precipice that overlooked the valley. It was, undoubtedly, the most suitable spot for a camp, had camping been advisable. But Mr. Oakhurst knew that scarcely half the journey to Sandy Bar was accomplished, and the party were not equipped or provisioned for delay. This fact he pointed out to his companions curtly, with a philosophic commentary on the folly of throwing up their hand before the game was played out.

But they were furnished with liquor, which in this emergency stood them in place of food, fuel, rest, and prescience. In spite of his remonstrances, it was not long before they were more or less under its influence. Uncle Billy passed rapidly from a bellicose state into one of stupor, the Duchess became maudlin, and Mother Shipton snored. Mr. Oakhurst alone remained erect, leaning against a rock, calmly surveying them.

Mr. Oakhurst did not drink. It interfered with a profession which required coolness, impassiveness, and presence of mind, and, in his own language, he "couldn't afford it." As he gazed at his recumbent fellow exiles, the loneliness begotten of his pariah trade, his habits of life, his very vices, for the first time seriously oppressed him. He bestirred himself in dusting his black clothes, washing his hands and face, and other acts characteristic of his studiously neat habits, and for a moment forgot his annoyance.

The thought of deserting his weaker and more pitiable companions never perhaps occurred to him. Yet he could not help feeling the want of that excitement which, singularly enough, was most conducive to that calm equanimity for which he was notorious. He looked at the gloomy walls that rose a thousand feet sheer above the circling pines around him, at the sky ominously clouded, at the valley below, already deepening into shadow; and, doing so, suddenly he heard his own name called.

A horseman slowly ascended the trail. In the fresh, open face of the newcomer Mr. Oakhurst recognized Tom Simson, otherwise known as "The Innocent," of Sandy Bar. He had met him some months before over a "little game," and had, with perfect equanimity, won the entire fortune—amounting to some forty dollars—of that guileless youth. After the game was finished, Mr. Oakhurst drew the youthful speculator behind the door and thus addressed him: "Tommy, you're a good little man, but you can't gamble worth a cent. Don't try it over again." He then handed him his money back, pushed him gently from the room, and so made a devoted slave of Tom Simson.

There was a remembrance of this in his boyish and enthusiastic greeting of Mr. Oakhurst. He had started, he said, to go to Poker Flat to seek his fortune. "Alone?" No, not exactly alone; in fact (a giggle), he had run away with Piney Woods. Didn't Mr. Oakhurst remember Piney? She that used to wait on the table at the Temperance House? They had been engaged a long time, but old Jake Woods had objected, and so they had run away, and were going to Poker Flat to be married, and here they were. And they were tired out, and how lucky it was they had found a place to camp, and company.

All this the Innocent delivered rapidly, while Piney, a stout, comely damsel of fifteen, emerged from behind the pine-tree, where she had been blushing unseen, and rode to the side of her lover.

Mr. Oakhurst seldom troubled himself with sentiment, still less with propriety; but he had a vague idea that the situation was not fortunate. He retained, however, his presence of mind sufficiently to kick Uncle Billy, who was about to say something, and Uncle Billy was sober enough to recognize in Mr. Oakhurst's kick a superior power that would not bear trifling.

He then endeavored to dissuade Tom Simson from delaying further, but in vain. He even pointed out the fact that there was no provision, nor means of making a camp. But, unluckily, the Innocent met this objection by assuring the party that he was provided with an extra mule loaded with provisions, and by the discovery of a rude attempt at a log house near the trail. "Piney can stay with Mrs. Oakhurst," said the Innocent, pointing to the Duchess, "and I can shift for myself."

Nothing but Mr. Oakhurst's admonishing foot saved

Uncle Billy from bursting into a roar of laughter. As it was, he felt compelled to retire up the cañon until he could recover his gravity. There he confided the joke to the tall pine-trees, with many slaps of his leg, contortions of his face, and the usual profanity. But when he returned to the party, he found them seated by a fire—for the air had grown strangely chill and the sky overcast—in apparently amicable conversation.

Piney was actually talking in an impulsive girlish fashion to the Duchess, who was listening with an interest and animation she had not shown for many days. The Innocent was holding forth, apparently with equal effect, to Mr. Oakhurst and Mother Shipton, who was actually relaxing into amiability.

"Is this yer a d—d picnic?" said Uncle Billy, with inward scorn, as he surveyed the sylvan group, the glancing firelight, and the tethered animals in the foreground.

Suddenly an idea mingled with the alcoholic fumes that disturbed his brain. It was apparently of a jocular nature, for he felt impelled to slap his leg again and cram his fist into his mouth.

As the shadows crept slowly up the mountain, a slight breeze rocked the tops of the pine-trees and moaned through their long and gloomy aisles. The ruined cabin, patched and covered with pine boughs, was set apart for the ladies. As the lovers parted, they unaffectedly exchanged a kiss, so honest and sincere that it might have been heard above the swaying pines. The frail Duchess and the malevolent Mother Shipton were probably too stunned to remark upon this last evidence of simplicity, and so turned without a word to the hut. The fire was replenished, the men lay down before the door, and in a few minutes were asleep.

Mr. Oakhurst was a light sleeper. Toward morning he awoke benumbed and cold. As he stirred the dying fire, the wind, which was now blowing strongly, brought to his cheek that which caused the blood to leave it—snow!

He started to his feet with the intention of awakening

the sleepers, for there was no time to lose. But turning to where Uncle Billy had been lying, he found him gone. A suspicion leaped to his brain, and a curse to his lips. He ran to the spot where the mules had been tethered—they were no longer there. The tracks were already rapidly disappearing in the snow.

The momentary excitement brought Mr. Oakhurst back to the fire with his usual calm. He did not waken the sleepers. The Innocent slumbered peacefully, with a smile on his good-humored, freckled face; the virgin Piney slept beside her frailer sisters as sweetly as though attended by celestial guardians; and Mr. Oakhurst, drawing his blanket over his shoulders, stroked his mustaches and waited for the dawn. It came slowly in a whirling mist of snowflakes that dazzled and confused the eye. What could be seen of the landscape appeared magically changed. He looked over the valley, and summed up the present and future in two words, "Snowed in!"

A careful inventory of the provisions, which, fortunately for the party, had been stored within the hut, and so escaped the felonious fingers of Uncle Billy, disclosed the fact that with care and prudence they might last ten days longer.

"That is," said Mr. Oakhurst *sotto voce* to the Innocent, "if you're willing to board us. If you ain't—and perhaps you'd better not—you can wait till Uncle Billy gets back with provisions."

For some occult reason, Mr. Oakhurst could not bring himself to disclose Uncle Billy's rascality, and so offered the hypothesis that he had wandered from the camp and had accidentally stampeded the animals. He dropped a warning to the Duchess and Mother Shipton, who of course knew the facts of their associate's defection.

"They'll find out the truth about us *all* when they find out anything," he added significantly, "and there's no good frightening them now."

Tom Simson not only put all his worldly store at the

disposal of Mr. Oakhurst, but seemed to enjoy the prospect of their enforced seclusion. "We'll have a good camp for a week, and then the snow'll melt, and we'll all go back together."

The cheerful gaiety of the young man and Mr. Oakhurst's calm infected the others. The Innocent, with the aid of pine boughs, extemporized a thatch for the roofless cabin, and the Duchess directed Piney in the rearrangement of the interior with a taste and tact that opened the blue eyes of that provincial maiden to their fullest extent.

"I reckon now you're used to fine things at Poker Flat," said Piney.

The Duchess turned away sharply to conceal something that reddened her cheeks through their professional tint, and Mother Shipton requested Piney not to "chatter." But when Mr. Oakhurst returned from a weary search for the trail, he heard the sound of happy laughter echoed from the rocks. He stopped in some alarm, and his thoughts first naturally reverted to the whiskey, which he had prudently cached. "And yet it don't somehow sound like whiskey," said the gambler. It was not until he caught sight of the blazing fire through the still blinding storm, and the group around it, that he settled to the conviction that it was "square fun."

Whether Mr. Oakhurst had cached his cards with the whiskey as something debarred the free access of the community, I cannot say. It was certain that, in Mother Shipton's words, he "didn't say 'cards' once" during that evening. Happily the time was beguiled by an accordion, produced somewhat ostentatiously by Tom Simson from his pack. Notwithstanding some difficulties attending the manipulation of this instrument, Piney Woods managed to pluck several reluctant melodies from its keys, to an accompaniment by the Innocent on a pair of bone castanets.

But the crowning festivity of the evening was reached in a rude camp-meeting hymn, which the lovers, joining hands, sang with great earnestness and vociferation. I fear that a certain defiant tone and Covenanter's swing to its chorus, rather than any devotional quality, caused it speedily to infect the others, who at last joined in the refrain:

> *I'm proud to live in the service of the Lord,*
> *And I'm bound to die in His army.*

The pines rocked, the storm eddied and whirled above the miserable group, and the flames of their altar leaped heavenward, as if in token of the vow.

At midnight the storm abated, the rolling clouds parted, and the stars glittered keenly above the sleeping camp. Mr. Oakhurst, whose professional habits had enabled him to live on the smallest possible amount of sleep, in dividing the watch with Tom Simson somehow managed to take upon himself the greater part of that duty. He excused himself to the Innocent by saying that he had "often been a week without sleep."

"Doing what?" asked Tom.

"Poker!" replied Oakhurst sententiously. "When a man gets a streak of luck—nigger-luck—he don't get tired. The luck gives in first. Luck," continued the gambler reflectively, "is a mighty queer thing. All you know about it for certain is that it's bound to change. And it's finding out when it's going to change that makes you. We've had a streak of bad luck since we left Poker Flat—you come along, and slap you get into it, too. If you can hold your cards right along you're all right. For," added the gambler, with cheerful irrelevance,

> *I'm proud to live in the service of the Lord,*
> *And I'm bound to die in His army.*

The third day came, and the sun, looking through the white-curtained valley, saw the outcasts divide their slowly decreasing store of provisions for the morning meal. It was one of the peculiarities of that mountain climate that its rays diffused a kindly warmth over the wintry landscape, as if in regretful commiseration of the past. But it revealed drift on drift of snow piled high around the hut—a hopeless, uncharted, trackless sea of white lying below the rocky shores to which the castaways still clung.

Through the marvelously clear air the smoke of the pastoral village of Poker Flat rose miles away. Mother Shipton saw it, and from a remote pinnacle of her rocky fastness hurled in that direction a final malediction. It was her last vituperative attempt, and perhaps for that reason was invested with a certain degree of sublimity. It did her good, she privately informed the Duchess. "Just you go out there and cuss, and see."

She then set herself to the task of amusing "the child," as she and the Duchess were pleased to call Piney. Piney was no chicken, but it was a soothing and original theory of the pair thus to account for the fact that she didn't swear and wasn't improper.

When night crept up again through the gorges, the reedy notes of the accordion rose and fell in fitful spasms and long-drawn gasps by the flickering campfire. But music failed to fill entirely the aching void left by insufficient food, and a new diversion was proposed by Piney—storytelling. Neither Mr. Oakhurst nor his female companions caring to relate their personal experiences, this plan would have failed, too, but for the Innocent.

Some months before he had chanced upon a stray copy of Mr. Pope's ingenious translation of the Iliad. He now proposed to narrate the principal incidents of that poem—having thoroughly mastered the argument and fairly forgotten the words—in the current vernacular of Sandy Bar. And so for the rest of that night the Homeric demigods again walked the earth. Trojan bully and wily Greek wrestled in the winds, and the great pines in the cañon seemed to bow to the wrath of the son of Peleus.

Mr. Oakhurst listened with quiet satisfaction. Most especially was he interested in the fate of "Ash-heels," as the

Innocent persisted in denominating the "swift-footed Achilles."

So, with small food and much of Homer and the accordion, a week passed over the heads of the outcasts. The sun again forsook them, and again from leaden skies the snowflakes were sifted over the land. Day by day closer around them drew the snowy circle, until at last they looked from their prison over drifted walls of dazzling white, that towered twenty feet above their heads. It became more and more difficult to replenish their fires, even from the fallen trees beside them, now half hidden in the drifts. And yet no one complained.

The lovers turned from the dreary prospect and looked into each other's eyes, and were happy. Mr. Oakhurst settled himself coolly to the losing game before him. The Duchess, more cheerful than she had been, assumed the care of Piney.

Only Mother Shipton—once the strongest of the party —seemed to sicken and fade. At midnight on the tenth day she called Oakhurst to her side. "I'm going," she said, in a voice of querulous weakness, "but don't say anything about it. Don't waken the kids. Take the bundle from under my head, and open it."

Mr. Oakhurst did so. It contained Mother Shipton's rations for the last week, untouched. "Give 'em to the child," she said, pointing to the sleeping Piney.

"You've starved yourself," said the gambler.

"That's what they call it," said the woman querulously, as she lay down again, and, turning her face to the wall, passed quietly away.

The accordion and the bones were put aside that day, and Homer was forgotten. When the body of Mother Shipton had been committed to the snow, Mr. Oakhurst took the Innocent aside, and showed him a pair of snowshoes, which he had fashioned from the old pack-saddle.

"There's one chance in a hundred to save her yet," he said, pointing to Piney; "but it's there," he added, pointing toward Poker Flat. "If you can reach there in two days she's safe." "And you?" asked Tom Simson.

"I'll stay here," was the curt reply.

The lovers parted with a long embrace. "You are not going, too?" said the Duchess, as she saw Mr. Oakhurst apparently waiting to accompany him.

"As far as the cañon," he replied. He turned suddenly and kissed the Duchess, leaving her pallid face aflame, and her trembling limbs rigid with amazement.

Night came, but not Mr. Oakhurst. It brought the storm again and the whirling snow. Then the Duchess, feeding the fire, found that someone had quietly piled beside the hut enough fuel to last a few days longer. The tears rose to her eyes, but she hid them from Piney.

The women slept but little. In the morning, looking into each other's faces, they read their fate. Neither spoke, but Piney, accepting the position of the stronger, drew near and placed her arm around the Duchess's waist. They kept this attitude for the rest of the day. That night the storm reached its greatest fury, and, rending asunder the protecting vines, invaded the very hut.

Toward morning they found themselves unable to feed the fire, which gradually died away. As the embers slowly blackened, the Duchess crept closer to Piney, and broke the silence of many hours: "Piney, can you pray?" "No, dear," said Piney simply. The Duchess, without knowing exactly why, felt relieved, and, putting her head upon Piney's shoulder, spoke no more. And so reclining, the younger and purer pillowing the head of her soiled sister upon her virgin breast, they fell asleep.

The wind lulled as if it feared to waken them. Feathery drifts of snow, shaken from the long pine boughs, flew like white winged birds, and settled about them as they slept. The moon through the rifted clouds looked down upon what had been the camp. But all human stain, all trace of earthly travail, was hidden beneath the spotless mantle mercifully flung from above.

They slept all that day and the next, nor did they waken when voices and footsteps broke the silence of the camp. And when pitying fingers brushed the snow from their wan faces, you could scarcely have told from the equal peace that dwelt upon them which was she that had sinned. Even the law of Poker Flat recognized this, and turned away, leaving them still locked in each other's arms.

But at the head of the gulch, on one of the largest pine-trees, they found the deuce of clubs pinned to the bark with a bowie-knife. It bore the following, written in pencil in a firm hand:

†

BENEATH THIS TREE

LIES THE BODY

OF

JOHN OAKHURST,

WHO STRUCK A STREAK OF BAD LUCK

ON THE 23D OF NOVEMBER 1850,

AND

HANDED IN HIS CHECKS

ON THE 7TH DECEMBER, 1850.

†

And pulseless and cold, with a derringer by his side and a bullet in his heart, though still calm as in life, beneath the snow lay he who was at once the strongest and yet the weakest of the outcasts of Poker Flat.

AN AFTERNOON MIRACLE

O. Henry

At the United States end of an international river bridge, four armed rangers sweltered in a little 'dobe hut, keeping a fairly faithful espionage upon the lagging trail of passengers from the Mexican side.

Bud Dawson, proprietor of the Top Notch Saloon, had, on the evening previous, violently ejected from his premises one Leandro Garcia, for alleged violation of the Top Notch code of behavior. Garcia had mentioned twenty-four hours as a limit, by which time he would call and collect a plentiful indemnity for personal satisfaction.

This Mexican, although a tremendous braggart, was thoroughly courageous, and each side of the river respected him for one of these attributes. He and a following of similar bravoes were addicted to the pastime of retrieving towns from stagnation.

The day designated by Garcia for retribution was to be further signalized on the American side by a cattlemen's convention, a bull fight, and an old settlers' barbecue and picnic. Knowing the avenger to be a man of his word, and believing it prudent to court peace while three such gently social relaxations were in progress, Captain McNulty, of the ranger company stationed there, detailed his lieutenant and three men for duty at the end of the bridge. Their instructions were to prevent the invasion of Garcia, either alone or attended by his gang.

Travel was slight that sultry afternoon, and the rangers swore gently, and mopped their brows in their convenient but close quarters. For an hour no one had crossed save an old woman enveloped in a brown wrapper and a black mantilla, driving before her a burro loaded with kindling wood tied in small bundles for peddling. Then three shots were fired down the street, the sound coming clear and snappy through the still air.

· The four rangers quickened from sprawling, symbolic figures of indolence to alert life, but only one rose to his feet. Three turned their eyes beseechingly but hopelessly upon the fourth, who had gotten nimbly up and was buckling his cartridge-belt around him. The three knew that Lieutenant Bob Buckley, in command, would allow no man of them the privilege of investigating a row when he himself might go.

The agile, broad-chested lieutenant, without a change of expression in his smooth, yellow-brown, melancholy face, shot the belt strap through the guard of the buckle, hefted his sixes in their holsters as a belle gives the finishing touches to her toilette, caught up his Winchester, and dived for the door. There he paused long enough to caution his comrades to maintain their watch upon the bridge, and then plunged into the broiling highway.

The three relapsed into resigned inertia and plaintive comment.

"I've heard of fellows," grumbled Broncho Leathers,

"what was wedded to danger, but if Bob Buckley ain't committed bigamy with trouble, I'm a son of a gun."

"Peculiarness of Bob is," inserted the Nueces Kid, "he ain't had proper trainin'. He never learned how to git skeered. Now, a man ought to be skeered enough when he tackles a fuss to hanker after readin' his name on the list of survivors, anyway."

"Buckley," commented Ranger No. 3, who was a misguided Eastern man, burdened with an education, "scraps in such a solemn manner that I have been led to doubt its spontaneity. I'm not quite onto his system, but he fights, like Tybalt, by the book of arithmetic."

"I never heard," mentioned Broncho, "about any of Dibble's ways of mixin' scrappin' and cipherin'."

"Triggernometry?" suggested the Nueces infant.

"That's rather better than I hoped from you," nodded the Easterner, approvingly. "The other meaning is that Buckley never goes into a fight without giving away weight. He seems to dread taking the slightest advantage. That's quite close to foolhardiness when you are dealing with horse-thieves and fence-cutters who would ambush you any night, and shoot you in the back if they could. Buckley's too full of sand. He'll play Horatius and hold the bridge once too often some day."

"I'm on there," drawled the Kid; "I mind that bridge gang in the reader. Me, I go instructed for the other chap —Spurious Somebody—the one that fought and pulled his freight, to fight 'em on some other date."

"Anyway," summed up Broncho, "Bob's about the gamest man I ever see along the Rio Bravo. Great Sam Houston! If she gets any hotter she'll sizzle!" Broncho whacked at a scorpion with his four-pound Stetson felt, and the three watchers relapsed into comfortless silence.

How well Bob Buckley had kept his secret, since these men, for two years his side comrades in countless border raids and dangers, thus spake of him, not knowing that he was the most arrant physical coward in all that Rio Bravo country! Neither his friends nor his enemies had suspected him of aught else than the finest courage. It was purely a physical cowardice, and only by an extreme, grim effort of will had he forced his craven body to do the bravest deeds. Scourging himself always, as a monk whips his besetting sin, Buckley threw himself with apparent recklessness into every danger, with the hope of some day ridding himself of the despised affliction. But each successive test brought no relief, and the ranger's face, by nature adapted to cheerfulness and good-humor, became set to the guise of gloomy melancholy. Thus, while the frontier admired his deeds, and his prowess was celebrated in print and by word of mouth in many camp-fires in the valley of the Bravo, his heart was sick within him. Only himself knew of the horrible tightening of the chest, the dry mouth, the weakening of the spine, the agony of the strung nerves—the never-failing symptoms of his shameful malady.

One mere boy in his company was wont to enter a fray with a leg perched flippantly about the horn of his saddle, a cigarette hanging from his lips, which emitted smoke and original slogans of clever invention. Buckley would have given a year's pay to attain that devil-may-care method. Once the debonair youth said to him: "Buck, you go into a scrap like it was a funeral. Not," he added, with a complimentary wave of his tin cup, "but what it generally is."

Buckley's conscience was of the New England order with Western adjustments, and he continued to get his rebellious body into as many difficulties as possible; wherefore, on that sultry afternoon he chose to drive his own protesting limbs to investigation of that sudden alarm that had startled the peace and dignity of the State.

Two squares down the street stood the Top Notch Saloon. Here Buckley came upon signs of recent upheaval. A few curious spectators pressed about its front entrance, grinding beneath their heels the fragments of a plate-glass window. Inside, Buckley found Bud Dawson utterly ignoring a bullet wound in his shoulder, while he feelingly wept at having to explain why he failed to drop the "blamed masquerooter," who shot him. At the entrance of the ranger Bud turned appealingly to him for confirmation of the devastation he might have dealt.

"You know, Buck, I'd 'a' plum got him, first rattle, if I'd thought a minute. Come in a-masque-rootin', playin' female till he got the drop, and turned loose. I never reached for a gun, thinkin' it was sure Chihuahua Betty, or Mrs. Atwater, or anyhow one of the Mayfield girls comin' a-gunnin', which they might, liable as not. I never thought of that blamed Garcia until—"

"Garcia!" snapped Buckley. "How did he get over here?"

Bud's bartender took the ranger by the arm and led him to the side door. There stood a patient gray burro cropping the grass along the gutter, with a load of kindling wood tied across its back. On the ground lay a black shawl and a voluminous brown dress.

"Masquerootin' in them things," called Bud, still resisting attempted ministrations to his wounds. "Thought he was a lady till he give a yell and winged me."

"He went down this side street," said the bartender. "He was alone, and he'll hide out till night when his gang comes over. You ought to find him in that Mexican lay-out below the depot. He's got a girl down there—Pancha Sales."

"How was he armed?" asked Buckley.

"Two pearl-handled sixes, and a knife."

"Keep this for me, Billy," said the ranger, handing over his Winchester. Quixotic, perhaps, but it was Bob Buckley's way. Another man—and a braver one—might have raised a posse to accompany him. It was Buckley's rule to discard all preliminary advantage.

The Mexican had left behind him a wake of closed doors and an empty street, but now people were beginning to emerge from their places of refuge with assumed unconsciousness of anything having happened. Many citizens who knew the ranger pointed out to him with alacrity the course of Garcia's retreat.

As Buckley swung along upon the trail he felt the beginning of the suffocating constriction about his throat, the cold sweat under the brim of his hat, the old, shameful, dreaded sinking of his heart as it went down, down, down in his bosom.

The morning train of the Mexican Central had that day been three hours late, thus failing to connect with the I. & G. N. on the other side of the river. Passengers for *Los Estados Unidos* grumblingly sought entertainment in the little swaggering mongrel town of two nations, for, until the morrow, no other train would come to rescue them. Grumblingly, because two days later would begin the great fair and races in San Antone. Consider that at that time San Antone was the hub of the wheel of Fortune, and the names of its spokes were Cattle, Wool, Faro, Running Horses, and Ozone. In those times cattlemen played at crack-loo on the sidewalks with double-eagles, and gentlemen backed their conception of the fortuitous card with stacks limited in height only by the interference of gravity. Wherefore, thither journeyed the sowers and the reapers—they who stampeded the dollars, and they who rounded them up. Especially did the caterers to the amusement of the people haste to San Antone. Two greatest shows on earth were already there, and dozens of smallest ones were on the way.

On a side track near the mean little 'dobe depot stood a private car, left there by the Mexican train that morning and doomed by an ineffectual schedule to ignobly await, amid squalid surroundings, connection with the next day's regular.

The car had been once a common day-coach, but those who had sat in it and cringed to the conductor's hatband slips would never have recognized it in its transformation. Paint and gilding and certain domestic touches had liberated it from any suspicion of public servitude. The whitest of lace curtains judiciously screened its windows. From its fore end drooped in the torrid air the flag of Mexico. From its rear projected the Stars and Stripes and a busy stovepipe, the latter reinforcing in its suggestion of culinary comforts the general suggestion of privacy and ease. The beholder's eye, regarding its gorgeous sides, found interest to culminate in a single name in gold and blue letters extending almost its entire length—a single name, the audacious privilege of royalty and genius. Doubly, then, was this arrogant nomenclature here justified; for the name was that of "Alvarita, Queen of the Serpent Tribe." This, her car, was back from a triumphant tour of the principal Mexican cities, and now headed for San Antonio, where, according to promissory advertisement, she would exhibit her "Marvelous Dominion and Fearless Control over Deadly and Venomous Serpents, Handling them with Ease as they Coil and Hiss to the Terror of Thousands of Tongue-tied Tremblers!"

One hundred in the shade kept the vicinity somewhat depeopled. This quarter of the town was a ragged edge; its denizens the bubbling froth of five nations; its architecture tent, *jacal,* and 'dobe; its distractions the hurdy-gurdy and the informal contribution to the sudden stranger's store of experience. Beyond this dishonorable fringe upon the old town's jowl rose a dense mass of trees, surmounting and filling a little hollow. Through this bickered a small stream that perished down the sheer and disconcerting side of the great cañon of the Rio Bravo del Norte.

In this sordid spot was condemned to remain for certain hours the impotent transport of the Queen of the Serpent Tribe.

The front door of the car was open. Its forward end was curtained off into a small reception-room. Here the admiring and propitiatory reporters were wont to sit and transpose the music of Señorita Alvarita's talk into the more florid key of the press. A picture of Abraham Lincoln hung against a wall; one of a cluster of school-girls grouped upon stone steps was in another place; a third was Easter lilies in a blood-red frame. A neat carpet was under foot. A pitcher, sweating cold drops, and a glass stood upon a fragile stand.

In a willow rocker, reading a newspaper, sat Alvarita.

Spanish, you would say; Andalusian, or, better still, Basque; that compound, like a diamond, of darkness and fire. Hair, the shade of purple grapes viewed at midnight. Eyes, long, dusky, and disquieting with their untroubled directness of gaze. Face, haughty and bold, touched with a pretty insolence that gave it life. To hasten conviction of her charm, but glance at the stacks of handbills in the corner, green, and yellow, and white. Upon them you see an incompetent presentment of the señorita in her professional garb and pose. Irresistible, in black lace and yellow ribbons, she faces you; a blue racer is spiraled upon each bare arm; coiled twice about her waist and once about her neck, his horrid head close to hers, you perceive Kuku, the great eleven-foot Asian python.

A hand drew aside the curtain that partitioned the car, and a middle-aged, faded woman holding a knife and a half-peeled potato looked in and said:

"Alviry, are you right busy?"

"I'm reading the home paper, ma. What do you think! That pale, tow-headed Matilda Price got the most votes in the *News* for the prettiest girl in Gallipo—*lees.*"

"Shuh! She wouldn't of done it if *you'd* been home, Alviry. Lord knows, I hope we'll be there before fall's over. I'm tired gallopin' round the world playin' we are dagoes, and givin' snake shows. But that ain't what I wanted to say. That there biggest snake's gone again. I've looked all over the car and can't find him. He must have been gone an hour. I remember hearin' somethin' rustlin' along the floor, but I thought it was you."

"Oh, blame that old rascal!" exclaimed the Queen, throwing down her paper. "This is the third time he's got away. George never *will* fasten down the lid to his box properly. I do believe he's *afraid* of Kuku. Now I've got to go hunt him."

"Better hurry; somebody might hurt him."

The Queen's teeth showed in a gleaming, contemptuous smile. "No danger. When they see Kuku outside they simply scoot away and buy bromides. There's a crick over between here and the river. That old scamp'd swap his skin any time for a drink of running water. I guess I'll find him there, all right."

A few minutes later Alvarita stepped upon the forward platform, ready for her quest. Her handsome black skirt was shaped to the most recent proclamation of fashion. Her spotless shirt-waist gladdened the eye in that desert of sunshine, a swelling oasis, cool and fresh. A man's split-straw hat sat firmly upon her coiled, abundant hair. Beneath her serene, round, impudent chin a man's four-in-hand tie was jauntily knotted about a man's high, stiff collar. A parasol she carried, of white silk, and its fringe was lace, yellowly genuine.

I will grant Gallipolis as to her costume, but firmly to Seville or Valladolid I am held by her eyes; castanets, balconies, mantillas, serenades, ambuscades, escapades—all these their dark depths guaranteed.

"Ain't you afraid to go out alone, Alviry?" queried the Queen-mother anxiously. "There's so many rough people about. Mebbe you'd better—"

"I never saw anything I was afraid of yet, ma. 'Specially people. And men in particular. Don't you fret. I'll trot along back as soon as I find that runaway scamp."

The dust lay thick upon the bare ground near the tracks. Alvarita's eye soon discovered the serrated trail of the escaped python. It led across the depot grounds and away down a smaller street in the direction of the little cañon, as predicted by her. A stillness and lack of excitement in the neighborhood encouraged the hope that, as yet, the inhabitants were unaware that so formidable a guest traversed their highways. The heat had driven them indoors, whence outdrifted occasional shrill laughs, or the depressing whine of a maltreated concertina. In the shade a few Mexican children, like vivified stolid idols in clay, stared from their play, vision-struck and silent, as Alvarita came and went. Here and there a woman peeped from a door and stood dumb, reduced to silence by the aspect of the white silk parasol.

A hundred yards and the limits of the town were passed, scattered chaparral succeeding, and then a noble grove, overflowing the bijou cañon. Through this a small bright stream meandered. Park-like it was, with a kind of cockney ruralness further endorsed by the waste papers and rifled tins of picknickers. Up this stream, and down it, among its pseudo-sylvan glades and depressions, wandered the bright and unruffled Alvarita. Once she saw evidence of the recreant reptile's progress in his distinctive trail across a spread of fine sand in the arroyo. The living water was bound to lure him; he could not be far away.

So sure was she of his immediate proximity that she perched herself to idle for a time in the curve of a great creeper that looped down from a giant water-elm. To reach this she climbed from the pathway a little distance up the side of a steep and rugged incline. Around her chaparral grew thick and high. A late-blooming ratama tree dispensed from its yellow petals a sweet and persistent odor. Adown the ravine rustled a sedative wind, melancholy with the taste of sodden, fallen leaves.

Alvarita removed her hat, and undoing the oppressive convolutions of her hair, began to slowly arrange it in two long, dusky plaits.

From the obscure depths of a thick clump of evergreen shrubs five feet away, two small jewel-bright eyes were steadfastly regarding her. Coiled there lay Kuku, the great python; Kuku, the magnificent, he of the plated muzzle, the grooved lips, the eleven-foot stretch of elegantly and brilliantly mottled skin. The great python was viewing his mistress without a sound or motion to disclose his presence. Perhaps the splendid truant forefelt his capture, but, screened by the foliage, thought to prolong the delight of his escapade. What pleasure it was, after the hot and dusty car, to lie thus, smelling the running water, and feeling the agreeable roughness of the earth and stones against his body!

Soon, very soon the Queen would find him, and he, power-less as a worm in her audacious hands, would be returned to the dark chest in the narrow house that ran on wheels.

Alvarita heard a sudden crunching of the gravel below her. Turning her head she saw a big, swarthy Mexican, with a daring and evil expression, contemplating her with an ominous, dull eye.

"What do you want?" she asked as sharply as five hair-pins between her lips would permit, continuing to plait her hair, and looking him over with placid contempt. The Mexican continued to gaze at her, and showed his teeth in a white, jagged smile.

"I no hurt-y you, Señorita," he said.

"You bet you won't," answered the Queen, shaking back one finished, massive plait. "But don't you think you'd better move on?"

"Not hurt-y you—no. But maybeso take one *beso*—one li'l kees, you call him."

The man smiled again, and set his foot to ascend the slope. Alvarita leaned swiftly and picked up a stone the size of a coconut.

"Vamoose, quick," she ordered peremptorily, "you *coon!*"

The red of insult burned through the Mexican's dark skin.

"*Hidalgo, Yo!*" he shot between his fangs. "I am not neg-r-ro! *Diabla bonita,* for that you shall pay me."

He made two quick upward steps this time, but the stone, hurled by no weak arm, struck him square in the chest. He staggered back to the footway, swerved half around, and met another sight that drove all thoughts of the girl from his head. She turned her eyes to see what had diverted his interest. A man with red-brown, curling hair and a melancholy, sunburned, smooth-shaven face was com-ing up the path, twenty yards away. Around the Mexican's waist was buckled a pistol belt with two empty holsters. He had laid aside his sixes—possibly in the *jacal* of the fair

Pancha—and had forgotten them when the passing of the fairer Alvarita had enticed him to her trail. His hands now flew instinctively to the holsters, but finding the weapons gone, he spread his fingers outward with the eloquent, abjuring, deprecating Latin gesture, and stood like a rock. Seeing his plight, the newcomer unbuckled his own belt containing two revolvers, threw it upon the ground, and continued to advance.

"Splendid!" murmured Alvarita, with flashing eyes.

As Bob Buckley, according to the mad code of bravery that his sensitive conscience imposed upon his cowardly nerves, abandoned his guns and closed in upon his enemy, the old, inevitable nausea of abject fear wrung him. His breath whistled through his constricted air passages. His feet seemed like lumps of lead. His mouth was dry as dust. His heart, congested with blood, hurt his ribs as it thumped against them. The hot June day turned to moist November. And still he advanced, spurred by a mandatory pride that strained its uttermost against his weakling flesh.

The distance between the two men slowly lessened. The Mexican stood, immovable, waiting. When scarce five yards separated them a little shower of loosened gravel rattled down from above to the ranger's feet. He glanced upward with instinctive caution. A pair of dark eyes, brilliantly soft, and fierily tender, encountered and held his own. The most fearful heart and the boldest one in all the Rio Bravo country exchanged a silent and inscrutable communication. Alvarita, still seated within her vine, leaned forward above the breast-high chaparral. One hand was laid across her bosom. One great dark braid curved forward over her shoulder. Her lips were parted; her face was lit with what seemed but wonder—great and absolute wonder. Her eyes lingered upon Buckley's. Let no one ask or presume to tell through what subtle medium the miracle was performed. As by a lightning flash two clouds will accomplish counterpoise and compensation of electric surcharge, so on that eyeglance the man received his complement of manhood, and the maid conceded what enriched her womanly grace by its loss.

The Mexican, suddenly stirring, ventilated his attitude of apathetic waiting by conjuring swiftly from his bootleg a long knife. Buckley cast aside his hat, and laughed once aloud, like a happy school-boy at a frolic. Then, empty-handed, he sprang nimbly, and Garcia met him without default.

So soon was the engagement ended that disappointment imposed upon the ranger's warlike ecstasy. Instead of dealing the traditional downward stroke, the Mexican lunged straight with his knife. Buckley took the precarious chance, and caught his wrist, fair and firm. Then he delivered the good Saxon knock-out blow—always so pathetically disastrous to the fistless Latin races—and Garcia was down and out, with his head under a clump of prickly pears. The ranger looked up again to the Queen of the Serpents.

Alvarita scrambled down to the path.

"I'm mighty glad I happened along when I did," said the ranger.

"He—he frightened me so!" cooed Alvarita.

They did not hear the long, low hiss of the python under the shrubs. Wiliest of the beasts, no doubt he was expressing the humiliation he felt at having so long dwelt in subjection to this trembling and coloring mistress of his whom he had deemed so strong and potent and fearsome.

Then came galloping to the spot the civic authorities; and to them the ranger awarded the prostrate disturber of the peace, whom they bore away limply across the saddle of one of their mounts. But Buckley and Alvarita lingered.

Slowly, slowly they walked. The ranger regained his belt of weapons. With a fine timidity she begged the indulgence of fingering the great .045's, with little "Ohs" and "Ahs" of new-born, delicious shyness.

The *cañoncito* was growing dusky. Beyond its terminus in the river bluff they could see the outer world yet suffused with the waning glory of sunset.

A scream—a piercing scream of fright from Alvarita. Back she cowered, and the ready, protecting arm of Buckley formed her refuge. What terror so dire as to thus beset the close of the reign of the never-before-daunted Queen?

Across the path there crawled a *caterpillar*—a horrid, fuzzy, two-inch caterpillar! Truly, Kuku, thou wert avenged. Thus abdicated the Queen of the Serpent Tribe—*viva la reina!*

TAPPAN'S BURRO

Zane Grey

I

Tappan gazed down upon the newly born little burro with something of pity and consternation. It was not a vigorous offspring of the redoubtable Jennie, champion of all the numberless burros he had driven in his desert-prospecting years. He could not leave it there to die. Surely it was not strong enough to follow its mother. And to kill it was beyond him.

"Poor little devil!" soliloquized Tappan. "Reckon neither Jennie nor I wanted it to be born. . . . I'll have to hole up in this camp a few days. You can never tell what a burro will do. It might fool us an' grow strong all of a sudden."

Whereupon Tappan left Jennie and her tiny, gray lop-eared baby to themselves, and leisurely set about making permanent camp. The water at this oasis was not much to his liking, but it was drinkable, and he felt he must put up with it. For the rest the oasis was desirable enough as a camping site. Desert wanderers like Tappan favored the lonely water holes. This one was up under the bold brow of the Chocolate Mountains, where rocky wall met the desert sand, and a green patch of *paloverdes* and mesquites proved the presence of water. It had a magnificent view down a many-leagued slope of desert growths, across the dark belt of green and the shining strip of red that marked the Rio Colorado, and on to the upflung Arizona land, range lifting to range until the saw-toothed peaks notched the blue sky.

Locked in the iron fastnesses of these desert mountains was gold. Tappan, if he had any calling, was a prospector. But the lure of gold did not bind him to this wandering life any more than the freedom of it. He had never made a rich strike. About the best he could ever do was to dig enough gold to grubstake himself for another prospecting trip into some remote corner of the American Desert. Tappan knew the arid Southwest from San Diego to the Pecos River and from Picacho on the Colorado to the Tonto Basin. Few prospectors had the strength and endurance of Tappan. He was a giant in build, and at thirty-five had never yet reached the limit of his physical force.

With hammer and pick and magnifying glass Tappan scaled the bare ridges. He was not an expert in testing minerals. He knew he might easily pass by a rich vein of ore. But he did his best, sure at least that no prospector could get more than he out of the pursuit of gold. Tappan was more of a naturalist than a prospector, and more of a dreamer than either. Many were the idle moments that he sat staring down the vast reaches of the valleys, or watching some creature of the wasteland, or marveling at the vivid hues of desert flowers.

Tappan waited two weeks at this oasis for Jennie's baby burro to grow strong enough to walk. And the very day that Tappan decided to break camp he found signs of gold at the head of a wash above the oasis. Quite by chance, as he was looking for his burros, he struck his pick into a place no

different from a thousand others there, and hit into a pocket
of gold. He cleaned out the pocket before sunset, the richer
for several thousand dollars.

"You brought me luck," said Tappan, to the little gray
burro staggering around its mother. "Your name is Jenet.
You're Tappan's burro, an' I reckon he'll stick to you."

Jenet belied the promise of her birth. Like a weed in
fertile ground she grew. Winter and summer Tappan pa-
trolled the sand beats from one trading post to another, and
his burros traveled with him. Jenet had an especially good
training. Her mother had happened to be a remarkably
good burro before Tappan had bought her. And Tappan had
patience; he found leisure to do things, and he had something of pride in Jenet. Whenever he happened to drop into
Ehrenberg or Yuma, or any freighting station, some prospector always tried to buy Jenet. She grew as large as a
medium-sized mule, and a three-hundred-pound pack was
no load to discommode her.

Tappan, in common with most lonely wanderers of the
desert, talked to his burro. As the years passed this habit
grew, until Tappan would talk to Jenet just to hear the sound
of his voice. Perhaps that was all which kept him human.

"Jenet, you're worthy of a happier life," Tappan would
say, as he unpacked her after a long day's march over the
barren land. "You're a ship of the desert. Here we are, with
grub an' water, a hundred miles from any camp. An' what
but you could have fetched me here? No horse! No mule! No
man! Nothin' but a camel, an' so I call you ship of the desert.
But for you an' your kind, Jenet, there'd be no prospectors,
and few gold mines. Reckon the desert would be still an
unknown waste. . . . You're a great beast of burden, Jenet,
an' there's no one to sing your praise."

And of a golden sunrise, when Jenet was packed and
ready to face the cool, sweet fragrance of the desert, Tappan
was wont to say:

"Go along with you, Jenet. The mornin's fine. Look at

the mountains yonder callin' us. It's only a step down there. All purple an' violet! It's the life for us, my burro, an' Tappan's as rich as if all these sands were pearls."

But sometimes, at sunset, when the way had been long and hot and rough, Tappan would bend his shaggy head over Jenet, and talk in different mood.

"Another day gone, Jenet, another journey ended—an' Tappan is only older, wearier, sicker. There's no reward for your faithfulness. I'm only a desert rat, livin' from hole to hole. No home! No face to see. . . . Some sunset, Jenet, we'll reach the end of the trail. An' Tappan's bones will bleach in the sands. An' no one will know or care!"

When Jenet was two years old she would have taken the blue ribbon in competition with all the burros of the Southwest. She was unusually large and strong, perfectly proportioned, sound in every particular, and practically tireless. But these were not the only characteristics that made prospectors envious of Tappan. Jenet had the common virtues of all good burros magnified to an unbelievable degree. Moreover, she had sense and instinct that to Tappan bordered on the supernatural.

During these years Tappan's trail crisscrossed the mineral region of the Southwest. But, as always, the rich strike held aloof. It was like the pot of gold buried at the foot of the rainbow. Jenet knew the trails and the water holes better than Tappan. She could follow a trail obliterated by drifting sand or cut out by running water. She could scent at long distance a new spring on the desert or a strange water hole. She never wandered far from camp so that Tappan had to walk far in search of her. Wild burros, the bane of most prospectors, held no charm for Jenet. And she had never yet shown any especial liking for a tame burro. This was the strangest feature of Jenet's complex character. Burros were noted for their habit of pairing off, and forming friendships for one or more comrades. These relations were permanent. But Jenet still remained fancy free.

Tappan scarcely realized how he relied upon this big, gray, serene beast of burden. Of course, when chance threw him among men of his calling he would brag about her. But he had never really appreciated Jenet. In his way Tappan was a brooding, plodding fellow, not conscious of sentiment. When he bragged about Jenet it was her good qualities upon which he dilated. But what he really liked best about her were the little things of every day.

During the earlier years of her training Jenet had been a thief. She would pretend to be asleep for hours just to get a chance to steal something out of camp. Tappan had broken this habit in its incipiency. But he never quite trusted her. Jenet was a burro.

Jenet ate anything offered her. She could fare for herself or go without. Whatever Tappan had left from his own meals was certain to be rich dessert for Jenet. Every meal time she would stand near the camp fire, with one great long ear drooping, and the other standing erect. Her expression was one of meekness, of unending patience. She would lick a tin can until it shone resplendent. On long, hard, barren trails Jenet's deportment did not vary from that where the water holes and grassy patches were many. She did not need to have grass or grain. Brittle-bush and sage were good fare for her. She could eat greasewood, a desert plant that pro-tected itself with a sap as sticky as varnish and far more dangerous to animals. She could eat cacti. Tappan had seen her break off leaves of the prickly pear cactus, and stamp upon them with her forefeet, mashing off the thorns, so that she could consume the succulent pulp. She liked mesquite beans, and leaves of willow, and all the trailing vines of the desert. And she could subsist in an arid waste land where a man would have died in short order.

No ascent or descent was too hard or dangerous for Jenet, provided it was possible of accomplishment. She would refuse a trail that was impassable. She seemed to have an uncanny instinct both for what she could do, and what was beyond a burro. Tappan had never known her to fail on something to which she stuck persistently. Swift streams of water, always bugbears to burros, did not stop Jenet. She hated quicksand, but could be trusted to navigate it, if that were possible. When she stepped gingerly, with little inch steps, out upon thin crust of ice or salty crust of desert sink hole, Tappan would know that it was safe, or she would turn back. Thunder and lightning, intense heat or bitter cold, the sirocco sand storm of the desert, the white dust of the alkali wastes—these were all the same to Jenet.

One August, the hottest and driest of his desert experience, Tappan found himself working a most promising claim in the lower reaches of the Panamint Mountains on the northern slope above Death Valley. It was a hard country at the most favorable season; in August it was terrible.

The Panamints were infested by various small gangs of desperadoes—outlaw claim jumpers where opportunity afforded—and out-and-out robbers, even murderers where they could not get the gold any other way.

Tappan had been warned not to go into this region alone. But he never heeded any warnings. And the idea that he would ever strike a claim or dig enough gold to make himself an attractive target for outlaws seemed preposterous and not worth considering. Tappan had become a wanderer now from the unbreakable habit of it. Much to his amaze he struck a rich ledge of free gold in a canyon of the Panamints; and he worked from daylight until dark. He forgot about the claim jumpers, until one day he saw Jenet's long ears go up in the manner habitual with her when she saw strange men. Tappan watched the rest of that day, but did not catch a glimpse of any living thing. It was a desolate place, shut in, red-walled, hazy with heat, and brooding with an eternal silence.

Not long after that Tappan discovered boot tracks of several men adjacent to his camp and in an out-of-the-way spot, which persuaded him that he was being watched. Claim jumpers who were not going to jump his claim in this torrid heat, but meant to let him dig the gold and then kill him. Tappan was not the kind of man to be afraid. He grew wrathful and stubborn. He had six small canvas bags of gold and did not mean to lose them. Still, he was worried.

"Now, what's best to do?" he pondered. "I mustn't give it away that I'm wise. Reckon I'd better act natural. But I can't stay here longer. My claim's about worked out. An' these jumpers are smart enough to know it. . . . I've got to make a break at night. What to do?"

Tappan did not want to cache the gold, for in that case, of course, he would have to return for it. Still, he reluctantly admitted to himself that this was the best way to save it. Probably these robbers were watching him day and night. It would be most unwise to attempt escaping by traveling up over the Panamints.

"Reckon my only chance is goin' down into Death Valley," soliloquized Tappan, grimly.

The alternative thus presented was not to his liking. Crossing Death Valley at this season was always perilous, and never attempted in the heat of day. And at this particular time of intense torridity, when the day heat was unendurable and the midnight furnace gales were blowing, it was an enterprise from which even Tappan shrank. Added to this were the facts that he was too far west of the narrow part of the valley, and even if he did get across he would find himself in the most forbidding and desolate region of the Funeral Mountains.

Thus thinking and planning, Tappan went about his mining and camp tasks, trying his best to act natural. But he did not succeed. It was impossible, while expecting a shot at any moment, to act as if there was nothing on his mind. His camp lay at the bottom of a rocky slope. A tiny spring of water made verdure of grass and mesquite, welcome green in all that stark iron nakedness. His camp site was out in the open, on the bench near the spring. The gold claim that Tappan was working was not visible from any vantage point either below or above. It lay back at the head of a break in the rocky wall. It had two virtues—one that the sun never got to it, and the other that it was well hidden. Once there, Tappan knew he could not be seen. This, however, did not diminish his growing uneasiness. The solemn stillness was a menace. The heat of the day appeared to be augmenting to a degree beyond his experience. Every few moments Tappan would slip back through a narrow defile in the rocks and peep from his covert down at the camp. On the last of these occasions he saw Jenet out in the open. She stood motionless. Her long ears were erect. In an instant Tappan became strung with thrilling excitement. His keen eyes searched every approach to his camp. And at last in the gully below to the right he discovered two men crawling along from rock to rock. Jenet had seen them enter that gully and was now watching for them to appear.

Tappan's excitement gave place to a grimmer emotion. These stealthy visitors were going to hide in ambush, and kill him as he returned to camp.

"Jenet, reckon what I owe you is a whole lot," muttered Tappan. "They'd have got me sure. . . . But now—"

Tappan left his tools, and crawled out of his covert into the jumble of huge rocks toward the left of the slope. He had a six-shooter. His rifle he had left in camp. Tappan had seen only two men, but he knew there were more than that, if not actually near at hand at the moment, then surely not far away. And his chance was to worm his way like an Indian down to camp. With the rifle in his possession he would make short work of the present difficulty.

"Lucky Jenet's right in camp!" said Tappan, to himself. "It beats hell how she does things!"

Tappan was already deciding to pack and hurry away. On the moment Death Valley did not daunt him. This matter of crawling and gliding along was work unsuited to his great stature. He was too big to hide behind a little shrub or a rock. And he was not used to stepping lightly. His hob-nailed boots could not be placed noiselessly upon the stones. Moreover, he could not progress without displacing little bits of weathered rock. He was sure that keen ears not too far distant could have heard him. But he kept on, making good progress around that slope to the far side of the canyon. Fortunately, he headed the gully up which his ambushers were stealing. On the other hand, this far side of the canyon afforded but little cover. The sun had gone down back of the huge red mass of the mountain. It had left the rocks so hot Tappan could not touch them with his bare hands.

He was about to stride out from his last covert and make a run for it down the rest of the slope, when, surveying the whole amphitheater below him, he espied the two men coming up out of the gully, headed toward his camp. They looked in his direction. Surely they had heard or seen him. But Tappan perceived at a glance that he was the closer to the camp. Without another moment of hesitation, he plunged from his hiding place, down the weathered slope. His giant strides set the loose rocks sliding and rattling. The men saw him. The foremost yelled to the one behind him. Then they both broke into a run. Tappan reached the level of the bench, and saw he could beat either of them into the camp. Unless he were disabled! He felt the wind of a heavy bullet before he heard it strike the rocks beyond. Then followed the boom of a Colt. One of his enemies had halted to shoot. This spurred Tappan to tremendous exertion. He flew over the rough ground, scarcely hearing the rapid shots. He could no longer see the man who was firing. But the first one was in plain sight, running hard, not yet seeing he was out of the race.

When he became aware of that he halted, and dropping on one knee, leveled his gun at the running Tappan. The distance was scarcely sixty yards. His first shot did not allow for Tappan's speed. His second kicked up the gravel in Tappan's face. Then followed three more shots in rapid succession. The man divined that Tappan had a rifle in camp. Then he steadied himself, waiting for the moment when Tappan had to slow down and halt. As Tappan reached his camp and dove for his rifle, the robber took time for his last aim, evidently hoping to get a stationary target. But Tappan did not get up from behind his camp duffel. It had been a habit of his to pile his boxes of supplies and roll of bedding together, and cover them with a canvas. He poked his rifle over the top of this and shot the robber.

Then, leaping up, he ran forward to get sight of the second one. This man began to run along the edge of the gully. Tappan fired rapidly at him. The third shot knocked the fellow down. But he got up, and yelling, as if for succor, he ran off. Tappan got another shot before he disappeared.

"Ahuh!" grunted Tappan, grimly. His keen gaze came back to survey the fallen robber, and then went out over the bench, across the wide mouth of the canyon. Tappan thought he had better utilize time to pack instead of pursuing the fleeing man.

Reloading the rifle, he hurried out to find Jenet. She was coming in to camp.

"Shore you're a treasure, old girl!" ejaculated Tappan.

Never in his life had he packed Jenet, or any other burro, so quickly. His last act was to drink all he could hold, fill his two canteens, and make Jenet drink. Then, rifle in hand, he drove the burro out of camp, round the corner of the red wall, to the wide gateway that opened down into Death Valley.

Tappan looked back more than he looked ahead. And he had traveled down a mile or more before he began to breathe more easily. He had escaped the claim jumpers. Even if they did show up in pursuit now, they could never catch him. Tappan believed he could travel faster and farther than any men of that ilk. But they did not appear. Perhaps the crippled one had not been able to reach his comrades in time. More likely, however, the gang had no taste for a chase in that torrid heat.

Tappan slowed his stride. He was almost as wet with sweat as if he had fallen into the spring. The great beads rolled down his face. And there seemed to be little streams of fire trickling down his breast. But despite this, and his labored panting for breath, not until he halted in the shade of a rocky wall did he realize the heat.

It was terrific. Instantly then he knew he was safe from pursuit. But he knew also that he faced a greater peril than that of robbers. He could fight evil men, but he could not fight this heat.

So he rested there, regaining his breath. Already thirst was acute. Jenet stood near by, watching him. Tappan, with his habit of humanizing the burro, imagined that Jenet looked serious. A moment's thought was enough for Tappan to appreciate the gravity of his situation. He was about to go down into the upper end of Death Valley—a part of that country unfamiliar to him. He must cross it, and also the Funeral Mountains, at a season when a prospector who knew the trails and water holes would have to be forced to undertake it. Tappan had no choice.

His rifle was too hot to hold, so he stuck it in Jenet's pack; and, burdened only by a canteen of water, he set out, driving the burro ahead. Once he looked back up the wide-mouthed canyon. It appeared to smoke with red heat veils. The silence was oppressive.

Presently he turned the last corner that obstructed sight of Death Valley. Tappan had never been appalled by any aspect of the desert, but it was certain that here he halted. Back in his mountain-walled camp the sun had passed behind the high domes, but here it still held most of the valley in its blazing grip. Death Valley looked a ghastly, glaring level of white, over which a strange dull leaden haze drooped like a blanket. Ghosts of mountain peaks appeared to show dim and vague. There was no movement of anything. No wind! The valley was dead. Desolation reigned supreme. Tappan could not see far toward either end of the valley. A few miles of white glare merged at last into leaden pall. A strong odor, not unlike sulphur, seemed to add weight to the air.

Tappan strode on, mindful that Jenet had decided opinions of her own. She did not want to go straight ahead or to

right or left, but back. That was the one direction impossible
for Tappan. And he had to resort to a rare measure—that of
beating her. But at last Jenet accepted the inevitable and
headed down into the stark and naked plain. Soon Tappan
reached the margin of the zone of shade cast by the mountain and was now exposed to the sun. The difference seemed
tremendous. He had been hot, oppressed, weighted. It was
now as if he was burned through his clothes, and walked on
red-hot sands.

When Tappan ceased to sweat and his skin became dry,
he drank half a canteen of water, and slowed his stride.
Inured to desert hardship as he was, he could not long stand
this. Jenet did not exhibit any lessening of vigor. In truth
what she showed now was an increasing nervousness. It was
almost as if she scented an enemy. Tappan never before had
such faith in her. Jenet was equal to this task.

With that blazing sun on his back, Tappan felt he was
being pursued by a furnace. He was compelled to drink the
remaining half of his first canteen of water. Sunset would
save him. Two more hours of such insupportable heat would
lay him prostrate.

The ghastly glare of the valley took on a reddish tinge.
The heat was blinding Tappan. The time came when he
walked beside Jenet with a hand on her pack, for his eyes
could no longer endure the furnace glare. Even with them
closed he knew when the sun sank behind the Panamints.
That fire no longer followed him. And the red left his eyelids.

With the sinking of the sun the world of Death Valley
changed. It smoked with heat veils. But the intolerable constant burn was gone. The change was so immense that it
seemed to have brought coolness.

In the twilight—strange, ghostly, somber, silent as
death—Tappan followed Jenet off the sand, down upon the
silt and borax level, to the crusty salt. Before dark Jenet
halted at a sluggish belt of fluid—acid, it appeared to Tappan. It was not deep. And the bottom felt stable. But Jenet

refused to cross. Tappan trusted her judgment more than his own. Jenet headed to the left and followed the course of the strange stream.

Night intervened. A night without stars or sky or sound, hot, breathless, charged with some intangible current! Tappan dreaded the midnight furnace winds of Death Valley. He had never encountered them. He had heard prospectors say that any man caught in Death Valley when these gales blew would never get out to tell the tale. And Jenet seemed to have something on her mind. She was no longer a leisurely, complacent burro. Tappan imagined Jenet seemed stern. Most assuredly she knew now which way she wanted to travel. It was not easy for Tappan to keep up with her, and ten paces beyond him she was out of sight.

At last Jenet headed the acid wash, and turned across the valley into a field of broken salt crust, like the roughened ice of a river that had broken and jammed, then frozen again. Impossible was it to make even a reasonable headway. It was a zone, however, that eventually gave way to Jenet's instinct for direction. Tappan had long ceased to try to keep his bearings. North, south, east, and west were all the same to him. The night was a blank—the darkness a wall—the silence a terrible menace flung at any leaving creature. Death Valley had endured them millions of years before living creatures had existed. It was no place for a man.

Tappan was now three hundred and more feet below sea level, in the aftermath of a day that had registered one hundred and forty-five degrees of heat. He knew, when he began to lose thought and balance—when only the primitive instincts directed his bodily machine. And he struggled with all his will power to keep hold of his sense of sight and feeling. He hoped to cross the lower level before the midnight gales began to blow.

Tappan's hope was vain. According to record, once in a long season of intense heat, there came a night when the furnace winds broke their schedule, and began early. The misfortune of Tappan was that he had struck this night.

Suddenly it seemed that the air, sodden with heat, began to move. It had weight. It moved soundlessly and ponderously. But it gathered momentum. Tappan realized what was happening. The blanket of heat generated by the day was yielding to outside pressure. Something had created a movement of the hotter air that must find its way upward, to give place for the cooler air that must find its way down.

Tappan heard the first, low, distant moan of wind and it struck terror to his heart. It did not have an earthly sound. Was that a knell for him? Nothing was surer than the fact that the desert must sooner or later claim him as a victim. Grim and strong, he rebelled against the conviction.

That moan was a forerunner of others, growing louder and longer until the weird sound became continuous. Then the movement of wind was accelerated and began to carry a fine dust. Dark as the night was, it did not hide the pale sheets of dust that moved along the level plain. Tappan's feet felt the slow rise in the floor of the valley. His nose recognized the zone of borax and alkali and niter and sulphur. He had reached the pit of the valley at the time of the furnace winds.

The moan augmented to a roar, coming like a mighty storm through a forest. It was hellish—like the woeful tide of Acheron. It enveloped Tappan. And the gale bore down in tremendous volume, like a furnace blast. Tappan seemed to feel his body penetrated by a million needles of fire. He seemed to dry up. The blackness of night had a spectral, whitish cast; the gloom was a whirling medium; the valley floor was lost in a sheeted, fiercely seeping stream of silt. Deadly fumes swept by, not lingering long enough to suffocate Tappan. He would gasp and choke—then the poison gas was gone on the gale. But hardest to endure was the heavy body of moving heat. Tappan grew blind, so that he had to hold to Jenet, and stumble along. Every gasping breath was a tortured effort. He could not bear a scarf over his face. His lungs heaved like great leather bellows. His heart pumped like an engine short of fuel. This was the supreme test for his never proven endurance. And he was all but vanquished. Tappan's senses of sight and smell and hearing failed him. There was left only the sense of touch—a feeling of rope and burro and ground—and an awful insulating pressure upon all his body. His feet marked a change from salty plain to sandy ascent and then to rocky slope. The pressure of wind gradually lessened: the difference in air made life possible; the feeling of being dragged endlessly by Jenet had ceased. Tappan went his limit and fell into oblivion.

When he came to, he was suffering bodily tortures. Sight was dim. But he saw walls of rocks, green growths of mesquite, tamarack, and grass. Jenet was lying down, with her pack flopped to one side. Tappan's dead ears recovered to a strange murmuring, babbling sound. Then he realized his deliverance. Jenet had led him across Death Valley, up into the mountain range, straight to a spring of running water.

Tappan crawled to the edge of the water and drank guardedly, a little at a time. He had to quell a terrific craving to drink his fill. Then he crawled to Jenet, and loosening the ropes of her pack, freed her from its burden. Jenet got up, apparently none the worse for her ordeal. She gazed mildly at Tappan, as if to say: "Well, I got you out of that hole."

Tappan returned her gaze. Were they only man and beast, alone in the desert? She seemed magnified to Tappan, no longer a plodding, stupid burro.

"Jenet, you—saved—my life," Tappan tried to enunciate. "I'll never—forget."

Tappan was struck then to a realization of Jenet's service. He was unutterably grateful. Yet the time came when he did forget.

II

Tappan had a weakness common to all prospectors: Any tale of a lost gold mine would excite his interest; and well-known legends of lost mines always obsessed him.

Peg-leg Smith's lost gold mine had lured Tappan to no less than half a dozen trips into the terrible shifting-sand country of southern California. There was no water near the region said to hide this mine of fabulous wealth. Many prospectors had left their bones to bleach white in the sun, finally to be buried by the ever blowing sands. Upon the occasion of Tappan's last escape from this desolate and forbidding desert, he had promised Jenet never to undertake it again. It seemed Tappan promised the faithful burro a good many things. It had been a habit.

When Tappan had a particularly hard experience or perilous adventure, he always took a dislike to the immediate country where it had befallen him. Jenet had dragged him across Death Valley, through incredible heat and the midnight furnace winds of that strange place; and he had promised her he would never forget how she had saved his life. Nor would he ever go back to Death Valley! He made his way over the Funeral Mountains, worked down through Nevada, and crossed the Rio Colorado above Needles, and entered Arizona. He traveled leisurely, but he kept going, and headed southeast toward Globe. There he cashed one of his six bags of gold, and indulged in the luxury of a complete new outfit. Even Jenet appreciated this fact, for the old outfit would scarcely hold together.

Tappan had the other five bags of gold in his pack; and after hours of hesitation he decided he would not cash them and entrust the money to a bank. He would take care of them. For him the value of this gold amounted to a small fortune. Many plans suggested themselves to Tappan. But in the end he grew weary of them. What did he want with a ranch, or cattle, or an outfitting store, or any of the businesses he now had the means to buy? Towns soon palled on Tappan. People did not long please him. Selfish interest and greed seemed paramount everywhere. Besides, if he acquired a place to take up his time, what would become of Jenet? That question decided him. He packed the burro and once more took to the trails.

A dim, lofty, purple range called alluringly to Tappan. The Superstition Mountains! Somewhere in that purple mass hid the famous treasure called the Lost Dutchman gold mine. Tappan had heard the story often. A Dutch prospector struck gold in the Superstitions. He kept the location secret. When he ran short of money, he would disappear for a few weeks, and then return with bags of gold. Wherever his strike, it assuredly was a rich one. No one ever could trail him or get a word out of him. Time passed. A few years made him old. During this time he conceived a liking for a young man, and eventually confided to him that some day he would tell him the secret of his gold mine. He had drawn a map of the landmarks adjacent to his mine. But he was careful not to put on paper directions how to get there. It chanced that he suddenly fell ill and saw his end was near. Then he summoned the young man who had been so fortunate as to win his regard. Now this individual was a ne'er-do-well, and upon this occasion he was half drunk. The dying Dutchman produced his map, and gave it with verbal directions to the young man. Then he died. When the recipient of this fortune recovered from the effects of liquor, he could not remember all the Dutchman had told him. He tortured himself to remember names and places. But the mine was up in the Superstition Mountains. He never remembered. He never found the lost mine, though he spent his life and died trying. Thus the story passed into the legend of the Lost Dutchman.

Tappan now had his try at finding it. But for him the shifting sands of the southern California desert or even the barren and desolate Death Valley were preferable to this Superstition Range. It was a harder country than the Pinacate of Sonora. Tappan hated cactus, and the Superstitions were full of it. Everywhere stood up the huge *saguaro,* the giant cacti of the Arizona plateaus, tall like branchless trees, fluted and columnar, beautiful and fascinating to gaze upon, but obnoxious to prospector and burro.

One day from a north slope Tappan saw afar a wonderful country of black timber, above which zigzagged for many miles a yellow, winding rampart of rock. This he took to be the rim of the Mogollon Mesa, one of Arizona's freaks of nature. Something called Tappan. He was forever victim to yearnings for the unattainable. He was tired of heat, glare, dust, bare rock, and thorny cactus. The Lost Dutchman gold mine was a myth. Besides, he did not need any more gold.

Next morning Tappan packed Jenet and worked down off the north slopes of the Superstition Range. That night about sunset he made camp on the bank of a clear brook, with grass and wood in abundance—such a camp site as a prospector dreamed of but seldom found.

Before dark Jenet's long ears told of the advent of strangers. A man and a woman rode down the trail into Tappan's camp. They had poor horses, and led a pack animal that appeared too old and weak to bear up under even the meager pack he carried.

"Howdy," said the man.

Tappan rose from his task to his lofty height and returned the greeting. The man was middle-aged, swarthy, and rugged, a mountaineer, with something about him that Tappan instinctively distrusted. The woman was under thirty, comely in a full-blown way, with rich brown skin and glossy dark hair. She had wide-open black eyes that bent a curious possession-taking gaze upon Tappan.

"Care if we camp with you?" she inquired, and she smiled.

That smile changed Tappan's habit and conviction of a lifetime.

"No indeed. Reckon I'd like a little company," he said.

Very probably Jenet did not understand Tappan's words, but she dropped one ear, and walked out of camp to the green bank.

"Thanks, stranger," replied the woman. "That grub shore smells good." She hesitated a moment, evidently waiting to catch her companion's eye, then she continued. "My name's Madge Beam. He's my brother Jake. . . . Who might you happen to be?"

"I'm Tappan, lone prospector, as you see," replied Tappan.

"Tappan! What's your front handle?" she queried, curiously.

"Fact is, I don't remember," replied Tappan, as he brushed a huge hand through his shaggy hair.

"Ahuh? Any name's good enough."

When she dismounted, Tappan saw that she had a tall, lithe figure, garbed in rider's overalls and boots. She unsaddled her horse with the dexterity of long practice. The saddlebags she carried over to the spot the man Jake had selected to throw the pack.

Tappan heard them talking in low tones. It struck him as strange that he did not have his usual reaction to an invasion of his privacy and solitude. Tappan had thrilled under those black eyes. And now a queer sensation of the unusual rose in him. Bending over his camp-fire tasks he pondered this and that, but mostly the sense of the nearness of a woman. Like most desert men, Tappan knew little of the other sex. A few that he might have been drawn to went out of his wandering life as quickly as they had entered it. This Madge Beam took possession of his thoughts. An evidence of Tappan's preoccupation was the fact that he burned his first batch of biscuits. And Tappan felt proud of his culinary ability. He was on his knees, mixing more flour and water, when the woman spoke from right behind him.

"Tough luck you burned the first pan," she said. "But it's a good turn for your burro. That shore is a burro. Biggest I ever saw."

She picked up the burned biscuits and tossed them over to Jenet. Then she came back to Tappan's side, rather embarrassingly close.

"Tappan, I know how I'll eat, so I ought to ask you to let me help," she said, with a laugh.

"No, I don't need any," replied Tappan. "You sit down on my roll of beddin' there. Must be tired, aren't you?"

"Not so very," she returned. "That is, I'm not tired of ridin'." She spoke the second part of this reply in lower tone.

Tappan looked up from his task. The woman had washed her face, brushed her hair, and had put on a skirt— a singularly attractive change. Tappan thought her younger. She was the handsomest woman he had ever seen. The look of her made him clumsy. What eyes she had! They looked through him. Tappan returned to his task, wondering if he was right in his surmise that she wanted to be friendly.

"Jake an' I drove a bunch of cattle to Maricopa," she volunteered. "We sold 'em, an' Jake gambled away most of the money. I couldn't get what I wanted."

"Too bad! So you're ranchers. Once thought I'd like that. Fact is, down here at Globe a few weeks ago I came near buyin' some rancher out an' tryin' the game."

"You did?" Her query had a low, quick eagerness that somehow thrilled Tappan. But he did not look up.

"I'm a wanderer. I'd never do on a ranch."

"But if you had a woman?" Her laugh was subtle and gay.

"A woman! For me? Oh, Lord, no!" ejaculated Tappan, in confusion.

"Why not? Are you a woman-hater?"

"I can't say that," replied Tappan, soberly. "It's just— I guess—no woman would have me."

"Faint heart never won fair lady."

Tappan had no reply for that. He surely was making a mess of the second pan of biscuit dough. Manifestly the woman saw this, for with a laugh she plumped down on her knees in front of Tappan, and rolled her sleeves up over shapely brown arms.

"Poor man! Shore you need a woman. Let me show you," she said, and put her hands right down upon Tappan's. The touch gave him a strange thrill. He had to pull his hands away, and as he wiped them with his scarf he looked at her. He seemed compelled to look. She was close to him now, smiling in good nature, a little scornful of man's encroachment upon the housewifely duties of a woman. A subtle something emanated from her—a more than kindness or gayety. Tappan grasped that it was just the woman of her. And it was going to his head.

"Very well, let's see you show me," he replied, as he rose to his feet.

Just then the brother Jake strolled over, and he had a rather amused and derisive eye for his sister.

"Wal, Tappan, she's not overfond of work, but I reckon she can cook," he said.

Tappan felt greatly relieved at the approach of this brother. And he fell into conversation with him, telling something of his prospecting since leaving Globe, and listening to the man's cattle talk. By and by the woman called, "Come an' get it!" Then they sat down to eat, and, as usual with hungry wayfarers, they did not talk much until appetite was satisfied. Afterward, before the camp fire, they began to talk again, Jake being the most discursive. Tappan conceived the idea that the rancher was rather curious about him, and perhaps wanted to sell his ranch. The woman seemed more thoughtful, with her wide black eyes on the fire.

"Tappan, what way you travelin'?" finally inquired Beam.

"Can't say. I just worked down out of the Superstitions. Haven't any place in mind. Where does this road go?"

"To the Tonto Basin. Ever heard of it?"

"Yes, the name isn't new. What's in this Basin?"

The man grunted. "Tonto once was home for the Apache. It's now got a few sheep an' cattlemen, lots of rustlers. An' say, if you like to hunt bear an' deer, come along with us."

"Thanks. I don't know as I can," returned Tappan, irresolutely. He was not used to such possibilities as this suggested.

Then the woman spoke up. "It's a pretty country. Wild

an' different. We live up under the rim rock. There's mineral in the canyons."

Was it that about mineral which decided Tappan or the
look in her eyes?

Tappan's world of thought and feeling underwent as
great a change as this Tonto Basin differed from the stark
desert so long his home. The trail to the log cabin of the
Beams climbed many a ridge and slope and foothill, all covered with manzanita, mescal, cedar, and juniper, at last to
reach the canyons of the Rim, where lofty pines and spruces
lorded it over the under forest of maples and oaks. Though
the yellow Rim towered high over the site of the cabin, the
altitude was still great, close to seven thousand feet above
sea level.

Tappan had fallen in love with this wild wooded and
canyoned country. So had Jenet. It was rather funny the way
she hung around Tappan, mornings and evenings. She ate
luxuriant grass and oak leaves until her sides bulged.

There did not appear to be any flat places in this landscape. Every bench was either up hill or down hill. The
Beams had no garden or farm or ranch that Tappan could
discover. They raised a few acres of sorghum and corn. Their
log cabin was of the most primitive kind, and outfitted
poorly. Madge Beam explained that this cabin was their
winter abode, and that up on the Rim they had a good house
and ranch. Tappan did not inquire closely into anything. If
he had interrogated himself, he would have found out that
the reason he did not inquire was because he feared something might remove him from the vicinity of Madge Beam.
He had thought it strange the Beams avoided wayfarers they
had met on the trail, and had gone round a little hamlet
Tappan had espied from a hill. Madge Beam, with woman's
intuition, had read his mind, and had said: "Jake doesn't get
along so well with some of the villagers. An' I've no han-
kerin' for gun play." That explanation was sufficient for Tappan. He had lived long enough in his wandering years to

appreciate that people could have reasons for being solitary.

This trip up into the Rim Rock country bade fair to become Tappan's one and only adventure of the heart. It was not alone the murmuring, clear brook of cold mountain water that enchanted him, nor the stately pines, nor the beautiful silver spruces, nor the wonder of the deep, yellow-walled canyons, so choked with verdure, and haunted by wild creatures. He dared not face his soul, and ask why this dark-eyed woman sought him more and more. Tappan lived in the moment.

He was aware that the few mountaineer neighbors who rode that way rather avoided contact with him. Tappan was not so dense that he did not perceive that the Beams preferred to keep him from outsiders. This perhaps was owing to their desire to sell Tappan the ranch and cattle. Jake offered to let it go at what he called a low figure. Tappan thought it just as well to go out into the forest and hide his bags of gold. He did not trust Jake Beam, and liked less the looks of the men who visited this wilderness ranch. Madge Beam might be related to a rustler, and the associate of rustlers, but that did not necessarily make her a bad woman. Tappan sensed that her attitude was changing, and she seemed to require his respect. At first, all she wanted was his admiration. Tappan's long unused deference for women returned to him, and when he saw that it was having some strange softening effect upon Madge Beam, he redoubled his attentions. They rode and climbed and hunted together. Tappan had pitched his camp not far from the cabin, on a shaded bank of the singing brook. Madge did not leave him much to himself. She was always coming up to his camp, on one pretext or another. Often she would bring two horses, and make Tappan ride with her. Some of these occasions, Tappan saw, occurred while visitors came to the cabin. In three weeks Madge Beam changed from the bold and careless woman who had ridden down into his camp that sunset, to a serious and appealing woman, growing more careful of her person and adornment, and manifestly bearing a burden on her mind.

October came. In the morning white frost glistened on the split-wood shingles of the cabin. The sun soon melted it, and grew warm. The afternoons were still and smoky, melancholy with the enchantment of Indian summer. Tappan hunted wild turkey and deer with Madge, and revived his boyish love of such pursuits. Madge appeared to be a woman of the woods, and had no mean skill with the rifle.

One day they were high on the Rim, with the great timbered basin at their feet. They had come up to hunt deer, but got no farther than the wonderful promontory where before they had lingered.

"Somethin' will happen to me to-day," Madge Beam said, enigmatically.

Tappan never had been much of a talker. But he could listen. The woman unburdened herself this day. She wanted freedom, happiness, a home away from this lonely country, and all the heritage of woman. She confessed it broodingly, passionately. And Tappan recognized truth when he heard it. He was ready to do all in his power for this woman and believed she knew it. But words and acts of sentiment came hard to him.

"Are you goin' to buy Jake's ranch?" she asked.

"I don't know. Is there any hurry?" returned Tappan.

"I reckon not. But I think I'll settle that," she said, decisively.

"How so?"

"Well, Jake hasn't got any ranch," she answered. And added hastily, "No clear title, I mean. He's only home-steaded one hundred an' sixty acres, an' hasn't proved up on it yet. But don't you say I told you."

"Was Jake aimin' to be crooked?"

"I reckon. . . . An' I was willin' at first. But not now."

Tappan did not speak at once. He saw the woman was in one of her brooding moods. Besides, he wanted to weigh her words. How significant they were! Today more than ever she had let down. Humility and simplicity seemed to

abide with her. And her brooding boded a storm. Tappan's
heart swelled in his broad breast. Was life going to dawn rosy
and bright for the lonely prospector? He had money to make
a home for this woman. What lay in the balance of the hour?
Tappan waited, slowly realizing the charged atmosphere.

Madge's somber eyes gazed out over the great void.
But, full of thought and passion as they were, they did not
see the beauty of that scene. But Tappan saw it. And in some
strange sense the color and wildness and sublimity seemed
the expression of a new state of his heart. Under him sheered
down the ragged and cracked cliffs of the Rim, yellow and
gold and gray, full of caves and crevices, ledges for eagles
and niches for lions, a thousand feet down to the upward
edge of the long green slopes and canyons, and so on down
and down into the abyss of forested ravine and ridge, rolling
league on league away to the encompassing barrier of purple mountain ranges.

The thickets in the canyons called Tappan's eye back to
linger there. How different from the scenes that used to be
perpetually in his sight! What riot of color! The tips of the
green pines, the crests of the silver spruces, waved about
masses of vivid gold of aspen trees, and wonderful cerise and
flaming red of maples, and crags of yellow rock, covered
with the bronze of frostbitten sumach. Here was autumn
and with it the colors of Tappan's favorite season. From
below breathed up the low roar of plunging brook; an eagle
screeched his wild call; an elk bugled his piercing blast.
From the Rim wisps of pine needles blew away on the
breeze and fell into the void. A wild country, colorful, beautiful, bountiful. Tappan imagined he could quell his wandering spirit here, with this dark-eyed woman by his side. Never
before had Nature so called him. Here was not the cruelty
or flinty hardness of the desert. The air was keen and sweet,
cold in the shade, warm in the sun. A fragrance of balsam
and spruce, spiced with pine, made his breathing a thing of
difficulty and delight. How for so many years had he endured vast open spaces without such eye-soothing trees as

these? Tappan's back rested against a huge pine that tipped the Rim, and had stood there, stronger than the storms, for many a hundred years. The rock of the promontory was covered with soft brown mats of pine needles. A juniper tree, with its bright green foliage and lilac-colored berries, grew near the pine, and helped to form a secluded little nook, fragrant and somehow haunting. The woman's dark head was close to Tappan, as she sat with her elbows on her knees, gazing down into the basin. Tappan saw the strained tensity of her posture, the heaving of her full bosom. He wondered, while his own emotions, so long darkened, roused to the suspense of that hour.

Suddenly she flung herself into Tappan's arms. The act amazed him. It seemed to have both the passion of a woman and the shame of a girl. Before she hid her face on Tappan's breast he saw how the rich brown had paled, and then flamed.

"Tappan! . . . Take me away. . . . Take me away from here—from that life down there," she cried, in smothered voice.

"Madge, you mean take you away—and marry you?" he replied.

"Oh, yes—yes—marry me, if you love me. . . . I don't see how you can—but you do, don't you?—Say you do."

"I reckon that's what ails me, Madge," he replied, simply.

"*Say* so, then," she burst out.

"All right, I do," said Tappan, with heavy breath. "Madge, words don't come easy for me. . . . But I think you're wonderful, an' I want you. I haven't dared hope for that, till now. I'm only a wanderer. But it'd be heaven to have you—my wife—an' make a home for you."

"Oh—Oh!" she returned, wildly, and lifted herself to cling round his neck, and to kiss him. "You give me joy. . . . Oh, Tappan, I love you. I never loved any man before. I know now. . . . An' I'm not wonderful—or good. But I love you."

The fire of her lips and the clasp of her arms worked

havoc in Tappan. No woman had ever loved him, let alone embraced him. To awake suddenly to such rapture as this made him strong and rough in his response. Then all at once she seemed to collapse in his arms and to begin to weep. He feared he had offended or hurt her, and was clumsy in his contrition. Presently she replied:

"Pretty soon—I'll make you—beat me. It's your love—your honesty—that's shamed me.... Tappan, I was party to a trick to—sell you a worthless ranch.... I agreed to—try to make you love me—to fool you—cheat you.... But I've fallen in love with you.—An' my God, I care more for your love—your respect—than for my life. I can't go on with it. I've double-crossed Jake, an' all of them.... Now, am I worth lovin'? Am I worth havin'?"

"More than ever, dear," he said.

"You will take me away?"

"Anywhere—any time, the sooner the better."

She kissed him passionately, and then, disengaging herself from his arms, she knelt and gazed earnestly at him. "I've not told all. I will some day. But I swear now on my soul —I'll be what you think me."

"Madge, you needn't say all that. If you love me—it's enough. More than I ever dreamed of."

"You're a man. Oh, why didn't I meet you when I was eighteen instead of now—twenty-eight, an' all that between.... But enough. A new life begins here for me. We must plan."

"You make the plans an' I'll act on them."

For a moment she was tense and silent, head bowed, hands shut tight. Then she spoke:

"Tonight we'll slip away. You make a light pack, that'll go on your saddle. I'll do the same. We'll hide the horses out near where the trail crosses the brook. An' we'll run off— ride out of the country."

Tappan in turn tried to think, but the whirl of his mind made any reason difficult. This dark-eyed, full-bosomed woman loved him, had surrendered herself, asked only his protection. The thing seemed marvelous. Yet she knelt there, those dark eyes on him, infinitely more appealing than ever, haunting with some mystery of sadness and fear he could not divine.

Suddenly Tappan remembered Jenet.

"I must take Jenet," he said.

That startled her. "Jenet—Who's she?"

"My burro."

"Your burro. You can't travel fast with that pack beast. We'll be trailed, an' we'll have to go fast. . . . You can't take the burro."

Then Tappan was startled. "What! Can't take Jenet?— Why, I—I couldn't get along without her."

"Nonsense. What's a burro? We must ride fast—do you hear?"

"Madge, I'm afraid I—I must take Jenet with me," he said, soberly.

"It's impossible. I can't go if you take her. I tell you I've got to get away. If you want *me* you'll have to leave your precious Jenet behind."

Tappan bowed his head to the inevitable. After all, Jenet was only a beast of burden. She would run wild on the ridges and soon forget him and have no need of him. Something strained in Tappan's breast. He did not see clearly here. This woman was worth more than all else to him.

"I'm stupid, dear," he said. "You see I never before ran off with a beautiful woman. . . . Of course my burro must be left behind."

Elopement, if such it could be called, was easy for them. Tappan did not understand why Madge wanted to be so secret about it. Was she not free? But then, he reflected, he did not know the circumstances she feared. Besides, he did not care. Possession of the woman was enough.

Tappan made his small pack, the weight of which was considerable owing to his bags of gold. This he tied on his saddle. It bothered him to leave most of his new outfit scat-

tered around his camp. What would Jenet think of that? He
looked for her, but for once she did not come in at meal
time. Tappan thought this was singular. He could not remember when Jenet had been far from his camp at sunset.
Somehow Tappan was glad.

After he had his supper, he left his utensils and supplies
as they happened to be, and strode away under the trees to
the trysting-place where he was to meet Madge. To his surprise she came before dark, and, unused as he was to the
complexity and emotional nature of a woman, he saw that
she was strangely agitated. Her face was pale. Almost a fury
burned in her black eyes. When she came up to Tappan, and
embraced him, almost fiercely, he felt that he was about to
learn more of the nature of womankind. She thrilled him to
his depths.

"Lead out the horses an' don't make any noise," she
whispered.

Tappan complied, and soon he was mounted, riding
behind her on the trail. It surprised him that she headed
down country, and traveled fast. Moreover, she kept to a
trail that continually grew rougher. They came to a road,
which she crossed, and kept on through darkness and brush
so thick that Tappan could not see the least sign of a trail.
And at length anyone could have seen that Madge had lost
her bearings. She appeared to know the direction she
wanted, but traveling upon it was impossible, owing to the
increasingly cut-up and brushy ground. They had to turn
back, and seemed to be hours finding the road. Once Tappan fancied he heard the thud of hoofs other than those
made by their own horses. Here Madge acted strangely, and
where she had been obsessed by desire to hurry she now
seemed to have grown weary. She turned her horse south on
the road. Tappan was thus enabled to ride beside her.
But they talked very little. He was satisfied with the fact of
being with her on the way out of the country. Some time in
the night they reached an old log shack by the roadside.
Here Tappan suggested they halt, and get some sleep

before dawn. The morrow would mean a long hard day.

"Yes, tomorrow will be hard," replied Madge, as she faced Tappan in the gloom. He could see her big dark eyes on him. Her tone was not one of a hopeful woman. Tappan pondered over this. But he could not understand, because he had no idea how a woman ought to act under such circumstances. Madge Beam was a creature of moods. Only the day before, on the ride down from the Rim, she had told him with a laugh that she was likely to love him madly one moment and scratch his eyes out the next. How could he know what to make of her? Still, an uneasy feeling began to stir in Tappan.

They dismounted, and unsaddled the horses. Tappan took his pack and put it aside. Something frightened the horses. They bolted down the road.

"Head them off," cried the woman, hoarsely.

Even on the instant her voice sounded strained to Tappan, as if she were choked. But, realizing the absolute necessity of catching the horses, he set off down the road on a run. And he soon succeeded in heading off the animal he had ridden. The other one, however, was contrary and cunning. When Tappan would endeavor to get ahead, it would trot briskly on. Yet it did not go so fast but what Tappan felt sure he would soon catch it. Thus walking and running, he put some distance between him and the cabin before he realized that he could not head off the wary beast. Much perturbed in mind, Tappan hurried back.

Upon reaching the cabin Tappan called to Madge. No answer! He could not see her in the gloom nor the horse he had driven back. Only silence brooded there. Tappan called again. Still no answer! Perhaps Madge had succumbed to weariness and was asleep. A search of the cabin and vicinity failed to yield any sign of her. But it disclosed the fact that Tappan's pack was gone.

Suddenly he sat down, quite overcome. He had been duped. What a fierce pang tore his heart! But it was for loss of the woman—not the gold. He was stunned, and then sick

with bitter misery. Only then did Tappan realize the meaning of love and what it had done to him. The night wore on,
and he sat there in the dark and cold and stillness until the
gray dawn told him of the coming of day.

The light showed his saddle where he had left it. Nearby
lay one of Madge's gloves. Tappan's keen eye sighted a bit
of paper sticking out of the glove. He picked it up. It was a
leaf out of a little book he had seen her carry, and upon it
was written in lead pencil:

> I am Jake's wife, not his sister. I double-crossed him an'
> ran off with you an' would have gone to hell for you. But
> Jake an' his gang suspected me. They were close on our
> trail. I couldn't shake them. So here I chased off the
> horses an' sent you after them. It was the only way I
> could save your life.

Tappan tracked the thieves to Globe. There he learned
they had gone to Phoenix—three men and one woman. Tappan had money on his person. He bought horse and saddle,
and setting out for Phoenix, he let his passion to kill grow
with the miles and hours. At Phoenix he learned Beam had
cashed the gold—twelve thousand dollars. So much of a fortune! Tappan's fury grew. The gang separated here. Beam
and his wife took stage for Tucson. Tappan had no trouble
in trailing their movements.

Gambling dives and inns and freighting posts and stage
drivers told the story of the Beams and their ill-gotten gold.
They went on to California, down into Tappan's country, to
Yuma, and El Cajon, and San Diego. Here Tappan lost track
of the woman. He could not find that she had left San Diego,
nor any trace of her there. But Jake Beam had killed a
Mexican in a brawl and had fled across the line.

Tappan gave up for the time being the chase of Beam,
and bent his efforts to find the woman. He had no resentment toward Madge. He only loved her. All that winter he
searched San Diego. He made of himself a peddler as a ruse

to visit houses. But he never found a trace of her. In the spring he wandered back to Yuma, raking over the old clues, and so on back to Tucson and Phoenix.

This year of dream and love and passion and despair and hate made Tappan old. His great strength and endurance were not yet impaired, but something of his spirit had died out of him.

One day he remembered Jenet. "My burro!" he soliloquized. "I had forgotten her. . . . Jenet!"

Then it seemed a thousand impulses merged in one drove him to face the long road toward the Rim Rock country. To remember Jenet was to grow doubtful. Of course she would be gone. Stolen or dead or wandered off! But then who could tell what Jenet might do? Tappan was both called and driven. He was a poor wanderer again. His outfit was a pack he carried on his shoulder. But while he could walk he would keep on until he found that last camp where he had deserted Jenet.

October was coloring the canyon slopes when he reached the shadow of the great wall of yellow rock. The cabin where the Beams had lived—or had claimed they lived—was a fallen ruin, crushed by snow. Tappan saw other signs of a severe winter and heavy snowfall. No horse or cattle tracks showed in the trails.

To his amaze his camp was much as he had left it. The stone fireplace, the iron pots, appeared to be in the same places. The boxes that had held his supplies were lying here and there. And his canvas tarpaulin, little the worse for wear of the elements, lay on the ground under the pine where he had slept. If any man had visited this camp in a year he had left no sign of it.

Suddenly Tappan espied a hoof track in the dust. A small track—almost oval in shape—fresh! Tappan thrilled through all his being.

"Jenet's track, so help me God!" he murmured.

He found more of them, made that morning. And, keen now as never before on her trail, he set out to find her. The tracks led up the canyon. Tappan came out into a little grassy clearing, and there stood Jenet, as he had seen her thousands of times. She had both long ears up high. She seemed to stare out of that meek, gray face. And then one of the long ears flopped over and drooped. Such perhaps was the expression of her recognition.

Tappan strode up to her.

"Jenet—old girl—you hung round camp—waitin' for me, didn't you?" he said, huskily, and his big hands fondled her long ears.

Yes, she had waited. She, too, had grown old. She was gray. The winter of that year had been hard. What had she lived on when the snow lay so deep? There were lion scratches on her back, and scars on her legs. She had fought for her life.

"Jenet, a man can never always tell about a burro," said Tappan. "I trained you to hang round camp an' wait till I came back. . . . 'Tappan's burro,' the desert rats used to say! An' they'd laugh when I bragged how you'd stick to me where most men would quit. But brag as I did, I never knew you, Jenet. An' I left you—an' forgot. Jenet, it takes a human bein'—a man—a woman—to be faithless. An' it takes a dog or a horse or a burro to be great. . . . Beasts? I wonder now. . . . Well, old pard, we're goin' down the trail together, an' from this day on Tappan begins to pay his debt."

III

Tappan never again had the old *wanderlust* for the stark and naked desert. Something had transformed him. The green and fragrant forests, and brown-aisled, pine-matted woodlands, the craggy promontories and the great colored canyons, the cold granite water springs of the Tonto seemed vastly preferable to the heat and dust and glare and the emptiness of the waste lands. But there was more. The ghost of his strange and only love kept pace with his wandering steps, a spirit that hovered with him as his shadow. Madge

Beam, whatever she had been, had showed to him the power of love to refine and ennoble. Somehow he felt closer to her here in the cliff country where his passion had been born. Somehow she seemed nearer to him here than in all those places he had tracked her.

So from a prospector searching for gold Tappan became a hunter, seeking only the means to keep soul and body together. And all he cared for was his faithful burro Jenet, and the loneliness and silence of the forest land.

He was to learn that the Tonto was a hard country in many ways, and bitterly so in winter. Down in the brakes of the basin it was mild in winter, the snow did not lie long, and ice seldom formed. But up on the Rim, where Tappan always lingered as long as possible, the storm king of the north held full sway. Fifteen feet of snow and zero weather were the rule in dead of winter.

An old native once warned Tappan: "See hyar, friend, I reckon you'd better not get caught up in the Rim Rock country in one of our big storms. Fer if you do you'll never get out."

It was a way of Tappan's to follow his inclinations, regardless of advice. He had weathered the terrible midnight storm of hot wind in Death Valley. What were snow and cold to him? Late autumn on the Rim was the most perfect and beautiful of seasons. He had seen the forest land brown and darkly green one day, and the next burdened with white snow. What a transfiguration! Then when the sun loosened the white mantling on the pines, and they had shed their burdens in drifting dust of white, and rainbowed mists of melting snow, and avalanches sliding off the branches, there would be left only the wonderful white floor of the woodland. The great rugged brown tree trunks appeared mightier and statelier in the contrast; and the green of foliage, the russet of oak leaves, the gold of the aspens, turned the forest into a world enchanting to the desert-seared eyes of this wanderer.

With Tappan the years sped by. His mind grew old

faster than his body. Every season saw him lonelier. He had a feeling, a vague illusive foreshadowing that his bones, instead of bleaching on the desert sands, would mingle with the pine mats and the soft fragrant moss of the forest. The idea was pleasant to Tappan.

One afternoon he was camped in Pine Canyon, a timber-sloped gorge far back from the Rim. November was well on. The fall had been singularly open and fair, with not a single storm. A few natives happening across Tappan had remarked casually that such autumns sometimes were not to be trusted.

This late afternoon was one of Indian summer beauty and warmth. The blue haze in the canyon was not all the blue smoke from Tappan's camp fire. In a narrow park of grass not far from camp Jenet grazed peacefully with elk and deer. Wild turkeys lingered there, loath to seek their winter quarters down in the basin. Gray squirrels and red squirrels barked and frisked, and dropped the pine and spruce cones, with thud and thump, on all the slopes.

Before dark a stranger strode into Tappan's camp, a big man of middle age, whose magnificent physique impressed even Tappan. He was a rugged, bearded giant, wide-eyed and of pleasant face. He had no outfit, no horse, not even a gun.

"Lucky for me I smelled your smoke," he said. "Two days for me without grub."

"Howdy, stranger," was Tappan's greeting. "Are you lost?"

"Yes an' no. I could find my way out down over the Rim, but it's not healthy down there for me. So I'm hittin' north."

"Where's your horse an' pack?"

"I reckon they're with the gang that took more of a fancy to them than me."

"Ahuh! You're welcome here, stranger," replied Tappan. "I'm Tappan."

"Ha! Heard of you. I'm Jess Blade, of anywhere. An'

I'll say, Tappan, I was an honest man till I hit the Tonto."

His laugh was frank, for all its note of grimness. Tappan liked the man, and sensed one who would be a good friend and bad foe.

"Come an' eat. My supplies are peterin' out, but there's plenty of meat."

Blade ate, indeed, as a man starved, and did not seem to care if Tappan's supplies were low. He did not talk. After the meal he craved a pipe and tobacco. Then he smoked in silence, in a slow realizing content. The morrow had no fears for him. The flickering ruddy light from the camp fire shone on his strong face. Tappan saw in him the drifter, the drinker, the brawler, a man with good in him, but over whom evil passion or temper dominated. Presently he smoked the pipe out, and with reluctant hand knocked out the ashes and returned it to Tappan.

"I reckon I've some news thet'd interest you," he said.

"You have?" queried Tappan.

"Yes, if you're the Tappan who tried to run off with Jake Beam's wife."

"Well, I'm that Tappan. But I'd like to say I didn't know she was married."

"Shore, I know thet. So does everybody in the Tonto. You were just meat for the Beam gang. They had played the trick before. But accordin' to what I hear thet trick was the last for Madge Beam. She never came back to this country. An' Jake Beam, when he was drunk, owned up thet she'd left him in California. Some hint at worse. Fer Jake Beam came back a harder man. Even his gang said thet."

"Is he in the Tonto now?" queried Tappan, with a thrill of fire along his veins.

"Yep, thar fer keeps," replied Blade, grimly. "Somebody shot him."

"Ahuh!" exclaimed Tappan with a deep breath of relief. There came a sudden cooling of the heat of his blood.

After that there was a long silence. Tappan dreamed of the woman who had loved him. Blade brooded over the camp fire. The wind moaned fitfully in the lofty pines on the slope. A wolf mourned as if in hunger. The stars appeared to obscure their radiance in haze.

"Reckon thet wind sounds like storm," observed Blade, presently.

"I've heard it for weeks now," replied Tappan.

"Are you a woodsman?"

"No, I'm a desert man."

"Wal, you take my hunch an' hit the trail fer low country."

This was well meant, and probably sound advice, but it alienated Tappan. He had really liked this hearty-voiced stranger. Tappan thought moodily of his slowly ingrowing mind, of the narrowness of his soul. He was past interest in his fellow men. He lived with a dream. The only living creature he loved was a lop-eared, lazy burro, growing old in contentment. Nevertheless that night Tappan shared one of his two blankets.

In the morning the gray dawn broke, and the sun rose without its brightness of gold. There was a haze over the blue sky. Thin, swift-moving clouds scudded up out of the southwest. The wind was chill, the forest shaggy and dark, the birds and squirrels were silent.

"Wal, you'll break camp today," asserted Blade.

"Nope. I'll stick it out yet a while," returned Tappan.

"But, man, you might get snowed in, an' up hyar thet's serious."

"Ahuh! Well, it won't bother me. An' there's nothin' holdin' you."

"Tappan, it's four days' walk down out of this woods. If a big snow set in, how'd I make it?"

"Then you'd better go out over the Rim," suggested Tappan.

"No. I'll take my chance the other way. But are you meanin' you'd rather not have me with you? Fer you can't stay hyar."

Tappan was in a quandary.

Some instinct bade him tell the man to go. Not empty-handed, but to go. But this was selfish, and entirely unlike Tappan as he remembered himself of old. Finally he spoke: "You're welcome to half my outfit—go or stay."

"Thet's mighty square of you, Tappan," responded the other, feelingly. "Have you a burro you'll give me?"

"No, I've only one."

"Ha! Then I'll have to stick with you till you leave."

No more was said. They had breakfast in a strange silence. The wind brooded its secret in the tree tops. Tappan's burro strolled into camp, and caught the stranger's eye.

"Wal, thet's shore a fine burro," he observed. "Never saw the like."

Tappan performed his camp tasks. And then there was nothing to do but sit around the fire. Blade evidently waited for the increasing menace of storm to rouse Tappan to decision. But the graying over of sky and the increase of wind did not affect Tappan. What did he wait for? The truth of his thoughts was that he did not like the way Jenet remained in camp. She was waiting to be packed. She knew they ought to go. Tappan yielded to a perverse devil of stubbornness. The wind brought a cold mist, then a flurry of wet snow. Tappan gathered firewood, a large quantity. Blade saw this and gave voice to earnest fears. But Tappan paid no heed. By nightfall sleet and snow began to fall steadily. The men fashioned a rude shack of spruce boughs, ate their supper, and went to bed early.

It worried Tappan that Jenet stayed right in camp. He lay awake a long time. The wind rose, and moaned through the forest. The sleet failed, and a soft, steady downfall of snow gradually set in. Tappan fell asleep. When he awoke it was to see a forest of white. The trees were mantled with blankets of wet snow, the ground covered two feet on a level. But the clouds appeared to be gone, the sky was blue, the storm over. The sun came up warm and bright.

"It'll all go in a day," said Tappan.

"If this was early October I'd agree with you," replied Blade. "But it's only akin' fer another storm. Can't you hear thet wind?"

Tappan only heard the whispers of his dreams. By now the snow was melting off the pines, and rainbows shone everywhere. Little patches of snow began to drop off the south branches of the pines and spruces, and then larger patches, until by mid-afternoon white streams and avalanches were falling everywhere. All of the snow, except in shaded places on the north sides of trees, went that day, and half of that on the ground. Next day it thinned out more, until Jenet was finding the grass and moss again. That afternoon the telltale thin clouds raced up out of the southwest and the wind moaned its menace.

"Tappan, let's pack an' hit it out of hyar," appealed Blade, anxiously. "I know this country. Mebbe I'm wrong, of course, but it feels like storm. Winter's comin' shore."

"Let her come," replied Tappan imperturbably.

"Say, do you want to get snowed in?" demanded Blade, out of patience.

"I might like a little spell of it, seein' it'd be new to me," replied Tappan.

"But man, if you ever get snowed in hyar you can't get out."

"That burro of mine could get me out."

"You're crazy. Thet burro couldn't go a hundred feet. What's more, you'd have to kill her an' eat her."

Tappan bent a strange gaze upon his companion, but made no reply. Blade began to pace up and down the small bare patch of ground before the camp fire. Manifestly, he was in a serious predicament. That day he seemed subtly to change, as did Tappan. Both answered to their peculiar instincts, Blade to that of self-preservation, and Tappan, to something like indifference. Tappan held fate in defiance. What more could happen to him?

Blade broke out again, in eloquent persuasion, giving proof of their peril, and from that he passed to amaze and then to strident anger. He cursed Tappan for a nature-loving idiot.

"An' I'll tell you what," he ended. "When mornin' comes I'll take some of your grub an' hit it out of hyar, storm or no storm."

But long before dawn broke that resolution of Blade's had become impracticable. Both men were awakened by a roar of storm through the forest, no longer a moan, but a marching roar, with now a crash and then a shriek of gale! By the light of the smoldering camp fire Tappan saw a whirling pall of snow, great flakes as large as feathers. Morning disclosed the setting in of a fierce mountain storm, with two feet of snow already on the ground, and the forest lost in a blur of white.

"I was wrong," called Tappan to his companion. "What's best to do now?"

"You damned fool!" yelled Blade. "We've got to keep from freezin' an' starvin' till the storm ends an' a crust comes on the snow."

For three days and three nights the blizzard continued, unabated in its fury. It took the men hours to keep a space cleared for their camp site, which Jenet shared with them. On the fourth day the storm ceased, the clouds broke away, the sun came out. And the temperature dropped to zero. Snow on the level just topped Tappan's lofty stature, and in drifts it was ten and fifteen feet deep. Winter had set in without compromise. The forest became a solemn, still, white world. But now Tappan had no time to dream. Dry firewood was hard to find under the snow. It was possible to cut down one of the dead trees on the slope, but impossible to pack sufficient wood to the camp. They had to burn green wood. Then the fashioning of snowshoes took much time. Tappan had no knowledge of such footgear. He could only help Blade. The men were encouraged by the piercing cold forming a crust on the snow. But just as they were about to pack and venture forth, the weather moderated, the crust refused to hold their weight, and another foot of snow fell.

"Why in hell didn't you kill an elk?" demanded Blade, sullenly. He had become darkly sinister. He knew the peril and he loved life. "Now we'll have to kill an' eat your precious Jenet. An' mebbe she won't furnish meat enough to last till this snow weather stops an' a good freeze'll make travelin' possible."

"Blade, you shut up about killin' an' eatin' my burro Jenet," returned Tappan, in a voice that silenced the other.

Thus instinctively these men became enemies. Blade thought only of himself. Tappan had forced upon him a menace to the life of his burro. For himself Tappan had not one thought.

Tappan's supplies ran low. All the bacon and coffee were gone. There was only a small haunch of venison, a bag of beans, a sack of flour, and a small quantity of salt left.

"If a crust freezes on the snow an' we can pack that flour, we'll get out alive," said Blade. "But we can't take the burro."

Another day of bright sunshine softened the snow on the southern exposures, and a night of piercing cold froze a crust that would bear a quick step of man.

"It's our only chance—an' damn slim at thet," declared Blade.

Tappan allowed Blade to choose the time and method, and supplies for the start to get out of the forest. They cooked all the beans and divided them in two sacks. Then they baked about five pounds of biscuits for each of them. Blade showed his cunning when he chose the small bag of salt for himself and let Tappan take the tobacco. This quantity of food and a blanket for each Blade declared to be all they could pack. They argued over the guns, and in the end Blade compromised on the rifle, agreeing to let Tappan carry that on a possible chance of killing a deer or elk. When this matter had been decided, Blade significantly began putting on his rude snowshoes, that had been constructed from pieces of Tappan's boxes and straps and burlap sacks.

"Reckon they won't last long," muttered Blade.

Meanwhile Tappan fed Jenet some biscuits and then began to strap a tarpaulin on her back.

"What you doin'?" queried Blade, suddenly.

"Gettin' Jenet ready," replied Tappan.

"Ready! For what?"

"Why, to go with us."

"Hell!" shouted Blade, and he threw up his hands in helpless rage.

Tappan felt a depth stirred within him. He lost his late taciturnity and silent aloofness fell away from him. Blade seemed on the moment no longer an enemy. He loomed as an aid to the saving of Jenet. Tappan burst into speech.

"I can't go without her. It'd never enter my head. Jenet's mother was a good faithful burro. I saw Jenet born way down there on the Rio Colorado. She wasn't strong. An' I had to wait for her to be able to walk. An' she grew up. Her mother died, an' Jenet an' me packed it alone. She wasn't no ordinary burro. She learned all I taught her. She was different. But I treated her same as any burro. An' she grew with the years. Desert men said there never was such a burro as Jenet. Called her Tappan's burro, an' tried to borrow an' buy an' steal her. . . . How many times in ten years Jenet has done me a good turn I can't remember. But she saved my life. She dragged me out of Death Valley. . . . An' then I forgot my debt. I ran off with a woman an' left Jenet to wait as she had been trained to wait. . . . Well, I got back in time. . . . An' now I'll not leave her here. It may be strange to you, Blade, me carin' this way. Jenet's only a burro. But I won't leave her."

"Man, you talk like thet lazy lop-eared burro was a woman," declared Blade, in disgusted astonishment.

"I don't know women, but I reckon Jenet's more faithful than most of them."

"Wal, of all the stark, starin' fools I ever run into you're the worst."

"Fool or not, I know what I'll do," retorted Tappan. The softer mood left him swiftly.

"Haven't you sense enough to see thet we can't travel

with your burro?" queried Blade, patiently controlling his temper. "She has little hoofs, sharp as knives. She'll cut through the crust. She'll break through in places. An' we'll have to stop to haul her out—mebbe break through ourselves. Thet would make us longer gettin' out."

"Long or short we'll take her."

Then Blade confronted Tappan as if suddenly unmasking his true meaning. His patient explanation meant nothing. Under no circumstances would he ever have consented to an attempt to take Jenet out of that snow-bound wilderness. His eyes gleamed.

"We've a hard pull to get out alive. An' hard-workin' men in winter must have meat to eat."

Tappan slowly straightened up to look at the speaker. "What do you mean?"

For answer Blade jerked his hand backward and downward, and when it swung into sight again it held Tappan's worn and shining rifle. Then Blade, with deliberate force, that showed the nature of the man, worked the lever and threw a shell into the magazine. All the while his eyes were fastened on Tappan. His face seemed that of another man, evil, relentless, inevitable in his spirit to preserve his own life at any cost.

"I mean to kill your burro," he said, in voice that suited his look and manner.

"No!" cried Tappan, shocked into an instant of appeal.

"Yes, I am, an' I'll bet, by God, before we get out of hyar you'll be glad to eat some of her meat!"

That roused the slow-gathering might of Tappan's wrath.

"I'd starve to death before I'd—I'd kill that burro, let alone eat her."

"Starve an' be damned!" shouted Blade, yielding to rage.

Jenet stood right behind Tappan, in her posture of contented repose, with one long ear hanging down over her gray meek face.

"You'll have to kill me first," answered Tappan, sharply.
"I'm good fer anythin'—if you push me," returned
Blade, stridently.

As he stepped aside, evidently so he could have unob-
structed aim at Jenet, Tappan leaped forward and knocked
up the rifle as it was discharged. The bullet sped harmlessly
over Jenet. Tappan heard it thud into a tree. Blade uttered
a curse. And as he lowered the rifle in sudden deadly intent,
Tappan grasped the barrel with his left hand. Then, clench-
ing his right, he struck Blade a sodden blow in the face. Only
Blade's hold on the rifle prevented him from falling. Blood
streamed from his nose and mouth. He bellowed in hoarse
fury, "I'll kill you—fer thet!"

Tappan opened his clenched teeth: "No, Blade—you're
not man enough."

Then began a terrific struggle for possession of the rifle.
Tappan beat at Blade's face with his sledge-hammer fist. But
the strength of the other made it imperative that he use
both hands to keep his hold on the rifle. Wrestling and pulling and jerking, the men tore round the snowy camp, scattering the camp fire, knocking down the brush shelter.
Blade had surrendered to a wild frenzy. He hissed his male-
dictions. His was the brute lust to kill an enemy that
thwarted him. But Tappan was grim and terrible in his re-
straint. His battle was to save Jenet. Nevertheless, there
mounted in him the hot physical sensations of the savage.
The contact of flesh, the smell and sight of Blade's blood, the
violent action, the beastly mien of his foe changed the fight
to one for its own sake. To conquer this foe, to rend him and
beat him down, blow on blow!

Tappan felt instinctively that he was the stronger. Suddenly he exerted all his muscular force into one tremendous
wrench. The rifle broke, leaving the steel barrel in his hands,
the wooden stock in Blade's. And it was the quicker-witted
Blade who used his weapon first to advantage. One swift
blow knocked Tappan down. As he was about to follow it up
with another, Tappan kicked his opponent's feet from under

him. Blade sprawled in the snow, but was up again as quickly as Tappan. They made at each other, Tappan waiting to strike, and Blade raining blows on Tappan. These were heavy blows aimed at his head, but which he contrived to receive on his arms and the rifle barrel he brandished. For a few moments Tappan stood up under a beating that would have felled a lesser man. His own blood blinded him. Then he swung his heavy weapon. The blow broke Blade's left arm. Like a wild beast, he screamed in pain; and then, without guard, rushed in, too furious for further caution. Tappan met the terrible onslaught as before, and watching his chance, again swung the rifle barrel. This time, so supreme was the force, it battered down Blade's arm and crushed his skull. He died on his feet—ghastly and horrible change!— and swaying backward, he fell into the upbanked wall of snow, and went out of sight, except for his boots, one of which still held the crude snowshoe.

Tappan stared, slowly realizing.

"Ahuh, stranger Blade!" he ejaculated, gazing at the hole in the snow bank where his foe had disappeared. "You were goin' to—kill an' eat—Tappan's burro!"

Then he sighted the bloody rifle barrel, and cast it from him. He became conscious of injuries which needed attention. But he could do little more than wash off the blood and bind up his head. Both arms and hands were badly bruised, and beginning to swell. But fortunately no bones had been broken.

Tappan finished strapping the tarpaulin upon the burro; and, taking up both his and Blade's supply of food, he called out, "Come on, Jenet."

Which way to go! Indeed, there was no more choice for him than there had been for Blade. Toward the Rim the snowdrift would be deeper and impassable. Tappan realized that the only possible chance for him was down hill. So he led Jenet out of camp without looking back once. What was it that had happened? He did not seem to be the same Tappan that had dreamily tramped into this woodland.

A deep furrow in the snow had been made by the men packing firewood into camp. At the end of this furrow the wall of snow stood higher than Tappan's head. To get out on top without breaking the crust presented a problem. He lifted Jenet up, and was relieved to see that the snow held her. But he found a different task in his own case. Returning to camp, he gathered up several of the long branches of spruce that had been part of the shelter, and carrying them out he laid them against the slant of snow he had to surmount, and by their aid he got on top. The crust held him.

Elated and with revived hope, he took up Jenet's halter and started off. Walking with his rude snowshoes was awkward. He had to go slowly, and slide them along the crust. But he progressed. Jenet's little steps kept her even with him. Now and then one of her sharp hoofs cut through, but not to hinder her particularly. Right at the start Tappan observed a singular something about Jenet. Never until now had she been dependent upon him. She knew it. Her intelligence apparently told her that if she got out of this snowbound wilderness it would be owing to the strength and reason of her master.

Tappan kept to the north side of the canyon, where the snow crust was strongest. What he must do was to work up to the top of the canyon slope, and then keeping to the ridge travel north along it, and so down out of the forest.

Travel was slow. He soon found he had to pick his way. Jenet appeared to be absolutely unable to sense either danger or safety. Her experience had been of the rock confines and the drifting sands of the desert. She walked where Tappan led her. And it seemed to Tappan that her trust in him, her reliance upon him, were pathetic.

"Well, old girl," said Tappan to her, "it's a horse of another color now—hey?"

At length he came to a wide part of the canyon, where a bench of land led to a long gradual slope, thickly studded with small pines. This appeared to be fortunate, and turned out to be so, for when Jenet broke through the crust Tappan had trees and branches to hold to while he hauled her out. The labor of climbing that slope was such that Tappan began to appreciate Blade's absolute refusal to attempt getting Jenet out. Dusk was shadowing the white aisles of the forest when Tappan ascended to a level. He had not traveled far from camp, and the fact struck a chill upon his heart.

To go on in the dark was foolhardy. So Tappan selected a thick spruce, under which there was a considerable depression in the snow, and here made preparation to spend the night. Unstrapping the tarpaulin, he spread it on the snow. All the lower branches of this giant of the forest were dead and dry. Tappan broke off many and soon had a fire. Jenet nibbled at the moss on the trunk of the spruce tree. Tappan's meal consisted of beans, biscuits, and a ball of snow, that he held over the fire to soften. He saw to it that Jenet fared as well as he. Night soon fell, strange and weirdly white in the forest, and piercingly cold. Tappan needed the fire. Gradually it melted the snow and made a hole, down to the ground. Tappan rolled up in the tarpaulin and soon fell asleep.

In three days Tappan traveled about fifteen miles, gradually descending, until the snow crust began to fail to hold Jenet. Then whatever had been his difficulties before, they were now magnified a hundredfold. As soon as the sun was up, somewhat softening the snow, Jenet began to break through. And often when Tappan began hauling her out he broke through himself. This exertion was killing even to a man of Tappan's physical prowess. The endurance to resist heat and flying dust and dragging sand seemed another kind from that needed to toil on in this snow. The endless snow-bound forest began to be hideous to Tappan. Cold, lonely, dreary, white, mournful—the kind of ghastly and ghostly winter land that had been the terror of Tappan's boyish dreams! He loved the sun—the open. This forest had deceived him. It was a wall of ice. As he toiled on, the state of his mind gradually and subtly changed in all except the fixed and absolute will to save Jenet. In some places he carried her. The fourth night found him dangerously near the end of his stock of food. He had been generous with Jenet. But now, considering that he had to do more work than she, he diminished her share. On the fifth day Jenet broke through the snow crust so often that Tappan realized how utterly impossible it was for her to get out of the woods by her own efforts. Therefore Tappan hit upon the plan of making her lie on the tarpaulin, so that he could drag her. The tarpaulin doubled once did not make a bad sled. All the rest of that day Tappan hauled her. And so all the rest of the next day he toiled on, hands behind him, clutching the canvas, head and shoulders bent, plodding and methodical, like a man who could not be defeated. That night he was too weary to build a fire, and too worried to eat the last of his food.

Next day Tappan was not unalive to the changing character of the forest. He had worked down out of the zone of the spruce trees; the pines had thinned out and decreased in size; oak trees began to show prominently. All these signs meant that he was getting down out of the mountain heights. But the fact, hopeful as it was, had drawbacks. The snow was still four feet deep on a level and the crust held Tappan only about half the time. Moreover, the lay of the land operated against Tappan's progress. The long, slowly descending ridge had failed. There were no more canyons, but ravines and swales were numerous. Tappan dragged on, stern, indomitable, bent to his toil.

When the crust let him down, he hung his snowshoes over Jenet's back, and wallowed through, making a lane for her to follow. Two days of such heart-breaking toil, without food or fire, broke Tappan's magnificent endurance. But not his spirit! He hauled Jenet over the snow, and through the snow, down the hills and up the slopes, through the thickets, knowing that over the next ridge, perhaps, was deliverance. Deer and elk tracks began to be numerous. Cedar and juniper trees now predominated. An occasional pine showed here and there. He was getting out of the forest land. Only such mighty and justifiable hope as that could have kept him on his feet.

He fell often, and it grew harder to rise and go on. The hour came when the crust failed altogether to hold Tappan and he had to abandon hauling Jenet. It was necessary to make a road for her. How weary, cold, horrible, the white reaches! Yard by yard Tappan made his way. He no longer sweat. He had no feeling in his feet or legs. Hunger ceased to gnaw at his vitals. His thirst he quenched with snow—soft snow now, that did not have to be crunched like ice. The pangs in his breast were terrible—cramps, constrictions, the piercing pains in his lungs, the dull ache of his overtaxed heart.

Tappan came to an opening in the cedar forest from which he could see afar. A long slope fronted him. It led down and down to open country. His desert eyes, keen as those of an eagle, made out flat country, sparsely covered with snow, and black dots that were cattle. The last slope! The last pull! Three feet of snow, except in drifts; down and down he plunged, making way for Jenet! All that day he toiled and fell and rolled down this league-long slope, wearing toward sunset to the end of his task, and likewise to the end of his will.

Now he seemed up and now down. There was no sense of cold or weariness. Only direction! Tappan still saw! The last of his horror at the monotony of white faded from his mind. Jenet was there, beginning to be able to travel for herself. The solemn close of endless day found Tappan arriving at the edge of the timbered country, where wind-bared patches of ground showed long, bleached grass. Jenet took to grazing.

As for Tappan, he fell with the tarpaulin, under a thick cedar, and with strengthless hands plucked and plucked at the canvas to spread it, so that he could cover himself. He looked again for Jenet. She was there, somehow a fading image, strangely blurred. But she was grazing. Tappan lay down, and stretched out, and slowly drew the tarpaulin over him.

A piercing cold night wind swept down from the snowy heights. It wailed in the edge of the cedars and moaned out toward the open country. Yet the night seemed silent. The stars shone white in a deep blue sky—passionless, cold, watchful eyes, looking down without pity or hope or censure. They were the eyes of Nature. Winter had locked the heights in its snowy grip. All night that winter wind blew down, colder and colder. Then dawn broke, steely, gray, with a fire in the east.

Jenet came back where she had left her master. Camp! As she had returned thousands of dawns in the long years of her service. She had grazed all night. Her sides that had been flat were now full. Jenet had weathered another vicissitude of her life. She stood for a while, in a doze, with one long ear down over her meek face. Jenet was waiting for Tappan.

But he did not stir from under the long roll of canvas. Jenet waited. The winter sun rose, in cold yellow flare. The snow glistened as with a crusting of diamonds. Somewhere in the distance sounded a long-drawn, discordant bray. Jenet's ears shot up. She listened. She recognized the call of one of her kind. Instinct always prompted Jenet. Sometimes she did bray. Lifting her gray head she sent forth a clarion: *"Hee-haw hee-haw-haw—hee-haw how-e-e-e!"*

That stentorian call started the echoes. They pealed down the slope and rolled out over the open country, clear as a bugle blast, yet hideous in their discordance. But this morning Tappan did not awaken.

WINE ON THE DESERT

Max Brand

There was no hurry, except for the thirst, like clotted salt, in the back of his throat, and Durante rode on slowly, rather enjoying the last moments of dryness before he reached the cold water in Tony's house. There was really no hurry at all. He had almost twenty-four hours' head start, for they would not find his dead man until this morning. After that, there would be perhaps several hours of delay before the sheriff gathered a sufficient posse and started on his trail. Or perhaps the sheriff would be fool enough to come alone.

Durante had been able to see the wheel and fan of Tony's windmill for more than an hour, but he could not make out the ten acres of the vineyard until he had topped the last rise, for the vines had been planted in a hollow. The lowness of the ground, Tony used to say, accounted for the water that gathered in the well during the wet season. The rains sank through the desert sand, through the gravels beneath, and gathered in a bowl of clay hardpan far below.

In the middle of the rainless season the well ran dry but, long before that, Tony had every drop of the water pumped up into a score of tanks made of cheap corrugated iron. Slender pipe lines carried the water from the tanks to the vines and from time to time let them sip enough life to keep them until the winter darkened overhead suddenly, one November day, and the rain came down, and all the earth made a great hushing sound as it drank. Durante had heard that whisper of drinking when he was here before; but he never had seen the place in the middle of the long drought.

The windmill looked like a sacred emblem to Durante, and the twenty stodgy, tar-painted tanks blessed his eyes; but a heavy sweat broke out at once from his body. For the air of the hollow, unstirred by wind, was hot and still as a bowl of soup. A reddish soup. The vines were powdered with thin red dust, also. They were wretched, dying things to look at, for the grapes had been gathered, the new wine had been made, and now the leaves hung in ragged tatters.

Durante rode up to the squat adobe house and right through the entrance into the patio. A flowering vine clothed three sides of the little court. Durante did not know the name of the plant, but it had large white blossoms with golden hearts that poured sweetness on the air. Durante hated the sweetness. It made him more thirsty.

He threw the reins off his mule and strode into the house. The water cooler stood in the hall outside the kitchen. There were two jars made of a porous stone, very ancient things, and the liquid which distilled through the pores kept the contents cool. The jar on the left held water; that on the right contained wine. There was a big tin dipper hanging on a peg beside each jar. Durante tossed off the cover of the vase on the left and plunged it in until the delicious coolness closed well above his wrist.

"Hey, Tony," he called. Out of his dusty throat the cry

was, "Throw some water into that mule of mine, would you, Tony?"

A voice pealed from the distance.

Durante, pouring down the second dipper of water, smelled the alkali dust which had shaken off his own clothes. It seemed to him that heat was radiating like light from his clothes, from his body, and the cool dimness of the house was soaking it up. He heard the wooden leg of Tony bumping on the ground, and Durante grinned; then Tony came in with that hitch and sideswing with which he accommodated the stiffness of his artificial leg. His brown face shone with sweat as though a special ray of light were focused on it.

"Ah, Dick!" he said. "Good old Dick! . . . How long since you came last! . . . Wouldn't Julia be glad! Wouldn't she be glad!"

"Ain't she here?" asked Durante, jerking his head suddenly away from the dripping dipper.

"She's away at Nogalez," said Tony. "It gets so hot. I said, 'You go up to Nogalez, Julia, where the wind don't forget to blow.' She cried, but I made her go."

"Did she cry?" asked Durante.

"Julia . . . that's a good girl," said Tony.

"Yeah. You bet she's good," said Durante. He put the dipper quickly to his lips but did not swallow for a moment; he was grinning too widely. Afterward he said: "You wouldn't throw some water into that mule of mine, would you, Tony?"

Tony went out with his wooden leg clumping loud on the wooden floor, softly in the patio dust. Durante found the hammock in the corner of the patio. He lay down in it and watched the color of sunset flush the mists of desert dust that rose to the zenith. The water was soaking through his body; hunger began, and then the rattling of pans in the kitchen and the cheerful cry of Tony's voice:

"What you want, Dick? I got some pork. You don't want pork. I'll make you some good Mexican beans. Hot. Ah ha, I know that old Dick. I have plenty of good wine for you,

Dick. Tortillas. Even Julia can't make tortillas like me. . . . And what about a nice young rabbit?"

"All blowed full of buckshot?" growled Durante.

"No, no. I kill them with the rifle."

"You kill rabbits with a rifle?" repeated Durante, with a quick interest.

"It's the only gun I have," said Tony. "If I catch them in the sights, they are dead. . . . A wooden leg cannot walk very far. . . . I must kill them quick. You see? They come close to the house about sunrise and flop their ears. I shoot through the head."

"Yeah? Yeah?" muttered Durante. "Through the head?" He relaxed, scowling. He passed his hand over his face, over his head.

Then Tony began to bring the food out into the patio and lay it on a small wooden table; a lantern hanging against the wall of the house included the table in a dim half circle of light. They sat there and ate. Tony had scrubbed himself for the meal. His hair was soaked in water and sleeked back over his round skull. A man in the desert might be willing to pay five dollars for as much water as went to the soaking of that hair.

Everything was good. Tony knew how to cook, and he knew how to keep the glasses filled with his wine.

"This is old wine. This is my father's wine. Eleven years old," said Tony. "You look at the light through it. You see that brown in the red? That's the soft that time puts in good wine, my father always said."

"What killed your father?" asked Durante.

Tony lifted his hand as though he were listening or as though he were pointing out a thought.

"The desert killed him. I found his mule. It was dead, too. There was a leak in the canteen. My father was only five miles away when the buzzards showed him to me."

"Five miles? Just an hour . . . Good Lord!" said Durante. He stared with big eyes. "Just dropped down and died?" he asked.

"No," said Tony. "When you die of thirst, you always die just one way. . . . First you tear off your shirt, then your undershirt. That's to be cooler. . . . And the sun comes and cooks your bare skin. . . . And then you think . . . there is water everywhere, if you dig down far enough. You begin to dig. The dust comes up your nose. You start screaming. You break your nails in the sand. You wear the flesh off the tips of your fingers, to the bone." He took a quick swallow of wine.

"Without you seen a man die of thirst, how d'you know they start to screaming?" asked Durante.

"They got a screaming look when you find them," said Tony. "Take some more wine. The desert never can get to you here. My father showed me the way to keep the desert away from the hollow. We live pretty good here? No?"

"Yeah," said Durante, loosening his shirt collar. "Yeah, pretty good."

Afterward he slept well in the hammock until the report of a rifle waked him and he saw the color of dawn in the sky. It was such a great, round bowl that for a moment he felt as though he were above, looking down into it.

He got up and saw Tony coming in holding a rabbit by the ears, the rifle in his other hand.

"You see?" said Tony. "Breakfast came and called on us!" He laughed.

Durante examined the rabbit with care. It was nice and fat and it had been shot through the head. Through the middle of the head. Such a shudder went down the back of Durante that he washed gingerly before breakfast; he felt that his blood was cooled for the entire day.

It was a good breakfast, too, with flapjacks and stewed rabbit with green peppers, and a quart of strong coffee. Before they had finished, the sun struck through the east window and started them sweating.

"Gimme a look at that rifle of yours, Tony, will you?" Durante asked.

"You take a look at my rifle, but don't you steal the luck that's in it," laughed Tony. He brought the fifteen-shot Winchester.

"Loaded right to the brim?" asked Durante.

"I always load it full the minute I get back home," said Tony.

"Tony, come outside with me," commanded Durante. They went out from the house. The sun turned the sweat of Durante to hot water and then dried his skin so that his clothes felt transparent.

"Tony, I gotta be damn mean," said Durante. "Stand right there where I can see you. Don't try to get close. ... Now listen. ... The sheriff's gunna be along this trail some time today, looking for me. He'll load up himself and all his gang with water out of your tanks. Then he'll follow my sign across the desert. Get me? He'll follow if he finds water on the place. But he's not gunna find water."

"What you done, poor Dick?" said Tony. "Now look. ... I could hide you in the old wine cellar where nobody ..."

"The sheriff's not gunna find any water," said Durante. "It's gunna be like this."

He put the rifle to his shoulder, aimed, fired. The shot struck the base of the nearest tank, ranging down through the bottom. A semicircle of darkness began to stain the soil near the edge of the iron wall.

Tony fell on his knees. "No, no, Dick! Good Dick!" he said. "Look! All the vineyard. It will die. It will turn into old, dead wood, Dick. ..."

"Shut your face," said Durante. "Now I've started, I kinda like the job."

Tony fell on his face and put his hands over his ears. Durante drilled a bullet hole through the tanks, one after another. Afterward, he leaned on the rifle.

"Take my canteen and go in and fill it with water out of the cooling jar," he said. "Snap into it, Tony!"

Tony got up. He raised the canteen, and looked around him, not at the tanks from which the water was pouring so that the noise of the earth drinking was audible, but at the rows of his vineyard. Then he went into the house.

Durante mounted his mule. He shifted the rifle to his left hand and drew out the heavy Colt from its holster. Tony came dragging back to him, his head down. Durante watched Tony with a careful revolver but he gave up the canteen without lifting his eyes.

"The trouble with you, Tony," said Durante, "is you're yellow. I'd of fought a tribe of wildcats with my bare hands, before I'd let 'em do what I'm doin' to you. But you sit back and take it."

Tony did not seem to hear. He stretched out his hands to the vines.

"Ah, my God," said Tony. "Will you let them all die?"

Durante shrugged his shoulders. He shook the canteen to make sure that it was full. It was so brimming that there was hardly room for the liquid to make a sloshing sound. Then he turned the mule and kicked it into a dogtrot.

Half a mile from the house of Tony, he threw the empty rifle to the ground. There was no sense packing that useless weight, and Tony with his peg leg would hardly come this far.

Durante looked back, a mile or so later, and saw the little image of Tony picking up the rifle from the dust, then staring earnestly after his guest. Durante remembered the neat little hole clipped through the head of the rabbit. Wherever he went, his trail never could return again to the vineyard in the desert. But then, commencing to picture to himself the arrival of the sweating sheriff and his posse at the house of Tony, Durante laughed heartily.

The sheriff's posse could get plenty of wine, of course, but without water a man could not hope to make the desert voyage, even with a mule or a horse to help him on the way. Durante patted the full, rounding side of his canteen. He might even now begin with the first sip but it was a luxury to postpone pleasure until desire became greater.

He raised his eyes along the trail. Close by, it was merely dotted with occasional bones, but distance joined the dots into an unbroken chalk line which wavered with a strange leisure across the Apache Desert, pointing toward the cool blue promise of the mountains. The next morning he would be among them.

A coyote whisked out of a gully and ran like a gray puff of dust on the wind. His tongue hung out like a little red rag from the side of his mouth; and suddenly Durante was dry to the marrow. He uncorked and lifted his canteen. It had a slightly sour smell; perhaps the sacking which covered it had grown a trifle old. And then he poured a great mouthful of lukewarm liquid. He had swallowed it before his senses could give him warning.

It was wine!

He looked first of all toward the mountains. They were as calmly blue, as distant as when he had started that morning. Twenty-four hours not on water, but on wine!

"I deserve it," said Durante. "I trusted him to fill the canteen. . . . I deserve it. Curse him!" With a mighty resolution, he quieted the panic in his soul. He would not touch the stuff until noon. Then he would take one discreet sip. He would win through.

Hours went by. He looked at his watch and found it was only ten o'clock. And he had thought that it was on the verge of noon! He uncorked the wine and drank freely and, corking the canteen, felt almost as though he needed a drink of water more than before. He sloshed the contents of the canteen. Already it was horribly light.

Once, he turned the mule and considered the return trip; but he could remember the head of the rabbit too clearly, drilled right through the center. The vineyard, the rows of old twisted, gnarled little trunks with the bark peeling off . . . every vine was to Tony like a human life. And Durante had condemned them all to death!

He faced the blue of the mountains again. His heart raced in his breast with terror. Perhaps it was fear and not the suction of that dry and deadly air that made his tongue cleave to the roof of his mouth.

The day grew old. Nausea began to work in his stomach, nausea alternating with sharp pains. When he looked down, he saw that there was blood on his boots. He had been spurring the mule until the red ran down from it flanks. It went with a curious stagger, like a rocking horse with a broken rocker; and Durante grew aware that he had been keeping the mule at a gallop for a long time. He pulled it to a halt. It stood with wide-braced legs. Its head was down. When he leaned from the saddle, he saw that its mouth was open.

"It's gunna die," said Durante. "It's gunna die. . . . What a fool I been. . . ."

The mule did not die until after sunset. Durante left everything except his revolver. He packed the weight of that for an hour and discarded it in turn. His knees were growing weak. When he looked up at the stars they shone white and clear for a moment only, and then whirled into little racing circles and scrawls of red.

He lay down. He kept his eyes closed and waited for the shaking to go out of his body, but it would not stop. And every breath of darkness was like an inhalation of black dust.

He got up and went on, staggering. Sometimes he found himself running.

Before you die of thirst, you go mad. He kept remembering that. His tongue had swollen big. Before it choked him, if he lanced it with his knife the blood would help him; he would be able to swallow. Then he remembered that the taste of blood is salty.

Once, in his boyhood, he had ridden through a pass with his father and they had looked down on the sapphire of a mountain lake, a hundred thousand million tons of water as cold as snow. . . .

When he looked up, now, there were not stars; and this frightened him terribly. He never had seen a desert night so dark. His eyes were failing, he was being blinded. When the morning came, he would not be able to see the mountains, and he would walk around and around in a circle until he dropped and died.

No stars, no wind; the air as still as the waters of a stale pool, and he in the dregs at the bottom. . . .

He seized his shirt at the throat and tore it away so that it hung in two rags from his hips.

He could see the earth only well enough to stumble on the rocks. But there were no stars in the heavens. He was blind: he had no more hope than a rat in a well. Ah, but Italian devils know how to put poison in wine that will steal all the senses or any one of them: and Tony had chosen to blind Durante.

He heard a sound like water. It was the swishing of the soft deep sand through which he was treading; sand so soft that a man could dig it away with his bare hands. . . .

Afterward, after many hours, out of the blind face of that sky the rain began to fall. It made first a whispering and then a delicate murmur like voices conversing, but after that, just at the dawn, it roared like the hoofs of ten thousand charging horses. Even through that thundering confusion the big birds with naked heads and red, raw necks found their way down to one place in the Apache Desert.

STAGE TO LORDSBURG

Ernest Haycox

This was one of those years in the Territory when Apache smoke signals spiraled up from the stony mountain summits and many a ranch cabin lay as a square of blackened ashes on the ground and the departure of a stage from Tonto was the beginning of an adventure that had no certain happy ending. . . .

The stage and its six horses waited in front of Weilner's store on the north side of Tonto's square. Happy Stuart was on the box, the ribbons between his fingers and one foot teetering on the brake. John Strang rode shotgun guard and an escort of ten cavalrymen waited behind the coach, half asleep in their saddles.

At four-thirty in the morning this high air was quite cold, though the sun had begun to flush the sky eastward. A small crowd stood in the square, presenting their final messages to the passengers now entering the coach. There was a girl going down to marry an infantry officer, a whisky drummer from St. Louis, an Englishman all length and bony corners and bearing with him an enormous sporting rifle, a gambler, a solid-shouldered cattleman on his way to New Mexico and a blond young man upon whom both Happy Stuart and the shotgun guard placed a narrow-eyed interest.

This seemed all until the blond man drew back from the coach door; and then a girl known commonly throughout the Territory as Henriette came quietly from the crowd. She was small and quiet, with a touch of paleness in her cheeks and her quite dark eyes lifted at the blond man's unexpected courtesy, showing surprise. There was this moment of delay and then the girl caught up her dress and stepped into the coach.

Men in the crowd were smiling but the blond one turned, his motion like the swift cut of a knife, and his attention covered that group until the smiling quit. He was tall, hollow-flanked, and definitely stamped by the guns slung low on his hips. But it wasn't the guns alone; something in his face, so watchful and so smooth, also showed his trade. Afterwards he got into the coach and slammed the door.

Happy Stuart kicked off the brakes and yelled, "Hi!" Tonto's people were calling out their last farewells and the six horses broke into a trot and the stage lunged on its fore and aft springs and rolled from town with dust dripping off its wheels like water, the cavalrymen trotting briskly behind. So they tipped down the long grade, bound on a journey no stage had attempted during the last forty-five days. Out below in the desert's distance stood the relay stations they hoped to reach and pass. Between lay a country swept empty by the quick raids of Geronimo's men.

The Englishman, the gambler and the blond man sat jammed together in the forward seat, riding backward to the course of the stage. The drummer and the cattleman occupied the uncomfortable middle bench; the two women shared the rear seat. The cattleman faced Henriette, his knees almost touching her. He had one arm hooked over the door's window sill to steady himself. A huge gold nugget slid gently back and forth along the watch chain slung across his wide chest and a chunk of black hair lay below his hat. His eyes considered Henriette, reading something in the girl that caused him to show her a deliberate smile. Henriette dropped her glance to the gloved tips of her fingers, cheeks unstirred.

They were all strangers packed closely together, with nothing in common save a destination. Yet the cattleman's smile and the boldness of his glance were something as audible as speech, noted by everyone except the Englishman, who sat bolt upright with his stony indifference. The army girl, tall and calmly pretty, threw a quick side glance at Henriette and afterwards looked away with a touch of color. The gambler saw this interchange of glances and showed the cattleman an irritated attention. The whisky drummer's eyes narrowed a little and some inward cynicism made a faint change on his lips. He removed his hat to show a bald head already beginning to sweat; his cigar smoke turned the coach cloudy and ashes kept dropping on his vest.

The blond man had observed Henriette's glance drop from the cattleman; he tipped his hat well over his face and watched her—not boldly but as though he were puzzled. Once her glance lifted and touched him. But he had been on guard against that and was quick to look away.

The army girl coughed gently behind her hand, whereupon the gambler tapped the whisky drummer on the shoulder. "Get rid of that." The drummer appeared startled. He grumbled, "Beg pardon," and tossed the smoke through the window.

All this while the coach went rushing down the ceaseless turns of the mountain road, rocking on its fore and aft springs, its heavy wheels slamming through the road ruts and whining on the curves. Occasionally the strident yell of Happy Stuart washed back. "Hi, Nellie! By God—!" The whisky drummer braced himself against the door and closed his eyes.

Three hours from Tonto the road, making a last round sweep, let them down upon the flat desert. Here the stage stopped and the men got out to stretch. The gambler spoke to the army girl, gently: "Perhaps you would find my seat more comfortable." The army girl said "Thank you," and changed over. The cavalry sergeant rode up to the stage, speaking to Happy Stuart.

"We'll be goin' back now—and good luck to ye."

The men piled in, the gambler taking the place beside Henriette. The blond man drew his long legs together to give the army girl more room, and watched Henriette's face with a soft, quiet care. A hard sun beat fully on the coach and dust began to whip up like fire smoke. Without escort they rolled across a flat earth broken only by cacti standing against a dazzling light. In the far distance, behind a blue heat haze, lay the faint suggestion of mountains.

The cattleman reached up and tugged at the ends of his mustache and smiled at Henriette. The army girl spoke to the blond man. "How far is it to the noon station?" The blond man said courteously: "Twenty miles." The gambler watched the army girl with the strictness of his face relaxing, as though the run of her voice reminded him of things long forgotten.

The miles fell behind and the smell of alkali dust got thicker. Henriette rested against the corner of the coach, her eyes dropped to the tip of her gloves. She made an enigmatic, disinterested shape there; she seemed past stirring, beyond laughter. She was young, yet she had a knowledge that put the cattleman and the gambler and the drummer and the army girl in their exact places; and she knew why the gambler had offered the army girl his seat. The army girl was in one world and she was in another, as everyone in the coach understood. It had no effect on her

for this was a distinction she had learned long ago. Only
the blond man broke through her indifference. His name
was Malpais Bill and she could see the wildness in the corners of his eyes and in the long crease of his lips; it was a
stamp that would never come off. Yet something flowed
out of him toward her that was different than the preda-
tory curiosity of other men; something unobtrusively gal-
lant, unexpectedly gentle.

Upon the box Happy Stuart pointed to the hazy out-
line two miles away. "Injuns ain't burned that anyhow."
The sun was directly overhead, turning the light of the
world a cruel brass-yellow. The crooked crack of a dry
wash opened across the two deep ruts that made this road.
Johnny Strang shifted the gun in his lap. "What's Malpais
Bill ridin' with us for?"

"I guess I wouldn't ask him," returned Happy Stuart
and studied the wash with a troubled eye. The road fell into
it roughly and he got a tighter grip on his reins and yelled:
"Hang on! Hi, Nellie! God damn you, hi!" The six horses
plunged down the rough side of the wash and for a moment
the coach stood alone, high and lonely on the break, and
then went reeling over the rim. It struck the gravel with a
roar, the front wheels bouncing and the back wheels skew-
ing around. The horses faltered but Happy Stuart cursed at
his leaders and got them into a run again. The horses lunged
up the far side of the wash two and two, their muscles
bunching and the soft dirt flying in yellow clouds. The front
wheels struck solidly and something cracked like a pistol
shot; the stage rose out of the wash, teetered crosswise and
then fell ponderously on its side, splintering the coach panels.

Johnny Strang jumped clear. Happy Stuart hung to the
handrail with one hand and hauled on the reins with the
other; and stood up while the passengers crawled through
the upper door. All the men, except the whisky drummer,
put their shoulders to the coach and heaved it upright again.
The whisky drummer stood strangely in the bright sunlight

shaking his head dumbly while the others climbed back in. Happy Stuart said, "All right, brother, git aboard."

The drummer climbed in slowly and the stage ran on. There was a low, gray dobe relay station squatted on the desert dead ahead with a scatter of corrals about it and a flag hanging limp on a crooked pole. Men came out of the dobe's dark interior and stood in the shade of the porch gallery. Happy Stuart rolled up and stopped. He said to a lanky man: "Hi, Mack. Where's the God-damned Injuns?"

The passengers were filing into the dobe's dining room. The lanky one drawled: "You'll see 'em before tomorrow night." Hostlers came up to change horses.

The little dining room was cool after the coach, cool and still. A fat Mexican woman ran in and out with the food platters. Happy Stuart said: "Ten minutes," and brushed the alkali dust from his mouth and fell to eating.

The long-jawed Mack said: "Catlin's ranch burned last night. Was a troop of cavalry around here yesterday. Came and went. You'll git to the Gap tonight all right but I do' know about the mountains beyond. A little trouble?"

"A little," said Happy, briefly, and rose. This was the end of rest. The passengers followed, with the whisky drummer straggling at the rear, reaching deeply for wind. The coach rolled away again, Mack's voice pursuing them. "Hit it a lick, Happy, if you see any dust rollin' out of the east."

Heat had condensed in the coach and the little wind fanned up by the run of the horses was stifling to the lungs; the desert floor projected its white glitter endlessly away until lost in the smoky haze. The cattleman's knees bumped Henriette gently and he kept watching her, a celluloid toothpick drooped between his lips. Happy Stuart's voice ran back, profane and urgent, keeping the speed of the coach constant through the ruts. The whisky drummer's eyes were round and strained and his mouth was open and all the color had gone out of his face. The gambler observed this without expression and without care; and once the cattleman, feeling the sag of the whisky drummer's shoulder, shoved him away. The Englishman sat bolt upright, staring emotionlessly at the passing desert. The army girl spoke to Malpais Bill: "What is the next stop?"

"Gap Creek."

"Will we meet soldiers there?"

He said: "I expect we'll have an escort over the hills into Lordsburg."

And at four o'clock of this furnace-hot afternoon the whisky drummer made a feeble gesture with one hand and fell forward into the gambler's lap.

The cattleman shrugged his shoulders and put a head through the window, calling up to Happy Stuart: "Wait a minute." When the stage stopped everybody climbed out and the blond man helped the gambler lay the whisky drummer in the sweltering patch of shade created by the coach. Neither Happy Stuart nor the shotgun guard bothered to get down. The whisky drummer's lips moved a little but nobody said anything and nobody knew what to do—until Henriette stepped forward.

She dropped to the ground, lifting the whisky drummer's shoulders and head against her breasts. He opened his eyes and there was something in them that they could all see, like relief and ease, like gratefulness. She murmured: "You are all right," and her smile was soft and pleasant, turning her lips maternal. There was this wisdom in her, this knowledge of the fears that men concelaed behind their manners, the deep hungers that rode them so savagely, and the loneliness that drove them to women of her kind. She repeated, "You are all right," and watched this whisky drummer's eyes lose the wildness of what he knew.

The army girl's face showed shock. The gambler and the cattleman looked down at the whisky drummer quite impersonally. The blond man watched Henriette through lids half closed, but the flare of a powerful interest broke the severe lines of his cheeks. He held a cigarette between his fingers; he had forgotten it.

Happy Stuart said: "We can't stay here."

The gambler bent down to catch the whisky drummer under the arms. Henriette rose and said, "Bring him to me," and got into the coach. The blond man and the gambler lifted the drummer through the door so that he was lying along the back seat, cushioned on Henriette's lap. They all got in and the coach rolled on. The drummer groaned a little, whispering: "Thanks—thanks," and the blond man, searching Henriette's face for every shred of expression, drew a gusty breath.

They went on like this, the big wheels pounding the ruts of the road while a lowering sun blazed through the coach windows. The mountain bulwarks began to march nearer, more definite in the blue fog. The cattleman's eyes were small and brilliant and touched Henriette personally, but the gambler bent toward Henriette to say: "If you are tired—"

"No," she said. "No. He's dead."

The army girl stifled a small cry. The gambler bent nearer the whisky drummer, and then they were all looking at Henriette; even the Englishman stared at her for a moment, faint curiosity in his eyes. She was remotely smiling, her lips broad and soft. She held the drummer's head with both her hands and continued to hold him like that until, at the swift fall of dusk, they rolled across the last of the desert floor and drew up before Gap Station.

The cattleman kicked open the door and stepped out, grunting as his stiff legs touched the ground. The gambler pulled the drummer up so that Henriette could leave. They all came out, their bones tired from the shaking. Happy Stuart climbed from the box, his face a gray mask of alkali and his eyes bloodshot. He said: "Who's dead?" and looked into the coach. People sauntered from the station yard, walking with the indolence of twilight. Happy Stuart said, "Well, he won't worry about tomorrow," and turned away.

A short man with a tremendous stomach shuffled

through the dusk. He said: "Wasn't sure you'd try to git through yet, Happy."

"Where's the soldiers for tomorrow?"

"Other side of the mountains. Everybody's chased out. What ain't forted up here was sent into Lordsburg. You men will bunk in the barn. I'll make out for the ladies somehow." He looked at the army girl and he appraised Henriette instantly. His eyes slid on to Malpais Bill standing in the background and recognition stirred him then and made his voice careful. "Hello, Bill. What brings you this way?"

Malpais Bill's cigarette glowed in the gathering dusk and Henriette caught the brief image of his face, serene and watchful. Malpais Bill's tone was easy, it was soft. "Just the trip."

They were moving on toward the frame house whose corners seemed to extend indefinitely into a series of attached sheds. Lights glimmered in the windows and men moved around the place, idly talking. The unhitched horses went away at a trot. The tall girl walked into the station's big room, to face a soldier in a disheveled uniform.

He said: "Miss Robertson? Lieutenant Hauser was to have met you here. He is at Lordsburg. He was wounded in a brush with the Apaches last night."

The tall army girl stood very still. She said: "Badly?"

"Well," said the soldier, "yes."

The fat man came in, drawing deeply for wind. "Too bad—too bad. Ladies, I'll show you the rooms, such as I got."

Henriette's dove-colored dress blended with the background shadows. She was watching the tall army girl's face whiten. But there was a strength in the army girl, a fortitude that made her think of the soldier. For she said quietly, "You must have had a bad trip."

"Nothing—nothing at all," said the soldier and left the room. The gambler was here, his thin face turning to the army girl with a strained expression, as though he were remembering painful things. Malpais Bill had halted in the doorway, studying the softness and the humility of Henriette's cheeks. Afterwards both women followed the fat host of Gap Station along a narrow hall to their quarters.

Malpais Bill wheeled out and stood indolently against the wall of this desert station, his glance quick and watchful in the way it touched all the men loitering along the yard, his ears weighing all the night-softened voices. Heat died from the earth and a definite chill rolled down the mountain hulking so high behind the house. The soldier was in his saddle, murmuring drowsily to Happy Stuart.

"Well, Lordsburg is a long ways off and the damn' mountains are squirmin' with Apaches. You won't have any cavalry escort tomorrow. The troops are all in the field."

Malpais Bill listened to the hoofbeats of the soldier's horse fade out, remembering the loneliness of a man in those dark mountain passes, and went back to the saloon at the end of the station. This was a low-ceilinged shed with a dirt floor and whitewashed walls that once had been part of a stable. Three men stood under a lantern in the middle of this little place, the light of the lantern palely shining in the rounds of their eyes as they watched him. At the far end of the bar the cattleman and the gambler drank in taciturn silence. Malpais Bill took his whisky when the bottle came, and noted the barkeep's obscure glance. Gap's host put in his head and wheezed, "Second table," and the other men in there began to move out. The barkeep's words rubbed together, one tone above a whisper. "Better not ride into Lordsburg. Plummer and Shanley are there."

Malpais Bill's lips were stretched to the long edge of laughter and there was a shine like wildness in his eyes. He said, "Thanks, friend," and went into the dining room.

When he came back to the yard night lay wild and deep across the desert and the moonlight was a frozen silver that touched but could not dissolve the world's incredible blackness. The girl Henriette walked along the Tonto road, swaying gently in the vague shadows. He went that way, the click of his heels on the hard earth bringing her around.

Her face was clear and strange and incurious in the

night, as though she waited for something to come, and knew what it would be. But he said: "You're too far from the house. Apaches like to crawl down next to a settlement and wait for strays."

She was indifferent, unafraid. Her voice was cool and he could hear the faint loneliness in it, the fatalism that made her words so even. "There's a wind coming up, so soft and good."

He took off his hat, long legs braced, and his eyes were both attentive and puzzled. His blond hair glowed in the fugitive light.

She said in a deep breath: "Why do you do that?"

His lips were restless and the sing and rush of strong feeling was like a current of quick wind around him. "You have folks in Lordsburg?"

She spoke in a direct, patient way as though explaining something he should have known without asking. "I run a house in Lordsburg."

"No," he said, "it wasn't what I asked."

"My folks are dead—I think. There was a massacre in the Superstition Mountains when I was young."

He stood with his head bowed, his mind reaching back to fill in that gap of her life. There was a hardness and a rawness to this land and little sympathy for the weak. She had survived and had paid for her survival, and looked at him now in a silent way that offered no explanations or apologies for whatever had been; she was still a pretty girl with the dead patience of all the past years in her eyes, in the expressiveness of her lips.

He said: "Over in the Tonto Basin is a pretty land. I've got a piece of a ranch there—with a house half built."

"If that's your country why are you here?"

His lips laughed and the rashness in him glowed hot again and he seemed to grow taller in the moonlight. "A debt to collect."

"That's why you're going to Lordsburg? You will never get through collecting those kind of debts. Everybody in the

Territory knows you. Once you were just a rancher. Then
you tried to wipe out a grudge and then there was a bigger
one to wipe out—and the debt kept growing and more men
are waiting to kill you. Someday a man will. You'd better run
away from the debts."

His bright smile kept constant, and presently she lifted
her shoulders with resignation. "No," she murmured, "you
won't run." He could see the sweetness of her lips and the
way her eyes were sad for him; he could see in them the
patience he had never learned.

He said, "We'd better go back," and turned her with his
arm. They went across the yard in silence, hearing the un-
dertone of men's drawling talk roll out of the shadows, seeing the glow of men's pipes in the dark corners. Malpais Bill
stopped and watched her go through the station door; she
turned to look at him once more, her eyes all dark and her
lips softly sober, and then passed down the narrow corridor
to her own quarters. Beyond her window, in the yard, a man
was murmuring to another man: "Plummer and Shanley are
in Lordsburg. Malpais Bill knows it." Through the thin parti-
tion of the adjoining room she heard the army girl crying
with a suppressed, uncontrollable regularity. Henriette
stared at the dark wall, her shoulders and head bowed; and
afterwards returned to the hall and knocked on the army
girl's door and went in.

Six fresh horses fiddled in front of the coach and the fat
host of Gap Station came across the yard swinging a lantern
against the dead, bitter black. All the passengers filed sleep-
dulled and miserable from the house. Johnny Strang
slammed the express box in the boot and Happy Stuart
gruffly said: "All right, folks."

The passengers climbed in. The cattleman came up and
Malpais Bill drawled: "Take the corner spot, mister," and
got in, closing the door. The Gap host grumbled: "If they
don't jump you on the long grade you'll be all right. You're
safe when you get to Al Schrieber's ranch." Happy's bronze

voice shocked the black stillness and the coach lurched forward, its leather springs squealing.

They rode for an hour in this complete darkness, chilled and uncomfortable and half asleep, feeling the coach drag on a heavy-climbing grade. Gray dawn cracked through, followed by a sunless light rushing all across the flat desert now far below. The road looped from one barren shoulder to another and at sunup they had reached the first bench and were slamming full speed along a boulder-strewn flat. The cattleman sat in the forward corner, the left corner of his mouth swollen and crushed, and when Henriette saw that her glance slid to Malpais Bill's knuckles. The army girl had her eyes closed, her shoulders pressing against the Englishman, who remained bolt upright with the sporting gun between his knees. Beside Henriette the gambler seemed to sleep, and on the middle bench Malpais Bill watched the land go by with a thin vigilance.

At ten they were rising again, with juniper and scrub pine showing on the slopes and the desert below them filling with the powdered haze of another hot day. By noon they reached the summit of the range and swung to follow its narrow rock-ribbed meadows. The gambler, long motionless, shifted his feet and caught the army girl's eyes.

"Schrieber's is directly ahead. We are past the worst of it."

The blond man looked around at the gambler, making no comment; and it was then that Henriette caught the smell of smoke in the windless air. Happy Stuart was cursing once more and the brake blocks began to cry. Looking through the angled vista of the window panel Henriette saw a clay and rock chimney standing up like a gaunt skeleton against the day's light. The house that had been there was a black patch on the ground, smoke still rising from pieces that had not been completely burnt.

The stage stopped and all the men were instantly out. An iron stove squatted on the earth, with one section of pipe stuck upright to it. Fire licked lazily along the collapsed fragments of what had been a trunk. Beyond the location of the house, at the foot of a corral, lay two nude figures grotesquely bald, with deliberate knife slashes marking their bodies. Happy Stuart went over there and had his look; and came back.

"Schriebers. Well—"

Malpais Bill said: "This morning about daylight." He looked at the gambler, at the cattleman, at the Englishman who showed no emotion. "Get back in the coach." He climbed to the coach's top, flattening himself full length there. Happy Stuart and Strang took their places again. The horses broke into a run.

The gambler said to the army girl: "You're pretty safe between those two fellows," and hauled a .44 from a back pocket and laid it over his lap. He considered Henriette more carefully than before, his taciturnity breaking. He said: "How old are you?"

Her shoulders rose and fell, which was the only answer. But the gambler said gently, "Young enough to be my daughter. It is a rotten world. When I call to you, lie down on the floor."

The Englishman had pulled the rifle from between his knees and laid it across the sill of the window on his side. The cattleman swept back the skirt of his coat to clear the holster of his gun.

The little flinty summit meadows grew narrower, with shoulders of gray rock closing in upon the road. The coach wheels slammed against the stony ruts and bounced high and fell again with a jar the springs could not soften. Happy Stuart's howl ran steadily above this rattle and rush. Fine dust turned all things gray.

Henriette sat with her eyes pinned to the gloved tips of her fingers, remembering the tall shape of Malpais Bill cut against the moonlight of Gap Station. He had smiled at her as a man might smile at any desirable woman, with the sweep and swing of laughter in his voice; and his eyes had been gentle. The gambler spoke very quietly and she didn't hear him until his fingers gripped her arm. He said again, not raising his voice: "Get down."

Henriette dropped to her knees, hearing gunfire blast through the rush and run of the coach. Happy Stuart ceased to yell and the army girl's eyes were round and dark. The walls of the canyon had tapered off. Looking upward through the window on the gambler's side, Henriette saw the weaving figure of an Apache warrior reel nakedly on a calico pony and rush by with a rifle raised and pointed in his bony elbows. The gambler took a cool aim; the stockman fired and aimed again. The Englishman's sporting rifle blasted heavy echoes through the coach, hurting her ears, and the smell of powder got rank and bitter. The blond man's boots scraped the coach top and round small holes began to dimple the paneling as the Apache bullets struck. An Indian came boldly abreast the coach and made a target that couldn't be missed. The cattleman dropped him with one shot. The wheels screamed as they slowed around the sharp ruts and the whole heavy superstructure of the coach bounced high into the air. Then they were rushing downgrade.

The gambler said quietly, "You had better take this," handing Henriette his gun. He leaned against the door with his small hands gripping the sill. Pallor loosened his cheeks. He said to the army girl: "Be sure and keep between those gentlemen," and looked at her with a way that was desperate and forlorn and dropped his head to the window's sill.

Henriette saw the bluff rise up and close in like a yellow wall. They were rolling down the mountain without brake. Gunfire fell off and the crying of the Indians faded back. Coming up from her knees then she saw the desert's flat surface far below, with the angular pattern of Lordsburg vaguely on the far borders of the heat fog. There was no more firing and Happy Stuart's voice lifted again and the brakes were screaming on the wheels, and going off, and screaming again. The Englishman stared out of the window sullenly; the army girl seemed in a deep desperate dream; the cattleman's face was shining with a strange sweat. Henriette reached over to pull the gambler up, but he had an unnatural weight to him and slid into the far corner. She saw that he was dead.

At five o'clock that long afternoon the stage threaded Lordsburg's narrow streets of dobe and frame houses, came upon the center square and stopped before a crowd of people gathered in the smoky heat. The passengers crawled out stiffly. A Mexican boy ran up to see the dead gambler and began to yell his news in shrill Mexican. Malpais Bill climbed off the top, but Happy Stuart sat back on his seat and stared taciturnly at the crowd. Henriette noticed then that the shotgun messenger was gone.

A gray man in a sleazy white suit called up to Happy. "Well, you got through."

Happy Stuart said: "Yeah. We got through."

An officer stepped through the crowd, smiling at the army girl. He took her arm and said, "Miss Robertson, I believe. Lieutenant Hauser is quite all right. I will get your luggage—"

The army girl was crying then, definitely. They were all standing around, bone-weary and shaken. Malpais Bill remained by the wheel of the coach, his cheeks hard against the sunlight and his eyes riveted on a pair of men standing under the board awning of an adjoining store. Henriette observed the manner of their waiting and knew why they were here. The blond man's eyes, she noticed, were very blue and flame burned brilliantly in them. The army girl turned to Henriette, tears in her eyes. She murmured: "If there is anything I can ever do for you—"

But Henriette stepped back, shaking her head. This was Lordsburg and everybody knew her place except the army girl. Henriette said formally, "Good-by," noting how still and expectant the two men under the awning remained. She swung toward the blond man and said, "Would you carry my valise?"

Malpais Bill looked at her, laughter remote in his eyes, and reached into the luggage pile and got her battered valise. He was still smiling as he went beside her, through the crowd and past the two waiting men. But when they turned into an anonymous and dusty little side street of the town, where the houses all sat shoulder to shoulder without grace or dignity, he had turned sober. He said: "I am obliged to you. But I'll have to go back there."

They were in front of a house no different from its neighbors; they had stopped at its door. She could see his eyes travel this street and comprehend its meaning and the kind of traffic it bore. But he was saying in that gentle, melody-making tone:

"I have watched you for two days." He stopped, searching his mind to find the thing he wanted to say. It came out swiftly. "God made you a woman. The Tonto is a pretty country."

Her answer was quite barren of feeling. "No. I am known all through the Territory. But I can remember that you asked me."

He said: "No other reason?" She didn't answer but something in her eyes pulled his face together. He took off his hat and it seemed to her he was looking through this hot day to that far-off country and seeing it fresh and desirable. He murmured: "A man can escape nothing. I have got to do this. But I will be back."

He went along the narrow street, made a quick turn at the end of it, and disappeared. Heat rolled like a heavy wave over Lordsburg's housetops and the smell of dust was very sharp. She lifted her valise, and dropped it and stood like that, mute and grave before the door of her dismal house. She was remembering how tall he had been against the moonlight at Gap Station.

There were four swift shots beating furiously along the sultry quiet, and a shout, and afterwards a longer and longer silence. She put one hand against the door to steady herself, and knew that those shots marked the end of a man, and the end of a hope. He would never come back; he would never stand over her in the moonlight with the long gentle smile on his lips and with the swing of life in his casual tone. She was thinking of all that humbly and with the patience life had beaten into her. . . .

She was thinking of all that when she heard the strike of boots on the street's packed earth; and turned to see him, high and square in the muddy sunlight, coming toward her with his smile.

A DAY IN TOWN

Ernest Haycox

They reached Two Dance around ten that morning and turned into the big lot between the courthouse and the Cattle King Hotel. Most of the homesteaders camped here when they came to town, for after a slow ride across the sage flats, underneath so hot and so yellow a sun, the shade of the huge locust trees was a comfort. Joe Blount unhitched and watered the horses and tied them to a pole. He was a long and loose and deliberate man who had worked with his hands too many years to waste motion, and if he dallied more than usual over his chores now it was because he dreaded the thing ahead of him.

His wife sat on the wagon's seat, holding the baby. She had a pin in her mouth and she was talking around it to young Tom: "Stay away from the horses on the street and don't you go near the railroad tracks. Keep hold of May's

159

hand. She's too little to be alone, you remember. Be sure to
come back by noon."

Young Tom was seven and getting pretty thin from
growth. The trip to town had him excited. He kept nodding
his sun-bleached head, he kept tugging at little May's hand,
and then both of them ran headlong for the street and
turned the corner of the Cattle King, shrilly whooping as
they disappeared.

Blount looked up at his wife. She was a composed
woman and not one to bother people with talk and sometimes it was hard for a man to know what was in her mind.
But he knew what was there now, for all their problems
were less than this one and they had gone over it pretty
thoroughly the last two-three months. He moved his fingers
up to the pocket of his shirt and dropped them immediately
away, searching the smoky horizon with his glance. He
didn't expect to see anything over there, but it was better
than meeting her eyes at this moment. He said in his patiently low voice: "Think we could make it less than three
hundred?"

The baby moved its arms, its warm-wet fingers aimlessly brushing Hester Blount's cheeks. She said: "I don't see
how. We kept figuring—and it never gets smaller. You know
best, Joe."

"No," he murmured, "it never gets any smaller. Well,
three hundred. That's what I'll ask for." And yet, with the
chore before him, he kept his place by the dropped wagon
tongue. He put his hands in his pockets and drew a long
breath and looked at the powdered earth below him with a
sustained gravity, and was like this when Hester Blount
spoke again. He noticed that she was pretty gentle with her
words: "Why, now, Joe, you go on. It isn't like you were
shiftless and hadn't tried. He knows you're a hard worker
and he knows your word's good. You just go ahead."

"Guess we've both tried," he agreed. "And I guess he
knows how it's been. We ain't alone." He went out toward
the street, reminding himself of this. They weren't alone. All

the people along Christmas Creek were burned out, so it wasn't as if he had failed because he didn't know how to farm. The thought comforted him a good deal; it restored a little of his pride. Crossing the street toward Dunmire's stable, he met Chess Roberts, with whom he had once punched cattle on the Hat outfit, and he stopped in great relief and palavered with Chess for a good ten minutes until, looking back, he saw his wife still seated on the wagon. That sight vaguely troubled him and he drawled to Chess, "Well, I'll see you later," and turned quite slowly toward the bank.

There was nothing in the bank's old-fashioned room to take a man's attention. Yet when he came into its hot, shaded silence Joe Blount removed his hat and felt ill at ease as he walked toward Lane McKercher. There was a pine desk here and on the wall a railroad map showing the counties of the Territory in colors. Over at the other side of the room stood the cage where McKercher's son waited on the trade.

McKercher was big and bony and gray and his eyes could cut. They were that penetrating, as everybody agreed. "Been a long time since you came to town. Sit down and have a talk," and his glance saw more about Joe Blount than the homesteader himself could ever tell. "How's Christmas Creek?"

Blount settled in the chair. He said, "Why, just fine," and laid his hands over the hat in his lap. Weather had darkened him and work had thinned him and gravity remained like a stain on his cheeks. He was, McKercher recalled, about thirty years old, had once worked as a puncher on Hat and had married a girl from a small ranch over in the Yellows. Thirty wasn't so old, yet the country was having its way with Joe Blount. When he dropped his head the skin around his neck formed a loose crease and his mouth had that half-severe expression which comes from too much trouble. This was what McKercher saw. This and the blue army shirt, washed and mended until it was as thin as cotton, and the man's long hard hands lying so loose before him. McKercher said, "A little dry over your way?"

"Oh," said Blount, "a little. Yeah, a little bit dry."

The banker sat back and waited, and the silence ran on a long while. Blount moved around in the chair and lifted his hand and reversed the hat on his lap. His eyes touched McKercher and passed quickly on to the ceiling. He stirred again, not comfortable. One hand reached up to the pocket of his shirt, dropping quickly back.

"Something on your mind, Joe?"

"Why," said Blount, "Hester and I have figured it out pretty close. It would take about three hundred dollars until next crop. Don't see how it could be less. There'd be seed and salt for stock and grub to put in and I guess some clothes for the kids. Seems like a lot but we can't seem to figure it any smaller."

"A loan?" said McKercher.

"Why, yes," said Blount, relieved that the explaining was over.

"Now let's see. You've got another year to go before you get title to your place. So that's no security. How was your wheat?"

"Burnt out. No rain over there in April."

"How much stock?"

"Well, not much. Just two cows. I sold off last fall. The graze was pretty skinny." He looked at McKercher and said in the briefest way, "I got nothing to cover this loan. But I'm a pretty good worker."

McKercher turned his eyes toward the desk. There wasn't much to be seen behind the cropped gray whiskers of his face. According to the country this was why he wore them—so that a man could never tell what he figured. But his shoulders rose and dropped and he spoke regretfully: "There's no show for you on that ranch, Joe. Dry farming— it won't do. All you fellows are burned out. This country never was meant for it. It's cattle land and that's about all."

He let it go like that, and waited for the homesteader

to come back with a better argument. Only, there was no argument. Joe Blount's lips changed a little and his hands flattened on the peak of his hat. He said in a slow, mild voice, "Well, I can see it your way all right," and got up. His mind strayed up to the shirt pocket again, and fell away—and McKercher, looking straight into the man's eyes, saw an expression there hard to define. The banker shook his head. Direct refusal was on his tongue and it wasn't like him to postpone it, which he did. "I'll think it over. Come back about two o'clock."

"Sure," said Blount, and turned across the room, his long frame swinging loosely, his knees springing as he walked, saving energy. After he had gone out of the place McKercher remembered the way the homesteader's hand had gone toward the pocket. It was a gesture that remained in the banker's mind.

Blount stopped outside the bank. Hester, at this moment, was passing down toward the dry-goods store with the baby in her arms. He waited until she had gone into the store and then walked on toward the lower end of town, not wanting her to see him just then. He knew McKercher would turn him down at two o'clock. He had heard it pretty plainly in the banker's tone, and he was thinking of all the things he had meant to explain to McKercher. He was telling McKercher that one or two bad years shouldn't count against a man. That the land on Christmas Creek would grow the best winter wheat in the world. That you had to take the dry with the wet. But he knew he'd never say any of this. The talk wasn't in him, and never had been. Young Tom and little May were across the street, standing in front of Swing's restaurant, seeing something that gripped their interest. Joe Blount looked at them from beneath the lowered brim of his hat; they were skinny with age and they needed some clothes. He went on by, coming against Chess Roberts near the saloon.

Chess said: "Well, we'll have a drink on this."

The smell of the saloon drifted out to Joe Blount, its odor of spilled whisky and tobacco smoke starting the saliva in his jaws, freshening a hunger. But Hester and the kids were on his mind and something told him it was unseemly, the way things were. He said: "Not right now, Chess. I got some chores to tend. What you doing?"

"You ain't heard? I'm riding for Hat again."

Blount said: "Kind of quiet over my way. Any jobs for a man on Hat?"

"Not now," said Chess. "We been layin' off summer help. A little bit tough this year, Joe. You havin' trouble on Christmas Creek?"

"Me? Not a bit, Chess. We get along. It's just that I like to keep workin'."

After Chess had gone, Joe Blount laid the point of his shoulder against the saloon wall and watched his two children walk hand in hand past the windows of the general store. Young Tom pointed and swung his sister around; and both of them had their faces against a window, staring in. Blount pulled his eyes away. It took the kids to do things that scraped a man's pride pretty hard, that made him feel his failure. Under the saloon's board awning lay shade, but sweat cracked through his forehead and he thought quickly of what he could do. Maybe Dunmire could use a man to break horses. Maybe he could get on hauling wood for the feed store. This was Saturday and the big ranch owners would be coming down the Two Dance grade pretty soon. Maybe there was a hole on one of those outfits. It was an hour until noon, and at noon he had to go back to Hester. He turned toward the feed store.

Hester Blount stood at the dry-goods counter of Vetten's store. Vetten came over, but she said, "I'm just trying to think." She laid the baby on the counter and watched it lift its feet straight in the air and aimlessly try to catch them with its hands; and she was thinking that the family needed a good many things. Underwear all around, and stockings and overalls. Little May had to have some material for a dress, and some ribbon. You couldn't let a girl grow up without a few pretty things, even out on Christmas Creek. It wasn't good for the girl. Copper-toed shoes for young Tom, and a pair for his father; and lighter buttoned ones for May. None of these would be less than two dollars and a half, and it was a crime the way it mounted up. And plenty of flannel for the baby.

She had not thought of herself until she saw the dark gray bolt of silk lying at the end of the counter, and when she saw it something happened to her heart. It wasn't good to be so poor that the sight of a piece of silk made you feel this way. She turned from it, ashamed of her thoughts—as though she had been guilty of extravagance. Maybe if she were young again and still pretty, and wanting to catch a man's eyes, it might not be so silly to think of clothes. But she was no longer young or pretty and she had her man. She could take out her love of nice things on little May, who was going to be a very attractive girl. As soon as Joe was sure of the three hundred dollars she'd come back here and get what they all had to have—and somehow squeeze out the few pennies for dress material and the hair ribbon.

She stood here thinking of these things and so many others—a tall and rather comely woman in her early thirties, dark-faced and carrying an even, sweet-lipped gravity while her eyes sought the dry-goods shelves and her hand unconsciously patted the baby's round middle.

A woman came bustling into the store and said in a loud, accented voice: "Why, Hester Blount, of all the people I never expected to see!"

Hester said, "Now, isn't this a surprise!" and the two took each other's hands, and fell into a quick half embrace. Ten years ago they had been girls together over in the Two Dance, Hester and this Lila Evenson who had married a town man. Lila was turning into a heavy woman and, like many heavy women, she loved white and wore it now, though it made her look big as a house. Above the tight collar of the dress, her skin was a flushed red and a second chin faintly trembled when she talked. Hester Blount stood motionless, listening to that outpour of words, feeling the quick search of Lila's eyes. Lila, she knew, would be taking everything in—her worn dress, her heavy shoes, and the lines of her face.

"And another baby!" said Lila and bent over it and made a long gurgling sound. "What a lucky woman! That's three? But ain't it a problem, out there on Christmas Creek? Even in town here I worry so much over my one darling."

"No," said Hester, "we don't worry. How is your husband?"

"So well," said Lila. "You know, he's bought the drugstore from old Kerrin, who is getting old. He had done so well. We are lucky, as we keep telling ourselves. And that reminds me. You must come up to dinner. You really must come this minute."

They had been brought up on adjoining ranches and had ridden to the same school and to the same dances. But that was so long ago, and so much had changed them. And Lila was always a girl to throw her fortunes in other people's faces. Hester said, gently, regretfully: "Now, isn't it too bad! We brought a big lunch in the wagon, thinking it would be easier. Joe has so many chores to do here."

"I have often wondered about you, away out there," said Lila. "Have you been well? It's been such a hard year for everybody. So many homesteaders going broke."

"We are well," said Hester slowly, a small, hard pride in her tone. "Everything's been fine."

"Now, that's nice," murmured Lila, her smile remaining fixed; but her eyes, Hester observed, were sharp and busy—and reading too much. Lila said, "Next time you come and see us," and bobbed her head and went out of the store, her clothes rustling in this quiet. Hester's lips went sharp-shut and quick color burned on her cheeks. She took up the baby and turned into the street again and saw that Tom hadn't come yet to the wagon. The children were out of sight and there was nothing to do but wait. Hearing the far-off halloo of a train's whistle, she walked on under the board galleries to the depot.

Heat swirled around her and light flashed up from polished spots on the iron rails. Around her lay the full monotony of the desert, so familiar, so wide—and sometimes so hard to bear. Backed against the yellow depot wall, she watched the train rush forward, a high plume of white steam rising to the sky as it whistled to warn them. And then it rushed by, engine and cars, in a great smash of sound that stirred the baby in her arms. She saw men standing on the platforms. Women's faces showed in the car windows, serene and idly curious and not a part of Hester's world at all; and afterward the train was gone, leaving behind the heated smell of steel and smoke. When the quiet came back it was lonelier than before. She turned back to the wagon.

It was then almost twelve. The children came up, hot and weary and full of excitement. Young Tom said: "The school is right in town. They don't have to walk at all. It's right next to the houses. Why don't they have to walk three miles like us?" And May said: "I saw a china doll with real clothes and painted eyelashes. Can I have a china doll?"

Hester changed the baby on the wagon seat. She said: "Walking is good for people, Tom. Why should you expect a doll now, May? Christmas is the time. Maybe Christmas we'll remember."

"Well, I'm hungry."

"Wait till your father comes," said Hester.

When he turned in from the street, later, she knew something was wrong. He was always a deliberate man, not much given to smiling. But he walked with his shoulders down and when he came up he said only: "I suppose we ought to eat." He didn't look directly at her. He had his own strong pride and she knew this wasn't like him—to stand by the wagon's wheel, so oddly watching his children. She reached under the seat for the box of sandwiches and the cups and the jug of cold coffee. She said: "What did he say, Joe?"

"Why, nothing yet. He said come back at two. He wanted to think about it."

She murmured, "It won't hurt us to wait," and laid out the sandwiches. They sat on the shaded ground and ate, the children with a quick, starved impatience, with an excited and aimless talk. Joe Blount looked at them carefully. "What was it you saw in the restaurant, sonny?"

"It smelled nice," said young May. "The smell came out the door."

Joe Blount cleared his throat. "Don't stop like that in front of the restaurant again."

"Can we go now? Can we go down by the depot?"

"You hold May's hand," said Blount, and watched them leave. He sat cross-legged before his wife, his big hands idle, his expression unstirred. The sandwich, which was salted bacon grease spread on Hester's potato bread, lay before him. "Ain't done enough this morning to be hungry," he said.

"I know."

They were never much at talking. And now there wasn't much to say. She knew that he had been turned down. She knew that at two o'clock he would go and come back empty-handed. Until then she wouldn't speak of it, and neither would he. And she was thinking with a woman's realism of what lay before them. They had nothing except this team and wagon and two cows standing unfed in the barn lot. Going back to Christmas Creek now would be going back only to pack up and leave. For they had delayed asking for this loan until the last sack of flour in the storehouse had been emptied.

He said: "I been thinking. Not much to do on the ranch this fall. I ought to get a little outside work."

"Maybe you should."

"Fact is, I've tried a few places. Kind of quiet. But I can look around some more."

She said, "I'll wait here."

He got up, a rangy, spare man who found it hard to be idle. He looked at her carefully and his voice didn't reveal anything: "If I were you I don't believe I'd order anything at the stores until I come back."

She watched the way he looked out into the smoky horizon, the way he held his shoulders. When he turned away, not meeting her eyes, her lips made a sweet line across her dark face, a softly maternal expression showing. She said, "Joe," and waited until he turned. "Joe, we'll always get along."

He went away again, around the corner of the Cattle King. She shifted her on the wagon's seat, her hand gently patting the baby who was a little cross from the heat. One by one she went over the list of necessary things in her mind, and one by one, erased them. It was hard to think of little May without a ribbon bow in her hair, without a good dress. Boys could wear old clothes, as long as they were warm; but a girl, a pretty girl, needed the touch of niceness. It was hard to be poor.

Coming out of the bank at noon, Lane McKercher looked into the corral space and saw the Blounts eating their lunch under the locust tree. He turned down Arapahoe Street, walking through the comforting shade of the poplars to the big square house at the end of the lane. At dinner hour his boy took care of the bank, and so he ate his meal with the housekeeper in a dining room whose shades had been tightly drawn—the heavy midday meal of a man who had developed his hunger and his physique from early days on the range. Afterward he walked to the living-room couch and lay down with a paper over his face for the customary nap.

A single fly made a racket in the deep quiet, but it was not this that kept him from sleeping. In some obscure manner the shape of Joe Blount came before him—the long, patient and work-stiffened shape of a man whose eyes had been so blue and so calm in face of refusal. Well, there had been something behind those eyes for a moment, and then it had passed away, eluding McKercher's sharp glance.

They were mostly all patient ones and seldom speaking —these men that came off the deep desert. A hard life had made them that way, as McKercher knew, who had shared that life himself. Blount was no different than the others and many times McKercher had refused these others, without afterthoughts. It was some other thing that kept his mind on Blount. Not knowing why, he lay quietly on the couch, trying to find the reason.

The country, he told himself, was cattle country, and those who tried to dry-farm it were bound to fail. He had seen them fail, year after year. They took their wagons and their families out toward Christmas Creek, loaded high with plunder; and presently they came back with their wagons baked and their eyebrows bleached and nothing left. With their wives sitting in the wagons, old from work, with their children long and thin from lack of food. They had always failed and always would. Blount was a good man, but so were most of the rest. Why should he be thinking of Blount?

He rose at one o'clock, feeling the heat and feeling his age; and washed his hands and face with good cold water. Lighting a cigar, he strolled back down Arapahoe and walked across the square toward the Cattle King. Mrs. Blount sat on the wagon's seat, holding a baby. The older youngsters, he noticed, were in the cool runway of Dunmire's stable. He went into the saloon, though not to drink.

"Nick," he said, "Joe Blount been in for a drink yet?"

The saloonkeeper looked up from an empty poker table. "No," he said.

McKercher went out, crossing to Billy Saxton's feed store. Deep in the big shed Billy Saxton weighed hay bales on his heavy scales. He stopped and sopped the sweat off his forehead, and smiled. "Bankin'," he stated, "is easier."

"Maybe it is," said Lane McKercher. "You know Joe Blount well?"

"Why, he's all right. Used to ride for Hat. Old man Dale liked him. He was in here a while back."

"To buy feed?"

"No, he wanted to haul wood for me."

McKercher went back up the street toward the bank. Jim Benbow was coming down the road from the Two Dance hills, kicking a long streamer of dust behind. Sun struck the windows on the north side of town, setting up a brilliant explosion of light. Joe Blount came out of the stable and turned over toward the Cattle King, waiting for Benbow.

In the bank, McKercher said to his son, "All right, you go eat," and sat down at his pine desk. Benbow put his head through the front door, calling: "I'll need five thousand this week, Mac—until the stock check comes in."

"All right."

He sat quite still at the desk, stern with himself because he could not recall why he kept thinking of Joe Blount. Men were everything to Lane McKercher, who watched them pass along this street year in and year out, who studied them with his sharp eyes and made his judgments concerning them. If there was something in a man, it had to come out. And what was it in Joe Blount he couldn't name? The echoes of the big clock on the wall rattled around the droning silence of the bank like the echo of feet striking the floor; it was then a quarter of two, and he knew he had to refuse Blount a second time. He could not understand why he had not made the first turndown final.

Blount met Jim Benbow on the corner of the Cattle King, directly after Hat's owner had left the bank. He shook Benbow's hand, warmed and pleased by the tall cattleman's smile of recognition. Benbow said: "Been a long time since I saw you. How's Christmas Creek, Joe?"

"Fine—just fine. You're lookin' good. You don't get old."

"Well, let's go have a little smile on that."

"Why, thanks, no. I was wonderin'. It's pretty quiet on my place right now. Not much to do till spring. You need a man?"

Benbow shook his head. "Not a thing doing, Joe. Sorry."

"Of course—of course," murmured Blount. "I didn't figure there would be."

He stood against the Cattle King's low porch rail after Benbow had gone down the street, his glance lifted and fixed on the smoky light of the desert beyond town. Shade lay around him but sweat began to creep below his hat brim. He was closely and quickly thinking of places that might be open for a man, and knew there were none in town and none on the range. This was the slack season of the year. The children were over in front of the grocery store, stopped by its door, hand in hand, round, dark cheeks lifted and still. Blount swung his shoulders around, cutting them out of his sight.

Sullen Ben Drury came out of the courthouse and passed Blount, removing his cigar and speaking, and replacing the cigar again. Its smell was like acid biting at Blount's jaw corners, and suddenly he faced the bank with the odd and terrible despair of a man who has reached the end of hope, and a strange thought came to him, which was that the doors of that bank were wide open and money lay on the counter inside for the taking.

He stood very still, his head down, and after a while he thought: "An unseemly thing for a man to hold in his head." It was two o'clock then and he turned over the square, going toward the bank with his legs springing as he walked and all his muscles loose. In the quietness of the room his boots dragged up odd sound. He stood by Lane McKercher's desk, waiting without any show of expression; he knew what McKercher would say.

McKercher said, slowly and with an odd trace of irritation: "Joe, you're wasting your time on Christmas Creek. And you'd waste the loan."

Blount said, mildly and courteously: "I can understand your view. Don't blame you for not loanin' without security." He looked over McKercher's head, his glance going through the window to the far strip of horizon. "Kind of difficult to give up a thing," he mused. "I figured to get away from ridin' for other folks and ride for myself. Well, that was why we went to Christmas Creek. Maybe a place the kids could have later. Man wants his children to have somethin' better than he had."

"Not on Christmas Creek," said McKercher. He watched Joe Blount with a closer and sharper interest, bothered by a feeling he could not name. Bothered by it and turned impatient by it.

"Maybe, maybe not," said Blount. "Bad luck don't last forever." Then he said, "Well, I shouldn't be talkin'. I thank you for your time." He put on his hat, and his big hand moved up across his shirt, to the pocket there—and dropped away. He turned toward the door.

"Hold on," said Lane. "Hold on a minute." He waited till Blount came back to the desk. He opened the desk's drawer and pulled out a can of cigars, holding them up. "Smoke?"

There was a long delay, and it was strange to see the way Joe Blount looked at the cigars, with his lips closely together. He said, his voice dragging on the words, "I guess not, but thanks."

Lane McKercher looked down at the desk, his expression breaking out of its maintained strictness. The things in a man had to come out, and he knew now why Joe Blount had stayed so long in his mind. It made him look up. "I have been considering this. It won't ever be a matter of luck on Christmas Creek. It's a matter of water. When I passed the feed store today I noticed a secondhand windmill in the back. It will do. You get hold of Plummer Bodry and find out his price for driving you a well. I never stake a man unless I stake him right. We will figure the three hundred and whatever it takes to put up a tank and windmill. When you buy your supplies today, just say you've got credit here."

"Why, now—" began Joe Blount in his slow, soft voice, "I—"

But Lane McKercher said to his son, just coming back from lunch, "I want you to bring your ledger over here." He kept on talking and Joe Blount, feeling himself pushed out, turned and left the bank.

McKercher's son came over. "Made that loan after all. Why?"

McKercher said only, "He's a good man, Bob." But he knew the real reason. A man that smoked always carried his tobacco in his shirt pocket. Blount had kept reaching, out of habit, for something that wasn't there. Well, a man like Blount loved this one small comfort and never went without it unless actually destitute. But Blount wouldn't admit it, and had been too proud to take a free cigar. Men were everything—and the qualities in them came out sooner or later, as with Blount. A windmill and water was a good risk with a fellow like that.

Hester watched him cross the square and come toward her, walking slowly, with his shoulders squared. She patted the baby's back and gently rocked it, and wondered at the change. When he came up he said, casually, "I'll hitch and drive around to the store, so we can load the stuff you buy."

She watched him carefully, so curious to know how it had happened. But she only said: "We'll get along."

He was smiling then, he who seldom smiled. "I guess you need a few things for yourself. We can spare something for that."

"Only a dress and some ribbon, for May. A girl needs something nice." She paused, and afterward added, because she knew how real his need was, "Joe, you buy yourself some tobacco."

He let out a long, long breath. "I believe I will," he said. They stood this way, both gently smiling. They needed no talk to explain anything to each other. They had been through so much these last few years. Hardship and trouble had drawn them so close together that words were unnecessary. So they were silent, remembering so much, and understanding so much, and still smiling. Presently he turned to hitch up.

THE INDIAN WELL

Walter Van Tilburg Clark

In this dead land, like a vast relief model, the only allegiance was to sun. Even night was not strong enough to resist; earth stretched gratefully under it, but had no hope that day would not return. Such living things as hoarded a little juice at their cores were secret about it, and only the most ephemeral existences, the air at dawn and sunset, the amethyst shadows in the mountains, had any freedom. The Indian Well alone, of lesser creations, was in constant revolt. Sooner or later all minor, breathing rebels came to its stone basin under the spring in the cliff, and from its overflow grew a meadow delta and two columns of willows and aspens holding a tiny front against the valley. The pictograph of a starving, ancient journey, cut in rock above the basin, a sun-warped shack on the south wing of the canyon, and an abandoned mine above it, were the last minute and practically contemporary tokens of man's participation in the cycles of the well's resistance, each of which was an epitome of centuries, and perhaps of the wars of the universe. The day before Jim Suttler came up in the early spring to take his part in one cycle was a busy day. The sun was merely lucid after four days of broken showers and one rain of an hour with a little cold wind behind it, and under the separate cloud shadows sliding down the mountain and into the valley, the canyon was alive. A rattler emerged partially from a hole in the mound on which the cabin stood, and having gorged in the darkness, rested with his head on a stone. A road-runner, stepping long and always about to sprint, came down the morning side of the mound, and his eye, quick to perceive the difference between the live and the inanimate of the same color, discovered the coffin-shaped head on the stone. At once he broke into a reaching sprint, his neck and tail stretched level, his beak agape with expectation. But his shadow arrived a step before him. The rattler recoiled, his head scarred by the sharp beak but his eye intact. The road-runner said nothing, but peered warily into the hole without stretching his neck, then walked off stiffly, leaning forward again as if about to run. When he had gone twenty feet he turned, balanced for an instant, and charged back, checking abruptly just short of the hole. The snake remained withdrawn. The road-runner paraded briefly before the hole, talking to himself, and then ran angrily up to the spring, where he drank at the overflow, sipping and stretching his neck, lifting his feet one at a time, ready to go into immediate action. The road-runner lived a dangerous and exciting life.

In the upper canyon the cliff swallows, making short sharp notes, dipped and shot between the new mud under the aspens and their high community on the forehead of the cliff. Electrical bluebirds appeared to dart the length of the canyon at each low flight, but turned up tilting half way down. Lizards made similar unexpected flights and stops on the rocks, and when they stopped did rapid push-ups, like men exercising on a floor. They were variably pugnacious and timid.

Two of them arrived simultaneously upon a rock below the road-runner. One of them immediately skittered to a rock two feet off, and they faced each other, exercising. A small hawk coming down over the mountain, but shadowless under a cloud, saw the lizards. Having overfled the difficult target, he dropped to the canyon mouth swiftly and banked back into the wind. His trajectory was cleared of swallows but one of them, fluttering hastily up, dropped a pellet of mud between the lizards. The one who had retreated disappeared. The other flattened for an instant, then sprang and charged. The road-runner was on him as he struck the pellet, and galloped down the canyon in great, tense strides on his toes, the lizard lashing the air from his beak. The hawk swooped at the road-runner, thought better of it, and rose against the wind to the head of the canyon, where he turned back and coasted out over the desert, his shadow a little behind him and farther and farther below.

The swallows became the voice of the canyon again, but in moments when they were all silent the lovely smaller sounds emerged, their own feathering, the liquid overflow, the snapping and clicking of insects, a touch of wind in the new aspens. Under these lay still more delicate tones, erasing, in the most silent seconds, the difference between eye and ear, a white cloud shadow passing under the water of the well, a dark cloud shadow on the cliff, the aspen patterns on the stones. Deepest was the permanent background of the rocks, those lost on the canyon floor, and those yet strong, the thinking cliffs. When the swallows began again it was impossible to understand the cliffs, who could afford to wait.

At noon a red and white range cow with one new calf, shining and curled, came slowly up from the desert, stopping often to let the calf rest. At each stop the calf would try vigorously to feed, but the cow would go on. When they reached the well the cow drank slowly for a long time; then she continued to wrinkle the water with her muzzle, drinking a little and blowing, as if she found it hard to leave. The calf worked under her with spasmodic nudgings. When she was done playing with the water, she nosed and licked him out from under her and up to the well. He shied from the surprising coolness and she put him back. When he stayed, she drank again. He put his nose into the water also, and bucked up as if bitten. She continued to pretend, and he returned, got water up his nostrils and took three jumps away. The cow was content and moved off toward the canyon wall, tonguing grass tufts from among the rocks. Against the cliff she rubbed gently and continuously with a mild voluptuous look, occasionally lapping her nose with a serpent tongue. The loose winter shag came off in tufts on the rock. The calf lost her, became panicked and made desperate noises which stopped prematurely, and when he discovered her, complicated her toilet. Finally she led him down to the meadow where, moving slowly, they both fed until he was full and went to sleep in a ball in the sun. At sunset they returned to the well, where the cow drank again and gave him a second lesson. After this they went back into the brush and northward into the dusk. The cow's size and relative immunity to sudden death left an aftermath of peace, rendered gently humorous by the calf.

Also at sunset, there was a resurgence of life among the swallows. The thin golden air at the cliff tops, in which there were now no clouds so that the eastern mountains and the valley were flooded with unbroken light, was full of their cries and quick maneuvers among a dancing myriad of insects. The direct sun gave them, when they perched in rows upon the cliff, a dramatic significance like that of men upon an immensely higher promontory. As dusk rose out of the canyon, while the eastern peaks were still lighted, the swallows gradually became silent creatures with slightly altered flight, until, at twilight, the air was full of velvet, swooping bats.

In the night jackrabbits multiplied spontaneously out of

the brush of the valley, drank in the rivulet, their noses and great ears continuously searching the dark, electrical air, and played in fits and starts on the meadow, the many young hopping like rubber, or made thumping love among the aspens and the willows. A coyote came down canyon on his belly and lay in the brush with his nose between his paws. He took a young rabbit in a quiet spring and snap, and went into the brush again to eat it. At the slight rending of his meal the meadow cleared of leaping shadows and lay empty in the starlight. The rabbits, however, encouraged by newcomers, returned soon, and the coyote killed again and went off heavily, the jack's great hind legs dragging.

In the dry-wash below the meadow an old coyote, without family, profited by the second panic, which came over him. He ate what his loose teeth could tear, leaving the open remnant in the sand, drank at the basin and, carefully circling the meadow, disappeared into the dry wilderness.

Shortly before dawn, when the stars had lost luster and there was no sound in the canyon but the rivulet and the faint, separate clickings of mice in the gravel, nine antelope in loose file, with three silently flagging fawns, came on trigger toe up the meadow and drank at the well, heads often up, muzzles dripping, broad ears turning. In the meadow they grazed and the fawns nursed. When there was as much gray as darkness in the air, and new wind in the canyon, they departed, the file weaving into the brush, merging into the desert, to nothing, and the swallows resumed the talkative day shift.

Jim Suttler and his burro came up into the meadow a little after noon, very slowly, though there was only a spring-fever warmth. Suttler walked pigeon-toed, like an old climber, but carefully and stiffly, not with the loose walk natural to such a long-legged man. He stopped in the middle of the meadow, took off his old black sombrero, and stared up at the veil of water shining over the edge of the basin. "We're none too early, Jenny," he said to the burro.

The burro had felt water for miles, but could show no excitement. She stood with her head down and her four legs spread unnaturally, as if to postpone a collapse. Her pack reared higher than Suttler's head, and was hung with casks, pails, canteens, a pick, two shovels, a crowbar and a rifle in a sheath. Suttler had the cautious uncertainty of his trade. His other burro had died two days before in the mountains east of Beatty, and Jenny and he bore its load.

Suttler shifted his old six-shooter from his rump to his thigh, and studied the well, the meadow, the cabin and the mouth of the mine as if he might choose not to stay. He was not a cinema prospector. If he looked like one of the probably mistaken conceptions of Christ, with his red beard and red hair to his shoulders, it was because he had been long away from barbers and without spare water for shaving. He was unlike Christ in some other ways also.

"It's kinda run down," he told Jenny, "but we'll take it."

He put his sombrero back on, let his pack fall slowly to the ground, showing the sweat patch in his bleached brown shirt, and began to unload Jenny carefully, like a collector handling rare vases, and put everything into one neat pile.

"Now," he said, "we'll have a drink." His tongue and lips were so swollen that the words were unclear, but he spoke casually, like a club-man sealing a minor deal. One learns to do business slowly with deserts and mountains. He picked up a bucket and started for the well. At the upper edge of the meadow he looked back. Jenny was still standing with her head down and her legs apart. He did not particularly notice her extreme thinness for he had seen it coming on gradually. He was thinner himself, and tall, and so round-shouldered that when he stood his straightest he seemed to be peering ahead with his chin out.

"Come on, you old fool," he said. "It's off you now."

Jenny came, stumbling in the rocks above the meadow, and stopping often as if to decide why this annoyance recurred. When she became interested, Suttler would not let her get to the basin, but for ten minutes gave her water from his cupped hands, a few licks at a time. Then he drove her off and she stood in the shade of the canyon wall watching him. He began on his thirst in the same way, a gulp at a time, resting between gulps. After ten gulps he sat on a rock by the spring and looked at the little meadow and the big desert, and might have been considering the courses of the water through his body, but noticed also the antelope tracks in the mud.

After a time he drank another half dozen gulps, gave Jenny half a pailful, and drove her down to the meadow, where he spread a dirty blanket in the striped sun and shadow under the willows. He sat on the edge of the blanket, rolled a cigarette and smoked it while he watched Jenny. When she began to graze with her rump to the canyon, he flicked his cigarette onto the grass, rolled over with his back to the sun and slept until it became chilly after sunset. Then he woke, ate a can of beans, threw the can into the willows and led Jenny up to the well, where they drank together from the basin for a long time. While she resumed her grazing, he took another blanket and his rifle from the pile, removed his heel-worn boots, stood his rifle against a fork, and, rolling up in both blankets, slept again.

In the night many rabbits played in the meadow in spite of the strong sweat and tobacco smell of Jim Suttler lying under the willows, but the antelope, when they came in the dead dark before dawn, were nervous, drank less, and did not graze but minced quickly back across the meadow and began to run at the head of the dry wash. Jenny slept with her head hanging, and did not hear them come or go.

Suttler woke lazy and still red-eyed, and spent the morning drinking at the well, eating and dozing on his blanket. In the afternoon, slowly, a few things at a time, he carried his pile to the cabin. He had a bachelor's obsession with order, though he did not mind dirt, and puttered until sundown making a brush bed and arranging his gear. Much of this time, however, was spent studying the records, on the cabin walls, of the recent human life of the well. He had to be careful, because among the still legible names and dates, after Frank Davis, 1893, Willard Harbinger, 1893, London, England, John Mason, June 13, 1887, Bucksport, Maine, Matthew Kenling from Glasgow, 1891, Penelope and Martin Reave, God Guide Us, 1885, was written Frank Hayward, 1492, feeling my age. There were other wits too. John Barr had written, Giv it back to the injuns, and Kenneth Thatcher, two years later, had written under that, Pity the noble redskin, while another man, whose second name was Evans, had written what was already a familiar libel, since it was not strictly true: Fifty miles from water, a hundred miles from wood, a million miles from God, three feet from hell. Someone unnamed had felt differently, saying, God is kind. We may make it now. Shot an antelope here July 10, 188—and the last number blurred. Arthur Smith, 1881, had recorded, Here berried my beloved wife Semantha, age 22, and my soul. God let me keep the child. J.M. said cryptically, Good luck, John, and Bill said, Ralph, if you come this way, am trying to get to Los Angeles. B. Westover said he had recovered from his wound there in 1884, and Galt said, enigmatically and without date, Bart and Miller burned to death in the Yellow Jacket. I don't care now. There were poets too, of both parties. What could still be read of Byron Cotter's verses, written in 1902, said,

> *. . . here alone*
> *Each shining dawn I greet,*
> *The Lord's wind on my forehead*
> *And where he set his feet*
> *One mark of heel remaining*
> *Each day filled up anew,*
> *To keep my soul from burning,*
> *With clear, celestial dew.*
> *Here in His Grace abiding*
> *The mortal years and few*
> *I shall . . .*

but you can't tell what he intended, while J.A. had printed,

> *My brother came out in '49*
> *I came in '51*
> *At first we thought we liked it fine*
> *But now, by God, we're done.*

Suttler studied these records without smiling, like someone reading a funny paper, and finally, with a heavy blue pencil, registered, Jim and Jenny Suttler, damn dried out, March—and paused, but had no way of discovering the day—1940.

In the evening he sat on the steps watching the swallows in the golden upper canyon turn bats in the dusk, and thought about the antelope. He had seen the new tracks also, and it alarmed him a little that the antelope could have passed twice in the dark without waking him.

Before false dawn he was lying in the willows with his carbine at ready. Rabbits ran from the meadow when he came down, and after that there was no movement. He wanted to smoke. When he did see them at the lower edge of the meadow, he was startled, yet made no quick movement, but slowly pivoted to cover them. They made poor targets in that light and backed by the pale desert, appearing and disappearing before his eyes. He couldn't keep any one of them steadily visible, and decided to wait until they made contrast against the meadow. But his presence was strong. One of the antelope advanced onto the green, but then threw its head up, spun, and ran back past the flank of the herd, which swung after him. Suttler rose quickly and raised the rifle, but let it down without firing. He could hear the light rattle of their flight in the wash, but had only a belief that he could see them. He had few cartridges, and the report and ponderous echo under the cliffs would scare them off for weeks.

His energies, however, were awakened by the frustrated hunt. While there was still more light than heat in the canyon, he climbed to the abandoned mine tunnel at the top of the alluvial wing of the cliff. He looked at the broken rock in the dump, kicked up its pack with a boot toe, and went into the tunnel, peering closely at its sides, in places black with old smoke smudges. At the back he struck two matches and looked at the jagged dead end and the fragments on the floor, then returned to the shallow beginning of a side tunnel. At the second match here he knelt quickly, scrutinized a portion of the rock, and when the match went out at once lit another. He lit six matches, and pulled at the rock with his hand. It was firm.

"The poor chump," he said aloud.

He got a loose rock from the tunnel and hammered at the projection with it. It came finally, and he carried it into the sun on the dump.

"Yessir," he said aloud, after a minute.

He knocked his sample into three pieces and examined each minutely.

"Yessir, yessir," he said with malicious glee, and, grinning at the tunnel, "The poor chump."

Then he looked again at the dump, like the mound before a gigantic gopher hole. "Still, that's a lot of digging," he said.

He put sample chips into his shirt pocket, keeping a small, black, heavy one that had fallen neatly from a hole like a borer's, to play with in his hand. After trouble he found the claim pile on the side hill south of the tunnel, its top rocks tumbled into the shale. Under the remaining rocks he found what he wanted, a ragged pice of yellowed paper between two boards. The writing was in pencil, and not diplomatic, "I hereby clame this whole damn side hill as far as I can shoot north and south and as far as I can dig in. I am a good shot. Keep off. John Barr, April 11, 1897."

Jim Suttler grinned. "Tough guy, eh?" he said.

He made a small ceremony of burning the paper upon a stone from the cairn. The black tinsel of ash blew off and broke into flakes.

"O.K., John Barr?" he asked.

"O.K., Suttler," he answered himself.

In blue pencil, on soiled paper from his pocket, he slowly printed, "Becus of the lamented desease of the late clament, John Barr, I now clame these diggins for myself and partner Jenny. I can shoot too." And wrote rather than printed, "James T. Suttler, March—" and paused.

"Make it an even month," he said, and wrote, "11, 1940." Underneath he wrote, "Jenny Suttler, her mark," and drew a skull with long ears.

"There," he said, and folded the paper, put it between the two boards, and rebuilt the cairn into a neat pyramid above it.

In high spirit he was driven to cleanliness. With scissors, soap and razor he climbed to the spring. Jenny was there, drinking.

"When you're done," he said, and when she lifted her head, pulled her ears and scratched her.

"Maybe we've got something here, Jenny," he said.

Jenny observed him soberly and returned to the meadow.

"She doesn't believe me," he said, and began to perfect himself. He sheared off his red tresses in long hanks, then cut closer, and went over yet a third time, until there remained a brush, of varying density, of stiff red bristles, through which his scalp shone whitely. He sheared the beard likewise, then knelt to the well for mirror and shaved painfully. He also shaved his neck and about his ears. He arose younger and less impressive, with jaws as pale as his scalp, so that his sunburn was a red domino. He burned tresses and beard ceremoniously upon a sage bush, and announced, "It is spring."

He began to empty the pockets of his shirt and breeches onto a flat stone, yelling, "In the spring a young man's fancy," to a kind of tune, and paused, struck by the facts.

"Oh, yeah?" he said. "Fat chance."

"Fat," he repeated with obscene consideration. "Oh,

well," he said, and finished piling upon the rock note-
books, pencil stubs, cartridges, tobacco, knife, stump pipe,
matches, chalk, samples, and three wrinkled photographs.
One of the photographs he observed at length before
weighting it down with a .45 cartridge. It showed a round,
blond girl with a big smile on a stupid face, in a patterned
calico housedress, in front of a blossoming rhododendron
bush.

He added to this deposit his belt and holster with the
big .45.

Then he stripped himself, washed and rinsed his gar-
ments in the spring, and spread them upon stones and
brush, and carefully arranged four flat stones into a platform
beside the trough. Standing there he scooped water over
himself, gasping, made it a lather, and at last, face and cop-
per bristles also foaming, gropingly entered the basin, and
submerged, flooding the water over in a thin and soapy
sheet. His head emerged at once. "My God," he whispered.
He remained under, however, till he was soapless, and goose
pimpled as a file, when he climbed out cautiously onto the
rock platform and performed a dance of small, revolving
patterns with a great deal of up and down.

At one point in his dance he observed the pictograph
journey upon the cliff, and danced nearer to examine it.

"Ignorant," he pronounced. "Like a little kid," he said.

He was intrigued, however, by more recent records,
names smoked and cut upon the lower rock. One of these,
in script, like a gigantic handwriting deeply cut, said AL-
VAREZ BLANCO DE TOLDEO, Anno Di 1624. A very
neat, upright cross was chiseled beneath it.

Suttler grinned. "Oh, yeah?" he asked, with his head
upon one side. "Nuts," he said, looking at it squarely.

But it inspired him, and with his jackknife he began
scraping beneath the possibly Spanish inscription. His knife,
however, made scratches, not incisions. He completed a bad
Jim and Jenny and quit, saying, "I should kill myself over a
phony wop."

Thereafter, for weeks, while the canyon became increasingly like a furnace in the daytime and the rocks stayed warm at night, he drove his tunnel farther into the mountain and piled the dump farther into the gully, making, at one side of the entrance, a heap of ore to be worked, and occasionally adding a peculiarly heavy pebble to the others in his small leather bag with a drawstring. He and Jenny thrived upon this fixed and well-watered life. The hollows disappeared from his face and he became less stringy, while Jenny grew round, her battleship-gray pelt even lustrous and its black markings distinct and ornamental. The burro found time from her grazing to come to the cabin door in the evenings and attend solemnly to Suttler playing with his samples and explaining their future.

"Then, old lady," Suttler said, "you will carry only small children, one at a time, for never more than half an hour. You will have a bedroom with French windows and a mattress, and I will paint your feet gold.

"The children," he said, "will probably be redheaded, but maybe blond. Anyway, they will be beautiful.

"After we've had a holiday, of course," he added. "For one hundred and thirty-three nights," he said dreamily. "Also," he said, "just one hundred and thirty-three quarts. I'm no drunken bum.

"For you, though," he said, "for one hundred and thirty-three nights a quiet hotel with other old ladies. I should drag my own mother in the gutter." He pulled her head down by the ears and kissed her loudly upon the nose. They were very happy together.

Nor did they greatly alter most of the life of the canyon. The antelope did not return, it is true, the rabbits were fewer and less playful because he sometimes snared them for meat, the little, clean mice and desert rats avoided the cabin they had used, and the road-runner did not come in daylight after Suttler, for fun, narrowly missed him with a piece of ore from the tunnel mouth. Suttler's violence was disproportionate perhaps, when he used his .45 to blow apart a creamy rat who did invade the cabin, but the loss was insignificant to the pattern of the well, and more than compensated when he one day caught the rattler extended at the foot of the dump in a drunken stupor from rare young rabbit, and before it could recoil held it aloft by the tail and snapped its head off, leaving the heavy body to turn slowly for a long time among the rocks. The dominant voices went undisturbed, save when he sang badly at his work or said beautiful things to Jenny in a loud voice.

There were, however, two more noticeable changes, one of which, at least, was important to Suttler himself. The first was the execution of the range cow's calf in the late fall, when he began to suggest a bull. Suttler felt a little guilty about this because the calf might have belonged to somebody, because the cow remained near the meadow bawling for two nights, and because the calf had come to meet the gun with more curiosity than challenge. But when he had the flayed carcass hung in the mine tunnel in a wet canvas, the sensation of providence overcame any qualms.

The other change was more serious. It occurred at the beginning of such winter as the well had, when there was sometimes a light rime on the rocks at dawn, and the aspens held only a few yellow leaves. Suttler thought often of leaving. The nights were cold, the fresh meat was eaten, his hopes had diminished as he still found only occasional nuggets, and his dreams of women, if less violent, were more nostalgic. The canyon held him with a feeling he would have called lonesome but at home, yet he probably would have gone except for this second change.

In the higher mountains to the west, where there was already snow, and at dawn a green winter sky, hunger stirred a buried memory in a cougar. He had twice killed antelope at the well, and felt there had been time enough again. He came down from the dwarfed trees and crossed the narrow valley under the stars, sometimes stopping abruptly to stare intently about, like a house-cat in a strange room. After each stop he would at once resume a quick, noiseless trot. From the top of the mountain above the spring he came down very slowly on his belly, but there was nothing at the well. He relaxed, and leaning on the rim of the basin, drank, listening between laps. His nose was clean with fasting, and he knew of the man in the cabin and Jenny in the meadow, but they were strange, not what he remembered about the place. But neither had his past made him fearful. It was only habitual hunting caution which made him go down into the willows carefully, and lie there head up, watching Jenny, but still waiting for antelope, which he had killed before near dawn. The strange smells were confusing and therefore irritating. After an hour he rose and went silently to the cabin, from which the strangest smell came strongly, a carnivorous smell which did not arouse appetite, but made him bristle nervously. The tobacco in it was like pins in his nostrils. He circled the cabin, stopping frequently. At the open door the scent was violent. He stood with his front paws up on the step, moving his head in serpent motions, the end of his heavy tail furling and unfurling constantly. In a dream Suttler turned over without waking, and muttered. The cougar crouched, his eyes intent, his ruff lifting. Then he swung away from the door, growling a little, and after one pause, crept back down to the meadow again and lay in the willows, but where he could watch the cabin also.

When the sky was alarmingly pale and the antelope had not come, he crawled a few feet at a time, behind the willows, to a point nearer Jenny. Then he crouched, working his hind legs slowly under him until he was set, and sprang, raced the three or four jumps to the drowsy burro, and struck. The beginning of her mortal scream was severed, but having made an imperfect leap, and from no height, the cat did not at once break her neck, but drove her to earth, where her small hooves churned futilely in the sod, and chewed and worried until she lay still.

Jim Suttler was nearly awakened by the fragment of scream, but heard nothing after it, and sank again.

The cat wrestled Jenny's body into the willows, fed with uncertain relish, drank long at the well, and went slowly over the crest, stopping often to look back. In spite of the light and the beginning talk of the swallows, the old coyote also fed and was gone before Suttler woke.

When Suttler found Jenny, many double columns of regimented ants were already at work, streaming in and out of the interior and mounting like bridge workers upon the ribs. Suttler stood and looked down. He desired to hold the small muzzle in the hollow of his hand, feeling that this familiar gesture would get through to Jenny, but couldn't bring himself to it because of what had happened to that side of her head. He squatted and lifted one hoof on its stiff leg and held that. Ants emerged hurriedly from the fetlock, their lines of communication broken. Two of them made disorganized excursions on the back of his hand. He rose, shook them off, and stood staring again. He didn't say anything because he spoke easily only when cheerful or excited, but a determination was beginning in him. He followed the drag to the spot torn by the small hoofs. Among the willows again, he found the tracks of both the cougar and the coyote, and the cat's tracks again at the well and by the cabin doorstep. He left Jenny in the willows with a canvas over her during the day, and did not eat.

At sunset he sat on the doorstep, cleaning his rifle and oiling it until he could spring the lever almost without sound. He filled the clip, pressed it home, and sat with the gun across his knees until dark, when he put on his sheepskin, stuffed a scarf into the pocket, and went down to Jenny. He removed the canvas from her, rolled it up and held it under his arm.

"I'm sorry, old woman," he said. "Just tonight."

There was a little cold wind in the willows. It rattled the upper branches lightly.

Suttler selected a spot thirty yards down wind, from which he could see Jenny, spread the canvas and lay down upon it, facing toward her. After an hour he was afraid of falling asleep and sat up against a willow clump. He sat there all night. A little after midnight the old coyote came into the dry-wash below him. At the top of the wash he sat down, and when the mingled scents gave him a clear picture of the strategy, let his tongue loll out, looked at the stars for a moment with his mouth silently open, rose and trotted back into the desert.

At the beginning of daylight the younger coyote trotted in from the north, and turned up toward the spring, but saw Jenny. He sat down and looked at her for a long time. Then he moved to the west and sat down again. In the wind was only winter, and the water, and faintly the acrid bat dung in the cliffs. He completed the circle, but not widely enough, walking slowly through the willows, down the edge of the meadow and in again not ten yards in front of the following muzzle of the carbine. Like Jenny, he felt his danger too late. The heavy slug caught him at the base of the skull in the middle of the first jump, so that it was amazingly accelerated for a fraction of a second. The coyote began it alive, and ended it quite dead, but with a tense muscular movement conceived which resulted in a grotesque final leap and twist of the hindquarters alone, leaving them propped high against a willow clump while the head was half buried in the sand, red welling up along the lips of the distended jaws. The cottony underpelt of the tail and rump stirred gleefully in the wind.

When Suttler kicked the body and it did not move, he suddenly dropped his gun, grasped it by the upright hind legs, and hurled it out into the sagebrush. His face appeared slightly insane with fury for that instant. Then he picked up his gun and went back to the cabin, where he ate, and drank half of one of his last three bottles of whiskey.

In the middle of the morning he came down with his pick and shovel, dragged Jenny's much lightened body down into the dry-wash, and dug in the rock and sand for two hours. When she was covered, he erected a small cairn of stone, like the claim post, above her.

"If it takes a year," he said, and licked the salt sweat on his lips.

That day he finished the half bottle and drank all of a second one, and became very drunk, so that he fell asleep during his vigil in the willows, sprawled wide on the dry turf and snoring. He was not disturbed. There was a difference in his smell after that day which prevented even the rabbits from coming into the meadow. He waited five nights in the willows. Then he transferred his watch to a niche in the cliff, across from and just below the spring.

All winter, while the day wind blew long veils of dust across the desert, regularly repeated, like waves or the smoke of line artillery fire, and the rocks shrank under the cold glitter of night, he did not miss a watch. He learned to go to sleep at sundown, wake within a few minutes of midnight, go up to his post and become at once clear-headed and watchful. He talked to himself in the mine and the cabin, but never in the niche. His supplies ran low, and he ate less, but would not risk a startling shot. He rationed his tobacco, and when it was gone worked up to a vomiting sickness every three days for nine days, but did not miss a night in the niche. All winter he did not remove his clothes, bathe, shave, cut his hair or sing. He worked the dead mine only to be busy, and became thin again, with sunken eyes which yet were not the eyes he had come with the spring before. It was April, his food almost gone, when he got his chance.

There was a half moon that night, which made the canyon walls black, and occasionally gleamed on wrinkles of the overflow. The cat came down so quietly that Suttler did not see him until he was beside the basin. The animal was suspicious. He took the wind, and twice started to drink, and didn't, but crouched. On Suttler's face there was a set grin which exposed his teeth.

"Not even a drink, you bastard," he thought.

The cat drank a little though, and dropped again, softly, trying to get the scent from the meadow. Suttler drew slowly upon his soul in the trigger. When it gave, the report was magnified impressively in the canyon. The cougar sprang straight into the air and screamed outrageously. The back of Suttler's neck was cold and his hands trembled, but he shucked the lever and fired again. This shot ricocheted from the basin and whined away thinly. The first, however, had struck near enough. The cat began to scramble rapidly on the loose stone, at first without voice, then screaming repeatedly. It doubled upon itself snarling and chewing in a small furious circle, fell and began to throw itself in short, leaping spasms upon the stones, stuck across the rim of the tank and lay half in the water, its head and shoulders raised in one corner and resting against the cliff. Suttler could hear it breathing hoarsely and snarling very faintly. The soprano chorus of swallows gradually became silent.

Suttler had risen to fire again, but lowered the carbine and advanced, stopping at every step to peer intently and listen for the hoarse breathing, which continued. Even when he was within five feet of the tank the cougar did not move, except to gasp so that the water again splashed from the basin. Suttler was calmed by the certainty of accomplishment. He drew the heavy revolver from his holster, aimed carefully at the rattling head, and fired again. The canyon boomed, and the east responded faintly and a little behind, but Suttler did not hear them, for the cat thrashed heavily in the tank, splashing him as with a bucket, and then lay still on its side over the edge, its muzzle and forepaws hanging. The water was settling quietly in the tank, but Suttler stirred it again, shooting five more times with great deliberation into the heavy body, which did not move except at the impact of the slugs.

The rest of the night, even after the moon was gone, he worked fiercely, slitting and tearing with his knife. In the morning, under the swallows, he dragged the marbled carcass, still bleeding a little in places, onto the rocks on the side away from the spring, and dropped it. Dragging the ragged hide by the neck, he went unsteadily down the canyon to the cabin, where he slept like a drunkard, although his whiskey had been gone for two months.

In the afternoon, with dreaming eyes, he bore the pelt to Jenny's grave, took down the stones with his hands, shoveled the earth from her, covered her with the skin, and again with earth and the cairn.

He looked at this monument. "There," he said.

That night, for the first time since her death, he slept through.

In the morning, at the well, he repeated his cleansing ritual of a year before, save that they were rags he stretched to dry, even to the dance upon the rock platform while drying. Squatting naked and clean, shaven and clipped, he looked for a long time at the grinning countenance, now very dirty, of the plump girl in front of the blossoming rhododendrons, and in the resumption of his dance he made singing noises accompanied by the words, "Spring, spring, beautiful spring." He was a starved but revived and volatile spirit.

An hour later he went south, his boot soles held on by canvas strips, and did not once look back.

The disturbed life of the spring resumed. In the second night the rabbits loved in the willows, and at the end of a week the rats played in the cabin again. The old coyote and a vulture cleaned the cougar, and his bones fell apart in the shale. The road-runner came up one day, tentatively, and in front of the tunnel snatched up a horned toad and ran with it around the corner, but no farther. After a month the antelope returned. The well brimmed, and in the gentle sunlight the new aspen leaves made a tiny music of shadows.

A MAN CALLED HORSE

Dorothy M. Johnson

He was a young man of good family, as the phrase went in the New England of a hundred-odd years ago, and the reasons for his bitter discontent were unclear, even to himself. He grew up in the gracious old Boston home under his grandmother's care, for his mother had died in giving him birth; and all his life he had known every comfort and privilege his father's wealth could provide.

But still there was the discontent, which puzzled him because he could not even define it. He wanted to live among his equals—people who were no better than he and no worse either. That was as close as he could come to describing the source of his unhappiness in Boston and his restless desire to go somewhere else.

In the year 1845, he left home and went out West, far beyond the country's creeping frontier, where he hoped to find his equals. He had the idea that in Indian country, where there was danger, all white men were kings, and he wanted to be one of them. But he found, in the West as in Boston, that the men he respected were still his superiors, even if they could not read, and those he did not respect weren't worth talking to.

He did have money, however, and he could hire the men he respected. He hired four of them, to cook and hunt and guide and be his companions, but he found them not friendly.

They were apart from him and he was still alone. He still brooded about his status in the world, longing for his equals.

On a day in June, he learned what it was to have no status at all. He became a captive of a small raiding party of Crow Indians.

He heard gunfire and the brief shouts of his companions around the bend of the creek just before they died, but he never saw their bodies. He had no chance to fight, because he was naked and unarmed, bathing in the creek, when a Crow warrior seized and held him.

His captor let him go at last, let him run. Then the lot of them rode him down for sport, striking him with their coup sticks. They carried the dripping scalps of his companions, and one had skinned off Baptiste's black beard as well, for a trophy.

They took him along in a matter-of-fact way, as they took the captured horses. He was unshod and naked as the horses were, and like them he had a rawhide thong around his neck. So long as he didn't fall down, the Crows ignored him.

On the second day they gave him his breeches. His feet were too swollen for his boots, but one of the Indians threw him a pair of moccasins that had belonged to the half-breed, Henri, who was dead back at the creek. The captive wore the moccasins gratefully. The third day they let him ride one of the spare horses so the party could move faster, and on that day they came in sight of their camp.

He thought of trying to escape, hoping he might be

killed in flight rather than by slow torture in the camp, but he never had a chance to try. They were more familiar with escape than he was and, knowing what to expect, they fore-stalled it. The only other time he had tried to escape from anyone, he had succeeded. When he had left his home in Boston, his father had raged and his grandmother had cried, but they could not talk him out of his intention.

The men of the Crow raiding party didn't bother with talk.

Before riding into camp they stopped and dressed in their regalia, and in parts of their victims' clothing; they painted their faces black. Then, leading the white man by the rawhide around his neck as though he were a horse, they rode down toward the tepee circle, shouting and singing, brandishing their weapons. He was unconscious when they got there; he fell and was dragged.

He lay dazed and battered near a tepee while the noisy, busy life of the camp swarmed around him and Indians came to stare. Thirst consumed him, and when it rained he lapped rain water from the ground like a dog. A scrawny, shrieking, eternally busy old woman with ragged graying hair threw a chunk of meat on the grass, and he fought the dogs for it.

When his head cleared, he was angry, although anger was an emotion he knew he could not afford.

It was better when I was a horse, he thought—when they led me by the rawhide around my neck. I won't be a dog, no matter what!

The hag gave him stinking, rancid grease and let him figure out what it was for. He applied it gingerly to his bruised and sun-seared body.

Now, he thought, I smell like the rest of them.

While he was healing, he considered coldly the advan-tages of being a horse. A man would be humiliated, and sooner or later he would strike back and that would be the end of him. But a horse had only to be docile. Very well, he would learn to do without pride.

He understood that he was the property of the screaming old woman, a fine gift from her son, one that she liked to show off. She did more yelling at him than at anyone else, probably to impress the neighbors so they would not forget what a great and generous man her son was. She was bossy and proud, a dreadful bag of skin and bones, and she was a devilish hard worker.

The white man, who now thought of himself as a horse, forgot sometimes to worry about his danger. He kept making mental notes of things to tell his own people in Boston about this hideous adventure. He would go back a hero, and he would say, "Grandmother, let me fetch your shawl. I've been accustomed to doing little errands for another lady about your age."

Two girls lived in the tepee with the old hag and her warrior son. One of them, the white man concluded, was his captor's wife and the other was his little sister. The daughter-in-law was smug and spoiled. Being beloved, she did not have to be useful. The younger girl had bright, wandering eyes. Often enough they wandered to the white man who was pretending to be a horse.

The two girls worked when the old woman put them at it, but they were always running off to do something they enjoyed more. There were games and noisy contests, and there was much laughter. But not for the white man. He was finding out what loneliness could be.

That was a rich summer on the plains, with plenty of buffalo for meat and clothing and the making of tepees. The Crows were wealthy in horses, prosperous and contented. If their men had not been so avid for glory, the white man thought, there would have been a lot more of them. But they went out of their way to court death, and when one of them met it, the whole camp mourned extravagantly and cried to their God for vengeance.

The captive was a horse all summer, a docile bearer of burdens, careful and patient. He kept reminding himself that he had to be better-natured than other horses, because he could not lash out with hoofs or teeth. Helping the old woman load up the horses for travel, he yanked at a pack and said, "Whoa, brother. It goes easier when you don't fight."

The horse gave him a big-eyed stare as if it understood his language—a comforting thought, because nobody else did. But even among the horses he felt unequal. They were able to look out for themselves if they escaped. He would simply starve. He was envious still, even among the horses.

Humbly he fetched and carried. Sometimes he even offered to help, but he had not the skill for the endless work of the women, and he was not trusted to hunt with the men, the providers.

When the camp moved, he carried a pack trudging with the women. Even the dogs worked then, pulling small burdens on travois of sticks.

The Indian who had captured him lived like a lord, as he had a right to do. He hunted with his peers, attended long ceremonial meetings with much chanting and dancing, and lounged in the shade with his smug bride. He had only two responsibilities: to kill buffalo and to gain glory. The white man was so far beneath him in status that the Indian did not even think of envy.

One day several things happened that made the captive think he might sometime become a man again. That was the day when he began to understand their language. For four months he had heard it, day and night, the joy and the mourning, the ritual chanting and sung prayers, the squabbles and the deliberations. None of it meant anything to him at all.

But on that important day in early fall the two young women set out for the river, and one of them called over her shoulder to the old woman. The white man was startled. She had said she was going to bathe. His understanding was so sudden that he felt as if his ears had come unstopped. Listening to the racket of the camp, he heard fragments of meaning instead of gabble.

On that same important day the old woman brought a pair of new moccasins out of the tepee and tossed them on the ground before him. He could not believe she would do anything for him because of kindness, but giving him moccasins was one way of looking after her property.

In thanking her, he dared greatly. He picked a little handful of fading fall flowers and took them to her as she squatted in front of her tepee, scraping a buffalo hide with a tool made from a piece of iron tied to a bone. Her hands were hideous—most of the fingers had the first joint missing. He bowed solemnly and offered the flowers.

She glared at him from beneath the short, ragged tangle of her hair. She stared at the flowers, knocked them out of his hand and went running to the next tepee, squalling the story. He heard her and the other women screaming with laughter.

The white man squared his shoulders and walked boldly over to watch three small boys shooting arrows at a target. He said in English, "Show me how to do that, will you?"

They frowned, but he held out his hand as if there could be no doubt. One of them gave him a bow and one arrow, and they snickered when he missed.

The people were easily amused, except when they were angry. They were amused, at him, playing with the little boys. A few days later he asked the hag, with gestures, for a bow that her son had just discarded, a man-size bow of horn. He scavenged for old arrows. The old woman cackled at his marksmanship and called her neighbors to enjoy the fun.

When he could understand words, he could identify his people by their names. The old woman was Greasy Hand, and her daughter was Pretty Calf. The other young woman's name was not clear to him, for the words were not in his vocabulary. The man who had captured him was Yellow Robe.

Once he could understand, he could begin to talk a little, and then he was less lonely. Nobody had been able to see any reason for talking to him, since he would not understand anyway. He asked the old woman, "What is my name?" Until he knew it, he was incomplete. She shrugged to let him know he had none.

He told her in the Crow language, "My name is Horse." He repeated it, and she nodded. After that they called him Horse when they called him anything. Nobody cared except the white man himself.

They trusted him enough to let him stray out of camp, so that he might have got away and, by unimaginable good luck, might have reached a trading post or a fort, but winter was too close. He did not dare leave without a horse; he needed clothing and a better hunting weapon than he had, and more certain skill in using it. He did not dare steal, for then they would surely have pursued him, and just as certainly they would have caught him. Remembering the warmth of the home that was waiting in Boston, he settled down for the winter.

On a cold night he crept into the tepee after the others had gone to bed. Even a horse might try to find shelter from the wind. The old woman grumbled, but without conviction. She did not put him out.

They tolerated him, back in the shadows, so long as he did not get in the way.

He began to understand how the family that owned him differed from the others. Fate had been cruel to them. In a short, sharp argument among the old women, one of them derided Greasy Hand by sneering. "You have no relatives!" and Greasy Hand raved for minutes of the deeds of her father and uncles and brothers. And she had had four sons, she reminded her detractor—who answered with scorn, "Where are they?"

Later the white man found her moaning and whimpering to herself, rocking back and forth on her haunches, staring at her mutilated hands. By that time he understood. A mourner often chopped off a finger joint. Old Greasy Hand had mourned often. For the first time he felt a twinge of pity, but he put it aside as another emotion, like anger, that he could not afford. He thought: What tales I will tell when I get home!

He wrinkled his nose in disdain. The camp stank of animals and meat and rancid grease. He looked down at his naked, shivering legs and was startled, remembering that he was still only a horse.

He could not trust the old woman. She fed him only because a starved slave would die and not be worth boasting about. Just how fitful her temper was he saw on the day when she got tired of stumbling over one of the hundred dogs that infested the camp. This was one of her own dogs, a large, strong one that pulled a baggage travois when the tribe moved camp.

Countless times he had seen her kick at the beast as it lay sleeping in front of the tepee, in her way. The dog always moved, with a yelp, but it always got in the way again. One day she gave the dog its usual kick and then stood scolding at it while the animal rolled its eyes sleepily. The old woman suddenly picked up her axe and cut the dog's head off with one blow. Looking well satisfied with herself, she beckoned her slave to remove the body.

It could have been me, he thought, if I were a dog. But I'm a horse.

His hope of life lay with the girl, Pretty Calf. He set about courting her, realizing how desperately poor he was both in property and honor. He owned no horse, no weapon but the old bow and the battered arrows. He had nothing to give away, and he needed gifts, because he did not dare seduce the girl.

One of the customs of courtship involved sending a gift of horses to a girl's older brother and bestowing much buffalo meat upon her mother. The white man could not wait for some far-off time when he might have either horses or meat to give away. And his courtship had to be secret. It was not for him to stroll past the groups of watchful girls, blowing a flute made of an eagle's wing bone, as the flirtatious young bucks did.

He could not ride past Pretty Calf's tepee, painted and bedizened; he had no horse, no finery.

Back home, he remembered, I could marry just about any girl I'd want to. But he wasted little time thinking about that. A future was something to be earned.

The most he dared do was wink at Pretty Calf now and then, or state his admiration while she giggled and hid her face. The least he dared do to win his bride was to elope with her, but he had to give her a horse to put the seal of tribal approval on that. And he had no horse until he killed a man to get one. . . .

His opportunity came in early spring. He was casually accepted by that time. He did not belong, but he was amusing to the Crows, like a strange pet, or they would not have fed him through the winter.

His chance came when he was hunting small game with three young boys who were his guards as well as his scornful companions. Rabbits and birds were of no account in a camp well fed on buffalo meat, but they made good targets.

His party walked far that day. All of them at once saw the two horses in a sheltered coulee. The boys and the man crawled forward on their bellies, and then they saw an Indian who lay on the ground, moaning, a lone traveler. From the way the boys inched forward, Horse knew the man was fair prey—a member of some enemy tribe.

This is the way the captive white man acquired wealth and honor to win a bride and save his life: He shot an arrow into the sick man, a split second ahead of one of his small companions, and dashed forward to strike the still-groaning man with his bow, to count first coup. Then he seized the hobbled horses.

By the time he had the horses secure, and with them his hope for freedom, the boys had followed, counting coup with gestures and shrieks they had practiced since boyhood, and one of them had the scalp. The white man was grimly amused to see the boy double up with sudden nausea when he had the thing in his hand. . . .

There was a hubbub in the camp when they rode in that evening, two of them on each horse. The captive was noticed. Indians who had ignored him as a slave stared at the brave man who had struck first coup and had stolen horses.

The hubbub lasted all night, as fathers boasted loudly of their young sons' exploits. The white man was called upon to settle an argument between two fierce boys as to which of them had struck second coup and which must be satisfied with third. After much talk that went over his head, he solemnly pointed at the nearest boy. He didn't know which boy it was and didn't care, but the boy did.

The white man had watched warriors in their triumph. He knew what to do. Modesty about achievements had no place among the Crow people. When a man did something big, he told about it.

The white man smeared his face with grease and char-coal. He walked inside the tepee circle, chanting and sing-ing. He used his own language.

"You heathens, you savages," he shouted. "I'm going to get out of here someday! I am going to get away!" The Crow people listened respectfully. In the Crow tongue he shouted, "Horse! I am Horse!" and they nodded.

He had a right to boast, and he had two horses. Before dawn, the white man and his bride were sheltered beyond a far hill, and he was telling her, "I love you, little lady. I love you."

She looked at him with her great dark eyes, and he thought she understood his English words—or as much as she needed to understand.

"You are my treasure," he said, "more precious than jewels, better than fine gold. I am going to call you Free-dom."

When they returned to camp two days later, he was bold but worried. His ace, he suspected, might not be high enough in the game he was playing without being sure of the rules. But it served.

Old Greasy Hand raged—but not at him. She complained loudly that her daughter had let herself go too cheap. But the marriage was as good as any Crow marriage. He had paid a horse.

He learned the language faster after that, from Pretty Calf, whom he sometimes called Freedom. He learned that his attentive, adoring bride was fourteen years old.

One thing he had not guessed was the difference that being Pretty Calf's husband would make in his relationship to her mother and brother. He had hoped only to make his position a little safer, but he had not expected to be treated with dignity. Greasy Hand no longer spoke to him at all. When the white man spoke to her, his bride murmured in dismay, explaining at great length that he must never do that. There could be no conversation between a man and his mother-in-law. He could not even mention a word that was part of her name.

Having improved his status so magnificently, he felt no need for hurry in getting away. Now that he had a woman, he had as good a chance to be rich as any man. Pretty Calf waited on him; she seldom ran off to play games with other young girls, but took pride in learning from her mother the many women's skills of tanning hides and making clothing and preparing food.

He was no more a horse but a kind of man, a half-Indian, still poor and unskilled but laden with honors, clinging to the buckskin fringes of Crow society.

Escape could wait until he could manage it in comfort, with fit clothing and a good horse, with hunting weapons. Escape could wait until the camp moved near some trading post. He did not plan how he would get home. He dreamed of being there all at once, and of telling stories nobody would believe. There was no hurry.

Pretty Calf delighted in educating him. He began to understand tribal arrangements, customs and why things

were as they were. They were that way because they had
always been so. His young wife giggled when she told
him, in his ignorance, things she had always known. But
she did not laugh when her brother's wife was taken by
another warrior. She explained that solemnly with words
and signs.

Yellow Robe belonged to a society called the Big Dogs.
The wife stealer, Cut Neck, belonged to the Foxes. They
were fellow tribesmen; they hunted together and fought
side by side, but men of one society could take away wives
from the other society if they wished, subject to certain
limitations.

When Cut Neck rode up to the tepee, laughing and
singing, and called to Yellow Robe's wife, "Come out! Come
out!" she did as ordered, looking smug as usual, meek and
entirely willing. Thereafter she rode beside him in ceremonial processions and carried his coup stick, while his other
wife pretended not to care.

"But why?" the white man demanded of his wife, his
Freedom. "Why did our brother let his woman go? He sits
and smokes and does not speak."

Pretty Calf was shocked at the suggestion. Her brother
could not possibly reclaim his woman, she explained. He
could not even let her come back if she wanted to—and she
probably would want to when Cut Neck tired of her. Yellow
Robe could not even admit that his heart was sick. That was
the way things were. Deviation meant dishonor.

The woman could have hidden from Cut Neck, she said.
She could even have refused to go with him if she had been
ba-wurokee—a really virtuous woman. But she had been his
woman before, for a little while on a berrying expedition,
and he had a right to claim her.

There was no sense in it, the white man insisted. He
glared at his young wife. "If you go, I will bring you back!"
he promised.

She laughed and buried her head against his shoulder.
"I will not have to go," she said. "Horse is my first man.
There is no hole in my moccasin."

He stroked her hair and said, *"Ba-wurokee."*

With great daring, she murmured, *"Hayha,"* and when he did not answer, because he did not know what she meant, she drew away, hurt.

"A woman calls her man that if she thinks he will not leave her. Am I wrong?"

The white man held her closer and lied, "Pretty Calf is not wrong. Horse will not leave her. Horse will not take another woman, either." No, he certainly would not. Parting from this one was going to be harder than getting her had been. *"Hayha,"* he murmured. "Freedom."

His conscience irked him, but not very much. Pretty Calf could get another man easily enough when he was gone, and a better provider. His hunting skill was improving, but he was still awkward.

There was no hurry about leaving. He was used to most of the Crow ways and could stand the rest. He was becoming prosperous. He owned five horses. His place in the life of the tribe was secure, such as it was. Three or four young women, including the one who had belonged to Yellow Robe, made advances to him. Pretty Calf took pride in the fact that her man was so attractive.

By the time he had what he needed for a secret journey, the grass grew yellow on the plains and the long cold was close. He was enslaved by the girl he called Freedom and, before the winter ended, by the knowledge that she was carrying his child. . . .

The Big Dog society held a long ceremony in the spring. The white man strolled with his woman along the creek bank, thinking: When I get home I will tell them about the chants and the drumming. Sometime. Sometime.

Pretty Calf would not go to bed when they went back to the tepee.

"Wait and find out about my brother," she urged. "Something may happen."

So far as Horse could figure out, the Big Dogs' were having some kind of election. He pampered his wife by staying up with her by the fire. Even the old woman, who was a great one for getting sleep when she was not working, prowled around restlessly.

The white man was yawning by the time the noise of the ceremony died down. When Yellow Robe strode in, garish and heathen in his paint and feathers and furs, the women cried out. There was conversation, too fast for Horse to follow, and the old woman wailed once, but her son silenced her with a gruff command.

When the white man went to sleep, he thought his wife was weeping beside him.

The next morning she explained.

"He wears the bearskin belt. Now he can never retreat in battle. He will always be in danger. He will die."

Maybe he wouldn't, the white man tried to convince her. Pretty Calf recalled that some few men had been honored by the bearskin belt, vowed to the highest daring, and had not died. If they lived through the summer, then they were free of it.

"My brother wants to die," she mourned. "His heart is bitter."

Yellow Robe lived through half a dozen clashes with small parties of raiders from hostile tribes. His honors were many. He captured horses in an enemy camp, led two successful raids, counted first coup and snatched a gun from the hand of an enemy tribesman. He wore wolf tails on his moccasins and ermine skins on his shirt, and he fringed his leggings with scalps in token of his glory.

When his mother ventured to suggest, as she did many times, "My son should take a new wife, I need another woman to help me," he ignored her. He spent much time in prayer, alone in the hills or in conference with a medicine man. He fasted and made vows and kept them. And before he could be free of the heavy honor of the bearskin belt, he went on his last raid.

The warriors were returning from the north just as the white man and two other hunters approached from the south, with buffalo and elk meat dripping from the bloody hides tied on their restive ponies. One of the hunters grunted, and they stopped to watch a rider on the hill north of the tepee circle.

The rider dismounted, held up a blanket and dropped it. He repeated the gesture.

The hunters murmured dismay. "Two! Two men dead!" They rode fast into the camp, where there was already wailing.

A messenger came down from the war party on the hill. The rest of the party delayed to paint their faces for mourning and for victory. One of the two dead men was Yellow Robe. They had put his body in a cave and walled it in with rocks. The other man died later, and his body was in a tree.

There was blood on the ground before the tepee to which Yellow Robe would return no more. His mother, with her hair chopped short, sat in the doorway, rocking back and forth on her haunches, wailing her heartbreak. She cradled one mutilated hand in the other. She had cut off another finger joint.

Pretty Calf had cut off chunks of her long hair and was crying as she gashed her arms with a knife. The white man tried to take the knife away, but she protested so piteously that he let her do as she wished. He was sickened with the lot of them.

Savages! he thought. Now I will go back! I'll go hunting alone, and I'll keep on going.

But he did not go just yet, because he was the only hunter in the lodge of the two grieving women, one of them old and the other pregnant with his child.

In their mourning, they made him a pauper again. Everything that meant comfort, wealth and safety they sacrificed to the spirits because of the death of Yellow Robe. The tepee, made of seventeen fine buffalo hides, the furs that should have kept them warm, the white deerskin dress, trimmed with elk teeth, that Pretty Calf loved so well, even their tools and Yellow Robe's weapons—everything but his sacred medicine objects—they left there on the prairie, and the whole camp moved away. Two of his best horses were killed as a sacrifice, and the women gave away the rest.

They had no shelter. They would have no tepee of their own for two months at least of mourning, and then the women would have to tan hides to make it. Meanwhile they could live in temporary huts made of willows, covered with skins given them in pity by their friends. They could have lived with relatives, but Yellow Robe's women had no relatives.

The white man had not realized until then how terrible a thing it was for a Crow to have no kinfolk. No wonder old Greasy Hand had only stumps for fingers. She had mourned, from one year to the next, for everyone she had ever loved. She had no one left but her daughter, Pretty Calf.

Horse was furious at their foolishness. It had been bad enough for him, a captive, to be naked as a horse and poor as a slave, but that was because his captors had stripped him. These women had voluntarily given up everything they needed.

He was too angry at them to sleep in the willow hut. He lay under a sheltering tree. And on the third night of the mourning he made his plans. He had a knife and a bow. He would go after meat, taking two horses. And he would not come back. There were, he realized, many things he was not going to tell when he got back home.

In the willow hut, Pretty Calf cried out. He heard rustling there, and the old woman's querulous voice.

Some twenty hours later his son was born, two months early, in the tepee of a skilled medicine woman. The child was born without breath, and the mother died before the sun went down.

The white man was too shocked to think whether he should mourn, or how he should mourn. The old woman screamed until she was voiceless. Piteously she approached him, bent and trembling, blind with grief. She held out her knife and he took it.

She spread out her hands and shook her head. If she cut

off any more finger joints, she could no more work. She could not afford any more lasting signs of grief.

The white man said, "All right! All right!" between his teeth. He hacked his arms with the knife and stood watching the blood run down. It was little enough to do for Pretty Calf, for little Freedom.

Now there is nothing to keep me, he realized. When I get home, I must not let them see the scars.

He looked at Greasy Hand, hideous in her grief-burdened age, and thought: I really am free now! When a wife dies, her husband has no more duty toward her family. Pretty Calf had told him so, long ago, when he wondered why a certain man moved out of one tepee and into another.

The old woman, of course, would be a scavenger. There was one other with the tribe, an ancient crone who had no relatives, toward whom no one felt any responsibility. She lived on food thrown away by the more fortunate. She slept in shelters that she built with her own knotted hands. She plodded wearily at the end of the procession when the camp moved. When she stumbled, nobody cared. When she died, nobody would miss her.

Tomorrow morning, the white man decided, I will go.

His mother-in-law's sunken mouth quivered. She said one word, questioningly. She said, *"Eero-oshay?"* She said, "Son?"

Blinking, he remembered. When a wife died, her husband was free. But her mother, who had ignored him with dignity, might if she wished ask him to stay. She invited him by calling him Son, and he accepted by answering Mother.

Greasy Hand stood before him, bowed with years, withered with unceasing labor, loveless and childless, scarred with grief. But with all her burdens, she still loved life enough to beg it from him, the only person she had any right to ask. She was stripping herself of all she had left, her pride.

He looked eastward across the prairie. Two thousand miles away was home. The old woman would not live forever. He could afford to wait, for he was young. He could afford to be magnanimous, for he knew he was a man. He gave her the answer. *"Eegya,"* he said. "Mother."

He went home three years later. He explained no more than to say, "I lived with Crows for a while. It was some time before I could leave. They called me Horse."

He did not find it necessary either to apologize or to boast, because he was the equal of any man on earth.

OUTLAW TRAIL

S. Omar Barker

The kid was rawboned, red-necked, straw-headed, small for sixteen and a long way from Arkansas. His name, if it mattered, was Elnathan Calhoun. The stump he sat on was the hip-high relic of a fallen patriarch, genus cottonwood. It was located in the noonday shade of a considerable *bosque* of its own glossy-leafed descendants, on the sunward side of the one-legged street of Bosque Largo, Territory of New Mexico, more or less U.S.A.

Old breast-yoke rings triple-stapled onto the top of the stump and hoof-trampled earth around its base bore witness to its sometime utility as a hitch rack. But there were no horses shading there now. There was only Elnathan Calhoun, who had judiciously cached his mount off up the draw and was now carelessly ensconced between hitch rings, blowing a soft whimsy of melody through a six-inch mouth harp. The tune was a tender ballad of hill-folk vintage called Barbara Allen, and it had a lonesome sound.

That the rider dust-jogging up the road from the southeast was a pilgrim seemed evidenced by a lightly packed bed horse. Distantly viewed, he looked to be tall in the saddle, weathered in the hat, and adequately armed. His calling name, if it mattered, was Tonk McSpadden, and Texas lay six days behind him.

That the nearer rider approaching from the opposite direction was no pilgrim was betrayed by the undusty spruceness of his garb and rigging, from burnished black boots to brim-broad black sombrero, including the gleam of a six-shooter's mother-of-pearl handle in between. His calling name was Pete Hadlock; he wore a deputy sheriff's badge, and he rode his sleek sorrel proud and prancy, like a man who doesn't much care who's watching him, just so it's somebody.

He was within ten feet of the hitch stump when Elnathan Calhoun took a sudden notion to see what a sorrel horse would think of a train whistle, with no train in sight. What the *whee-oo-whee-whee-oo-oo* of Elnathan's mouth harp lacked in steam, it made up for in surprise. The sorrel did not think well of it. He promptly, as the cowboys say, "swallered his head," and his equally surprised rider sailed off over it.

"Mister," said Elnathan Calhoun with the friendliest of grins, "you couldn't have flew off purtier if you had wings!"

For a moment Deputy Sheriff Hadlock sat in the dust calling a wrathful roll of swear words. By the time he arose from disgrace and advanced upon the person of Elnathan Calhoun, he was beginning to repeat himself, and the boy's Arkansas grin was half an inch wider.

A brawny hand gathered up a fistful of Elnathan Calhoun's shirt front and hoisted him ungently off the stump.

"You think spookin' horses is funny, huh?" said the burly buckaroo-deputy. "Darned if I know whether to slap your face, kick your pants or throw you in jail!"

From the way he drew back his right hand it was evident that Deputy Hadlock aimed to try the slapping first.

Six days' ride from the Texas line, two weeks from the scene of a bitterly lost love, and headed for hell-don't-care, Tonk McSpadden arrived just in time to mind his own business—but didn't. Approaching unobserved, he flicked a midget lasso-rope loop over Hadlock's ready-to-smack arm and yanked.

"I do declare," he remarked with a dryness not wholly due to a dusty throat, "if it ain't ol' Pearl-Handled Pete!"

Hadlock whirled around.

"Tonk, you damn Injun!" His greeting smacked only a little of brotherly cordiality. "What you doin' in New Mexico?"

"Right now I'm takin' a census—countin' the growed-up men that come in big over kids—and it looks like you're number one." Tonk obligingly let out enough slack for Hadlock to slip the noose off his arm. "Somethin' rile you, Pete?"

"My train whistle spooked his bronc." Elnathan Calhoun's grin widened again at the memory. "He couldn't have flew off purtier if he'd had wings. But I don't need no thirty-dollar help, cowboy."

Tonk McSpadden stepped off his horse and stood between them.

"Tonk," said red-in-the-face Hadlock, "I'd just as soon. wallop you as the kid. And I kinder think I can do it!"

"Someday when you ain't got on your big behavior maybe I'll accommodate you. Right now I don't hate nobody but myself. Besides you look over-het and I'm over-dry. If that sign yonder don't lie, I'll buy you a beer and let you tell me your secret of success."

"There's two things," declared Hadlock, preening his brown mustache, "that tally big in this Territory, Injun: straight pistol-pointin' and crooked politics. You're lookin' at a he-wolf expert in both. There ain't been a holdup nor a horse stole in Tuloso County since I hired out to the law. Nor there won't be. Not even with Curly Jack Marcotte and his wild bunch rendezvousin' not a hundred miles north, and the sheriff away."

"If I could admire myself thataway I wouldn't speak to nobody but me—and that only on a Sunday." Elnathan Calhoun batted his crockery-blue eyes and grinned engagingly.

The grin appeased Pete Hadlock not at all. "Buster," he said, "this is one fair city where bums ain't welcome. You've got just ten minutes to start goin' someplace else—or to jail as a hobo!"

"And me without no watch," sighed Elnathan Calhoun. "Just good looks and money." He tossed a silver dollar—his last—in the air, caught it, returned it debonairly to his pocket, and addressed himself to Tonk McSpadden as if Hadlock no longer even existed.

"I can't buy you no beer, mister—my daddy was a pure-water preacher and he'd ha'nt me. But let's you and me go cut a can of pork and beans. I got the money to pay for it. We can talk about robbin' banks, shootin' sheriffs and huggin' purty girls."

"I'm a crackers-and-sardines man myself, Buzzsaw," said the black-eyed cowboy. "Let's go."

The patched kid from Arkansas and the part-Tonkawa-Indian cowboy from Texas sat on the steps of Ike Bamberger's store spooning pork and beans and sardines onto crackers with their pocketknives. Cooling tomatoes they slupped direct from the can.

Elnathan Calhoun's silver dollar now reposed in Ike Bamberger's cash drawer, but Elnathan didn't care. Tonk's letting him stand treat for the grub gave him that precious grown-man feeling. Pete Hadlock's horse now stood hitched in front of the Bosque saloon.

"I could have whipped ol' shiny-boots if you'd have let me," Elnathan complained mildly. "I make a big show with my fists, then kick 'em in the groin."

"That's as good a way as any to get yourself shot," said Tonk dryly. "But there ain't nothing wrong with Pete ex-

cept he fancies himself. Him and me went up the trail together. He drifted out here and finagled him a badge. Me,
I went back to Texas, but things had changed some, so I lit
out for new country."

"Meanin' your girl had went back on you?"

"You finish them termaters, Buzzsaw. I'm running over
You aiming to get out of town like you was told? You've done
used up twenty of your ten minutes."

"Tonk," said Elnathan Calhoun earnestly, "I'm goin' to
tell you a secret. I never had no girl go back on me, but I got
plumb wearied of my stepdaddy's whippin's. I've been a
month gettin' this far. From what I hear, it ain't much farther." Elnathan Calhoun lowered his voice. "I'm fixin' to join
up with that Curly Jack outfit and be an outlaw!"

For a long moment Tonk McSpadden sat silent, feeling
a resurge of lonely bitterness within him—the bitterness
that had ridden with him every foot of the long miles from
a homey little town deep in the live-oak hills of Texas. When
finally he spoke, his tone was short and abrupt. "Outlawin'
is a risky business, kid."

"Bug on a buzzsaw!" retorted Elnathan Calhoun scornfully. "You think I ain't got the guts?"

Again Tonk took a long time to answer. "I hate to see
a man afoot," he said finally. "My bed horse is packed light.
You reckon you could straddle him behind the pack?"

Pete Hadlock's horse was still hitched in front of the
saloon when they rode out of Bosque Largo. A mile out,
Elnathan Calhoun slid off the pack horse.

"I've got another secret, Tonk," he said. "You wait
here."

With a gangling gait not unlike that of a loping jackrab-
bit, the boy hurried into a dense *bosque* of young cottonwoods. He emerged a few minutes later astraddle a bony red
mule, without a saddle, but with an ancient six-shooter
belted around his skinny middle. Before him on the mare

mule's high withers he carried a bundle rolled in a rusty-black preacher's coat. A crudely fashioned rope hackamore served for bridle.

"Kid," said Tonk, "it ain't polite to mention it, but I left my good manners in Texas. Hiding out that mule and gun while you went into town could smell to a man with a long nose like maybe you stole 'em."

"I bought the pistol and a piece of rope from a Mexkin with—with my next to last dollar. The mule just follered me."

"It's a habit mules have got," commented Tonk dryly, "specially with somebody leadin' 'em."

Elnathan didn't answer. As they rode on, he got out his mouth harp and tenderly revived Barbara Allen.

"I knew a gal that used to sing that tune," said Tonk sharply. "Play something else or shut up!"

"Tonk"—Elnathan Calhoun put away the harmonica—"are you goin' with me to join up with ol' Curly Jack?"

"Might." The cowboy pinched out his half-smoked brown cigarette and threw it down. "Me and Curly Jack growed up together, back in Texas."

"Bug on a buzzsaw!" exclaimed young Mr. Calhoun. "That makes it a cinch! I was scared Curly Jack might suspect I was a detective out to betray him to the law. Thisaway he'll know it's all right, won't he?"

Tonk McSpadden didn't answer. He and Curly Jack Marcotte had been friends before Marcotte took to the outlaw trail. It had been strong in Tonk's mind that they could be friends again out in the wilds of New Mexico. The thought had been a sort of salve to the soreness of his heart —and of his pride. To hell with untrue women, to hell with honest wages, to hell with Texas, to hell with everything.

Word of the bold bravado of the Curly Jack Wild Bunch had drifted as far away as the Texas Hill Country—apparently also all the way to Arkansas. It was a savage purpose in Tonk McSpadden's heart that more of the same word, his name with it, would one day come to the ears of the blue-eyed girl he had meant to marry—just to let her know that he didn't give a damn. Of such bitterness of heart, in those hard horseback days, was the fabric of outlaw character all too often woven.

Tonk McSpadden rode with a six-shooter at his hip, a short thirty-thirty in his saddle scabbard, and he knew how to shoot them. What Curly Jack had learned to do, Tonk McSpadden could learn. So could a buzzsaw kid from Arkansas—and who would there be to care?

They camped together that night in a draw twenty miles from Bosque Largo. For an hour after they had eaten, the wild, weird howl of coyotes played intermittent accompaniment to the tunes of Elnathan Calhoun's mouth harp— none of them, this time, Barbara Allen.

The kid had no bedroll. Tonk unspooled his own for double.

"You don't need to bed me," said Elnathan. "I'm used to sleepin' wild."

"Suit yourself," said Tonk shortly, and turned in.

He was still awake an hour later when the kid came crawling under the bed tarp.

"A mite chilly out there," he apologized. "You ain't been asleep anyhow, have you, Tonk?"

For answer the cowboy made a brief, grunting sound. Tonk had seen stray dogs take up with a man after no more than one kind word, then stay with him whether he liked it or not. Already the kid seemed to consider them pardners in adventure—which, in that day and time, meant considerably more than if you pronounced partner with a "t." Whatever the nature of the attachment, there was admiration in it that made Tonk uneasy.

"Tonk"—Elnathan spoke timorously in the darkness— "you reckon that deputy sheriff suspicioned where we're headin' for?"

"My reckon machine don't work after dark. Now shut up and go to sleep!"

* * *

Samuel W. Loftis, long on hard luck and short on cow savvy, was having bull trouble—big trouble for a granger with only a slim fourteen-year-old daughter on a work horse for cowhand help. On money borrowed from the so-far-unrobbed bank at Tuloso, county seat of the same-named county, Loftis had ventured a small start in the cattle business: thirty crazy-quilt cows and one rangy bull of ungentle temper, which Janie, with a young girl's whimsy, had christened Sir Roanyred.

Now, still five miles from home with the cattle, the bull had sulled on them. He had put both Loftis and the girl on the skedaddle, then waded out into a cattail marsh from which neither hurled rocks, cuss words nor sweet persuasion could budge him.

Topping a nearby rise, Tonk McSpadden appraised the situation thusly to Elnathan Calhoun:

"When you ride the outlaw trail, Buzzsaw, you don't help nobody's bull out of a bog. You pull your hat down real low and ride 'way 'round 'em, Shep, hoping they won't notice you."

"Bug on a buzzsaw, Tonk!" Elnathan pocketed his mouth harp. "The little one in overalls looks like a girl!"

"For a lad of your tender years," said Tonk, ".you've got mighty growed-up eyesight."

Instead of "riding 'way 'round 'em," Tonk made spur-jingling entry upon the scene, the boy close behind him. At their approach Janie Loftis ducked behind her horse, plainly bashful about being seen in two-legged clothing.

"Mister," Tonk addressed the harassed homesteader, "you look right pestered."

"Just purt' near pestered enough to borrow your pistol and shoot the dang-dratted criter!"

"Dead bulls don't daddy no calves," observed Tonk. "Too bad my rope won't reach him from solid ground or I might drag him out for you."

"Tonk," said Elnathan Calhoun, sliding off his mule, "you git your rope ready!"

Without further powwow, the boy struck out into the marsh, leaping from one grass hummock to another. By the time he got within ten yards, Sir Roanyred's front hoofs were slinging mud. His tail was up and his neck was bowed.

"You better watch out!" Janie called out shrill warning. "He's on the fight!"

From ten feet away Elnathan Calhoun's handful of mud splattered Sir Roanyred smack between the eyes. There may be more provocative methods of insulting an angry bull, but Sir Roanyred wasn't choosy. With a big whoosh of wind he lowered his sharp-horned head and charged.

With hardly a six-foot safety zone between bull's horns and boy's behind, Elnathan headed for solid ground.

"Here come us wildies, Tonk!" he yelled. "Git ready with your doggone rope!"

Slogging almost knee-deep in muck, neither boy nor bull could make much speed, but the race was evenly matched.

Six yards from solid ground Elnathan hit a deep spot. A dagger-sharp horn tip ripped his shirttail within an inch of live meat. As the bull's massive head swung for another gouge, Tonk's loop snugged suddenly around the base of his horns, jerked tight, and yanked Sir Roanyred over on his side.

In response to this further insult, the roan bull lurched on out of the bog in a head-on charge at Tonk's horse. But that wise Texas pony had side-stepped belligerent bovines before. As the momentum of blind rage carried the bull on past, Tonk squalled his wildest cowboy squall, grabbed and bent his tail in such a painful kink that the anguished animal kept on going.

Tonk ran him a few yards, flipped the rope over his high hindquarters and fair-grounded him so hard they could hear all the wind whoosh out of him as he hit the ground. Tonk waited, let him get up, then wind-busted him hard again.

"Texas cure for big behavior," remarked Tonk. "Buzzsaw, will you kindly slip my rope off before the gentleman ketches his wind? I do believe he won't give these good folks no more trouble."

The cowboy believed right. Sir Roanyred lurched up and hightailed it to the other cattle without even looking back.

"I sure am obliged to you!" The granger sounded like he meant it. "My name's Sam Loftis. This is my daughter Janie. Time we get these cattle home it'll be comin' on night. We'd be mighty proud to lodge you boys, Mr.—"

"Smith—John Smith. No, let's make it Bill Jones. Too many pilgrims ridin' under John Smith's hat already." Tonk said it sober-faced. "My pardner here goes by the name of Cadwallader Casanova when the sheriff ain't after him, so maybe you'd better call him Johnson. And we thank you kindly, but us owl-hooters like to ride by night, don't we—Johnson?"

"Bug on a buzzsaw, Tonk!" exclaimed Elnathan. "You gone plumb crazy?"

A troubled look came into Sam Loftis' eyes. In it suspicion and fear battled with stubborn good will—and lost.

"Boys," he said evenly, "I don't take you to be the kind that have to hide behind fake names. You come to my house for the night—and welcome."

"I sure wish you would," put in Janie timidly. "We don't ever have no company any more. With that Curly Jack Marcotte and his outlaws terrifyin' the country, ma's plumb scared to let a stranger step inside the door."

"Hush, child!" said Loftis gently.

Here it is again, thought Tonk. *Curly Jack . . . a name to be whispered in fear; a shadow of dread across a sunny land. And what the hell do you care, Tonk McSpadden?*

Aloud he said: "You see, Buzzsaw? We fooled 'em. All right, let's get on with the man's cattle—and see if this little junie-bird's ma makes good biscuits!"

She did. With fresh fried ham and eggs, Mrs. Loftis' biscuits were manna and ambrosia, and her look of suspicion relaxed when Loftis and Janie took enthusiastic turns telling her and three wide-eyed littler girls how the bull came out of the bog.

"He purt' near got Buzzsaw—I mean Mr. Johnson, ma!" Janie favored Elnathan with an admiring smile. "Scared me purt' near to death!"

"Shucks"—Elnathan buttered another biscuit like a man who trusts his own capacity—"that's the way I used to toll wild razorbacks out of the brush back in Arkinsaw. They're a heap dangerouser than bulls. Anyhow, I knew Tonk's rope would ketch him before he yamped me."

"He plays the mouth organ, too, ma—real pretty."

"Well, now!" Mrs. Loftis' smile was warm and motherly. "Maybe he'll play some for us after supper. Pass Mr. Jones the biscuits, Janie."

While Janie and her mother washed dishes, Elnathan Calhoun sat on the woodbox breathing tender mountain melodies through his harmonica, and now not even Barbara Allen had a lonesome sound.

In the cool dark outside, well out of kitchen hearing, Tonk McSpadden meshed mixed strands of inner torment into firm resolution and spoke his piece.

"Mr. Loftis," he said, "of course you know my name ain't Jones. What it is don't matter. What does matter is that this kid has took to me like a stray pup—and it ain't good."

"I doubt that, young man."

"Put it this way, Mr. Loftis: when a growed man gets his hair ruffed the wrong way, the trail he picks to get away from it is his own business. But this young Arkansas stray is a good solid boy, except he's got some wild and venturesome notion and he don't know which from 'tother about the whys and wherefores. What I'm asking is for you to home him in off the rough trail right here and now. Work him. Feed him. Daddy him what you can. It could turn out some-day he'll do you for a son."

"You puzzle me, young man." The granger's answer came slowly. "But I'll do what you ask—if the boy will stay."

"Work it this way: bed him in the house tonight if you can. Tell him I can't stand his infernal kickin'. Time he wakes up in the morning, I'll be long gone from here. Thanks, Mr. Loftis, and I wish you good night."

"Hold on, Jones, Tonk, or whatever your right name is." The homesteader's tone turned suddenly stern. "I'm no hand to pry, but one thing I want to know: are you scoutin' for Curly Jack Marcotte—or ain't you?"

"You're smart enough to know that if I was I wouldn't tell you."

"If Curly Jack should clean out that bank at Tuloso," Loftis went on grimly, "it would ruin me and some other honest folks around here."

"From what I hear, no bank is plumb safe with Marcotte around," Tonk said dryly. "As for me, Mr. Loftis, let's just say I'm a bug on a buzzsaw. Whichaway I jump ain't nobody's business but my own."

The homesteader's shrug was a gesture of bafflement. "So be it," he said. "But I know which way I'm fixin' to jump all right: I'm going in and draw what savings I've got out of that bank while it's still got a chance to be there—just in case."

Half old in sun-browned adobe, half new in sun-warping pine, the village of Tuloso, Territory of New Mexico, couched itself peacefully and with some prosperity in the embrace of rimrocked mesas gapped widely by a two-way valley whose green embroidery of tule marshes gave the oasis its name.

Leaving the Loftis place, Tonk had first thought to give all settlements a wide berth. He had foxed his trail and camped last night among remote rocky hills, hoping thus to lose the Buzzsaw Kid if that misguided youngster should try to follow him. Now that he seemed to have succeeded, the cowboy had re-estimated the hazards of an empty grubsack and was riding into Tuloso to replenish it.

Looking down on the placid settlement, Tonk remembered similar hill-country villages in faraway Texas, and tried hard to clamp down on the nostalgic pang under his ribs.

How far must a lonely man ride to rid himself of bitterness, how far harden himself to callus his soul against old hurt? That he had managed to turn the kid aside on a better trail was good—much as he missed him. As for himself, close ahead lay the outlaw trail. By tomorrow night he would reach Curly Jack Marcotte's reputed hideout—and for better or worse, the die would be cast.

"Hey, Tonk!" The red mare mule brought Elnathan dusting up beside him at a gangling gallop. "Bug on a buzzsaw, Tonk! If I'd knowed you aimed to sneak out on me, I'd have hobbled you instead of the mule! Maybe I'm a cockleburr in your tail, but wherever you go, I'm going', Tonk— and—and nothin' can stop me!"

"For two cents and a ticket to hell," Tonk told him dryly, "I'd turn you over to Pete Hadlock for stealing that mule!"

Elnathan's only answer was an ingratiating grin. In a mutual stubbornness of silence, they rode into Tuloso together, hitched their mounts in cottonwood shade and started up the street toward a sign that said GENERAL MERCHANDISE.

Across the street Tonk recognized Sam Loftis' team, hitched to a rickety buckboard, dozing at a hitch rack. Evidently the homesteader had come to town after his money just as he had threatened. Straight ahead in front of the Tuloso County Bank, a whiskery man with a six-shooter in one hand stood holding the reins of five saddled horses with the other. Nearby, a second black-shirted *hombre* had two men and a woman backed up against the wall, held there, their hands high in the air, by the threat of his six-shooter.

The man holding the horses waved his gun warningly at Tonk and Buzzsaw as they approached.

"Face to the wall and hands high, boys!" he ordered in a tone of insolent confidence. "Curly Jack's in town!"

It was sound advice—but wasted.

* * *

A shot sounded inside the bank. Three men came rushing out. Two carried loot-laden gunnysacks. The third shoved a valiantly kicking and clawing Janie Loftis along beside them, a shield against possible attack.

The outlaws' sudden rush excited the horses, making them hard to hold.

"Hang onto the gal till we get mounted, Cuff!"

To Tonk McSpadden the leader's voice had a familiar sound that somehow sickened him, and suddenly he knew whose side he was on. Grimly his hand dropped to his six-shooter.

"You skedaddle, Buzz!" He spoke with quiet urgency back over his shoulder. "Hell's fixin' to pop!"

This, too, was sound advice—but wasted.

Quick as a cat, Elnathan Calhoun had already darted in among the lunging horses, harmonica in hand.

"*Whee-oo-whee-whee-oo-oo!   Whee-oo-whee-whee-oo-oo!*"

At the train-whistle screech of the boy's mouth harp, the outlaws' already nervous horses went crazy-wild. One lunged against the man holding them, knocking his gun off aim so that his quick shot at Tonk McSpadden flew wild. The whirled-around rump of another bumped into the outlaw who held the girl and knocked him down.

Thus abruptly freed, Janie wasted no time. Grabbing the fallen outlaw's gun, she hit him over the head with it just as Elnathan Calhoun's big old pistol, having failed to fire, dealt a like cranial wallop to another one. A third outlaw went down with one of Tonk's well-aimed bullets through both legs.

Two of the outlaws somehow managed to mount and take off down the street. The last bullet in Tonk McSpadden's wheel tumbled one of them. The other ran head-on into a new arrival galloping in from a side street. Arriving late, but not too late, Deputy Sheriff Pete Hadlock was not on prancy-parade this time—and he knew how to shoot.

In the strange brevity of swift violence, the battle was

over and Curly Jack Marcotte's last bank robbery foiled, with the grim tally of one outlaw dead and four safely captured, three of them wounded.

Janie Loftis paused to give Elnathan Calhoun a hasty squeeze, then ran to her father as he came limping out of the bank between two white-faced tellers, bleeding from a bullet wound in his leg—his reward for trying to balk the robbery.

Tonk paused to stare briefly down at the lifeless face of a curly-haired outlaw leader he had once known as an honest cowboy.

"Well, Buzzsaw," he said, deep-down soberly, "now we know about outlawin'!"

"Injun," said Deputy Sheriff Hadlock, and there was no bluster in it, "it looks like you and the kid saved the bacon. If either of you wants to kick me for my big behavior the other day, I'll bend over for it."

"Bug on a buzzsaw!" Elnathan Calhoun managed a faint grin. "Wouldn't I look purty kickin' a law officer, and me with a stole mule I've got to take back before I can start over sure 'nough honest!"

BLOOD ON THE SUN

Thomas Thompson

We hadn't expected him. He stood there in the doorway of Doc Isham's store, his lips thin and tight. He looked more like the trouble man I had first figured him to be than like the Preacher we had come to know. He was built like a cowboy, tall and lean-hipped. He was about thirty-five years old, I'd judge. It was hard to tell, and he wasn't a man to say. With all his gentleness, he had never quite lost the cold steadiness that had been in his eyes the night he first came to our valley with a bullet in his chest and more blood on his saddle than there was in his body. He had been a dead man that night, but Grace Beaumont had refused to let him die.

That coldness was in his eyes now as he looked at us, and it bothered me. It was those eyes and his hands, long and tapered and almost soft, that had made me pick him as a gun fighter. "Howdy, neighbors," he said. "I hear you've decided to fight Corby Lane." His voice was soft, but everybody heard it and they all stopped talking.

We were all there. Jim Peterson, tall and blond and nervous, thinking of the bride he had left at home. Fedor Marios, with his great mat of kinky white hair; Mel Martin, the oldest man in the valley. Ted Beaumont was down at the end of the counter with the two farmers from Rincón Valley. They were the ones who had come across the ridge to tell us there was no use trying to deal with Corby Lane. They had tried it, and Corby Lane had moved his sheep through their valley and wiped out their crops completely.

Frank Medlin, the young cowboy who worked for the Walking R over at Seventeen Mile, was also there. It was Frank Medlin who had gotten Ted Beaumont into his latest trouble. The two of them had served six months in jail on a cattle-rustling charge just a few months back.

Ted moved away from the counter, walking a little unsteady. "So help me," he said, "it's the Preacher come to pray!"

I keep calling him the Preacher. He wasn't one, really. His name was Johnny Calaveras, but us folks here in the valley had nearly forgotten that. To us he was the Preacher. It wasn't that he actually held church. It was just in the way he looked at things, calm and peaceful, always expecting the best. That's all right when you're fighting something like weather or grasshoppers, but it wouldn't work against Corby Lane and his hired gunmen, and nobody knew it any better than I did. I had been a sheriff in a boom town before I married and settled down. I knew about men like Corby Lane.

The Preacher looked at Ted, remembering that this boy was Grace Beaumont's brother, and then he looked around the room, measuring every man, and there wasn't a man there who didn't grow restless under that gaze.

"Here's the Preacher," Mel Martin said needlessly. "I reckon that makes all of us." His lie was there in his voice.

We hadn't asked the Preacher to join us. We didn't figure he'd want to.

The two farmers from Rincón Valley were standing between Mel Martin and Ted Beaumont. Ted pushed one of them away roughly and stood there peering at the Preacher. "Let's get things out in the open, Preacher," Ted said. "You're always mighty full of high-flown advice, especially for me. I just want you to know that I'm running this show."

The Preacher didn't show any signs of how he had taken that. "Which end of the show you running, Ted?" he said. "The fighting end?"

There was a lot of nervousness and tension in that room. The Preacher's remark struck everybody funny, just as a remark will sometimes when men are keyed to the breaking point. We all laughed, and the color came into Ted Beaumont's cheeks. But Ted wasn't a boy who backed down easy. He took a step closer to the Preacher and he let his eyes run over the man. "Where's your gun, Preacher?" Ted said.

The Preacher stood there, and I saw the half smile on his lips; it was the kind of smile I never like to see on a man. There was bad blood between the Preacher and Ted Beaumont. I caught myself wondering if that was the reason Grace Beaumont and the Preacher had never married, and I figured it must be. They had been in love ever since Grace had nursed him back to health from that gunshot wound he had when he came into the valley.

"I don't wear a gun when I'm talking to my friends, Ted," the Preacher said easily.

It made Ted mad. He was a handsome kid, stocky-built. He had wavy blond hair. He was just twenty, but he had done a man's work from the day his dad had been gored to death by a bull four years back, and all of us accepted him as a man. Ted had set himself up as a sort of leader here, and that was all right with most of us. We were going to need his kind of fire before this day was over.

There wasn't a man in the valley wouldn't have been glad to forget the scrapes the kid had been in, even if only for his sister Grace's sake. But Ted wouldn't let you. He always looked like he was mad at the world. Now he got that nasty twist to his lips and said, "What you gonna do, Preacher? Sing church songs to them sheep?"

When you're standing there thinking that within a few hours you'll maybe be killing a fellow human being or getting killed yourself, that kind of talk sounds childish. We all felt it. The Preacher said, "Why not? I've heard you and Frank Medlin singin' to cows on night herd. How do you know sheep don't like music?"

The way he said it made Ted look a little foolish. The muscles of his face tightened. Until the Preacher had come in nobody had questioned any of Ted's decisions, and Ted didn't want his decisions questioned now. He said, "Look, Preacher. We've decided on a line. They go one step beyond it and maybe we'll club a few sheep. Maybe we'll hang a few sheepherders." He slapped the gun he had strapped around his middle. "We don't need no sermon from you. This gun will do the talkin'."

The Preacher gave him a long look and then deliberately turned away. He spoke to those two farmers from the other valley. "What happened in Rincón?" he asked.

The two Rincón men started to talk at once, stopped, and then one went ahead. "There's six Mexican herders with the band," the farmer said, "but they won't cause no trouble. It's this Corby Lane and the three men with him. They're gun fighters, neighbor, and they come on ahead of the sheep."

"We know the setup, Preacher," Ted Beaumont said. His voice was ugly.

The kid was getting under my skin. "The Preacher ain't heard it," I said. "Let him hear it."

"Why?" Ted Beaumont said, turning to me. "So he'll know what verse in the Bible to read? Let's get out of here. I warned you last month a couple of us had to put on guns and fix a boundary if we wanted to keep this valley clear of sheep."

"You mean you and Frank Medlin decided you needed an excuse to wear guns?" the Preacher said.

"If Frank and me are the only two not afraid to wear guns, yes," Ted said bluntly.

The Preacher shook his head. "You're not tough, Ted," he said. "I've told you that before. You're just mixed up."

I saw the wicked anger in Ted's eyes and it wasn't a man's anger. It was the flaring temper of a kid. "I told you I'd handle this without your sermons, Preacher," Ted said.

"You're not going to handle it, Ted," the Preacher said. "Not you or anyone here, the way you got it laid out."

I kept my mouth shut. I liked the Preacher. I wanted to give him his chance. It was old Mel Martin who bristled. "Hold on a minute," Mel said. "There's gettin' to be too much palaver."

"Looks to me like you need some palaver," the Preacher said. "You're gonna expose yourself, let Corby Lane know just how many men you got and what you plan—"

"You got a better idea, Preacher?" Mel said.

"I have," the Preacher said. "Let me go up there and talk to Corby Lane."

It surprised all of us and there was a loud hoot of derision from Ted Beaumont. "You and who else, Preacher?" Ted scoffed. "You and God, maybe?"

I saw the brittle hardness come into the Preacher's eyes, and I could see him fighting to control his temper. "A man could do worse than picking God for a saddle partner, Ted," the Preacher said. "But I figured on taking one man with me."

"Who you want to take with you, Preacher?" Ted said, his voice sarcastic. "Old Fedor, maybe?"

The deep red of Fedor Marios' complexion turned to a saddle tan and I thought he would hit Ted. He didn't have a chance. The Preacher's voice was so soft we barely heard it, but it filled the room like a solid block: "Why don't you come along with me, Ted?"

The color ran out of Ted Beaumont's cheeks. I looked

at the Preacher, and I was looking at a man who had fought a losing battle with his temper. He hadn't planned on taking Ted Beaumont up there with him. He had planned on taking me, maybe. I was his best friend. But a man could stand just so much. Even a man like the Preacher. Ever since he had known Grace Beaumont, the Preacher had tried to be friendly with her brother. He had taken things from Ted no other man would have taken.

I saw the conflict in Ted Beaumont's face. It was one thing to go up to that sheep camp with ten men back of him. It was another to go it alone with a man like the Preacher. I saw the conflict and I saw Ted make his decision. It was the wrong one. He figured the Preacher was bluffing and he was going to call that bluff.

"Sure, Preacher," Ted said. "I'd like to see you run. What are we waiting for?"

"I got a little business to attend to," the Preacher said. "I'll be back in five minutes and we'll go."

"You sure you'll get back, Preacher?" Ted said.

The Preacher had started toward the door. He stopped and turned. In his eyes was an anger so great that I knew it wasn't aimed at Ted Beaumont alone. It was a bigger thing. An anger toward the thing that made Ted Beaumont the way he was. I couldn't think of the man as the Preacher any more. He was Johnny Calaveras again, a man who had ridden in out of the night with a bullet in his chest. I wouldn't have wanted to cross him right then. He looked at me and said, "You better come with me, Luke, to see I get back all right." He went outside and mounted and I followed him.

He wanted to see Grace and tell her what had happened. That's the way Johnny and Grace were with each other. He headed for the schoolhouse up at the end of the street and I followed.

Grace must have expected him. She had let the kids out for an early recess and I saw her standing by the oak tree out by the pump.

She was one of those women who became really beautiful after you knew them. The trouble Ted had caused her showed in her eyes and in the way she smiled, but the grief she had known was a part of her beauty. Johnny swung down easy and walked over to her, and she put out both her hands and he took them. I loosened my reins and let my horse crop at the grass. I didn't want to listen to what they had to say. It was none of my business.

I glanced at them a couple of times, and they were standing there close together, still holding hands, the Preacher tall and straight and serious.

The kids had spotted them now and they were all standing there, staring like a bunch of calves at a corral fence.

Maybe the wind changed. Maybe Johnny spoke louder. Anyway, I heard him, though I wasn't trying to listen. "Maybe I could have handled it without a gun, the way we planned," he said. "Maybe I couldn't have. I won't risk it with Ted along."

Suddenly it was as if the two of them had reached the end of a dream and they were all alone in the world, and it wasn't the world as they had wanted it, but the world as it was. I saw Johnny bend his head swiftly and kiss her, and I heard those blasted kids giggle, and it wasn't anything to giggle about.

I saw Grace break away from Johnny's embrace, reluctantly and yet quickly, and then she left the schoolyard and went across the street to the Perkins house, where the schoolteachers always lived. She walked rapidly. When she came back out of the house she had a folded belt and a holstered gun in her hand. She came across the street and handed it to Johnny Calaveras, and I knew it was the same gun he had worn into the valley. No one had seen it since that first night.

"I'll take care of him, Grace," I heard him say. "Maybe it's best this way." He buckled on the gun belt. The dark-brown stains of Johnny's own blood were still on the leather. I felt old and tired and somehow useless, and then I saw Grace Beaumont's eyes and I saw the worry and the end of a dream in them. I didn't have to make any decision. I thought of my own wife and of the love I had seen between Johnny and Grace, a love that was maybe ending here today.

I rode over close to them. "I'm going, too, Johnny," I said.

"I didn't ask you," he said flatly.

"You couldn't stop me."

We rode back to the store, and everyone was out in front. Ted Beaumont was in the street, mounted, a little uncertain. He said, "I see Luke didn't let you get away from him."

Suddenly I felt sorry for Ted Beaumont. He was nothing but a darn-fool kid itching to get his fingers on a gun. I had seen the signs before. A gun could be a dangerous thing with a kid like Ted. I wondered if Johnny had known what it was like to want a gun more than anything else.

"Get this, kid," Johnny said, and now his eyes were holding Ted. "From here on out I give the orders. Make up your mind to it or drop out now."

I saw Ted bluster, wanting to give a scoffing answer, but that gun, the new look about the Preacher, held him from it. And he couldn't back down now. He said, "What's holding us up?"

"Nothing," Johnny Calaveras said. "Not a thing."

The sheep were an undistinguishable blot against the brown grass, and as Johnny and Ted and I climbed the hill the animals took form and shape and became separate bunches. We could see the herders, men on foot, and their dogs stretched in shady patches, tongues lolling, ears alert. The herders, half asleep under the trees, hadn't noticed us yet. We couldn't be seen from Corby Lane's camp because there was a shoulder of the hill between us and the camp. Ted looked at me. There was an amused, indulgent swagger in his glance, but there were white patches at the corners of his mouth, and I knew he had been watching Johnny Calaveras.

The only thing Johnny had done was to strap on that gun and take off his gloves, but that made the difference. He wasn't the Preacher any more. I could see his right hand just hanging limp at his side almost as if his elbow were broken. Johnny Calaveras was a gun fighter. It was marked on him as clearly as if it had been printed in red letters.

I watched his right hand opening and closing, loosening fingers that had been long unused in their deadly business. I saw Ted Beaumont's lip move, and I knew the fear he was beginning to feel. I had felt it myself.

We had dropped down into a draw, out of sight of the sheep, and Johnny Calaveras reined up sharply. He didn't waste words. "I know Corby Lane," he said. "I can ride into his camp and talk to him without getting shot at. What good it will do, I don't know, but that's the way it has to be." A little of the harshness went out of his voice. "If it should come to a fight," he said, "I want the odds on our side."

He was talking straight to Ted now. There was something cold and deathlike about Johnny's voice. I felt as if I were watching the opening of a grave.

"A gun fighter that stays alive," Johnny said, "never gives a sucker a break. Luke, you ride up this draw and come in behind the camp. Keep your ears open, and don't make a move unless I give the sign, but don't be afraid to shoot if I do."

I think he was trying to make Ted see that there was nothing glamorous about gun fighting. It was brutal stuff with nothing of trust or decency about it. I looked at Ted, wondering if he had seen through this, and I knew he hadn't. He still had that cocky swagger in his eyes, but those white patches at the corners of his mouth were more noticeable. "You want me to ride along with Luke to cover for you?" he said.

"No," Johnny said. "I want you to come along with me. Maybe Luke couldn't hold you if you started to run."

That was like slapping the kid in the face, but it was a smart move. Ted Beaumont would be twice as determined now. He was a little scared, and a little anger right now wouldn't hurt him. I headed on down the draw, riding slow enough not to attract attention, and I saw Johnny and Ted ride up on the ridge to within full sight of the sheep camp.

Luck was with me and my timing was perfect. I came up behind the sheep camp just as Johnny and Ted rode in. The three men standing there by the oak didn't even suspect I was around. They were too busy watching Johnny and Ted, and I was able to dismount and move up into the brush not fifty feet behind them.

One of the men looked more like a sheepherder than he did a gunman, but he kept his hand near his gun as he slouched there against the tree. Another was thick through, a brutal-looking man with shaggy hair and crossed gun belts and blue lips.

The other gunman was slender to the point of being emaciated, and at first I picked this one to be Corby Lane. His clothes seemed to hang on his frame. His shirt moved in the imperceptible breeze, and he gave the impression that if his clothes were removed he would be revealed as a skeleton strung together with spring wire. "You boys just ridin'?" he said. "Or did you want something?"

"I want to talk to Corby Lane," Johnny Calaveras said slowly.

The thin man shifted his position slightly and I felt my finger tightening on the trigger of my rifle. "Corby's taking a siesta," the thin man said. "You can say it to me."

"I'll wait for Corby," Johnny said, smiling. It was a cold, thin smile.

I had watched this kind of thing before. The thin man was measuring Johnny, seeing the things I had seen. He had recognized Johnny for what he was, or for what he had been in the past, and the thin man was smart enough to take it easy. There wouldn't be any fast gunplay. Both men had respect for the damage a .45 slug could do.

"You might have quite a wait," the thin man said. He

had glanced across the fire they had burning and beyond to the tent that stood under the oaks.

"I got time," Johnny said.

The other two gunmen were standing back, letting the thin man do all the talking. Johnny and the thin man sparred, making small talk, each one looking for a weak spot in the other. It would have gone on like that until Johnny found the opening he wanted, except for Ted Beaumont.

I had been so busy watching the play between Johnny and the thin man and keeping my rifle ready on the other two gunmen that I had nearly forgotten Ted. He had behaved himself up to this point and any fool could see what Johnny was doing, stalling, waiting for Corby Lane to show. But I had misjudged Ted just the way I had misjudged the Preacher. Ted said, "We're wasting time, Preacher." Every eye except Johnny's turned toward him.

I saw Johnny tense. "I'll handle this," he snapped.

"You talk too much, Preacher," Ted said. "We come here to run these sheepers out. I do my talking with this!"

Ted's hand slapped down awkwardly and his fingers closed around the butt of his gun. Telling it now, I can see every move. I couldn't then. I threw myself out of the brush, my rifle hip level, and I yelled out for them to throw up their hands. I saw the thin man drop into a half crouch and I saw his gun half clear leather, and then Johnny was sailing out of his saddle and he landed on Ted Beaumont's shoulders. The kid went down hard, the gun spinning out of its holster.

I rammed my rifle barrel against the thin man's back and I heard his grunt of pain. The thin man let his half-drawn gun slip from his fingers, and Johnny had snapped to his feet, his cocked gun in his hand, and he was covering that tent beyond the fire, his eyes sweeping the other two gunmen, warning them.

Johnny didn't even look at Ted. "You're so anxious to get the feel of that gun," Johnny said across his shoulder, "pick it up and see if you can keep them covered." The kid did as he was told.

I knew what had happened to Ted and I felt like taking a club to him. It was as Johnny said. Ted was too blasted anxious to get the feel of his gun, and if he had gotten away with his crazy plan he would have figured himself quite a gunman. I was glad he had failed. I saw him standing there, the wind half knocked out of him, and for a minute I was afraid he was going to be sick. The gunmen had raised their hands and I moved around behind them and took their guns.

The thin man laughed, a high, wild sound. "Where I come from, punk," he said to Ted, "you wouldn't live to be as tall as you think you are."

Ted swallowed hard but he kept his gun trained on the thin man.

Johnny moved over toward the tent. He kept his gun in his hand and he walked toward the door of the tent, walking slowly on the balls of his feet, making no sound. When he was near the tent he moved to one side and he stood there, his hand gripping the butt of the gun. "Come out, Corby," he said softly. "It's Johnny Calaveras."

The flap of the tent moved aside and a man came out. He was round and fat. His eyes were a striking pale blue and his skin looked as if it had never seen the sun. He reminded me of a well-fed snake that had lived too long in the dark. He stood there on his thick legs and stared, his tongue darting in and out. "Is it you, Johnny?" he asked.

"You want to touch me, Corby?" Johnny said. "You want to feel the flesh and bone?"

"Johnny, I figured—"

"You figured I was dead," Johnny said. "Otherwise I would have come after you before this."

Corby Lane looked at his gunmen lined up there under Ted's and my guns. I saw that Corby Lane was a man who was weak without guns to back him up. "Johnny," he said, "it was all a mistake. It was a mix-up."

"It was that," Johnny Calaveras said. "And you did the mixing. You set a gun trap, and me and Steve walked into it."

This talk didn't make sense, except to tell me that Corby Lane was part of the past that was always in Johnny's eyes. Corby Lane's voice was steadier now. "All right," he said. "So it was planned. But I didn't plan it. It was Steve's idea. He was tired of the way you kept riding him. He was tired of your preaching."

There was a wicked ruthlessness on Johnny's face now, and I thought I was going to see a man killed. For that second Johnny Calaveras was a man without a heart or a soul. His lips were thin, tight against his teeth, and I saw his trigger finger tightening. I saw the sweat on his forehead. I watched him trying to keep from squeezing the trigger. His voice came out on his expelled breath.

"You're a liar," he said. "Steve didn't know anything about it. You told him to raid my camp. He did it because that was what you were paying him for and because he liked to fight. You counted on that. You told him me and my boys were part of the XB outfit. He couldn't tell in the dark that it was my camp he was raiding any more than I could tell it was Steve who was raiding me. You double-crossed us both, Corby, because you wanted to get rid of me and Steve and you knew there was no other way."

Sometimes a certain dignity comes to a man standing on the edge of eternity. It came to Corby Lane now. His shoulders squared and he faced Johnny Calaveras. "All right," he said flatly. "That's the way it was, and it worked. Steve's dead. He caught a bullet right between the eyes that night." There was perspiration on Corby Lane's moon face, but there was a growing confidence in his voice. "Maybe you fired the bullet that killed him, Johnny," Corby Lane said quietly. "Did you ever think of that?"

Whatever it was, I knew that Corby Lane had hit Johnny Calaveras with everything he had. I saw the old tiredness come into Johnny's eyes, and an old hurt was there in the sag of his shoulders. "Yes," Johnny said. "I've thought of that. And I figured if I hunted you down and killed you it would give me something else to think about."

"I would have been easy to find," Corby Lane said. In some way he had gained the upper hand, and as I watched I realized these two men had known each other not only well but completely. Corby Lane knew of some twist in Johnny's nature that would be a weakness in a gun fighter. I figured I knew what it was. Corby Lane knew that Johnny was a man who would ask himself questions, and that, for a gun fighter, was a dangerous thing. Someday he might ask himself if it was worthwhile killing again. Corby Lane was gambling that Johnny had already asked himself that question. And Johnny had, I knew. Otherwise he wouldn't have become the man we called the Preacher.

"Why didn't you come after me, Johnny?" Corby Lane said.

"Because I decided there was only one way to really hurt you, Corby," Johnny said, "and that's the way I'm going to hurt you now. I want that money belt you always carry. Without money to hire guns you're nothing. You're not even worth hunting down."

"If this is a plain holdup why didn't you say so?" Corby Lane said. "They'll excuse a gun fight quicker than they will a robbery."

"Go to the law, Corby," Johnny said. "When you do I'll start talking. The law is still trying to find out what happened to those six soldiers that got killed. The law still wants to know what happened to that payroll the soldiers were packing."

I saw the surprise in Corby Lane's face and then the terror, and I knew Johnny had pulled something out of Corby Lane's past, something that had been long dead. "You can't tie that to me," Corby Lane shouted. "It happened before I even knew you. You don't know anything about it."

"Don't I?" Johnny said. "It didn't happen before you knew Steve. Maybe Steve told me all about it. Maybe it was on Steve's mind so strong he had to talk about it."

I watched Corby Lane. I knew he was trying to decide if Johnny was bluffing or not, and I saw he was afraid to take the chance. He made one last gesture. "If you know so much," he said, "you know Steve was in it. You're admitting that."

"I am," Johnny said. "But Steve is dead. They can't hang a dead man, Corby, but they can sure hang you."

"What money you've got," Johnny said. "We'll call it wages you owed me and Steve. After that, turn those sheep out through the canyon and keep 'em on open graze. I reckon you can't make a living running sheep legitimate, Corby. I reckon you'll go broke. That's good enough for me, and it would be for Steve. Someday you're going to slip and say the wrong thing, and the government will know what happened to that payroll pack train. I'll count on it happening. If I ever hear of you making a slip, I'll see that it happens sooner. Give me the money belt, Corby."

The gunmen watched their boss back down. I watched Corby Lane, too, and I watched Johnny Calaveras. I wondered if Johnny really did know enough to hang this man, and Corby Lane was wondering the same thing. I decided I would never know for sure; I knew Corby Lane would never take the chance of finding out. Johnny had him whipped. Lane took off the heavy money belt and handed it to Johnny Calaveras.

The tall, thin gunman spit between his wide-spaced teeth. "So you're Johnny Calaveras," he said. "I've heard of you."

"Move those sheep down into the valley and you'll hear a lot more," Johnny said.

"I reckon I would," the tall gunman said. "But I won't be around." He glanced toward the fire where I had thrown the guns. "If you're finished with me and my boys here," the tall gunman said, "I reckon we'll mosey along." He looked at the money belt Johnny was strapping around his middle. "I don't work for a man that ain't got no money," the gunman said.

As we rode back to town I looked at Ted and his face was serious and ashamed, and I knew he was thinking of the fool he had made of himself. Ted Beaumont had lived a long time in those few minutes back there.

Maybe the Preacher figured he owed us an explanation, but I never thought that was it. Rather, I think he wanted Ted to see everything in the right light. The Preacher stared straight ahead. "I worked for Corby Lane down in New Mexico," he said. "There was a cattle war on and any man who took a job took a gun job." It didn't sound like the rest was really meant for us. "Steve was already working for Corby," he said. "I figured it would be best if I was with Steve."

He was trying to say a lot more, but suddenly it was hard for him to talk. "This Steve," I said. "He was your buddy?"

The tiredness in the Preacher's eyes was something you could feel. "Steve was my brother," he said. "He was a kid who couldn't leave guns alone."

It hit me like a sledge hammer, and I looked at Ted and saw the impact of it numbing him. I thought of Johnny Calaveras, this quiet man we called the Preacher, living with the thought that he might have killed his own brother in a gun trap set by Corby Lane. And suddenly I knew what the fight inside Johnny was as he stood there with a gun held on Corby Lane, and I knew why he had let Corby Lane live. It was his way of proving to himself that he had whipped the past, his way of paying a debt he felt he owed. And I knew now why Johnny Calaveras and Grace Beaumont had never married.

"I used to be pretty proud of my gun speed," the Preacher said quietly. "But spending the rest of your life wondering whether you killed your own brother is quite a price to pay for pride." I glanced at Ted Beaumont; he looked sick.

Everybody was out on the street when we got back to Doc Isham's store. They were standing there looking up toward the south end of the valley. There wasn't any worry in their eyes any more, and I knew that band of sheep had turned east, toward the mouth of the canyon.

Grace was there, and when she looked at Johnny and Ted she knew, without being told, that the two men she loved had reached an understanding. She knew that Johnny had won his right to live his new life. I knew now what it was that had made Grace and Johnny's love for each other so compelling. It was the understanding between them. There wasn't anything about Johnny's past that Grace didn't know, and that knowledge had drawn them together, and at the same time it had held them apart. Johnny would never ask a girl like Grace to marry him until he was sure his past was gone, until he was sure he could settle a fight without killing.

Johnny dismounted, and for a second his shoulder touched Ted Beaumont's shoulder. I saw Ted glance toward the money belt, his eyes questioning. I saw Johnny's quick understanding and I saw his grin, amused, pleased. He unbuckled the belt and tossed it to one of the farmers from Rincón Valley. "Here," he said, "Corby Lane sent this down. Said he hoped it would pay for the damage his sheep did to your crops." He turned then to Ted. I saw Ted stiffen, waiting for the lacing he knew he had coming.

The Preacher said, "If you've a mind to grub out that oak on your place, Ted, I could give you a hand with it tomorrow."

"Thanks, Johnny," Ted said, and he tried to grin.

Johnny took Grace's arm and the two of them walked off together.

I left the valley about ten years back. Johnny and Grace are married now, still in love, still amazed at the goodness of the world. Ted Beaumont married my oldest girl, Lucy. Ted's a good, steady boy now. Outside of that, things haven't changed much. Folks around here still call Johnny Calaveras the Preacher. It's surprising how much respect men can cram into a nickname like that.

STUBBY PRINGLE'S CHRISTMAS

Jack Schaefer

High on the mountainside by the little line cabin in the crisp clean dusk of evening Stubby Pringle swings into saddle. He has shape of bear in the dimness, bundled thick against cold. Double socks crowd scarred boots. Leather chaps with hair out cover patched corduroy pants. Fleece-lined jacket with wear of winters on it bulges body and heavy gloves blunt fingers. Two gay red bandannas folded together fatten throat under chin. Battered hat is pulled down to sit on ears and in side pocket of jacket are rabbit-skin earmuffs he can put to use if he needs them.

Stubby Pringle swings up into saddle. He looks out and down over worlds of snow and ice and tree and rock. He spreads arms wide and they embrace whole ranges of hills. He stretches tall and hat brushes stars in sky. He is Stubby Pringle, cowhand of the Triple X, and this is his night to howl. He is Stubby Pringle, son of the wild jackass, and he is heading for the Christmas dance at the schoolhouse in the valley.

Stubby Pringle swings up and his horse stands like rock. This is the pride of his string, flop-eared ewe-necked cat-hipped strawberry roan that looks like it should have died weeks ago but has iron rods for bones and nitroglycerin for blood and can go from here to doomsday with nothing more than mouthfuls of snow for water and tufts of winter-cured bunch-grass snatched between drifts for food. It stands like rock. It knows the folly of trying to unseat Stubby. It wastes no energy in futile explosions. It knows that twenty-seven miles of hard winter going are foreordained for this evening and twenty-seven more of harder uphill return by morning. It has done this before. It is saving the dynamite under its hide for the destiny of a true cow pony which is to take its rider where he wants to go—and bring him back again.

Stubby Pringle sits his saddle and he grins into cold and distance and future full of festivity. Join me in a look at what can be seen of him despite the bundling and frosty breath vapor that soon will hang icicles on his nose. Those are careless haphazard scrambled features under the low hat brim, about as handsome as a blue boar's snout. Not much fuzz yet on his chin. Why, shucks, is he just a boy? Don't make that mistake, though his twentieth birthday is still six weeks away. Don't make the mistake Hutch Handley made last summer when he thought this was young unseasoned stuff and took to ragging Stubby and wound up with ears pinned back and upper lip split and nose mashed flat and the whole of him dumped in a rainbarrel. Stubby has been taking care of himself since he was orphaned at thirteen. Stubby has been doing man's work since he was fifteen. Do you think Hardrock Harper of the Triple X would have anything but an all-around hard-proved hand up here at his farthest winter line camp siding Old Jake Hanlon, toughest hard-bitten old cowman ever to ride range?

Stubby Pringle slips gloved hand under rump to wipe

frost off the saddle. No sense letting it melt into patches of corduroy pants. He slaps rightside saddlebag. It contains a burlap bag wrapped around a two-pound box of candy, of fancy chocolates with variegated interiors he acquired two months ago and has kept hidden from Old Jake. He slaps leftside saddlebag. It holds a burlap bag wrapped around a paper parcel that contains a close-folded piece of dress goods and a roll of pink ribbon. Interesting items, yes. They are ammunition for the campaign he has in mind to soften the affections of whichever female of the right vintage among those at the schoolhouse appeals to him most and seems most susceptible.

Stubby Pringle settles himself firmly into the saddle. He is just another of far-scattered poorly-paid patched-clothes cowhands that inhabit these parts and likely marks and smells of his calling have not all been scrubbed away. He knows that. But this is his night to howl. He is Stubby Pringle, true-begotten son of the wildest jackass, and he has been riding line through hell and high water and winter storms for two months without a break and he has done his share of the work and more than his share because Old Jake is getting along and slowing some and this is his night to stomp floorboards till schoolhouse shakes and kick heels up to lanterns above and whirl a willing female till she is dizzy enough to see past patched clothes to the man inside them. He wriggles toes deep into stirrups and settles himself firmly in the saddle.

"I could of et them choc'lates," says Old Jake from the cabin doorway. "They wasn't hid good," he says. "No good at all."

"An' be beat like a drum," says Stubby. "An' wrung out like a dirty dishrag."

"By who?" says Old Jake. "By a young un like you? Why, I'd of tied you in knots afore you knew what's what iffen you tried it. You're a dang-blatted young fool," he says. "A ding-busted dang-blatted fool. Riding out a night like this iffen it is Chris'mas eve. A dong-bonging ding-busted dang-blatted fool," he says. "But iffen I was your age again, I reckon I'd be doing it too." He cackles like an old rooster. "Squeeze one of 'em for me," he says and he steps back inside and he closes the door.

Stubby Pringle is alone out there in the darkening dusk, alone with flop-eared ewe-necked cat-hipped roan that can go to the last trumpet call under him and with cold of wicked winter wind around him and with twenty-seven miles of snow-dumped distance ahead of him. "Wahoo!" he yells. "Skip to my Loo!" he shouts. "Do-si-do and round a-bout!"

He lifts reins and the roan sighs and lifts feet. At easy warming-up amble they drop over the edge of benchland where the cabin snugs into tall pines and on down the great bleak expanse of mountainside.

Stubby Pringle, spurs a jingle, jogs upslope through crusted snow. The roan, warmed through, moves strong and steady under him. Line cabin and line work are far forgotten things back and back and up and up the mighty mass of mountain. He is Stubby Pringle, rooting tooting hard-working hard-playing cowhand of the Triple X, heading for the Christmas dance at the schoolhouse in the valley.

He tops out on one of the lower ridges. He pulls rein to give the roan a breather. He brushes an icicle off his nose. He leans forward and reaches to brush several more off sidebars of old bit in the bridle. He straightens tall. Far ahead, over top of last and lowest ridge, on into the valley, he can see tiny specks of glowing allure that are schoolhouse windows. Light and gaiety and good liquor and fluttering skirts are there. "Wahoo!" he yells. "Gals an' women an' grandmothers!" he shouts. "Raise your skirts and start askipping! I'm acoming!"

He slaps spurs to roan. It leaps like mountain lion, out and down, full into hard gallop downslope, rushing, reckless of crusted drifts and ice-coated bush-branches slapping at them. He is Stubby Pringle, born with spurs on, nursed on tarantula juice, weaned on rawhide, at home in the saddle of a hurricane in shape of horse that can race to outer edge of eternity and back, heading now for high-jinks two months overdue. He is ten feet tall and the horse is gigantic, with wings, iron-boned and dynamite-fueled, soaring in forty-foot leaps down the flank of the whitened wonder of a winter world.

They slow at the bottom. They stop. They look up the rise of the last low ridge ahead. The roan paws frozen ground and snorts twin plumes of frosty vapor. Stubby reaches around to pull down fleece-lined jacket that has worked a bit up back. He pats rightside saddlebag. He pats leftside saddlebag. He lifts reins to soar up and over last low ridge.

Hold it, Stubby. What is that? Off to the right.

He listens. He has ears that can catch snitch of mouse chewing on chunk of bacon rind beyond the log wall by his bunk. He hears. Sound of ax striking wood.

What kind of dong-bonging ding-busted dang-blatted fool would be chopping wood on a night like this and on Christmas Eve and with a dance underway at the school-house in the valley? What kind of chopping is this anyway? Uneven in rhythm, feeble in stroke. Trust Stubby Pringle, who has chopped wood enough for cook stove and fireplace to fill a long freight train, to know how an ax should be handled.

There. That does it. That whopping sound can only mean that the blade has hit at an angle and bounced away without biting. Some dong-bonged ding-busted dang-blatted fool is going to be cutting off some of his own toes.

He pulls the roan around to the right. He is Stubby Pringle, born to tune of bawling bulls and blatting calves, branded at birth, cowman raised and cowman to the marrow, and no true cowman rides on without stopping to check anything strange on range. Roan chomps on bit, annoyed at interruption. It remembers who is in saddle. It sighs and obeys. They move quietly in dark of night past boles of trees jet black against dim grayness of crusted snow on ground. Light shows faintly ahead. Lantern light through a small oiled-paper window. Yes. Of course. Just where it has been for eight months now. The Henderson place. Man and woman and small girl and waist-high boy. Homesteaders. Not even fools, homesteaders. Worse than that. Out of their minds altogether. All of them. Out here anyway. Betting the government they can stave off starving for five years in exchange for one hundred sixty acres of land. Land that just might be able to support seven jackrabbits and two coyotes and nine rattlesnakes and maybe all of four thin steers to a whole section. In a good year. Homesteaders. Always out of almost everything, money and food and tools and smiles and joy of living. Everything. Except maybe hope and stubborn endurance.

Stubby Pringle nudges the reluctant roan along. In patch-light from the window by a tangled pile of dead tree branches he sees a woman. Her face is gray and pinched and tired. An old stocking-cap is pulled down on her head. Ragged man's jacket bumps over long woolsey dress and clogs arms as she tries to wing an ax into a good-sized branch on the ground.

Whopping sound and ax bounces and barely misses an ankle.

"Quit that!" says Stubby, sharp. He swings the roan in close. He looks down at her. She drops ax and backs away, frightened. She is ready to bolt into two-room bark-slab shack. She looks up. She sees that haphazard scrambled features under low hat brim are crinkled in what could be a grin. She relaxes some, hand on door latch.

"Ma'am," says Stubby. "You trying to cripple yourself?" She just stares at him. "Man's work," he says. "Where's your man?"

"Inside," she says; then, quick, "He's sick."

"Bad?" says Stubby.

"Was," she says. "Doctor that was here this morning

thinks he'll be all right now. Only he's almighty weak. All wobbly. Sleeps most of the time."

"Sleeps," says Stubby, indignant. "When there's wood to be chopped."

"He's been almighty tired," she says, quick, defensive. "Even afore he was took sick. Wore out." She is rubbing cold hands together, trying to warm them. "He tried," she says, proud. "Only a while ago. Couldn't even get his pants on. Just fell flat on the floor."

Stubby looks down at her. "An' you ain't tired?" he says.

"I ain't got time to be tired," she says. "Not with all I got to do."

Stubby Pringle looks off past dark boles of trees at last row ridge-top that hides valley and schoolhouse. "I reckon I could spare a bit of time," he says. "Likely they ain't much more'n started yet," he says. He looks again at the woman. He sees gray pinched face. He sees cold-shivering under bumpy jacket. "Ma'am," he says. "Get on in there an' warm your gizzard some. I'll just chop you a bit of wood."

Roan stands with dropping reins, ground-tied, disgusted. It shakes head to send icicles tinkling from bit and bridle. Stopped in midst of epic run, wind-eating, mile-gobbling, iron-boned and dynamite-fueled, and for what? For silly chore of chopping.

Fifteen feet away Stubby Pringle chops wood. Moon is rising over last low ridgetop and its light, filtered through trees, shines on leaping blade. He is Stubby Pringle, moon-struck maverick of the Triple X, born with ax in hands, with strength of stroke in muscles, weaned on whetstone, fed on cordwood, raised to fell whole forests. He is ten feet tall and ax is enormous in moonlight and chips fly like stormflakes of snow and blade slices through branches thick as his arm, through logs thick as his thigh.

He leans ax against a stump and he spreads arms wide and he scoops up whole cords at a time and strides to door and kicks it open. . . .

Both corners of front room by fireplace are piled full now, floor to ceiling, good wood, stout wood, seasoned wood, wood enough for a whole wicked winter week. Chore done and done right, Stubby looks around him. Fire is burning bright and well-fed, working on warmth. Man lies on big old bed along opposite wall, blanket over, eyes closed, face gray-pale, snoring long and slow. Woman fusses with something at old woodstove. Stubby steps to doorway to backroom. He pulls aside hanging cloth. Faint in dimness inside he sees two low bunks and in one, under an old quilt, a curly-headed small girl and in the other, under the old quilt, a boy who would be waist-high awake and standing. He sees them still and quiet, sleeping sound. "Cute little devils," he says.

He turns back and the woman is coming toward him, cup of coffee in hand, strong and hot and steaming. Coffee the kind to warm the throat and gizzard of chore-doing hard-chopping cowhand on a cold cold night. He takes the cup and raises it to his lips. Drains it in two gulps. "Thank you, ma'am," he says. "That was right kindly of you." He sets cup on table. "I got to be getting along," he says. He starts toward outer door.

He stops, hands on door latch. Something is missing in two-room shack. Trust Stubby Pringle to know what. "Where's your tree?" he says. "Kids got to have a Christmas tree."

He sees the woman sink down on chair. He hears a sigh come from her. "I ain't had time to cut one," she says.

"I reckon not," says Stubby. "Man's job anyway," he says. "I'll get it for you. Won't take a minute. Then I got to be going."

He strides out. He scoops up ax and strides off, upslope some where small pines climb. He stretches tall and his legs lengthen and he towers huge among trees swinging with ten-foot steps. He is Stubby Pringle, born an expert on Christmas trees, nursed on pine needles, weaned on pine cones, raised with an eye for size and shape and symmetry. There. A beauty. Perfect. Grown for this and for nothing else. Ax blade slices keen and swift. Tree topples. He strides back with tree on shoulder. He rips leather whangs from his saddle and lashes two pieces of wood to tree bottom, crosswise, so tree can stand upright again.

Stubby Pringle strides into shack, carrying tree. He sets it up, center of front-room floor, and it stands straight, trim and straight, perky and proud and pointed. "There you are, ma'am," he says. "Get your things out an' start decorating. I got to be going." He moves toward outer door.

He stops in outer doorway. He hears the sigh behind him. "We got no things," she says. "I was figuring to buy some but sickness took the money."

Stubby Pringle looks off at last low ridge-top hiding valley and schoolhouse. "Reckon I still got a bit of time," he says. "They'll be whooping it mighty late." He turns back, closing door. He sheds hat and gloves and bandannas and jacket. He moves about checking everything in the sparse front room. He asks for things and the woman jumps to get those few of them she has. He tells her what to do and she does. He does plenty himself. With this and with that magic wonders arrive. He is Stubby Pringle, born to poverty and hard work, weaned on nothing, fed on less, raised to make do with least possible and make the most of that. Pinto beans strung on thread brighten tree in firelight and lantern light like strings of store-bought beads. Strips of one bandanna, cut with shears from sewing-box, bob in bows on branchends like gray red flowers. Snippets of fleece from jacketlining sprinkled over tree glisten like fresh fall of snow. Miracles flow from strong blunt fingers through bits of old paper-bags and dabs of flour paste into link chains and twisted small streamers and two jaunty little hats and two smart little boats with sails.

"Got to finish it right," says Stubby Pringle. From strong blunt fingers comes five-pointed star, triple-thickness to make it stiff, twisted bit of old wire to hold it upright. He fastens this to topmost tip of topmost bough. He wraps lone bandanna left around throat and jams battered hat on head and shrug into now-skimpy-lined jacket. "A right nice little tree," he says. "All you got to do now is get out what you got for the kids and put it under. I really got to be going." He starts toward outer door.

He stops in open doorway. He hears the sigh behind him. He knows without looking around the woman has slumped into old rocking chair. "We ain't got anything for them," she says. "Only now this tree. Which I don't mean it isn't a fine grand tree. It's more'n we'd of had 'cept for you."

Stubby Pringle stands in open doorway looking out into cold clean moonlit night. Somehow he knows without turning head two tears are sliding down thin pinched cheeks. "You go on along," she says. "They're good young uns. They know how it is. They ain't expecting a thing."

Stubby Pringle stands in doorway looking out at last ridge-top that hides valley and schoolhouse. "All the more reason," he says soft to himself. "All the more reason something should be there when they wake." He sighs too. "I'm a dong-bonging ding-busted dang-blatted fool," he says. "But I reckon I still got a mite more time. Likely they'll be sashaying around till it's most morning."

Stubby Pringle strides on out, leaving door open. He strides back, closing door with heel behind him. In one hand he has burlap bag wrapped around paper parcel. In other hand he has squarish chunk of good pine wood. He tosses bag-parcel into lap-folds of woman's apron.

"Unwrap it," he says. "There's the makings for a right cute dress for the girl. Needle-and-threader like you can whip it up in no time. I'll just whittle me out a little something for the boy."

Moon is high in cold cold sky. Frosty clouds drift up there with it. Tiny flakes of snow float through upper air. Down below by a two-room shack droops a disgusted cowpony roan, ground-tied, drooping like statue snow-crusted. It is accepting the inescapable destiny of its kind which is to wait for its rider, to conserve deep-bottomed dynamite en-

ergy, to be ready to race to the last margin of motion when
waiting is done.

Inside the shack fire in fireplace cheerily gobbles wood,
good wood, stout wood, seasoned wood, warming two-rooms
well. Man lies on bed, turned on side, curled up some, snoring slow and steady. Woman sits in rocking chair, sewing.
Her head nods slow and drowsy and her eyelids sag weary
but her fingers fly, stitch-stitch-stitch. A dress has shaped
under her hands, small and flounced and with little puff-
sleeves, fine dress, fancy dress, dress for smiles and joy of
living. She is sewing pink ribbon around collar and down
front and into fluffy bow on back.

On a stool nearby sits Stubby Pringle, piece of good pine
wood in one hand, knife in other hand, fine knife, splendid
knife, all-around-accomplished knife, knife he always has
with him, seven-bladed knife with four for cutting from
little to big and corkscrew and can opener and screwdriver.
Big cutting blade has done its work. Little cutting blade is
in use now. He is Stubby Pringle, born with feel for knives
in hand, weaned on emery wheel, fed on shavings, raised to
whittle his way through the world. Tiny chips fly and shavings flutter. There in his hands, out of good pine wood,
something is shaping. A horse. Yes. Flop-eared ewe-necked
cat-hipped horse. Flop-eared head is high on ewe neck,
stretched out, sniffing wind, snorting into distance. Cat-hips
are hunched forward, caught in crouch for forward leap. It
is a horse fit to carry a waist-high boy to uttermost edge of
eternity and back.

Stubby Pringle carves swift and sure. Little cutting
blade makes final little cutting snitches. Yes. Tiny mottlings
and markings make no mistaking. It is a strawberry roan. He
closes knife and puts it in pocket. He looks up. Dress is
finished in woman's lap. But woman's head has dropped
down in exhaustion. She sit slumped deep in rocking chair
and she too snores slow and steady.

Stubby Pringle stands up. He takes dress and puts it
under tree, fine dress, fancy dress, dress waiting now for

small girl to wake and wear it with smiles and joy of living. He sets wooden horse beside it, fine horse, proud horse, snorting-into-distance horse, cat-hips crouched, waiting now for waist-high boy to wake and ride it around the world. Quietly he piles wood on fire and banks ashes around to hold it for morning. Quietly he pulls on hat and wraps bandanna around and shrugs into skimpy-lined jacket. He looks at old rocking chair and tired woman slumped in it. He strides to outer door and out, leaving door open. He strides back, closing door with heel behind. He carries other burlap bag wrapped around box of candy, of fine chocolates, fancy chocolates with variegated interiors. Gently he lays this in lap of woman. Gently he takes big old shawl from wall nail and lays this over her. He stands by big old bed and looks down at snoring man. "Poor devil," he says. "Ain't fair to forget him." He takes knife from pocket, fine knife, seven-bladed knife, and lays this on blanket on bed. He picks up gloves and blows out lantern and swift as sliding moon shadow he is gone.

High high up frosty clouds scuttle across face of moon. Wind whips through topmost tips of tall pines. What is it that hurtles like hurricane far down there on upslope of last low ridge, scattering drifts, smashing through brush, snorting defiance at distance? It is flop-eared ewe-necked cat-hipped roan, iron-boned and dynamite-fueled, ramming full gallop through the dark of night. Firm in saddle is Stubby Pringle, spurs ajingle, toes atingle, out on prowl, ready to howl, heading for the dance at the schoolhouse in the valley. He is ten feet tall, great as a grizzly, and the roan is gigantic, with wings, soaring upward in thirty-foot leaps. They top out and roan rears high, pawing stars out of sky, and drops down, cat-hip hunched for fresh leap out and down.

Hold it, Stubby. Hold hard on reins. Do you see what is happening on out there in the valley?

Tiny lights that are schoolhouse windows are winking

out. Tiny dark shapes moving about are horsemen riding off, are wagons pulling away.

Moon is dropping down the sky, haloed in frosty mist. Dark gray clouds dip and swoop around sweep of horizon. Cold winds weave rustling through ice-coated bushes and trees. What is that moving slow and lonesome up snow-covered mountainside? It is a flop-eared ewe-necked cat-hipped roan, just that, nothing more, small cow pony, worn and weary, taking its rider back to clammy bunk in cold line cabin. Slumped in saddle is Stubby Pringle, head down, shoulders sagged. He is just another of far-scattered poorly-paid patched-clothes cowhands who inhabit these parts. Just that. And something more. He is the biggest thing there is in the whole wide roster of the human race. He is a man who has given of himself, of what little he has and is, to bring smiles and joy of living to others along his way.

He jogs along, slump-sagged in saddle, thinking of none of this. He is thinking of dances undanced, of floorboards unstomped, of willing women left unwhirled.

He jogs along, half-asleep in saddle, and he is thinking now of bygone Christmas seasons and of a boy born to poverty and hard work and make-do poring in flicker of firelight over ragged old Christmas picturebook. And suddenly he hears something. The tinkle of sleigh bells.

Sleigh bells?

Yes. I am telling this straight. He and roan are weaving through thick-clumped brush. Winds are sighing high overhead and on up the mountainside and lower down here they are whipping mists and snow flurries all around him. He can see nothing in mystic moving dimness. But he can hear. The tinkle of sleigh bells, faint but clear, ghostly but unmistakable. And suddenly he sees something. Movement off to the left. Swift as wind, glimmers only through brush and mist and whirling snow, but unmistakable again. Antlered heads high, frosty breath streaming, bodies rushing swift and silent, floating in flash of movement past, seeming to leap in air alone needing no touch of ground beneath. Reindeer? Yes. Reindeer strong and silent and fleet out of some far frozen northland marked on no map. Reindeer swooping down and leaping past and rising again and away, strong and effortless and fleeting. And with them, hard on their heels, almost lost in swirling snow mist of their passing, vague and formless but there, something big and bulky with runners like sleigh and flash of white beard whipping in wind and crack of long whip snapping.

Startled roan has seen something too. It stands rigid, head up, staring left and forward. Stubby Pringle, body atingle, stares too. Out of dark of night ahead, mingle with moan of wind, comes a long-drawn chuckle, deep deep chuckle, jolly and cheery and full of smiles and joy of living. And with it long-drawn words.

We-e-e-l-l-l do-o-o-ne . . . pa-a-a-artner!

Stubby Pringle shakes his head. He brushes an icicle from his nose. "An' I didn't have a single drink," he says. "Only coffee an' can't count that. Reckon I'm getting soft in the head." But he is cowman through and through, cowman through to the marrow. He can't ride on without stopping to check anything strange on his range. He swings down and leads off to the left. He fumbles in jacket pocket and finds a match. Strikes it. Holds it cupped and bends down. There they are. Unmistakable. Reindeer tracks.

Stubby Pringle stretches up tall. Stubby Pringle swings into saddle. Roan needs no slap of spurs to unleash strength in upward surge, up up up steep mountainside. It knows. There in saddle once more is Stubby Pringle, moonstruck maverick of the Triple X, all-around hard-proved hard-honed cowhand, ten feet tall, needing horse gigantic, with wings, iron-boned and dynamite-fueled, to take him home to little line cabin and some few winks of sleep before another day's hard work. . . .

Stubby Pringle slips into cold clammy bunk. He wriggles vigorous to warm blanket under and blanket over.

"Was it worth all that riding?" comes voice of Old Jake Hanlon from other bunk on other wall.

"Why, sure," says Stubby. "I had me a right good time."

All right, now. Say anything you want. I know, you know, any dong-bonged ding-busted dang-blatted fool ought to know, that icicles breaking off branches can sound to drowsy ears something like sleigh bells. That blurry eyes half-asleep can see strange things. That deer and elk make tracks like those of reindeer. That wind sighing and soughing and moaning and maundering down mountains and through piny treetops can sound like someone shaping words. But we could talk and talk and it would mean nothing to Stubby Pringle.

Stubby is wiser than we are. He knows, he will always know, who it was, plump and jolly and belly-bouncing, that spoke to him that night out on wind-whipped winter-worn mountainside.

We-e-e-l-l-l do-o-o-ne . . . pa-a-a-rt-ner!

THE WINTER OF HIS LIFE

Lewis B. Patten

In afternoon, the porch was shaded by the shabby red-brick wall of the house. The old man sat in the padded rocker, his gentle motion making a steady and unchanging squeak. Sun heat beat against the pavement beyond the small square of lawn, to rise in shimmering layers that had the effect of distorting shapes across the street. A red and white jeep tinnily announced its presence to the tune of "Yankee Doodle," and the shabby, overcrowded houses along River Street erupted unbelievable numbers of small, dirty children, who ran to the curb, nickels clutched in grimy hands, to wait for the man with the ice-cream sticks.

A truck made its throaty racket, passing the ice-cream wagon, and from long habit the old man held his breath for the children's safety. When the truck had passed, he resumed his rocking.

Inside the house he could hear the busy whir of Mary's sewing machine. He thought of Mary, his mind seeing her black-haired and young, with a devil of merriment dancing in her eyes. She was not like that any more. She was aged and weathered, as he himself was.

Time made its changes, in people as in trees and houses and cities. Those two great cottonwoods that shaded the yard had been but saplings when the old man came here. The street in front had been dusty. Quite a nice new neighborhood, it had been. Respectable.

Now there was the slaughterhouse down next to the river, reddening the stream for a half-mile below it. There were warehouses, a trucking company's dock, a beer joint on either corner. There were the familiar sounds of violence at night, the wail of the police sirens.

A car prowled along the street, hesitated before the old man's house, and finally stopped. A youngish man got out and sauntered up the walk, casually and unhurriedly opening the wrought-iron gate.

His tone was deferential. "Mr. Handy? Pete Handy?"

"Yep." This was an old story to old Pete Handy. Another newspaperman—maybe a writer of fiction. Poking around in the rubble of the past he had become interested in Pete Handy, perhaps in some happening to which Pete Handy had been witness. He wanted Pete Handy to talk.

But there was no stimulation in recalling the past now. It was too long dead, too long buried. He had hashed and rehashed too many times the things he had done, the things he had seen, until at last they assumed in his mind the unreality of lurid fiction.

This one would be no different from the others. He would ask Pete about something and, when Pete answered, would disagree, would politely argue, for some of the things he had read would not jibe with what Pete told him. Pete might say, as he had often said before, "Man, I was there," and that would draw the courteous but skeptical, "Yes, sir. I know you were. But perhaps you've forgotten. North's *Old Time Gunmen* says . . ."

The conversation took the pattern he had known it would take. He made his answers to the questions wearily, giving this only a part of his mind. The noise of the city went on, trucks, distant locomotives, the roar of a motor back in the alley and the squeal of tires against hot pavement, the interminable whir of Mary's sewing machine, the drone of a fly.

The young man went away, wearing an expression that was both puzzled and pitying, and the old man rocked away the afternoon, tall and gaunt, his skin like cracked, old leather stretched tightly over a bony frame. His eyes were faded blue, his hands blue-veined and frail on the rocker's arms. Only his mind was active.

Abilene, Dodge City, Deadwood, Tombstone. The trouble centers of the early West. Wyatt Earp, Bat Masterson, Hickok, Billy the Kid. Lincoln County War, Johnson County War. The sight of a million ponderous buffalo in one herd. Ninety-six, the old man was, and these were the things he had seen.

He had felt the kick of a Colt's single action against his palm, had seen a man fall before him—more than once. He carried bullet scars, and knife scars, and the scars of a long-horn's hooves.

His name had inspired respect, and sometimes fear. But that was past. Oddly, it was not the people he recalled now, nor the conflict. It was the everlasting peace of a thousand miles of unfenced, unpeopled land. It was the brassy blue of the sky on a hot day, the yellow rippling movement of an infinity of virgin grass. It was the freedom a man could know. . . .

A bunch of boys, teen-agers, moved past on the walk, their faces molded into the conscious pattern of toughness, their words secret and softly spoken. The old man watched them and drew their hostile stares. One of them, Joe Nemecek, he knew, for he had ridden him on his old and bony knee as a baby so many years ago. He knew Frank Sanchez, too. The others were familiar but unknown strangers, come to the community during these last ten years, the years of final deterioration. Joe Nemecek was a stranger too, impatient of age, busy with his own dark pursuits, forgetful of a childhood friendship.

Pete Handy could see the pattern of viciousness in the group, the immature, childish savagery so dangerous when the body is grown, when the mind still retains the cruelty of childhood and has not yet learned to pity.

He shrugged, and the boys passed from his sight. These things were no longer the old man's problems. There had been a time when he would have carefully catalogued each boy as a potential source of danger to himself. But that, too, was long ago, when he had been a peace officer himself.

The sewing machine stopped its whirring. In the depths of the house, in the kitchen, he heard the metallic clang of a skillet being withdrawn from a cupboard. Afterward he heard the sizzle of frying meat and smelled its sharp and friendly odor.

The shadows lengthened along the street. Brief, home-going traffic clogged the artery that was River Street, and then the quiet of dusk came down.

Frank Sanchez said: "See that old buzzard? I was in the store this morning when he came in after a loaf of bread. He carries his change in a black pocketbook, but he didn't have no change this morning. He pulled out a roll of bills two inches thick, tied with a rubber band."

Joe Nemecek broke in. "He goes for a walk every night at eight. Down to the slaughterhouse for a word with the night watchman. He skirts the truck dock and goes to the river bank, where he stands and has a smoke. Then he goes home."

A third broke in with hopeful wickedness, "Tonight?"

"All right."

Joe Nemecek felt a stir of excitement, but he felt none of the fear which the prospect of the first attack had stirred in him some months before. They were so easy—so damned easy. They crawled and they begged and they whimpered.

You got so you could feel nothing but contempt for them. It got so it was like stepping on a beetle, and you felt nothing afterward. Yet, in prospect, there was always this excitement, this tingling anticipation.

Some of them died, some recovered. You left them in the shadows limp and inert and bloody, and what happened after that didn't matter.

The planning was brief. "Down behind the slaughterhouse at eight," said Sanchez. "We'll spot him as he goes around the truck dock and slip ahead of him to the river bank."

They broke up at the corner. Sanchez and a couple of others went into the beer joint. Joe Nemecek went home.

Joe's home was one of the old ones, new at the same time the old man's house had been new. Joe's father, stolid and round-backed from a long lifetime of hard work, was puttering in the neat, postage-stamp plot of grass before the house.

There was too much age-difference between Joe and his father for there to be any closeness. Joe was seventeen; his father, sixty. Joe said, "Hi," and drew his father's habitually unfriendly stare. Jan Nemecek had no patience with the indolence and wastrel prowling of his son.

Nor did the boy feel patience for his father's stolidity, his unimaginative beast-of-burden attitude toward his work. Mainly the gulf between them was there because of Jan Nemecek's patient acceptance which he had learned in his hard sixty years—because of the restless reaching for something better which stirred in the boy.

"You better get them fool notions outa your head," Jan would say. "Livin' is work—an' work—an' more damn work. Stay away from them bums you run with. Git yourself a job."

And be like you? Joe would think. Be a damned old work horse like Sol Levy's junk horse an' stand with your head down while they lay on the whip? Starve and work and worry until you don't know anything else? Not me!

Resentment was the seed of his discontent, resentment

against monotony that could dull your mind, rob you of courage, make you grovel and beg like the ones Joe remembered, bleeding and dying in the ugly shadows.

He tramped up the flagstone walk, across the sagging porch that needed paint, and into the musty house, a tall boy, stringy from sudden, upshooting growth, wearing dirty levis and a white T-shirt.

At eight o'clock, the old man laid aside his paper and got up. His wife looked at him over the sock she was darning in her grave and unsmiling way, and weariness showed in her eyes, weariness that never left her these days. "You shouldn't walk alone in the dark. This is not the same neighborhood that it was when we came here. There's a bad gang of boys . . ."

"Joe Nemecek? I used to ride him on my knee, and often enough found it wet afterward. Frank Sanchez? I taught him how to catch a baseball. The others? They're not bad, Mary. They're only young."

The things that youth felt and dreamed did not change with the years. The heady wine of adventure stirred forever in their growing and active bodies. They needed something to pit themselves against, and in the old days these things had been plentiful. Then it had been adventure just to stay alive. There had been the long cattle drives, monotonous and back-breaking to be sure, but filled with danger and excitement. Living had been a battle against the elements. Running cattle had been a battle against those who would enrich themselves at your expense. Youth needed something to fight.

Pete Handy could remember Dodge, filled to overflowing with trail hands no older than Joe Nemecek, wanting perhaps the same things Joe Nemecek wanted: a drink, a fight, a spin of the wheel. Excitement.

There was little enough of that to be had any more. The country was tamed. You conformed to the pattern or you ran afoul of the law. Yet civilization could not still the eternal longings of youth. . . .

The night was cool, and the old man took a light sweater from its hook in the hall closet. His hand touched something hard and smooth, groped, and drew out the worn leather cartridge belt and holstered .45. The tools of his trade. He fingered them for a moment, then hung them back in the closet. They had an unfamiliar feel in his hands, an unfamiliar and slightly unpleasant feel.

He went out into the cool darkness, hardly hearing the clang of the iron gate behind him.

Slowly he walked, his mind fallow and inactive. The slaughterhouse was a dim and untidy shape of clustered buildings against the aurora cast in the sky by the city's lights. The truck dock was brightly lighted, busy and noisy. Great, long trailers stood backed against it, side by side. On both corners the beer joints put the red neon glow of their signs on walk and pavement. The river lifted its cool, dank smell.

At the slaughterhouse, a dark shape waited behind the chainlink gate, shadowy and still. The light and pleasant odor of pipe tobacco smoke came to Pete Handy and he said: "Hello, Ben. How does it go tonight?"

"All right. Quiet."

Pete Handy packed his pipe and lighted it. They smoked in silence for a while, companionable silence. The breeze shifted, bringing the smell of the slaughterhouse, and even this had the power to stir Pete Handy's memory. The smell of death. The smell of ten thousand naked and blackened buffalo carcasses rotting slowly on the plain. The smell that hung over the land the spring after the big die-up.

He murmured something to Ben and moved away, stiff and old in the winter of his life. He skirted the truck dock at the circle of its light and took the narrow path through the brush to the river's bank.

Out of his past came the old tingle of premonition, the sixth sense that had half a dozen times saved his life. It was uneasiness, it was a stirring in the follicles of the hair that grew on the back of his neck. An animal sense, one he had not felt for fifty years.

This time he reasoned it away. The smell of the slaughterhouse with its attendant memories had caused it. It was nothing. This was the city.

Sudden movement came from the shadows. Against the light on the water's surface was dimly silhouetted the shape of a man—no, not a man, but one of those mixtures of man and boy. Man's body, boy's mind. Man's strength, boy's cruelty.

A voice, clear and soft, said: "All right. Get him!"

They came in from all sides, uncounted by the old man, who stepped back, whose hand went automatically from some ancient prompting to his side where no gun hung tonight.

A fist slammed against his jaw, snapped his head to one side. He was slow with age, but all of the old, remembered things came back. Groggy, he still went through the motions, and while there was no hope in him, neither was there fear, or even regret.

Waiting in the high willows beside the whispering river, Frank Sanchez asked: "Who the hell is he anyway? Where's he get his money? Old-age pension?"

The tension was upon Joe Nemecek, the tension that always preceded these things. "What difference does it make? He used to be some kind of a cop. Maybe he's got a cop's pension." Cop or not, he would die, cringing and begging against the hard-eyed lack of pity that surrounded him. His body would go into the river and would catch on the rocks beneath the viaduct three hundred yards below.

Movement stirred along the path, and the old man came out of the willows. Frank Sanchez said: "All right. Get him!"

Frank moved close, and his fist slammed against the side of the old man's jaw. Joe Nemecek came in, wanting part of this, and was briefly surprised at the way the old man stood, spraddle-legged, a little crouched. A couple of the gang moved behind him to close the path, to cut off retreat; but there was no retreat in the old man.

Even as this flurry of action moved toward its inevitable climax, Joe Nemecek could feel surprise at this, for it was something new. There was only silence from the old man, the harsh bellows of his breath dragging in and out. Frank Sanchez moved his body too close, and the old man's knee came savagely into Frank's crotch and put him down on the ground, rolling and groaning.

They beat the old man inexorably backward. Joe came close, his hands fisted and ready to strike. Suddenly it was very important to him that he make the old man break, that he make him beg and crawl as the others had done.

The dull shine of the river put its glow on the old man's face, put its pinpoint of sparkle in the fierce old eyes— uncompromising, bitter, yet showing some strange and savage pleasure. Fear had not touched him, and suddenly Joe Nemecek knew that fear would never touch him.

Joe dropped his hands and yelled: "Stop it! Cut it out!"

Frank Sanchez, rising, snarled, "What the hell?" and came in, fisting a rock the size of an orange in his hand. The rock came against the side of the old man's head with a sodden crack, and Pete Handy tottered and fell, limp on the wet sand. Frank straddled him immediately, drawing back the fisted rock.

The brutality of it infected them all, lusting and bright-eyed, all save Joe Nemecek. He caught the upraised hand of Sanchez and twisted the rock away. He brought it around against Frank's head, and felt the slump of the older boy. He flung Sanchez aside, then stood himself straddling the old man, but facing the gang.

He did not know what to say; he could not even fathom his own foolishness. "He wasn't afraid," he said. "He didn't beg. Let him alone."

It was a tight and touchy moment, but Joe Nemecek found an intoxicating excitement in it. This was something new for Joe.

The way the old man stood, unyielding, turned them back, turned them unsure and boyish again and sent them slinking away. Joe knelt over the limp and lifeless body of the old man, feeling pity for the first time in his life.

A siren wailed distantly. Frank Sanchez rose, cursed him, and went away. The siren wailed again. Joe looked at the old man. Joe hated cops, and this one had been a cop. Yet, for an instant, he could not help wondering how the years had been with this one, what he had done and what he had seen, what he had learned that had made him able to die so courageously. For an instant he imagined himself, Joe Nemecek, blue-clad, behind the wheel of that distant police car, no work horse, but a man with a job to do.

He rose and walked toward home, frowning.

The old man lay by the river bank and stared sightlessly at the sky. He had found again the everlasting peace of a thousand miles of unfenced, unpeopled land.

ISLEY'S STRANGER

Clay Fisher

He rode a mule. He was middling tall, middling spare, middling young. He wore a soft dark curly beard. His bedroll was one thready army blanket wound round a coffee can, tin cup, plate, razor, camp ax, Bible, copy of the *Rubáiyát*, a mouth harp, some other few treasures of like necessity in the wilderness.

Of course, Isley didn't see all those things when the drifter rode up to his fire that night on Wolf Mountain flats. They came out later, after Isley had asked him to light down and dig in, the same as any decent man would do with a stranger riding up on him out of the dark and thirty miles from the next shelter. Isley always denied that he was smote with Christian charity, sweet reason, or unbounding brother love in issuing the invite. It was simply that nobody turns anybody away out on the Wyoming range in late fall. Not

with a norther building over Tongue River at twilight and
the wind beginning to snap like a trapped weasel come full
dark. No, sir. Not, especially, when that somebody looks at
you with eyes that would make a kicked hound seem happy
and asks only to warm his hands and hear a friendly voice
before riding on.

Well, Isley had a snug place. Anyway, it was for a line
rider working alone in that big country. Isley could tell you
that holes were hard to find out there in the wide open. And
this one he had was ample big for two, or so he figured.

It was a sort of outcrop of the base rock, making a
three-sided room at the top of a long, rolling swell of ground
about midway of the twenty-mile flats. It had been poled
and sodded over by some riders before Isley and was not the
poorest place in that county to bed down by several. Oh,
what the heck, it wasn't the Brown Hotel in Denver, or even
the Drover's in Cheyenne. Sure, the years had washed the
roof sods. And, sure, in a hard rain you had to wear your hat
tipped back to keep the drip from spiking you down the
nape of your shirt collar. But the three rock sides were
airtight and the open side was south-facing. Likewise, the
old grass roof, seepy or not, still cut out 90 and 9 per cent
of the wind. Besides, it wasn't raining that night or about to.
Moreover, Isley was a man who would see the sun with his
head in a charcoal sack during an eclipse. It wasn't any
effort, then, for him to ease up off his hunkers, step around
the fire, bat the smoke out of his eyes, grin shy, and say:

"Warm your hands, hell, stranger; unrope your bedroll
and move in!"

They hit it off from scratch.

While the wanderer ate the grub Isley insisted on fixing
for him—eating wasn't exactly what he did with it; it was
more like inhaling—the little K-Bar hand had a chance to
study his company. Usually Isley was pretty fair at sizing a
man, but this one had him winging. Was he tall? No, he
wasn't tall. Was he short then? No, you wouldn't say he was
exactly short either. Middling, that's what he was. What kind

of a face then? Long? Thin? Square? Horsy? Fine? Handsome? Ugly? No, none of these things, and all of them too.
He just had a face. It was like his build, just middling. So it
went; the longer Isley looked at him, the less he saw that he
could hang a guess on. With one flicker of the fire he looked
sissy as skim milk. Then, with the next, he looked gritty as
fish eggs rolled in sand. Cock your head one way and the
fellow seemed so helpless he couldn't drive nails in a snow-
bank. Cock it the other and he appeared like he might haul
hell out of its shuck. Isley decided he wouldn't bet either
way on him in a tight election. One thing was certain,
though. And that thing Isley would take bets on all winter.
This curly-bearded boy hadn't been raised on the short
grass. He wouldn't know a whiffle-tree from a wagon tongue
or a whey-belly bull from a bred heifer. He was as out of
place in Wyoming as a cow on a front porch.

Isley was somewhat startled, then, when his guest got
down the final mouthful of beans, reached for a refill from
the coffeepot, and said quietly:

"There's bad trouble hereabouts, is there not, friend?"

Well, there was for a fact, but Isley couldn't see how this
fellow, who looked like an out-of-work schoolteacher riding
a long ways between jobs, could know anything about *that*
kind of trouble.

"How come you to know that?" he asked. "It sure don't
look to me like trouble would be in your line. No offense,
mind you, mister. But around here—well, put it this way—
there ain't nobody looking up the trouble we got. Most of us
does our best to peer over it or around it. What's your stake
in the Wolf Mountain War, pardner?"

"Is that what it's called?" the other said softly. Then,
with that sweet-sad smile which lighted up his pale face like
candle shine, "Isn't it wonderful what pretty names men can
think up for such ugly things? 'The Wolf Mountain War.' It
has alliteration, poetry, intrigue, beauty . . ."

Isley began to get a little edgy. This bearded one he had
invited in out of the wind was not quite all he ought to be,

he decided. He had best move careful. Sometimes these nutty ones were harmless; other times they would kill you quicker than anthrax juice.

He tried sending a return smile with his reply.

"Well, yes, whatever you say, friend. It's just another fight over grass and water, whatever you want to call it for a name. There's them as has the range and them as wants the range. It don't change none."

"Which side are you on, Isley?"

"Well, now, you might say that—" Isley broke off to stare at him. "*Isley?*" he said. "How'd you know my name?"

The stranger looked uncomfortable, just for a moment. He appeared to glance around as though stalling for a good answer. Then he nodded and pointed to Isley's saddle propped against the rear wall.

"I read it on your stirrup fender just now."

Isley frowned. He looked over at the saddle. Even knowing where he had worked in that *T-o-m I-s-l-e-y* with copper-head rivets and a starnose punch, he couldn't see it. It lay up under the fender on the saddle skirt about an inch or so, purposely put there so he could reveal it to prove ownership in case somebody borrowed it without asking.

"Pretty good eyes," he said to the stranger. "That's mighty small print, considering it's got to be read through a quarter inch of skirting leather."

The stranger only smiled.

"The skirt is curled a little, Isley, and the rivets catch the firelight. Call it that, plus a blind-luck guess."

The small puncher was not to be put off.

"Well," he said, "if you're such a powerful good blind-luck guesser, answer me this: how'd you know to call me Isley, instead of Tom?"

"Does it matter? Would you prefer Tom?"

"No, hell, no, that ain't what I mean. Everybody calls me Isley. I ain't been called Tom in twenty years." His querulously knit brows drew in closer yet. "And by the way," he added, "while it ain't custom to ask handles in these parts, I never did cotton to being put to the social disadvantage. Makes a man feel he ain't been give his full and equal American rights. I mean, where the other feller knows who you are, but you ain't any idea who he might be. You follow me, friend?"

"You wish me to give you a name. Something you can call me. Something more tangible than friend."

"No, it don't have to be nothing more tangle-able than friend. Friend will do fine. I ain't trying to trap you."

"I know you aren't, Isley. I will tell you what. You call me Eben."

"Eben? That's an off-trail name. I never heard of it."

"It's an old Hebrew name, Isley."

"Oh? I ain't heard of them neither. Sounds like a southern tribe. Maybe Kioway or Comanche strain. Up here we got mostly Sioux and Cheyenne."

"The Hebrews weren't Indians exactly, though they were nomadic and fierce fighters. We call them Jews today."

"Oh, sure. Now, I knowed that."

"Of course you did."

They sat silent a spell, then Isley nodded.

"Well, Eben she is. Eben what?"

"Just Eben."

"You mean like I'm just Isley?"

"Why not?"

"No good reason." Isley shrugged it off, while still bothered by it. "Well," he said, "that brings us back to where we started. How come you knowed about our trouble up here? And how come you got so far into the country without crossing trails with one side or the other? I would say this would be about the onhealthiest climate for strangers since the Grahams and Tewkesburys had at it down in Arizony Territory. I don't see how you got ten miles past Casper, let alone clear up here into the Big Horn country."

Eben laughed. It was a quiet laugh, soft and friendly.

"You've provided material to keep us up all night," he

said. "Let us just say that I go where trouble is and that I know how to fin my way to it."

Isley squinted at him, his own voice soft with seriousness.

"You're right; we'd best turn in. As for you and finding trouble, I got just this one thing to say: I hope you're as good at sloping away from it as you are at stumbling onto it."

The other nodded thoughtfully, face sad again.

"Then this Wolf Mountain War is as bad as I believed," he said.

"Mister," replied Isley, "when you have put your foot into this mess, you have not just stepped into *anybody's* cow chip; you have lit with both brogans square in the middle of granddaddy pasture flapjack of them all."

"Colorful"—Eben smiled wryly—"but entirely accurate, I fear. I hope I'm not too late."

"For what?" asked Isley. "It can't be stopped, for it's already started."

"I didn't mean too late to stop it. I meant too late to see justice done. That's the way I was in Pleasant Valley—too late, too late . . ."

He let it trail off, as Isley's eyes first widened, then narrowed, with suspicion.

"You was *there*?" he said. "In that Graham-Tewkesbury feud?"

"I was there. I was not in the feud."

"Say," said Isley enthusiastically, curiosity overcoming doubt, "who the hell won that thing, anyways—the sheepmen or the cattlemen? Naturally we're some interested, seeings how we got the same breed of cat to skin up here."

"Neither side won," said Eben. "Neither side ever wins a war. The best that can be done is that some good comes out of the bad, that in some small way the rights of the innocent survive."

Isley, like most simple men of his time, had had the Bible read to him in his youth. Now he nodded again.

"You mean 'the meek shall inherit the earth?' " he asked.

"That's close," admitted his companion. "But they never inherit anything but the sins of the strong, unless they have help in time. That's what worries me. There's always so much trouble and so little time."

"That all you do, mister? Go around looking for trouble to mix into?"

"It's enough, Isley." The other smiled sadly. "Believe me, it is enough."

The little cowboy shook his head.

"You know something, Eben," he said honestly. "I think you're a mite touched."

The pale youth sighed, his soft curls moving in assent. "Do you know something, Isley?" he answered. "I have never been to any place where the men did not say the same thing. . . ."

Next morning the early snow clouds were still lying heavy to the north, but the wind had quieted. Breakfast was a lot cheerier than last night's supper, and it turned out the newcomer wasn't such a nut as Isley had figured. He wasn't looking for trouble at all but for a job the same as everybody else. What he really wanted was some place to hole in for the winter. He asked Isley about employment prospects at the K-Bar and was informed they were somewhat scanter than bee tracks in a blizzard. Especially, said Isley, for a boy who looked as though he had never been caught on the blister end of a shovel.

Eben assured the little rider that he could work, and Isley, more to show him to the other hands than thinking Old Man Reston would put him on, agreed to let him ride along in with him to the home place. Once there, though, things took an odd turn and Isley was right back to being confused about his discovery.

As far as the other hands went, they didn't make much of the stranger. They thought he looked as though he had wintered pretty hard last year, hadn't come on with the spring grass. Most figured he wouldn't make it through the cold snap. To the man they allowed that the Old Man would eat him alive. That is, providing he showed the gall to go on up to the big house and insult the old devil's intelligence by telling him to his bare face that he aimed to hit him for work. A cow ranch in October is no place to be looking for gainful employment. The fact this dauncy stray didn't know that stamped him a real rare tinhorn. Naturally the whole bunch traipsed up to the house and spied through the front-room window to see the murder committed. Isley got so choused up over the roostering the boys were giving his protégé that, in a moment of sheer inspiration, he offered to cover all Reston money in the crowd. He was just talking, but his pals decided to charge him for the privilege. By the time he had taken the last bet, he was in hock for his wages up to the spring roundup. And, by the time he had gotten up to the house door with Eben in tow, he would have gladly given twice over that amount to be back out on the Wolf Mountain flats or, indeed, any other place as many miles from the K-Bar owner's notoriously lively temperament.

He was stuck, though, and would not squeal. With more courage than Custer's bugler blowing the second charge at the Little Big Horn, he raised his hand and rapped on the ranch house door. He did bolster himself with an under-breath blasphemy, however, and Eben shook his head and said, "Take not the name of the Lord thy God in vain, Isley. Remember, your strength is as the strength of ten." Isley shot him a curdled look. Then he glanced up at the sky. "Lord, Lord," he said, "what have I done to deserve this?" He didn't get any answer from above but did draw one from within. It suggested in sulphuric terms that they come in and close the door after them. As well, it promised corporal punishment for any corral mud or shred of critter matter stomped into the living-room rug or any time consumed, past sixty seconds, in stating the grievance, taking no for an answer, and getting the hell back outside where they belonged.

Since the offer was delivered in the range bull's bellow

generally associated with H. F. Reston, Senior, in one of his
mellower states, Isley hastened to take it up.

"Mr. Reston," he said, once safe inside and the door
heeled shut, "this here is Eben, and he's looking for work."

Henry Reston turned red, then white. He made a sound
like a sow grizzly about to charge. Then he strangled it,
waited for his teeth to loosen their clamp on one another,
waved toward the door, and said, "Well, he couldn't be
looking for it in better company, Isley. Good luck to the both
of you."

"What?" said Isley in a smothered way.

"You heard me. And don't slam the door on your way
out."

"But, Mr. Reston, sir—"

"Isley." The other man got up from his desk. He was the
size of an aged buffalo and the sweetness too. "You remember damned well what I told you when you drug that last
bum in here. Now you want to run a rest camp for all the
drifters and sick stock that comes blowing into the barnyard
with every first cold spell, you hop right to it. I'm trying to
run a cow ranch, not a winter resort. Now you get that
pilgrim out of here. You come back in twenty minutes. I'll
have your check."

Isley was a man who would go so far. He wasn't a fighter,
but he didn't push too well. When he got his tail up and
dropped his horns, he would stand his ground with most.

"I'll wait for it right here," he said.

"Why, you banty-legged little sparrow hawk, who the
hell do you think you're telling what you'll do? *Out!*"

"*Mr. Reston* . . ." The stranger said it so quietly that it
hit into the angry air louder than a yell. "Mr. Reston," he
went on, "you're frightened. There is no call to take out your
fears on Isley. Why not try me?"

"*You?*"

The Old Man just stared at him.

Isley wished he was far, far away. He felt very foolish
right then. He couldn't agree more with the way the Old

Man had said, "You." Here was this pale-faced, skinny drifter with the downy beard, soft eyes, quiet voice, and sweet smile standing there in his rags and tatters and patches and, worst of all, his farmer's run-over flat boots; here he was standing there looking like something the cat would have drug in but didn't have the nerve to; and here he was standing there with all that going against him and still telling the biggest cattleman in Big Horn Basin to wind up and have a try at *him*! Well, Isley thought, in just about two seconds the Old Man was going to tie into him with a list of words that would raise a blood blister on a rawhide boot. That is, if he didn't just reach in the desk drawer, fetch out his pistol, and shoot him dead on the spot.

But Isley was only beginning to be wrong.

"Well," breathed Henry Reston at last, "try you, eh?" He rumbled across the room to come to a halt in front of the slight and silent mule rider. He loomed wide as a barn door, tall as a wagon tongue. But he didn't fall in on the poor devil the way Isley had feared. He just studied him with a very curious light in his faded blue eyes and finally added, "And just what, in God's name, would you suggest I try you *at*?"

"Anything. Anything at all."

Reston nodded. "Pretty big order."

The other returned the nod. "Would a man like you take a small order?"

The owner of the K-Bar jutted his jaw. "You ain't what you let on to be," he challenged. "What do you want here?"

"What Isley told you—a job."

"What brought you here?"

"There's trouble here."

"You like trouble?"

"No."

"Maybe you're a troublemaker."

"No. I make peace when I can."

"And when you can't?"

"I still try."

"You think me giving you a winter's work is going to help you along that path?"

"Yes. Otherwise I wouldn't be here."

Again Henry Reston studied him. Reston was not, like Tom Isley, a simple man. He was a very complicated and powerful and driving man, and a dangerous man too.

"I make lot of noise when I'm riled," he said to the drifter. "Don't let that fool you. I'm a thinking man."

"If you weren't," said the other, "I wouldn't be asking to work for you. I know what you are."

"But I don't know what you are, eh, is that it?"

"No, I'm just a man looking for work. I always pay my way. If there's no work for me, I travel on. I don't stay where there's no job to do."

"Well, there's no job for you here in Big Horn Basin."

"You mean not that you know of."

"By God! Don't try to tell me what I mean, you ragamuffin!"

"What we are afraid of we abuse. Why do you fear me?"

Reston looked at him, startled.

"I? Fear you? You're crazy. You're not right in the head. I'm Henry F. Reston. I own this damned country!"

"I know. That's why I'm here."

"Now what the devil do you mean by that?"

"Would the men in the valley give me work? They're poor. They haven't enough for themselves."

"How the hell do you know about the men in the valley?"

"I told you, Mr. Reston. There's trouble here. It's why I came. Now will you give me work so that I may stay?"

"No! I'm damned if I will. Get out. The both of you!"

Isley started to sneak for the door, but Eben reached out and touched him on the arm. "Wait," he said.

"By God!" roared Reston, and started for the desk drawer.

But Eben stopped him, too, as easily as he had Isley.

"Don't open the drawer," he said. "You don't need a pistol. A pistol won't help you."

Reston came around slowly. To Isley's amazement he

showed real concern. This white-faced tumbleweed had him winging.

"Won't help me what?" he asked scowlingly.

"Decide about me."

"Oh? Well, now, you ain't told me yet what it is I've got to decide about you. Except maybe whether to kill you or have you horsewhipped or drug on a rope twice around the bunkhouse. Now you tell me what needs deciding past that."

"I want work."

Henry Reston started to turn red again, and Isley thought he would go for the drawer after all. But he did not.

"So you want work?" he said. "And you claim you can do anything? And you got the cheek to hair up to me and say, slick and flip, 'Try me.' Well, all right, by God, I'll do it. Isley . . ."

"Yes, sir, Mr. Reston?"

"Go put that Black Bean horse in the bronc chute. Hang the bucking rig on him and clear out the corral."

"Good Lord, Mr. Reston, that outlaw ain't been rode since he stomped Charlie Tackaberry. He's ruint three men and—"

"You want your job back, Isley, saddle him."

"But—"

"Right now."

"No, sir," Isley began, hating to face the cold with no job, but knowing he couldn't be party to feeding the mule rider to Black Bean. "I don't reckon I need your pay, Mr. Reston. Me and Eben will make out. Come on, Ebe."

He began to back out, but Eben shook his head.

"We need the work, Isley. Go saddle the horse."

"You don't know this devil! He's a killer."

"I've faced them before, Isley. Lots of them. Saddle him."

"You, a bronc stomper? Never. I bet you ain't been on a bucker in your whole life."

"I wasn't talking about horses, Isley, but about killers."

"No, sir," insisted the little cowboy stoutly. "I ain't a-

going to do it. Black Bean will chew you up fine. It ain't
worth it to do it for a miserable winter's keep. Let's go."
    Eben took hold of his arm again. Isley felt the grip. It
took him like the talons of an eagle. Eben nodded.
    "Isley," he said softly, *"saddle the horse."*

    The K-Bar hands got the old horse in the chute and
saddled without anybody getting crippled. He had been
named Black Bean from the Texas Ranger story of Bigfoot
Wallace, where the Mexican general made the captive rangers draw a bean each, from a pottery jug of mixed black and
white ones, and the boys who got white beans lived and the
boys who got black ones got shot. It was a good name for that
old horse.
    Isley didn't know what to expect of his friend by now.
But he knew of long experience what to expect of Black
Bean. The poor drifter would have stood a better chance
going against the Mexican firing squad.
    The other K-Bar boys *thought* they knew what was
bound to take place. This dude very plainly had never been
far enough around the teacup to find the handle. He was
scarce man enough to climb over the bronc chute to get on
Black Bean, let alone to stay on him long enough for them
to get the blindfold off and the gate swung open.
    But Isley wasn't off the pace as far as that. He knew
Eben had *something* in mind. And when the thin youth had
scrambled over the chute poles and more fallen then fitted
into the bucking saddle, the other hands sensed this too.
They quit roostering and hoorawing the pilgrim and got
downright quiet. One or two—Gant Callahan and Deece
McKayne, first off—actually tried helping at the last. Grant
said, "Listen, buddy, don't try to stay with him. Just flop off
the minute he gets clear of the gates. We'll scoop you up
'fore he can turn on you." Deece hung over the chute bars
and whispered his advice, but Isley, holding Black Bean's
head, heard him. What he said was, "See that top bar crost
the gateposts? Reach for it the minute Isley whips off the

blind. Hoss will go right on out from under you, and all you got to is skin on up over the pole and set tight. You'll get spurred some by the boys, but I don't want to be buryin' you in a feed sack, you hear?"

Fact was that, between Gant and Deece giving him last-minute prayers and the other boys getting quiet, the whole operation slowed down to where the Old Man yelled at Isley to pull the blind and for Wil Henniger to jerk the gate pin or get out of the way and leave somebody else do it—while they were on their ways up to the big house to pick up their pay. Being October, and with that early blizzard threatening, he had them where the hair was short. Wil yelled out, "Powder River, let 'er buck!" and flung wide the gate. Isley pulled the blind and jumped for his life.

Well, what followed was the biggest quiet since Giggles La Chance decided to show up for Church on Easter Sunday. And seeing that Giggles hadn't heard a preacher, wore a hat, or been seen abroad in daylight for six years, that was some quiet.

What Black Bean did sure enough deserved the tribute, however. And every bit as much as Giggles La Chance.

Moreover, there was a connection between the two; the devil seemed involved, somehow, with both decisions.

That old horse, which had stomped more good riders into the corral droppings than any sunfisher since the Strawberry Roan, came out of that bucking chute on a sidesaddle trot, mincy and simpery as an old-maid bell mare. He went around the corral bowing his neck and blowing out through his nostrils and rolling back those wally-mean eyes of his soft and dewy as a cow elk with a new calf. He made the circuit once around and brought up back in front of the chute gate and stopped and spread out and stood like a five-gaited Kentucky saddlebred on the show stand; and that big quiet got so deep-still that when Dutch Hafner let out his held wind and said, "*Great Gawd Almighty!*" you'd have thought he'd shot off a cannon in a cemetery four o'clock on Good Friday morning.

Isley jumped and said, "Here, don't beller in a man's ear

trumpet thataway!" and then got down off the chute fence and wandered off across the ranch lot, talking to himself.

The others weren't much better off, but it was Old Man Reston who took it hardest of all.

That horse had meant a lot to him. He'd always sort of looked up to him. He was a great deal the same temperament as Old Henry. Mean and tough and smart and fearing neither God nor devil nor any likeness of either which walked on two legs. Now there he was out there making moony eyes at the seedy drifter and damn fools out of Henry F. Reston and the whole K-Bar crew.

It never occurred to Old Henry, as it later did to Isley, that Eben had done about the same thing to him, Reston, in his living room up to the ranch house as he'd done to Black Bean in the bucking chute: which was to buffalo him out of a full gallop right down to a dead walk, without raising either voice or hand to do it. But by the time Isley got this figured out, there wasn't much of a way to use the information. Old Henry, cast down by losing his outlaw horse and made powerful uneasy by the whole performance, had given Isley his pay and Eben fifteen dollars for his ride—the normal fee for bronc breaking in those parts—and asked them both to be off the K-Bar by sunset. Eben had offered the fifteen dollars to the Old Man for Black Bean when he had heard him order Deece and Gant to take the old horse out and shoot him for wolf bait. Old Henry had allowed it was a Pecos swap to take anything for such a shambles, by which he meant an outright steal. But he was always closer with a dollar than the satin over a cancan dancer's seat, and so he took the deal, throwing in the bucking saddle, a good split-ear bridle, and a week's grub in a greasy sack to boot. It was maybe an hour short of sundown when Isley, riding Eben's mule, and Eben astride the denatured killer, Black Bean, came to the west line of the K-Bar, in company with their escort.

"Well," said Dutch Hafner, "yonder's Bull Pine. Good luck, but don't come back."

Isley looked down into the basin of the Big Horn,

sweeping from the foot of the ridge upon which they sat their horses, as far as the eye might reach, westward to Cody, Pitchfork, Meeteetse, and the backing saw teeth of the Absoroka Range. The little puncher shook his head, sad, like any man, to be leaving home at only age forty-four.

"I dunno, Dutch," he mourned, "what's to become of us? There ain't no work in Bull Pine. Not for a cow hand. Not, especially, for a K-Bar cowhand."

"That's the gospel, Isley," said Deece McKayne helpfully. "Fact is, was I you, I wouldn't scarce dast go inter Bull Pine, let alone inquire after work."

Gant Callahan, the third member of the honor guard, nodded his full agreement. "You cain't argue them marbles, Isley. Bull Pine ain't hardly nothing but one big sheep camp. I wisht there was something I could add to what Dutch has said, but there ain't. So good luck, and ride wide around them woolies."

Isley nodded back in misery. "My craw's so shrunk it wouldn't chamber a piece of pea gravel," he said. "I feel yellow as mustard without the bite."

"Yellow, hell!" snapped big Dutch, glaring at Deece and Gant. "These two idjuts ain't to be took serious, Isley. Somebody poured their brains in with a teaspoon and got his arm joggled at that. Ain't no sheepman going to go at a cowboy in broad day, and you'll find work over yonder in the Pitchfork country. Lots of ranches there."

"Sure," said Isley, "and every one of them on the sharp lookout for a broke-down line rider and a pale-face mule wrangler to put on for the winter. Well, anyways, so long."

The three K-Bar hands raised their gloves in a mutually waved "So long, Isley" and turned their horses back for the snug home-place bunkhouse. Isley pushed up the collar of his worn blanket coat. The wind was beginning to spit a little sleet out of the north. It was hardly an hour's ride down the ridge and out over the flat to Bull Pine. Barring that, the next settlement—in cow country—was Greybull, on the river. That would take them till midnight to reach, and if this sleet turned to snow and came on thick—well, the hell with that; they had no choice. A K-Bar cowboy's chances in a blue norther were better than he could expect in a small-flock sheep town like Bull Pine. Shivering, he turned to Eben.

"Come on," he said. "We got a six-hour ride."

The gentle drifter held back, shading his eyes and peering out across the basin. "Strange," he said, "it doesn't appear to be that far."

"Whoa up!" said Isley, suddenly alarmed. "What don't appear to be that far?"

"Why, Bull Pine, of course," replied the other, with his sad, soft smile. "Where else would we go?"

Isley could think of several places, one of them a sight warmer than the scraggly ridge they were sitting on. But he didn't want to be mean or small with the helpless pilgrim, no matter he had gotten him sacked and ordered off the K-Bar for good. So he didn't mention any of the options but only shivered again and made a wry face and said edgily:

"I'd ought to know better than to ask, Ebe, but why for we want to go to Bull Pine?"

"Because," said the bearded wanderer, "that's where the trouble is."

Eben was right. Bull Pine was where the trouble was.

All the past summer and preceding spring the cattlemen had harassed the flocks of the sheepmen in the lush pastures of the high country around the basin. Parts of flocks and whole flocks had been stampeded and run to death. Some had been put over cliffs. Some cascaded into the creeks. Others just plain chased till their hearts stopped. Nor had it been all sheep. A Basque herder had died and five Valley men had been hurt defending their flocks. So far no cattleman had died, or even been hit, for it was they who always made the first jump and mostly at night. Now the sheepmen had had all they meant to take.

Those high country pastures were 90 percent government land, and the sheep had just as much right to them as the cattle. More right, really, because they were better suited to use by sheep than cattle. But the country, once so open and free and plenty for all, was filling up. Even in the twenty years since Isley was young the Big Horn Basin had grown six new towns and God alone knew how many up-creek, shoestring cattle ranches. The sheep had come in late, though, only about ten years back. Bull Pine was the first, and sole, sheep town in northwest Wyoming, and it wasn't yet five years old. The cattlemen, headed by Old Henry Reston, meant to see that it didn't get another five years older too. And Isley knew what Eben couldn't possibly know: that the early blizzard threatening now by the hour was all the cattlemen had been waiting for. Behind its cover they meant to sweep down on Bull Pine in a fierce raid of the haying pens and winter sheds along the river. These shelters had been built in a community effort of the valley sheep ranchers working together to accomplish what no two or three or ten of them could do working alone. They were a livestockmen's curiosity known about as far away as Colorado, Utah, and Montana. They had proved unbelievably successful, and if allowed to continue uncontested, it might just be that the concept of winter-feeding sheep in that country would catch on. If it did, half the honest cattlemen in Wyoming could be out of business. On the opposite hand, if some natural disaster should strike the Bull Pine feed lots—say, like the fences giving way in a bad snowstorm—why, then the idea of winter-feeding sheep in the valley would suffer a setback like nothing since old Brigham Young's sea gulls had sailed into those Mormon crickets down by Deseret.

Knowing what he knew of the cattlemen's plan to aid nature in this matter of blowing over the sheepmen's fences during the first hard blizzard, Isley followed Eben into Bull Pine with all ten fingers and his main toes crossed.

By good luck they took a wrong turn or two of the trail on the way down off the ridge. Well, it wasn't exactly luck either. Isley had something to do with it. But, no matter, when they came into Bull Pine it was so dark a man needed both hands to find his nose. Isley was more than content to have it so. Also, he would have been well pleased to have been allowed to stay out in front of the general store, holding the mounts, while Eben went within to seek the loan of some kind soul's shearing shed to get in out of the wind and snow for the night. But Eben said no, that what he had in mind would require Isley's presence. The latter would simply have to gird up his courage and come along.

Groaning, the little K-Bar puncher got down. From the number of horses standing humpbacked to the wind at the hitch rail, half the sheepmen in the basin must be inside. That they would be so, rather than home getting set to hay their sheep through the coming storm, worried Isley a great deal. Could it be that the Bull Piners had some warning of the cattlemen's advance? Was this a council of range war they were stepping into the middle of? Isley shivered.

"Ebe," he pleaded, "please leave me stay out here and keep our stock company. Me and them sheepmen ain't nothing in common saving for two legs and one head and maybe so a kind word for motherhood. Now, be a good feller, and rustle on in there by your ownself and line us up a woodshed or sheep pen or hayrick to hole up in for the night."

Eben shook his head. "No," he insisted, "you must come in with me. You are essential to the entire situation."

Isley shivered again but stood resolute. "Listen, Ebe," he warned, "this here blizzard is a-going to swarm down the valley like Grant through Cumberland Gap. We don't get under cover we're going to be froze as the back of a bronze statue's lap. Or like them poor sheep when Old Henry and his boys busts them loose in the dark of dawn tomorroy."

"It's Old Henry and the others I'm thinking of," said Eben quietly. "We must be ready for them. Come along."

But Isley cowered back. "Ebe," he said, "I know that kicking never done nobody but a mule no good. Still, I got to plead self-defense here. So don't crowd me. I'm all rared back, and I ain't a-going in there conscious."

He actually drew up one wrinkled boot as though he would take a swing at the drifter. But Eben only smiled and, for the second time, put his thin hand on Isley's arm. Isley felt the power of those slender fingers. They closed on his arm, and his will, like a No. 6 lynx trap.

"Come on, Isley," said the soft voice, "I need your testimony." And Isley groaned once more and put his head down into his collar as deep as it would go and followed his ragged guide into the Bull Pine General Store.

"Friends," announced Eben, holding up his hands as the startled sheepmen looked up at him from their places around the possum-belly stove, "Brother Isley and I have come from afar to help you in your hour of need. Please hear us out."

"That bent-legged little stray," dissented one member immediately, "never come from no place to help no sheepman. I smell cowboy! Fetch a rope, men."

Eben gestured hurriedly, but it did no good. A second valley man growled, "Ain't that Tom Isley as works for Henry Reston?" And a third gnarled herder rasped, "You bet it is! Never mind the rope, boys. I'll knock his head open, barehanded."

The group surged forward, the hairy giant who had spoken last in the lead. Eben said no more but did not let them beyond him to the white-faced K-Bar cowboy.

As the burly leader drew abreast of him, the drifter reached out and took him gently by one shoulder. He turned him around, got a hip into his side, threw him hard and far across the floor and up against the dry-goods counter, fifteen feet away. The frame building shook to its top scantling when the big man landed. He knocked a three-foot hole in the floor, ending up hip-deep in a splintered wedging of boards from which it took the combined efforts of three friends and the storekeeper's two-hundred-pound daughter to extract him.

By the time he was freed and being revived by a stimulant-restorative composed of equal parts of sheep-dip and spirits of camphorated oil, the rest of the assemblage was commencing to appreciate the length and strength of the drifter's throw. And, realizing these things, they were politely moving back to provide him the room he had requested in the first place. Eben made his address direct and nippy.

They had come down out of the hills, he said, bearing news of invading Philistines. They were not there to become a part of the Wolf Mountain War but to serve in what small way they might to bring that unpleasantness to a peaceful conclusion, with freedom and justice for all. Toward that end, he concluded, his bowlegged friend had something to say which would convince the sheep raisers that he came to them, not as a kineherd bearing false prophecies, but as a man of their own simple cloth, who wanted to help them as were too honest and God-fearing to help themselves at the cattlemen's price of killing and maiming their fellow men by gunfire and in the dead of night when decent men were sleeping and their flocks on peaceful, unguarded graze.

This introduction served to interest the Bull Pine men and terrify Tom Isley. He was not up on kineherds, Philistines, and false prophets, but he knew sheepmen pretty well. He reckoned he had maybe thirty seconds to fill the flush Eben had dealt him before somebody thought of that rope again. Glancing over, he saw Big Sam Yawkey—the fallen leader of the meeting—beginning to snort and breathe heavy from the sheep-dip fumes. Figuring Big Sam to be bright-eyed and bushy-tailed again in about ten of those thirty seconds, it cut things really fine.

Especially when he didn't have the least, last notion what the heck topic it was that Eben expected him to take off on. "Ebe!" he got out in a strangulated whisper, "what in the name of Gawd you expect me to talk about?" But the Good Samaritan with the moth-eaten mule and the one thin army blanket wasn't worried a whit. He just put out his bony hand, touched his small companion on the shoulder, and said, with his soft smile, as the sheepmen closed in:

"Never fear, Isley. You will think of something."

And, for a fact, Isley did.

"Hold off!" he yelled, backing to the hardware counter and picking himself a pick handle out of a barrel of assorted tool hafts. "I'll law you out like Samson with that jackass jawbone!"

The sheepmen coagulated, came to a halt.

"Now, see here," Isley launched out. "Ebe's right. I'm down here to do what I can to settle this fight. There's been far too much blood spilt a'ready. And I got an idee, like Ebe says, how to stop this here war quicker'n you can spit and holler howdy. But it ain't going to be risk-free. Monkeying around with them cattlemen is about as safe as kicking a loaded polecat. They're touchier than a teased snake, as I will allow you all know."

Several of the sheepmen nodded, and one said, "Yes, we know, all right. And so do you. You're one of them!"

"No," denied Isley, "that ain't so. Mr. Reston threw me off the K-Bar this very day. Ebe, here, made him look some small in front of the boys, and the Old Man ordered us both took to the west line and told to keep riding. I got included on account I drug Ebe in off the range, and Old Henry, he said I could keep him, seeings I'd found him first."

His listeners scowled and looked at one another. This bowlegged little man had been punching cattle too long. He had clearly gone astray upstairs and been given his notice because of it. But they would hear him out, as none of them wanted to be flung against the dry-goods counter or skulled with that pick handle.

"Go ahead," growled Big Sam Yawkey, coming up groggily to take his place in front of the Bull Piners. "But don't be overlong with your remarks. I done think you already stretched the blanket about as far as she will go. But, by damn, if there's a sick lamb's chance that you *do* have some way we can get back at them murderers, we ain't going to miss out on it. Fire away."

"Thank you, Mr. Yawkey," said Isley, and fired.

The idea he hit them with was as much a surprise to him as to them. He heard the words coming out of his mouth, but it was as though somebody else was pulling the wires and making his lips flap. He found himself listening with equal interest to the Bull Pine sheepmen, to his wild-eyed plan for ambushing the cattlemen in Red Rock Corral.

It was beautifully simple:

Red Rock Corral was a widened-out place in the middle of that squeezed-in center part of Shell Canyon called the Narrows. If you looked at the Narrows as a sort of rifle barrel of bedrock, then Red Rock Corral would be like a place midways of the barrel where a bullet with a weak charge had stuck, then been slammed into by the following, full-strength round, bulging the barrel at that spot. It made a fine place to catch range mustangs, for example. All you had to do was close off both ends of the Narrows, once you had them in the bulge. Then just leave them there to starve down to where they would lead out peaceful as muley cows.

Isley's idea was that what would work for tough horses would work for tough men.

The sheepmen knew for a fact, he said, that the hill trail came down to the basin through Shell Canyon. Now, if added to this, they also knew for a fact, as Isley did, that Old Henry and his boys were coming down that trail early tomorrow to knock over their winter feed pens and stampede their sheep into the blizzard's deep snow, why, then they would be catching up to the first part of the Isley plan.

Pausing, the little cowboy offered them a moment to consider the possibilities. Big Sam was the first to recover.

"You meaning to suggest," he said, heavy voice scraping like a burro with a bad cold, "that we bottle them cattlemen up in Red Rock Corral and starve them into agreeing to leave us be? Why, I declare you're balmier than you look, cowboy. In fact, you're nervier than a busted tooth. You think we need you to tell us about ambushing? That's the cattlemen's speed. And you can't do it without people getting hurt, kilt likely. Boys," he said, turning to the others, "some deck is shy a joker, and this is him. Fetch the rope."

"No! Wait!" cried Isley, waving his pick handle feebly. "I ain't done yet."

"Oh, yes you are," rumbled Big Sam, moving forward. Yet, as before, he did not reach Tom Isley.

Eben raised his thin, pale hand and Big Sam brought up as short as though he had walked into an invisible wall.

"What the hell?" he muttered, rubbing his face, frightened. "I must be losing my marbles. Something just clouted me acrost the nose solid as a low limb."

"It was your conscience." Eben smiled. "Isley has more to say. Haven't you, Isley?"

The little cowboy shook his head, bewildered.

"Hell, don't ask me, Ebe. You're the ventrillyquist."

"Speak on"—his friend nodded—"and be not afraid."

"Well," said Isley, "I'll open my mouth and see what comes out. But I ain't guaranteeing nothing."

Big Sam Yawkey, still rubbing his nose, glared angrily.

"Something better come out," he promised, "or I'll guarantee you something a sight more substantial than nothing, and that's to send you out of town with your toes down. You've got me confuseder than a blind dog in a butcher shop, and I'm giving you one whole minute more to hand me the bone, or down comes your doghouse."

"Yeah!" snapped a burly herder behind him. "What you take us for, a flock of ninnies? Jest because we run sheep don't mean we got brains to match. And you suggesting that we set a wild-hoss trap for them gun slingers and night riders of Old Man Reston's is next to saying we're idjuts. You think we're empty-headed enough to buy any such sow bosom as holding them cattlemen in that rock hole with a broomtail brush fence on both ends?"

"*No,*" said Isley calmly, and to his own amazement, "*but you might try doing it with blasting powder.*"

"What?" shouted Yawkey.

"Yes, sir," said Isley meekly. "A half can of DuPont number nine at each end, touched off by signal from the bluff above. When all of them have rode into Red Rock Corral, down comes the canyon wall, above and below, and there they are, shut off neat as a newborn calf, and nobody even scratched. I'd say that with this big snow that's coming, and with the thermometer dropping like a gut-shot elk, they'd sign the deed to their baby sister's virtue inside of forty-eight hours."

There was a silence then, as profound as the pit.

It was broken presently by Big Sam's awed nod and by him clearing his throat, shaky and overcome, as though asked to orate in favor of the flag on Independence Day.

"Great Gawd A'mighty, boys," he said, "it might work!"

And the rush for the front door and the horses standing back-humped at the hitch rail was on.

As a matter of Big Horn Basin record, it did work.

The Bull Piners got their powder planted by three A.M., and about four down the trail came the deputation from the hills. The snow was already setting in stiff, and they were riding bunched tight. Big Sam Yawkey fired his Winchester three times when they were all in the middle of Red Rock Corral, and Jase Threepersons, the storekeeper, and Little Ginger, his two-hundred-pound daughter, both lit off their respective batches of DuPont number 9 above and below the corral so close together the cattlemen thought it was one explosion and Judgment Day come at last.

Well, it had, in a way.

And, as Isley had predicted, it came in less than forty-eight hours.

The sheepmen were mighty big about it. They lowered down ropes with all sorts of bedding and hot food and even whisky for the freezing ranchers, as well as some of their good baled sheep hay for the horses. But they made it clear, through Big Sam's bellowed-down advice, that they meant

to keep their friends and neighbors from the hills bottled up
in that bare-rock bulge till the new grass came, if need be.
They wouldn't let them starve, except slowly, or freeze,
unless by accident. But they had come out from Bull Pine
to get a truce, plus full indemnity for their summer's sheep
losses, and they were prepared to camp up on that bluff—
in the full comfort of their heated sheep wagons—from right
then till hell, or Red Rock Corral, froze over.

That did it.

There was some hollering back and forth between the
two camps for most of that first day. Then it got quiet for the
better part of the second. Then, along about sundown, Old
Henry Reston yelled up and said, "What's the deal, Yawkey?
We don't get back to our stock right quick, we won't have
enough left to hold a barbecue."

Big Sam read them the terms, which Isley wasn't close
enough to hear. Reston accepted under profane duress, and
he and Big Sam shook on the matter. Naturally such a grip
had the force of law in the basin. Once Old Henry and Big
Sam had put their hands to an agreement, the man on either
side who broke that agreement might just as well spool his
bed and never stop moving.

Realizing this, Isley modestly stayed out of the affair.
There were other inducements toward laying low and keeping back from the rim while negotiations went forward and
concluded. One of these was the little cowboy's certain
knowledge of what his fellow K-Bar riders would think of a
cowman who sold out to a bunch of sheepherders. Even
more compelling was the cold thought as to what they
would *do* to such a hero, should they ever catch up to the
fact he had plotted the whole shameful thing. All elements,
both of charming self-effacement and outright cowardice,
considered, Isley believed himself well-advised to saddle up
and keep traveling. This he planned to do at the first opportunity—which would be with that night's darkness in about
twenty minutes. It was in carrying out the first part of this
strategy—rounding up Eben and their two mounts—that he

ran into the entertainment committee from the Bull Pine camp: three gentleman sheepherders delegated by their side to invite Isley to the victory celebration being staged in his honor at the Ram's Horn Saloon later that evening.

Isley, confronted with this opportunity, refused to be selfish. He bashfully declined the credit being so generously offered, claiming that it rightfully belonged to another. When pressed for the identity of this hidden champion, he said that of course he meant his good friend Eben. "You know," he concluded, "the skinny feller with the white face and curly whiskers. Ebe," he called into the gathering dusk past the hay wagon where they had tied Black Bean and the mule, "come on out here and take a bow!"

But Eben did not come out, and Jase Threepersons, the chairman of the committee, said to Isley, "What skinny feller with what white face and what curly whiskers?"

He said it in a somewhat uncompromising manner, and Isley retorted testily, "The one that was with me in the store; the one what thrun Big Sam acrost the floor. Damn it, what you trying to come off on me, anyhow?"

Jase looked at him and the other two sheepmen looked at him, and Jase said, in the same flat way as before, "*You* thrun Big Sam agin that counter. There wasn't nobody in that store with you. What *you* trying to come off on *us*, Tom Isley?"

"Blast it!" cried Isley. "I never laid a finger on Big Sam. You think I'd be crazy enough to try that?"

The three shook their heads, looking sorrowful.

"Evidently so," said Jase Threepersons.

"No, now you all just hold up a minute," said Isley, seeing their pitying looks. "Come on, I'll show you. Right over here ahint the hay wagon. Me and Ebe was bedded here last night and boilt our noon coffee here today. I ain't seen him the past hour or so, and he may have lost his nerve and lit out, but, by damn, I can show you where his mule was tied and I'll fetch *him* for you, give time."

They were all moving around the wagon as he spoke,

Isley in the lead. He stopped dead. "No!" they heard him say. "My God, it cain't be!" But when they got up to him, it was. There was no sign of a double camp whatever. And no sign of the bearded stranger or of his moth-eaten mule. "He was right here!" yelled Isley desperately. "Damn it, you saw him, you're just funning, just hoorawing me. You seen him and you seen that broke-down jackass he rides. Who the hell you think I been talking to the past three days, *myself?*"

"'Pears as if." Jase nodded sympathetically. "Too bad, too. Little Ginger had kind of took a shine to you. Wanted me to see you stuck around Bull Pine a spell. But, seeings the way things are with you, I reckon she'd best go back to waiting out Big Sam."

"Yes, sir, thank you very much, sir," said Isley gratefully, "but I still aim to find Ebe and that damn mule for you." He bent forward with sudden excitement. "Say, lookit here! Mule tracks leading off! See? What'd I tell you? Old Ebe, he's a shy cuss and mightily humble. He didn't want no thanks. He'd done what he come for—stopped the trouble —and he just naturally snuck off when nobody was a-watching him. Come on! We can catch him easy on that stove-up old jack."

The three men came forward, stooped to examine the snow. There were some tracks there, all right, rapidly being filled by the fresh fall of snow coming on, but tracks all the same. They could have been mule tracks too. It was possible. But they could also have been smallish horse tracks. Like say left by Pettus Teague's blue-blood race mare. Or by that trim Sioux pony belonging to Charlie Bo-peep, the Basque half-breed. Or by Coony Simm's little bay. Or Nels Bofors' slim Kentucky-bred saddler. Or two, three others in the camp.

Straightening from its consideration of the evidence, the committee eyed Tom Isley.

"Isley," said Jase Threepersons, "I'll tell you what we'll do. All things took into account, you've been under considerable strain. Moreover, that strain ain't apt to get any less when word gets back up into the hills that you come down here and hatched this ambush idea. We owe you a-plenty, and we ain't going to argue with you about that there feller and his mule. But them cowboys of Old Henry's might take a bit more convincing. Now suppose you just don't be here when Big Sam and the others comes up out of the corral with the K-Bar outfit. We'll say you was gone when we got here to the hay wagon and that you didn't leave no address for sending on your mail. All right?"

Isley took a look at the weather.

It was turning off warmer, and this new snow wouldn't last more than enough to cover his tracks just nice. The wind was down, the sun twenty minutes gone, and from the rim of the bluff above the corral sounds were floating which indicated the roping parties were pulling up the first of the K-Bar sheep raiders. To Isley it looked like a fine night for far riding. And sudden.

He pulled his coat collar up, his hat brim down, and said to Jase Threepersons, "All right."

"We'll hold the boys at the rim to give you what start we can," said Jase. And Isley stared at him and answered, "No, don't bother. You've did more than enough for me a'ready. Good-by, boys, and if I ever find any old ladies or dogs that need kicking, I will send them along to you."

Being sheepherders, they didn't take offense but set off to stall the rescue party at the rim, true to their word.

Isley didn't linger to argue the morals of it. He got his blanket out from under the hay wagon, rolled it fast, hurried to tie it on behind old Black Bean's saddle. By this time he wasn't even sure who *he* was but didn't care to take any chances on it. He just might turn out to be Tom Isley, and then it would be close work trying to explain to Dutch and Gant and Deece and the rest what it was he was doing bedded down in the sheep camp.

He had the old black outlaw swung around and headed in the same direction as the fading mule tracks—or whatever they were—in something less than five minutes flat.

The going was all downhill to the river, and he made good time. About eight o'clock he came to the Willow Creek Crossing of the Big Horn, meaning to strike the Pitchfork Trail there. He was hungry and cold and the old black needed a rest, so he began to look around for a good place to lie up for the night. Imagine his surprise and pleasure, then, to spy ahead the winky gleam and glow of a campfire, set in a snug thicket of small timber off to the right of the crossing. Following its cheery guide, he broke through the screening brush and was greeted by a sight that had him bucked up quicker than a hatful of hot coffee.

"Ebe!" he cried delightedly. "I knowed you wouldn't run out on me. God bless it, I am that pleased to see you!"

"And I likewise, Isley." The gentle-voiced drifter smiled. "Alight and thrice welcome to my lowly board."

Well, he had a windtight place there. It was nearly as warm and shut in from the cold as the old rock house out on Wolf Mountain flat, and he had added to it with a neat lean-to of ax-cut branches, as pretty as anything Isley had ever seen done on the range. And the smell of the rack of lamb he had broiling over the flames of his fire was enough to bring tears to the eyes of a Kansas City cow buyer.

Isley could see no legitimate reason for declining the invitation.

Falling off Black Bean, he said, "You be a-saying grace, Ebe, while I'm a-pulling this hull. I don't want to hold you up none when we set down. . . ."

While they ate, things were somewhat quiet. It was very much the same as it had been when Eben came in, cold and hungry, to Isley's fire out on the flats. Afterward, though, with the blackened coffeepot going the rounds, Isley rolling his rice-paper smokes, and Eben playing some of the lonesomest pretty tunes on his old mouth harp that the little cowboy had ever heard, the talk started flowing at a better rate.

There were several things Isley wanted to know, chief among them being the matter of the Bull Pine men letting on as if he had jumped his head hobbles. But he kept strong on this point at first, leading off with some roundabout inquiries which wouldn't tip his hand to Eben. These were such things as how come he didn't recognize any of the tunes Eben was playing on the harp? Or how did Eben manage to evaporate from the sheep camp at Red Rock Corral without any of the Bull Piners seeing him. Or why didn't he let Isley know he was going? And how come him, Eben, to have lamb on the fire in October, when there wasn't any lamb?

To this tumble of questions Eben only replied with his soft laugh and such put-offers as that the tunes were sheep-herder songs from another land, that the fresh snowfall had hidden his departure from the hay-wagon bed spot, that he knew the Bull Piners planned a party for Isley and didn't wish to stand in his way of enjoying the tribute due him, and that for him, Eben, lamb was always in season and always he could put his hand to some just about as he pleased.

Well, Isley was a little mystified by this sort of round-the-barn business. But when Eben made the remark about the Bull Pine party being due him, Isley, he quit slanting his own talk, off-trail, and brought it right to the bait.

"Ebe," he said, "I'm going to ask you one question. And you mighten as well answer it, for I'm going to hang onto it like an Indian to a whisky jug."

"Gently, gently." The other smiled. "You'll have your answer, but not tonight. In the morning, Isley, I promise you."

"Promise me what?" demanded the little cowboy. "I ain't even said what I wanted."

"But I know what you want, and you shall have it—in the morning."

Isley eyed him stubbornly.

"I'll have what in the morning?" he insisted.

Eben smiled that unsettling sad-sweet smile and shrugged.

"Proof that I was with you all the while," he said.

Isley frowned then nodded.

"All right, Ebe, you want to save her for sunup, that's fine with me. I'm a little wore down myself."

"You rest, then," said the drifter. "Lie back upon your saddle and your blanket, and I will read to you from a book I have." He reached in his own blanket, still curiously unrolled, and brought forth two volumes: one a regular-sized black leather Bible, the other a smallish red morocco-bound tome with some sort of outlandish foreign scripting on the cover. "The Book of the Gospel," he said, holding up the Bible, then, gesturing with the little red book, "the *Rubáiyát* of Omar Khayyám. Which will you have, Isley?"

"Well," said the latter, "I can tell by some of your talk, Ebe, that you favor the Good Book, and I ain't denying that it's got some rattling-tall yarns in it. But if it's all the same to you, I'll have a shot of the other. I'm a man likes to see both sides of the billiard ball."

Eben nodded soberly but without any hint of reproval.

"You have made your choice, Isley," he said, "and so be it. Listen."

He opened the small volume then and began to read selected lines for his raptly attentive companion. Lazing back on his blanket, head propped on his saddle, the warmth of the fire reflecting in under the lean-to, warm and fragrant as fresh bread, Isley listened to the great rhymes of the ancient Persian:

> *. . . And as the Cock crew, those who stood before*
> *The Tavern shouted—"Open then the Door!*
> *"You know how little while we have to stay*
> *"And once departed, may return no more! . . ."*

> *. . . Come, fill the Cup, and in the fire of Spring*
> *Your winter-garment of Repentance fling:*
> *The Bird of Time has but a little way*
> *To flutter—and the Bird is on the Wing. . . .*

> *. . . A Book of Verses underneath the Bough,*
> *A Jug of Wine, a Loaf of Bread—and Thou*

Beside me singing in the Wilderness—   .
Oh, Wilderness were Paradise enow! . .

. . . Yesterday this Day's Madness did prepare,
Tomorrow's Silence, Triumph, or Despair:
Drink! for you know not whence you came, nor why:
Drink! for you know not why you go, nor where . . .

. . . The moving Finger writes; and, having writ,
Moves on: nor all your Piety nor Wit
Shall lure it back to cancel half a line,
Nor all your Tears wash out a Word of it. . . .

The poetry was done then, and Eben was putting down the little red book to answer some drowsy questions from Isley as to the nature of the man who could write such wondrously true things about life as she is actually lived, just on a piece of ordinary paper and in such a shriveled little old leather book.

Eben reached over and adjusted Isley's blanket more closely about the dozing cowboy, then told him the story of Omar Khayyám. But Isley was tired and his thoughts dimming. He remembered later some few shreds of the main idea, such as that Old Omar was a tentmaker by trade, that he didn't set much store by hard work, that he didn't know beans about horses, sheep, or cattle but was a heller on women and grape juice. Past that he faded out and slept gentle as a dead calf. The sun was an hour high and shining square in his eyes when he woke up.

He lay still a minute, not recalling where he was. Then it came to him and he sat up with a grin and a stretch and a *"Morning, Ebe!"* that was warm and cheerful enough to light a candle from. But Eben didn't answer to it. And never would. For when Tom Isley blinked to get the climbing sun out of his eyes, and took a second frowning look around the little campsite, all he saw was the unbroken stretch of the new snow which had fallen quiet as angel's wings during the night. There was no Eben, no mule, no threadbare army-blanket bedroll. And this time there were not even any half-filled hoofprints leading away into the snow. This time there was only the snow. And the stillness. And the glistening beauty of the new day.

Oh, and there was one other small thing which neither Tom Isley nor anybody else in Big Horn Basin was ever able to explain. It was a little red morocco book about four by six inches in size, which Isley found in his blanket when he went to spool it for riding on. Nobody in northwest Wyoming had ever heard of it, including Tom Isley.

It was called the *Rubáiyát* of Omar Khayyám.

LOST SISTER

Dorothy M. Johnson

Our household was full of women, who overwhelmed my uncle Charlie and sometimes confused me with their bustle and chatter. We were the only men on the place. I was nine years old when still another woman came—Aunt Bessie, who had been living with the Indians.

When my mother told me about her, I couldn't believe it. The savages had killed my father, a cavalry lieutenant, two years before. I hated Indians and looked forward to wiping them out when I got older. (But when I was grown, they were no menace any more.)

"What did she live with the hostiles for?" I demanded.

"They captured her when she was a little girl," Ma said. "She was three years younger than you are. Now she's coming home."

High time she came home, I thought. I said so, promising, "If they was ever to get me, I wouldn't stay with 'em long."

Ma put her arms around me. "Don't talk like that. They won't get you. They'll never get you."

I was my mother's only real tie with her husband's family. She was not happy with those masterful women, my aunts Margaret, Hannah, and Sabina, but she would not go back East where she came from. Uncle Charlie managed the store the aunts owned, but he wasn't really a member of the family—he was just Aunt Margaret's husband. The only man who had belonged was my father, the aunts' younger brother. And I belonged, and someday the store would be mine. My mother stayed to protect my heritage.

None of the three sisters, my aunts, had ever seen Aunt Bessie. She had been taken by the Indians before they were born. Aunt Mary had known her—Aunt Mary was two years older—but she lived a thousand miles away now and was not well.

There was no picture of the little girl who had become a legend. When the family had first settled here, there was enough struggle to feed and clothe the children without having pictures made of them.

Even after army officers had come to our house several times and there had been many letters about Aunt Bessie's delivery from the savages, it was a long time before she came. Major Harris, who made the final arrangements, warned my aunts that they would have problems, that Aunt Bessie might not be able to settle down easily into family life.

This was only a challenge to Aunt Margaret, who welcomed challenges. "She's our own flesh and blood," Aunt Margaret trumpeted. "Of course she must come to us. My poor, dear sister Bessie, torn from her home forty years ago!"

The major was earnest but not tactful. "She's been with the savages all those years," he insisted. "And she was only a little girl when she was taken. I haven't seen her myself, but it's reasonable to assume that she'll be like an Indian woman."

My stately aunt Margaret arose to show that the audience was ended. "Major Harris," she intoned, "I cannot permit anyone to criticize my own dear sister. She will live in my home, and if I do not receive official word that she is coming within a month, I shall take steps."

Aunt Bessie came before the month was up.

The aunts in residence made valiant preparations. They bustled and swept and mopped and polished. They moved me from my own room to my mother's—as she had been begging them to do because I was troubled with nightmares. They prepared my old room for Aunt Bessie with many small comforts—fresh doilies everywhere, hairpins, a matching pitcher and bowl, the best towels, and two new nightgowns in case hers might be old. (The fact was that she didn't have any.)

"Perhaps we should have some dresses made," Hannah suggested. "We don't know what she'll have with her."

"We don't know what size she'll take, either," Margaret pointed out. "There'll be time enough for her to go to the store after she settles down and rests for a day or two. Then she can shop to her heart's content."

Ladies of the town came to call almost every afternoon while the preparations were going on. Margaret promised them that, as soon as Bessie had recovered sufficiently from her ordeal, they should all meet her at tea.

Margaret warned her anxious sisters, "Now, girls, we mustn't ask her too many questions at first. She must rest for a while. She's been through a terrible experience." Margaret's voice dropped 'way down with those last two words, as if only she could be expected to understand.

Indeed Bessie had been through a terrible experience, but it wasn't what the sisters thought. The experience from which she was suffering, when she arrived, was that she had been wrenched from her people, the Indians, and turned over to strangers. She had not been freed. She had been made a captive.

Aunt Bessie came with Major Harris and an interpreter,

a half-blood with greasy black hair hanging down to his shoulders. His costume was half army and half primitive. Aunt Margaret swung the door open wide when she saw them coming. She ran out with her sisters following, while my mother and I watched from a window. Margaret's arms were outstretched, but when she saw the woman closer, her arms dropped and her glad cry died.

She did not cringe, my aunt Bessie who had been an Indian for forty years, but she stopped walking and stood staring, helpless among her captors.

The sisters had described her often as a little girl. Not that they had ever seen her, but she was a legend, the captive child. Beautiful blond curls, they said she had, and big blue eyes—she was a fairy child, a pale-haired little angel who ran on dancing feet.

The Bessie who came back was an aging woman who plodded in moccasins, whose dark dress did not belong on her bulging body. Her brown hair hung just below her ears. It was growing out; when she was first taken from the Indians, her hair had been cut short to clean out the vermin.

Aunt Margaret recovered herself and, instead of embracing this silent, stolid woman, satisfied herself by patting an arm and crying, "Poor dear Bessie, I am your sister Margaret. And here are our sisters Hannah and Sabina. We do hope you're not all tired out from your journey!"

Aunt Margaret was all graciousness, because she had been assured beyond doubt that this was truly a member of the family. She must have believed—Aunt Margaret could believe anything—that all Bessie needed was to have a nice nap and wash her face. Then she would be as talkative as any of them.

The other aunts were quick-moving and sharp of tongue. But this one moved as if her sorrows were a burden on her bowed shoulders, and when she spoke briefly in answer to the interpreter, you could not understand a word of it.

Aunt Margaret ignored these peculiarities. She took the

party into the front parlor—even the interpreter, when she understood there was no avoiding it. She might have gone on battling with the major about him, but she was in a hurry to talk to her lost sister.

"You won't be able to converse with her unless the interpreter is present," Major Harris said. "Not," he explained hastily, "because of any regulation, but because she has forgotten English."

Aunt Margaret gave the half-blood interpreter a look of frowning doubt and let him enter. She coaxed Bessie. "Come, dear, sit down."

The interpreter mumbled, and my Indian aunt sat cautiously on a needlepoint chair. For most of her life she had been living with the people who sat comfortably on the ground.

The visit in the parlor was brief. Bessie had had her instructions before she came. But Major Harris had a few warnings for the family. "Technically, your sister is still a prisoner," he explained, ignoring Margaret's start of horror. "She will be in your custody. She may walk in your fenced yard, but she must not leave it without official permission.

"Mrs. Raleigh, this may be a heavy burden for you all. But she has been told all this and has expressed willingness to conform to these restrictions. I don't think you will have any trouble keeping her here." Major Harris hesitated, remembered that he was a soldier and a brave man, and added, "If I did, I wouldn't have brought her."

There was the making of a sharp little battle, but Aunt Margaret chose to overlook the challenge. She could not overlook the fact that Bessie was not what she had expected.

Bessie certainly knew that this was her lost white family, but she didn't seem to care. She was infinitely sad, infinitely removed. She asked one question: "Ma-ry?" and Aunt Margaret almost wept with joy.

"Sister Mary lives a long way from here," she explained, "and she isn't well, but she will come as soon as she's able. Dear sister Mary!"

The interpreter translated this, and Bessie had no more to say. That was the only understandable word she ever did say in our house, the remembered name of her older sister.

When the aunts, all chattering, took Bessie to her room, one of them asked, "But where are her things?"

Bessie had no things, no baggage. She had nothing at all but the clothes she stood in. While the sisters scurried to bring a comb and other oddments, she stood like a stooped monument, silent and watchful. This was her prison. Very well, she would endure it.

"Maybe tomorrow we can take her to the store and see what she would like," Aunt Hannah suggested.

"There's no hurry," Aunt Margaret declared thoughtfully. She was getting the idea that this sister was going to be a problem. But I don't think Aunt Margaret ever really stopped hoping that one day Bessie would cease to be different, that she would end her stubborn silence and begin to relate the events of her life among the savages, in the parlor over a cup of tea.

My Indian aunt accustomed herself, finally, to sitting on the chair in her room. She seldom came out, which was a relief to her sisters. She preferred to stand, hour after hour, looking out the window—which was open only about a foot, in spite of all Uncle Charlie's efforts to budge it higher. And she always wore moccasins. She never was able to wear shoes from the store, but seemed to treasure the shoes brought to her.

The aunts did not, of course, take her shopping after all. They made her a couple of dresses; and when they told her, with signs and voluble explanations, to change her dress, she did.

After I found that she was usually at the window, looking across the flat land to the blue mountains, I played in the yard so I could stare at her. She never smiled, as an aunt should, but she looked at me sometimes, thoughtfully, as if measuring my worth. By performing athletic feats, such as

walking on my hands, I could get her attention. For some
reason, I valued it.

She didn't often change expression, but twice I saw her
scowl with disapproval. Once was when one of the aunts
slapped me in a casual way. I had earned the slap, but the
Indians did not punish children with blows. Aunt Bessie was
shocked, I think, to see that white people did. The other
time was when I talked back to someone with spoiled, small-
boy insolence—and that time the scowl was for me.

The sisters and my mother took turns, as was their Christian duty, in visiting her for half an hour each day. Bessie
didn't eat at the table with us—not after the first meal.

The first time my mother took her turn, it was under
protest. "I'm afraid I'd start crying in front of her," she
argued, but Aunt Margaret insisted.

I was lurking in the hall when Ma went in. Bessie said
something, then said it again, peremptorily, until my
mother guessed what she wanted. She called me and put her
arm around me as I stood beside her chair. Aunt Bessie
nodded, and that was all there was to it.

Afterward, my mother said, "She likes you. And so do
I." She kissed me.

"I don't like her," I complained. "She's queer."

"She's a sad old lady," my mother explained. "She had
a little boy once, you know."

"What happened to him?"

"He grew up and became a warrior. I suppose she was
proud of him. Now the Army has him in prison somewhere.
He's half Indian. He was a dangerous man."

He was indeed a dangerous man, and a proud man, a
chief, a bird of prey whose wings the Army had clipped after
bitter years of trying.

However, my mother and my Indian aunt had that one
thing in common: they both had sons. The other aunts were
childless.

There was a great to-do about having Aunt Bessie's photograph taken. The aunts, who were stubbornly and val-

iantly trying to make her one of the family, wanted a picture of her for the family album. The government wanted one too, for some reason—perhaps because someone realized that a thing of historic importance had been accomplished by recovering the captive child.

Major Harris sent a young lieutenant with the greasy-haired interpreter to discuss the matter in the parlor. (Margaret, with great foresight, put a clean towel on a chair and saw to it the interpreter sat there.) Bessie spoke very little during that meeting, and of course we understood only what the half-blood *said* she was saying.

No, she did not want her picture made. No.

But your son had his picture made. Do you want to see it? They teased her with that offer, and she nodded.

If we let you see his picture, then will you have yours made?

She nodded doubtfully. Then she demanded more than had been offered: If you let me keep his picture, then you can make mine.

No, you can only look at it. We have to keep his picture. It belongs to us.

My Indian aunt gambled for high stakes. She shrugged and spoke, and the interpreter said, "She not want to look. She will keep or nothing."

My mother shivered, understanding as the aunts could not understand what Bessie was gambling—all or nothing.

Bessie won. Perhaps they had intended that she should. She was allowed to keep the photograph that had been made of her son. It has been in history books many times—the half-white chief, the valiant leader who was not quite great enough to keep his Indian people free.

His photograph was taken after he was captured, but you would never guess it. His head is high, his eyes stare with boldness but not with scorn, his long hair is arranged with care—dark hair braided on one side and with a tendency to curl where the other side hangs loose—and his hands hold the pipe like a royal scepter.

That photograph of the captive but unconquered warrior had its effect on me. Remembering him, I began to control my temper and my tongue, to cultivate reserve as I grew older, to stare with boldness but not scorn at people who annoyed or offended me. I never met him, but I took silent pride in him—Eagle Head, my Indian cousin.

Bessie kept his picture on her dresser when she was not holding it in her hands. And she went like a docile, silent child to the photograph studio, in a carriage with Aunt Margaret early one morning, when there would be few people on the street to stare.

Bessie's photograph is not proud but pitiful. She looks out with no expression. There is no emotion there, no challenge, only the face of an aging woman with short hair, only endurance and patience. The aunts put a copy in the family album.

But they were nearing the end of their tether. The Indian aunt was a solid ghost in the house. She did nothing because there was nothing for her to do. Her gnarled hands must have been skilled at squaws' work, at butchering meat and scraping and tanning hides, at making tepees and beading ceremonial clothes. But her skills were useless and unwanted in a civilized home. She did not even sew when my mother gave her cloth and needles and thread. She kept the sewing things beside her son's picture.

She ate (in her room) and slept (on the floor) and stood looking out the window. That was all, and it could not go on. But it had to go on, at least until my sick aunt Mary was well enough to travel—Aunt Mary, who was her older sister, the only one who had known her when they were children.

The sisters' duty visits to Aunt Bessie became less and less visits and more and more duty. They settled into a bearable routine. Margaret had taken upon herself the responsibility of trying to make Bessie talk. Make, I said, not teach. She firmly believed that her stubborn and unfortunate sister needed only encouragement from a strong-willed person. So Margaret talked, as to a child, when she bustled in:

"Now there you stand, just looking, dear. What in the world is there to see out there? The birds—are you watching the birds? Why don't you try sewing? Or you could go for a little walk in the yard. Don't you want to go out for a nice little walk?"

Bessie listened and blinked.

Margaret could have understood an Indian woman's not being able to converse in a civilized tongue, but her own sister was not an Indian. Bessie was white, therefore she should talk the language her sisters did—the language she had not heard since early childhood.

Hannah, the put-upon aunt, talked to Bessie too, but she was delighted not to get any answers and not to be interrupted. She bent over her embroidery when it was her turn to sit with Bessie and told her troubles in an unending flow. Bessie stood looking out the window the whole time.

Sabina, who had just as many troubles, most of them emanating from Margaret and Hannah, went in like a martyr, firmly clutching her Bible, and read aloud from it until her time was up. She took a small clock along so that she would not, because of annoyance, be tempted to cheat.

After several weeks Aunt Mary came, white and trembling and exhausted from her illness and the long, hard journey. The sisters tried to get the interpreter in but were not successful. (Aunt Margaret took that failure pretty hard.) They briefed Aunt Mary, after she had rested, so the shock of seeing Bessie would not be too terrible. I saw them meet, those two.

Margaret went to the Indian woman's door and explained volubly who had come, a useless but brave attempt. Then she stood aside, and Aunt Mary was there, her lined white face aglow, her arms outstretched. "Bessie! Sister Bessie!" she cried.

And after one brief moment's hesitation, Bessie went into her arms and Mary kissed her sun-dark, weathered cheek. Bessie spoke. "Ma-ry," she said. "Ma-ry." She stood with tears running down her face and her mouth working.

So much to tell, so much suffering and fear—and joy and triumph, too—and the sister there at last who might legitimately hear it all and understand.

But the only English word that Bessie remembered was "Mary," and she had not cared to learn any others. She turned to the dresser, took her son's picture in her work-hardened hands, reverently, and held it so her sister could see. Her eyes pleaded.

Mary looked on the calm, noble, savage face of her half-blood nephew and said the right thing: "My, isn't he handsome!" She put her head on one side and then the other. "A fine boy, sister," she approved. "You must"—she stopped, but she finished—"be awfully proud of him, dear!"

Bessie understood the tone if not the words. The tone was admiration. Her son was accepted by the sister who mattered. Bessie looked at the picture and nodded, murmuring. Then she put it back on the dresser.

Aunt Mary did not try to make Bessie talk. She sat with her every day for hours, and Bessie did talk—but not in English. They sat holding hands for mutual comfort while the captive child, grown old and a grandmother, told what had happened in forty years. Aunt Mary said that was what Bessie was talking about. But she didn't understand a word of it and didn't need to.

"There is time enough for her to learn English again," Aunt Mary said. "I think she understands more than she lets on. I asked her if she'd like to come and live with me, and she nodded. We'll have the rest of our lives for her to learn English. But what she has been telling me—she can't wait to tell that. About her life, and her son."

"Are you sure, Mary dear, that you should take the responsibility of having her?" Margaret said dutifully, no doubt shaking in her shoes for fear Mary would change her mind now that deliverance was in sight. "I do believe she'd be happier with you, though we've done all we could."

Margaret and the older sisters would certainly be happier with Bessie somewhere else. And so, it developed, would the United States Government.

Major Harris came with the interpreter to discuss details, and they told Bessie she could go, if she wished, to live with Mary a thousand miles away. Bessie was patient and willing, stolidly agreeable. She talked a great deal more to the interpreter than she had ever done before. He answered at length and then explained to the others that she had wanted to know how she and Mary would travel to this far country. It was hard, he said, for her to understand just how far they were going.

Later we knew that the interpreter and Bessie had talked about much more than that.

Next morning, when Sabina took breakfast to Bessie's room, we heard a cry of dismay. Sabina stood holding the tray, repeating, "She's gone out the window! She's gone out the window!"

And so she had. The window that had always stuck so that it would not raise more than a foot was open wider now. And the photograph of Bessie's son was gone from the dresser. Nothing else was missing except Bessie and the decent dark dress she had worn the day before.

My uncle Charlie got no breakfast that morning. With Margaret shrieking orders, he leaped on a horse and rode to the telegraph station.

Before Major Harris got there with half a dozen cavalrymen, civilian scouts were out searching for the missing woman. They were expert trackers. Their lives had depended, at various times, on their ability to read the meaning of a turned stone, a broken twig, a bruised leaf. They found that Bessie had gone south. They tracked her for ten miles. And then they lost the trail, for Bessie was as skilled as they were. Her life had sometimes depended on leaving no stone or twig or leaf marked by her passage. She traveled fast at first. Then, with time to be careful, she evaded the followers she knew would come.

The aunts were stricken with grief—at least Aunt Mary

was—and bowed with humiliation about what Bessie had done. The blinds were drawn, and voices were low in the house. We had been pitied because of Bessie's tragic folly in having let the Indians make a savage of her. But now we were traitors because we had let her get away.

Aunt Mary kept saying pitifully, "Oh, why did she go? I thought she would be contented with me!"

The others said that it was, perhaps, all for the best. Aunt Margaret proclaimed, "She has gone back to her own." That was what they honestly believed, and so did Major Harris.

My mother told me why she had gone. "You know that picture she had of the Indian chief, her son? He's escaped from the jail he was in. The fort got word of it, and they think Bessie may be going to where he's hiding. That's why they're trying so hard to find her. They think," my mother explained, "that she knew of his escape before they did. They think the interpreter told her when he was here. There was no other way she could have found out."

They scoured the mountains to the south for Eagle Head and Bessie. They never found her, and they did not get him until a year later, far to the north. They could not capture him that time. He died fighting.

After I grew up, I operated the family store, disliking storekeeping a little more every day. When I was free to sell it, I did, and went to raising cattle. And one day, riding in a canyon after strayed steers, I found—I think—Aunt Bessie. A cowboy who worked for me was along, or I would never have let anybody know.

We found weathered bones near a little spring. They had a mystery on them, those nameless human bones suddenly come upon. I could feel old death brushing my back.

"Some prospector," suggested my riding partner.

I thought so too until I found, protected by a log, sodden scraps of fabric that might have been a dark, respectable dress. And wrapped in them was a sodden something that might have once been a picture.

The man with me was young, but he had heard the story of the captive child. He had been telling me about it, in fact. In the passing years it had acquired some details that surprised me. Aunt Bessie had become once more a fair-haired beauty, in this legend that he had heard, but utterly sad and silent. Well, sad and silent she really was.

I tried to push the sodden scrap of fabric back under the log, but he was too quick for me. "That ain't no shirt, that's a dress!" he announced. "This here was no prospector—it was a woman!" He paused and then announced with awe, "I bet you it was your Indian aunt!"

I scowled and said, "Nonsense. It could be anybody."

He got all worked up about it. "If it was *my* aunt," he declared, "I'd bury her in the family plot."

"No," I said, and shook my head.

We left the bones there in the canyon, where they had been for forty-odd years if they were Aunt Bessie's. And I think they were. But I would not make her a captive again. She's in the family album. She doesn't need to be in the family plot.

If my guess about why she left us is wrong, nobody can prove it. She never intended to join her son in hiding. She went in the opposite direction to lure pursuit away.

What happened to her in the canyon doesn't concern me, or anyone. My aunt Bessie accomplished what she set out to do. It was not her life that mattered, but his. She bought him another year.

PASÓ POR AQUÍ

Eugene Manlove Rhodes

I

Exceptions are so inevitable that no rule is without them—
except the one just stated. Neglecting fractions then, not to
insult intelligence by specifying the obvious, trained nurses
are efficient, skillful, devoted. It is a noble calling. Nevertheless, it is notorious that the official uniform is of reprehensi-
ble charm. This regulation is variously explained by men,
women, and doctors. "No fripperies, curlicues, and didos—
bully!" say the men. "Ah! Yes! But why? Artful minxes!" say
the women, who should know best. "Cheerful influence in
the sick room," say the doctors.

Be that as it may, such uniform Jay wore, spotless and
starched, crisp and cool; Jay Hollister, now seated on the
wide portico of the Alamogordo Hospital; not chief nurse,
but chief ornament, according to many, not only of that
hospital, but also of the great railroad which maintained it.

323

Alamogordo was a railroad town, a new town, a ready-made and highly painted town, direct from Toyland.

Ben Griggs was also a study in white—flannels, oxfords, and panama; a privileged visitor who rather overstepped his privileges; almost a fixture in that pleasant colonnade.

"Lamp of life," said Ben, "let's get down to brass tacks. You're homesick!"

"Homesick!" said Jay scornfully. *"Homesick!* I'm heart-sick, bankrupt, shipwrecked, lost, forlorn—here in this terrible country, among these dreadful people. Homesick? Why, Ben, I'm just damned!"

"Never mind, heart's delight—you've got me."

Miss Hollister seemed in no way soothed by this reassuring statement.

"Your precious New Mexico! Sand!" she said. "Sand, snakes, scorpions; wind, dust, glare, and heat; lonely, desolate, and forlorn!"

"Under the circumstances," said Ben, "you could hardly pay me a greater compliment, 'Whither thou goest, I will go,' and all that. Good girl! This unsolicited tribute—"

"Don't be a poor simpleton," advised the good girl. "I shall stick it out for my year, of course, since I was foolish enough to undertake it. That is all. Don't you make any mistakes. These people shall never be my people."

"No better people on earth. In all the essentials—"

"Oh, who cares anything about essentials?" cried Jay impatiently—voicing, perhaps, more than she knew. "A tin plate will do well enough to eat out of, certainly, if that is what you mean. I prefer china, myself. I'm going back where I can see flowers and the green grass, old gardens and sundials."

"I know not what others may say," observed Ben grandly, "but as for me, you take the sundials and give me the sun. Right here, too, where they climb for water and dig for wood. Peevish, my fellow townsman; peevish, waspy, crabbed. You haven't half enough to do. In this beastly climate people simply will not stay sick. They take up their bed and beat it, and you can't help yourself. Nursing is a mere sinecure." His hands were clasped behind his head, his slim length reclined in a steamer chair, feet crossed, eyes half closed, luxurious. "Ah, idleness!" he murmured. "Too bad, too bad! You never were a grouch back home. Rather good company, if anything."

Ben's eyes were blue and dreamy. They opened a trifle wider now, and rolled slowly till they fell upon Miss Hollister, both upright and haughty in her chair, her lips pressed to a straight line. She regarded him sternly. He blinked, his hands came from behind his head, he straightened up and adjusted his finger-tips to meet with delicate precision. "But the main trouble, the fount and origin of your disappointing conduct is, as hereinbefore said, homesickness. It is, as has been observed, a nobler pang than indigestion, though the symptoms are of striking similarity. Nostalgia, more than any other feeling, is fatal to the judicial faculties, and I think," said Ben, "I think, my dear towny, that when you look at this fair land, your future home, you regard all things with a jaundiced eye."

"Oh-h!" gasped Jay, hotly indignant. "Look at it yourself! Look at it!"

The hospital was guarded and overhung by an outer colonnade of cottonwoods; she looked through a green archway across the leagues of shimmering desert, somber, wavering, and dim; she saw the long bleak range beyond, saw-toothed and gray; saw in the midway levels the unbearable brilliance of the White Sands, a dazzle and tumult of wild light, a blinding mirror with two score miles for diameter.

But Ben's eyes widened with delight, their blue darkened to a deeper blue of exultation, not to be feigned.

"More than beautiful—fascinating," he said.

"Repulsive, hateful, malignant, appalling!" cried Jay Hollister bitterly. "The starved, withered grass, the parched earth, the stunted bushes—miserable, hideous—the abomination of desolation!"

"Girl, by all good rights I ought to shut your wild, wild mouth with kisses four—that's what I orter do—elocutin' that way. But you mean it, I guess." Ben nodded his head sagely. "I get your idea. Blotched and leprous, eh? Thin, starved soil, poisoned and mildewed patches—thorns and dwarfed scrub, red leer of the sun. Oh, *si!* Like that bird in Browning? Hills like giants at a huntin' lay—the round squat turret—all the lost adventurers, my peers—the Dark Tower, weird noises just offstage, increasin' like a bill, I mean a bell —increasin' like a bell, fiddles a-moanin', 'O-o-o-h-h-h! What did you do-o-o with your summer's wa-a-a-ges? So this is Paris!' Yes, yes! But why not shed the secondhand stuff and come down to workaday?"

"Ben Griggs," said Miss Hollister with quiet and deadly conviction, "you are absolutely the most blasphemous wretch that ever walked in shoe leather. You haven't anything even remotely corresponding to a soul."

"When we are married," said Ben, and paused, reflecting. "That is, if I don't change my mind—"

"Married!" said Miss Hollister derisively. *"When! You!"* Her eyes scorned him.

"Woman," said Ben, "beware! You make utter confusion with the parts of speech. You make mere interjections of pronouns, prepositions, and verbs and everything. You use too many shockers. More than that—mark me, my lass —isn't it curious that no one has ever thought to furnish printed words with every phonograph record of a song? Just a little sheet of paper—why, it needn't cost more than a penny apiece at the outside. Then we could know what it was all about."

"The way you hop from conversational crag to crag," said Jay, "is beyond all praise."

"Oh, well, if you insist, we can go back to our marriage again."

"My poor misguided young friend," said Jay, "make no mistakes. I put up with you because we played together when we were kids, and because we are strangers here in a strange land, townies together—"

Ben interrupted her. "Two tawny townies twisting twill together!" he chanted happily, beating slow time with a gentle finger. "Twin turtles twitter tender twilight twaddle. Twice twenty travelers—"

"Preposterous imbecile!" said Jay, dimpling nevertheless, adorably. "Here is something to put in your little book. Jay Hollister will never marry an idler and a wastrel. Why, you're not even a ne'er-do-well. You're a do-nothing, net."

"All the world loves a loafer," Ben protested. "Still, as Alice remarked, if circumstances were different they would be quite otherwise. If frugal industry—"

"There comes your gambler friend," said Jay coldly.

"Who, Monte? Where?" Ben turned eagerly.

"Across the street. No, the other way." Though she fervently disapproved of Monte, Jay was not sorry for the diversion. It was daily more difficult to keep Ben in his proper place, and she had no desire to discuss frugal industry.

"Picturesque rascal, what? Looking real pleased about something, too. Say, girl, you've made me forget something I was going to tell you."

"He is laughing to himself," said Jay.

"I believe he is, at that." Ben raised his voice. "Hi, Monte! Come over and tell us the joke."

II

Monte's mother had known him as Rosalio Marquez. The overname was professional. He dealt monte wisely but not too well. He was nearing thirty-five, the easiest age of all; he was slender and graceful; he wore blue serge and a soft black hat, low-crowned and wide-brimmed. He carried his hat in his hand as he came up the steps. He bowed courteously to Jay, with murmured greetings in Spanish, soft syllables of lingering caress; he waved a friendly salute to Ben.

"Yes, indeed," said Ben. "With all my heart. Your statement as to the beauty of the day is correct in every particular, and it affords me great pleasure to endorse an opinion so just. But, after all, dear heart, that is hardly the point, is it? The giddy jest, the merry chuckles—those are the points on which we greatly desire information."

Monte hesitated, almost imperceptibly, a shrewd questioning in his eyes.

"Yes, have a chair," said Jay, "and tell us the joke."

"Thees is good, here, thank you," said Monte. He sat on the top step and hung the black hat on his knee; his face lit up with soft low laughter. "The joke? O, eet ees upon the sheriff, Jeem Hunter. I weel tell it."

He paused to consider. In his own tongue Monte's speech sounded uncommonly like a pack of firecrackers lit at both ends. In English it was leisured, low, and thoughtful. The unslurred vowels, stressed and piquant, the crisp consonants, the tongue-tip accents—these things combined to make the slow caressing words into something rich and colorful and strange, all unlike our own smudged and neutral speech. The customary medium of the Southwest between the two races is a weird and lawless hodge-podge of the two tongues—a barbarous *lingua franca*.

As Miss Hollister had no Spanish, Monte drew only from his slender stock of English; and all unconsciously he acted the story as he told it.

"When Jeem was a leetle, small boy," said Monte, his hand knee-high to show the size in question, "he dream manee times that he find those marbles—oh, many marbles! That mek heem ver' glad, thees nize dream. Then he get older"—Monte's hand rose with the sheriff's maturity—"and some time he dream of find money lak thoss marble. And now Jeem ees grown and sheriff—an' las' night he come home ver' late, ver' esleepy. I weel tell you now how eet ees, but Jeem he did not know eet. You see, Melquiades he have a leetle, litla game." He glanced obliquely at Miss Hollister, his shoulders and down-drawn lips expressed apology for the little game, and tolerance for it. "Just neeckles and dimes. An' some fellow he go home weener, and there ees hole een hees pocket. But Jeem he do not know. *Bueno,* Jeem has been to Tularosa, Mescalero, Fresnal, all places, to leef word to look out for thees fellow las' week what rob the bank at Belen, and he arrive back on a freight train las' night, mebbe so about three in the morning—oh, veree tired, ver' esleepy. So when he go up the street een the moonlight he see there a long streeng of neeckles and dimes under hees feet." Without moving, Monte showed the homeward progress of that drowsy man and his faint surprise. "So Jeem he laugh and say, 'There ees that dream again.' And he go on. But bimeby he steel see thoss neeckles, and he peench heemself, so— and he feel eet." Monte's eyes grew round with astonishment. "And he bend heemself to peek eet, and eet ees true money, and not dreaming at all. Yais. He go not back, but on ahead he peek up one dollar seexty-five cents of thees neeckles and dimes."

"I hadn't heard of any robbery, Monte," said Ben. "What about it?"

"Yes, and where is Belen?" said Jay. "Not around here, surely. I've never heard of the place."

"Oh, no, *muy lejos*—a long ways. Belen, what you call Bethlehem, ees yonder thees side of Albuquerque, a leetle. I have been there manee times, but not estraight—round about." He made a looping motion of his hand to illustrate. "Las Vegas, and then down, or by Las Cruces, and then up. Eet is hundred feefty, two hundred miles in estraight line— I do not know."

"Anybody hurt?" asked Ben.

"Oh, no—no fuss! Eet ees veree funnee. Don Numa Frenger and Don Nestor Trujillo, they have there beeg estore to sell all theengs, leetle bank, farms, esheep ranch, freighting for thoss mines, buy wool and hides—all theengs for get the monee what ees there een thees place. And las' week, maybe Friday, Saturday, Nestor he ees go to deennair, and Numa Frenger ees in the estore, *solito*.

"Comes een a customer, *un colorado*—esscusa me, a red-head. He buy tomatoes, cheese, crackers, sardines, sooch things, and a nose bag, and he ask to see shotgun. Don Numa, he exheebit two, three, and thees red he peek out nize shotgun. So he ask for shells, bird-eshot, buck-eshot, and he open the buck-eshot and sleep two shells een barrel, and break eet to throw out thoss sheel weeth extractor, and sleep them een again. 'Eet work fine!' he say. 'Have you canteen?'

"Then Numa Frenger he tek long pole weeth hook to get thoss canteen where eet hang from the *viga*, the r-rafter, the beams. And when he get eet, he turn around an' thees estranger ees present thees shotgun at hees meedle. Yais.

" 'Have you money een your esafe?' say the *estranjero*, the estr-ranger. And Numa ees bite hees mouth. 'Of your kindness,' say the customer, 'weel you get heem? I weel go weeth you?'

"So they get thees money from the esafe. And thees one eel not tek onlee the paper money. 'Thees gold an' seelver ees so heav-ee,' he tell Numa Frenger. 'I weel not bozzer.' Then he pay for those theengs of which he mek purchase an' correc' Don Numa when he mek meestake in the *adición*, and get hees change back. And then he say to Numa, 'Weel you not be so good to come to eshow me wheech ees best road out from thees town to the ford of the reever?' And Numa, he ees ge-nash hees teeth, but there ees no *remedio*.

"And so they go walking along thees lane between the orchards, these two togezzer, and the leetle bir-rds es-sing een the *árboles*—thees red fellow laughing and talkin' weeth Numa, ver' gay—leading hees horse by the bridle, and weeth the shotgun een the crook of hees arm. So the people loog out from the doors of their house and say, 'Ah! Don Numa ees diverrt heemself weeth hees friend.''

"And when they have come beyond the town, thees fellow ees mount hees horse. 'For your courtesy,' he say, 'I thank you. At your feet,' he say. 'Weeth God!' And he ride off laughing, and een a leetle way he toss hees shotgun een a bush, and he ride on to cross the reever, eslow. But when Numa Frenger see thees, he run queeckly, although he ees a ver' fat man, an' not young; he grab thees gun, he point heem, he pull the triggle—Nozzing! He break open the gun to look wizzen side—Nozzing! *O caballeros y conci-*

udadanos!" Monte threw down the gun; both hands grabbed his locks and tugged with the ferocity of despair.

"Ah-h! What a lovely cuss-word," cried Jay. "How trippingly it goes upon the tongue. I must learn that. Say it again!"

"But eet ees not a bad word, that," said Monte sheepishly. "Eet ees onlee idle word, to feel up. When thees *politicos* go up an' down, talking nonsense een the nose, when they weesh to theenk of more, then they say with *emoción,* '*O caballeros y conciudadanos*'; that ees, 'gentlemen and fellow ceetizens.' No more."

"Well, now, the story?" said Ben. "He crossed the river, going east—was that it?"

"Oh, yes. Well, when Numa Frenger see that thees gun ees emptee, he ees ver' ángree man. He ees more enr-rage heemself for that than for all what gone befor-re. He ees ar-rouse all Belen, he ees send telegraph to Sabinal, La Joya, Socorro, San Marcial, ever wheech way, to meek queek the posse, to send queek to the mesa to catch thees man, to mek *proclamación* to pay for heem three thousand dollar of rewar-rd. 'Do not keel heem, I entr-reat you,' say Don Numa. 'Breeng heem back. I want to fry heem.' "

"Now isn't that New Mexico for you?" demanded Jay. "A man commits a barefaced robbery, and you make a joke of it."

Monte placed the middle finger of his right hand in the palm of his left, pressed firmly as if to hold something there, and looked up under his brows at Miss Hollister.

"Then why do you laugh?" said Monte.

"You win," said Jay. "Go on with the story."

"Well, then," said Monte, "thees fellow he go up on the high plain on thees side of the reever, and he ride east and south by Sierra Montoso, and over the mountains of Los Piños, and he mek to go over Chupadero Mesa to thoss ruins of Gran Quivira. But he ride onlee *poco a poco,* easalee. And already a posse from La Joya, San Acacia is ride up the Alamillo Cañon, and across the plain." His swift hands fash-

ioned horseman, mountain, mesa, and plain. "Page Otero
and six, five other men. And they ride veree fast so that
already they pass in front of him to the south. They are now
before heem on Chupadero, and there they see heem. Eet
ees almost sundown.

"*Inmediatamente* he turn and go back. And their horses
are not so tired lak hees horse, and they spread out and ride
fast, and soon they are about to come weetheen gunshot
weeth the rifle. And when he see eet, thees *colorado* ees ride
oopon a reedge that all may see, and he tek that paper
money from the nose bag at the head of the saddle and he
toss eet up—pouf! The weend is blow gentle and thees
money it go joomp, joomp, here, there, een the booshes.
Again he ride a leetle way, and again he scatter thees money
lak a man to feed the hen een hees yard. So then he go on
away, thees red one. And when thees posse come to that
place, thees nize money is go hop, hop, along the ground
and over the booshes. There ees feefty-dollar beel een the
mesquite, there ees twenty-dollar beel een the tar-bush,
there ees beels blow by, roll by, slide by. So thees posse ees
deesmount heemself to peek heem, *muy enérgico*—lively.
And the weend ees come up faster at sundown, *como siempre* 'Come on!' says Page Otero. 'Come on, thees fellow weel
to escape!' Then the posse loog up surprise, and say, 'Who,
me?' and they go on to peek up thees monee. So that red-
head get clear away thees time."

"Did they get all the money?" asked Ben.

"Numa he say yes. He do not know just how mooch
thees bandit ees take, but he theenk they breeng back all,
or most nearly all."

"Do they know who he was?" asked Jay.

"*Por cierto*, no. But from the deescreepcion and hees
horse and saddle, they theenk eet ees a cowboy from
Quemado, name—I cannot to pr-ronounce thees name, Meester Ben. You say heem. I have eet here een 'La Voz del
Pueblo.' " From a hip pocket he produced a folded newspaper printed in Spanish, and showed Ben the place.

"Ross McEwen—about twenty-five or older, red hair, gray eyes, five feet nine inches—humph!" he returned the paper. "Will they catch him, do you think?"

Monte considered. He looked slowly at the far dim hills; he bent over to watch an inch-high horseman at his feet, toiling through painful immensities.

"The world ees ver' beeg een thees country," he said at last. "I theenk most mebbe not. *Quién sabe?* Onlee thees fellow must have water—and there ees not much water. Numa Frenger ees send now to all places, to Leencoln County; to Jeem Hunter here, and he meks every one to loog out; to Pat Garrett in Doña Ana Countee, and Pat watches by Parker Lake and the pass of San Agustin; to El Paso, and they watch there most of all that he pass not to Mexico Viejo. Eet may be at some water place they get heem. Or that he get them. He seem lak a man of some enterpr-rize, no?" He rose to go. "But I have talk too much. I mus' go now to my beesness."

"A poor business for a man as bright as you are," said Jay, and sniffed.

"But I geeve a square deal," said Monte serenely. "Eet ees a good beesness. At your feet, señorita! Unteel then, Meester Ben."

"Isn't he a duck? I declare, it's a shame to laugh at his English," said Jay.

"Don't worry. He gets to hear our Spanish, even if he is too polite to laugh."

"I hate to think of that man being chased for blood money," said Jay. "Hunter and that Pat Garrett you think so much of are keen after that reward, it seems. It is dreadful the way these people here make heroes out of their killers and man-hunters."

"Let's get this straight," said Ben. "You're down on the criminal for robbing and down on the sheriff for catching him. Does that sound like sense? If there was no reward offered, it's the sheriff's duty to catch him, isn't it? And if there is a reward, it's still his duty. The reward doesn't make him a man-hunter. Woman, you ain't right in your head. And as for Pat Garrett and some of these other old-timers—they're enjoying temporary immortality right now. They've become a tradition while they still live. Do you notice how all these honest-to-goodness old-timers talk? All the world is divided into three parts. One part is old-timers and the other two are not. The most clannish people on earth. And that brings us, by graceful and easy stages, to the main consideration, which I want to have settled before I go. And when I say settled, I mean that nothing is ever settled till it is settled right—get me?" He stood up; as Jay rose he took both her hands. "If circumstances were otherwise, Jay?"

She avoided his eyes. "Don't ask me now. I don't know, Ben—honest, I don't. You mustn't pester me now. It isn't fair when I'm so miserable." She pulled her hands away.

"Gawd help all poor sailors on a night like this!" said Ben fervently. "Listen, sister, I'm going to work, see? Goin' to fill your plans and specifications, every damn one, or bust a tug."

"I see you at it," jeered Jay, with an unpleasant laugh. "Work? You?"

"Me. I, myself. A faint heart never filled a spade flush," said Ben. "Going to get me a job and keep it. Lick any man that tries to fire me. Put that in your hope chest. Bye-bye, little didums. At your feet!"

As he went down the street his voice floated back to her:

> *But now my hair is falling out,*
> *And down the hill we'll go,*
> *And sleep together at the foot—*
> *John Barleycorn, my Jo!*

III

A high broad tableland lies east of the Rio Grande, and mountains make a long unbroken wall to it, with cliffs that front the west. This mesa is known locally as El Corredor. It is a pleasing and wholesome country. Zacatón and salt grass are gray green upon the level plain, checkered with patches of bare ground, white and glaring. On those bare patches, when the last rains fell, weeks, months, or years ago, an oozy paste filmed over the glossy levels, glazed by later suns, cracking at last to shards like pottery. But in broken country, on ridges and slopes, was a thin turf of buffalo and mesquite grass, curly, yellow, and low. There was iron beneath this place and the sand of it was red, the soil was ruddy white, the ridges and the lower hill slopes were granite red, yellowed over with grass. Even the high crowning cliffs were faintly cream, not gray, as limestone is elsewhere. Sunlight was soft and mellow there, sunset was red upon these cliffs. And Ross McEwen fled down that golden corridor.

If he had ridden straight south, he might have been far ahead by this time, well on the road to Mexico. But his plan had been to reach the Panhandle of Texas; he had tried for easting and failed. Three times he had sought to work through the mountain barrier to the salt plains—a bitter country of lava flow and sinks, of alkali springs, salt springs, magnesia springs, soda springs; of soda lakes, salt lakes, salt marshes, salt creeks; of rotten and crumbling ground, of greasy sand, of chalk that powdered and rose on the lightest airs, to leave no trace that a fugitive had passed this way.

He had been driven back once by the posse on Chupadero. Again at night he had been forced back by men who did not see him. He had tried to steal through by the old Ozanne stage road over the Oscuro, and found the pass guarded; and the last time, today, had been turned back by men that he did not even see. In the mouth of Mockingbird

Pass he had found fresh-shod tracks of many horses going
east. Mockingbird was held against him.

He could see distinctly, and in one eye-flight, every
feature of a country larger than all England. He could look
north to beyond Albuquerque, past the long ranges of Man-
zano, Montoso, Sandia, Oscuro; southward, between his
horse's ears, the northern end of the San Andrés was high
and startling before him, blue black with cedar brake and
piñon, except for the granite-gold top of Salinas Peak. Westward was the great valley of the Jornado del Muerto, the
Journey of the Dead, its width the fifty miles which lay
between the San Andrés and the Rio Grande.

And beyond the river was a bright enormous expanse,
bounded only by the dozen ranges that made the crest of the
Continental Divide—Dátil, Magdalena, San Mateo, the
Black Range, the Mimbres, Florida.

Between, bordering the midway river, other mountain
ranges lay tangled: Cuchillo Negro, Fra Cristóbal, Sierra de
los Caballos, Doña Ana, Robelero. It was over the summits
of these ranges that he saw the Continental Divide.

Here was irony indeed. With that stupendous panorama
outspread before him, he was being headed off, driven,
herded! He cocked an eyebrow aslant at the thought, and
spoke of it to his horse, who pricked back an ear in attention.
He was a honey-colored horse, and his name was Miel; which
is, by interpretation, Honey.

"Wouldn't you almost think, sweetness," said Ross
McEwen in a plaintive drawl, "that there was enough el-
bow-room here to satisfy every reasonable man? And yet
these lads are crowdin' me like a cop after an alley cat."

He sensed that an unusual effort was being made to take
him, and he smiled—a little ruefully—at the reflection that
the people at Mockingbird might well have been mere
chance comers upon their lawful occasions, and with no
designs upon him, no knowledge of him. Every man was a
possible enemy. He was out of law.

This was the third day of his flight. The man was still

brisk and bold, the honey-colored horse was still sturdy, but both lacked something of the sprightly resilience they had brought to the fords of Belen. There had been brief grazing and scant sleep, night riding, doubling and twisting to slip into lonely water holes. McEwen had chosen, as the lesser risk, to ride openly to Prairie Springs. He had found no one there and had borrowed grub for himself and several feeds of corn for the Honey horse. There had been no fast riding, except for the one brief spurt with the posse on Chupadero. But it had been a steady grind, doubly tiresome that they might not keep to the beaten trails. Cross-country traveling on soft ground is rough on horseflesh.

And now they left the plain and turned through tar-bush up the long slope to the San Andrés. A thousand ridges and hollows came plunging and headlong against them; and with that onset, at once and suddenly the tough little horse was tiring, failing.

Halfway to the hill foot they paused for a brief rest. High on their slim lances, banners of yucca blossoms were white and waxen, and wild bees hummed to their homes in the flower stalks of last year; flaunting afar, cactus flowers flamed crimson or scarlet through the black tar-bush.

Long since McEwen had given up the Panhandle. He planned now to bear far to the southeast, crossing the salt plains below the White Sands to the Guadalupe Mountains, where they straddled the boundary between the territory and Texas, and so east to the Staked Plains. He knew the country ahead, or had known it ten years before. But there would be changes. There was a new railroad, so he had heard, from El Paso to Tularosa, and so working north toward the States. There would be other things, too—new ranches, and all that. For sample, behind him, just where this long slope merged with the flats, three unexpected windmills, each five miles from the other, had made a line across his path; he had made a weary detour to pass unseen.

The San Andrés made here a twenty-mile offset where they joined the Oscuro, with the huge round mass of Salinas

Peak as their mutual corner. Lava Gap, the meeting-place
of the two ranges, was now directly at his left and ten miles
away. The bleak and mile-high walls of it made a frame for
the tremendous picture of Sierra Blanca, sixty long miles to
the east, with a gulf of nothingness between. Below that
nothingness, as McEwen knew, lay the black lava river of
the Mal Pais. But Lava Gap was not for him. Unless pursuit
was quite abandoned, Lava Gap and Dripping Springs
would be watched and guarded. He was fenced in by
probabilities.

But the fugitive was confident yet, and by no means at
the end of his resources. He knew a dim old Indian trail over
a high and improbable pass beyond Salinas Peak. It started
at Grapevine Spring, Captain Jack Crawford's ranch.

"And at Grapevine," said Ross aloud, "I'll have to buy,
beg, borrow, or get me a horse. Hope there's nobody at
home. If there's any one there I'll have to get his gun first
and trade afterwards. Borrowing horses is not highly recom-
mended, but it beats killing 'em."

To the right and before him the Jornado was hazy, vast,
and mysterious. To the right and behind him, the lava flow
of San Pascual sprawled black and sinister in the lowlands;
and behind him—Far behind him, far below him, a low line
of dust was just leaving the central windmill of those three
new ranches, a dozen miles away. McEwen watched this
dust with some interest while he rolled and lit a cigarette.
He drank the last water from his canteen.

"Come on, me bold outlaw," he said, "Keep moving.
You've done made your bed, but these hellhounds won't let
you sleep in it." He put foot to stirrup; he stroked the Honey
horse.

"Miel, old man, you tough it out four or five miles more,
and your troubles will be over. Me for a fresh horse at Grapevine, come hell or high water. Take it easy. No hurry. Just
shuffle along."

The pursuing dust did not come fast, but it came
straight his way. "I'll bet a cookie," said Ross sagely, "that

some of these gay bucks have got a spyglass. Wonder if that ain't against the rules? And new men throwin' in with them at every ranch. Reckon I would, too, if it wasn't for this red topknot of mine. Why couldn't they meet up with some other redheaded hellion and take him back? Wouldn't that be just spiffin'? One good thing, anyway—I didn't go back to the Quemado country. Some of the boys would sure have got in Dutch, hidin' me out. This is better."

He crossed the old military road that had once gone through Lava Gap to Fort Stanton; he smiled at the shod tracks there; he came to the first hills, pleasingly decorated with bunches of mares—American mares, gentle mares—Corporal Tanner's mares. He picked a bunch with four or five saddle horses in it and drove them slowly up Grapevine Cañon. The Miel horse held up his head and freshened visibly. He knew what this meant. The sun dropped behind the hills. It was cool and fresh in Grapevine.

The outlaw took his time. He had a long hour or more. He turned for a last look at the north and the cliffs of Oscuro Mountain blazing in the low sun to fiery streamers of red light. You would have seen, perhaps, only a howling wilderness; but this man was to look back, waking and in dream, and to remember that brooding and sunlit silence as the glowing heart of the world. From this place alone he was to be an exile.

"Nice a piece of country as ever laid outdoors," said Ross McEwen. "I've seen some several places where it would be right pleasant to have a job along with a bunch of decent punchers—good grub and all that, mouth organ by the firelight after supper—or herding sheep."

Grapevine Spring is at the very head of the cañon. To east, south, and west the hills rise directly from the corral fences. McEwen drove the mares into the water pen and called loudly to the house. The hail went unanswered. Eagles screamed back from a cliff above him.

"A fool for luck," said McEwen.

He closed the bars, he gave Miel his first installment of

water. Then he went to the house. It was unlocked and there
was no one there. The ashes on the hearth were cold. He
borrowed two cans of beans and some bacon; he borrowed
and ground a little coffee. There was a slender store of corn,
and he borrowed one feed of this to make tomorrow's breakfast for the new horse he was soon to acquire. He found an
old saddle and he borrowed that, with an old bridle as well;
he brought his own to replace them; he lit the little lamp on
the table and grinned happily.

"They'll find Miel and my saddle and the light," he said,
"and they'll make sure I've taken to the brush."

He went back to the pen, he roped and saddled a sad-
dle-marked brown, broad-chested and short-coupled, unshod. Shod tracks are too easily followed. Then he scratched
his red head and grinned again. The pen was built of poles
laid in panels, except at the front; the cedar brake grew to
the very sides of it. He went to the back and took down two
panels, laying the poles aside; he let the mares drift out
there, seeing to it that some of them went around by the
house, and the rest on the other side of the pen. It was almost
dark by now.

"There," he said triumphantly. "The boys will drive in
a bunch of stock when they come, for remounts, and they'll
go right on through. Fine mess in the dark. And it'll puzzle
them to find which way I went, with all these here tracks.
Time I was gone."

He came back to the watering-trough; he washed his
hands and face and filled his canteen; he went on where
Miel stood weary and huddled in the dusk. His hand was
gentle on that drooping neck.

"Miel, old fellow," he said, "you've been one good little
horse to me. *Buena suerte.*" He led the brown to the bars.
"I hate a fool," said Ross McEwen.

He took down the bars and rode into the cedar brush
at right angles to the cañon, climbing steadily from the first.
It was a high and desperate pass, and branches had grown
across the unused trail; long before he had won halfway to

the summit he heard, far below him, the crashing of horses in the brush, the sound of curses and laughter. The pursuit had arrived at Grapevine.

He topped the summit of that nameless pass an hour later, and turned down the dark cañon to the east—to meet grief at once. Since his time a cloudburst had been this way. Where once had been fair footing the flood had cut deep and wide, and every semblance of soil had washed away, leaving only a wild moraine, a loose rubble of rocks and tumbled boulders. But it was the only way. The hillsides were impossibly steep and sidelong, glassy granite and gneiss, or treacherous slides of porphyry. Ross led his horse. Every step was a hazard in that narrow and darkened place, with crumbling ridge and pit and jump off, with wind-rows of smooth round rock to roll and turn under their feet. It took the better part of two hours to win through the narrows, perhaps two miles. The cañon widened then, the hillsides were lower and Ross could ride again, picking his doubtful way in the starlight. He turned on a stepladder of hills to the north, and came about midnight to Dripstone, high in a secret hollow of the hills. The prodigious bulk of Salinas loomed mysterious and incredible above him in the starlight.

He tied the brown horse securely and named him Porch Climber. He built a tiny fire and toasted strips of bacon on the coals; he opened and ate one can of his borrowed beans. Then he spread out his saddle blankets with hat and saddle for pillow, and so lay down to untroubled sleep.

IV

He awoke in that quiet place before the first stirring of dawn. A low thin moon was in the sky and the mountains were dim across the east. He washed his eyes out with water from the canteen. He made a nose bag from the corn sack and hung it on Porch Climber's brown head. The Belen nose bag had gone into the discard days before. He washed out the empty bean can for coffeepot. He built a fire of twigs and hovered over it while his precious coffee came to a boil; his coat was thin and the night air was fresh, almost chilly. He smacked his lips over the coffee; he saddled and watered Porch Climber at Dripstone and refilled his canteen there. Porch Climber drank sparingly.

"Better fill up, old-timer," Ross advised him. "You're sure going to need it."

Knuckled ridges led away from Salinas like fingers of a hand. The eastern flat was some large fraction of a mile nearer to sea level than the high plain west of the mountain, and these ridges were massive and steep accordingly. He made his way down one of them. The plain was dark and cold below him; the mountains took shape and grew, the front range of the Rockies—Capitan, Carrizo, Sierra Blanca, Sacramento, with Guadalupe low and dim in the south; the White Sands were dull and lifeless in the midway plain. Bird twitter was in the air. Rabbits scurried through the brush, a quail whirred by and sent back a startled call; crimson streaks shot up the sky, and day grew broad across the silent levels. The cutbanks of Salt Creek appeared, wandering away southeast toward the marshes. Low and far against the black base of the Sacramento, white feathers lifted and fluffed, the smoke of the first fires at Tularosa, fifty miles away. Flame tipped the far-off crests, the sun leaped up from behind the mountain wall, the level light struck on the White Sands, glanced from those burnished bevels and splashed on the western cliffs; the desert day blazed over this new half-world.

He had passed a few cows on the ridges, but now, as he came close to the flats, he was suddenly aware of many cattle before him, midges upon the vast plain; more cattle than he had found on the western side of the mountains. He drew rein, instantly on the alert, and began to quarter the scene with a keen scrutiny. At once a silver twinkling showed to northward—the steel fans of a windmill, perhaps six miles out from the foot of the main mountain. His eye moved slowly across the plain. He was shocked to find a second windmill tower some six or eight miles south of the first, keeping at the same distance from the hills, and when he made out the faint glimmer of a third, far in the south, he gave way to indignation. It was a bald plain with no cover for the quietly disposed, except a few clumps of soapweed here and there. And this line of windmills was precisely the line of the road to El Paso. Where he had expected smooth going he would have to keep to the roughs; to venture into the open was to court discovery. He turned south across the ridges.

He had talked freely to Miel, but until now he had been reticent with Porch Climber, who had not yet won his confidence. At this unexpected reverse he opened his heart.

"Another good land gone wrong," he said. "I might have known it. This side of Salt Creek is only half-bad cow country, so of course it's all settled up, right where we want to go. Of course no one would live east of Salt Creek, not even sheepherders. And we couldn't possibly make it, goin' on the other side of Salt Creek with all that marsh country and the hell of the White Sands. Why, this is plumb ridiculous!"

He meditated for a while upon his wrongs and then broke out afresh: "When I was here, the only water east of the mountains was the Wildy Well at the corner of the damn White Sands. Folks drove along the road, and when they wanted water they nicely went up in the hills. It's no use to cross over to Tularosa. They'll be waiting for us there. No, sir, we've pointedly got to skulk down through the brush. And you'll find it heavy going, up one ridge and down another, like a flea on a washboard."

Topping the next ridge, he reined back swiftly into a hollow place. He dismounted and peered through a mesquite bush, putting the branches aside to look. A mile to the south two horsemen paced soberly down a ridge—and it was a ridge which came directly from the pass to Grapevine.

"Now ain't them the bright lads?" said the runaway,

divided between chagrin and admiration. "What are you
going to do with fellows like that? I ask you. I left plain word
that I done took to the hills afoot, without the shadow of a
doubt. Therefore, they reasoned, I hadn't. They've cop-
pered every bet. Now that's what I call clear thinkin'. I
reckon some of 'em did stay there, but these two crossed
over that hell-gate at night, just in case.

"I'll tell a man they had a ride where that cloudburst
was. Say, they'll tell their grandchildren about that—if they
live that long, which I misdoubt, the way they're carryin' on.
This gives me what is technically known as the willies.
Hawse," said McEwen, "let's us tarry a spell and see what
these hirelin' bandogs are goin' to do now."

He took off the bridle and saddle, he staked Porch
Climber to rest and graze while he watched. What the bandogs did was to ride straight to the central windmill, where
smoke showed from the house. McEwen awaited develop-
ments. Purely from a sense of duty he ate the other can of
beans while he waited.

"They'll take word to every ranch," he prophesied
gloomily. "Leave a man to watch where there isn't any one
there—take more men along when they find more than one
at a well. Wish to God I was a drummer."

His prognostications were verified. After a long wait,
which meant breakfast, a midget horseman rode slowly
north toward the first windmill. A little later two men rode
slowly south toward the third ranch.

"That's right, spread the news, dammit, and make everybody hate you," said Ross. He saddled and followed
them, paralleling their course, but keeping to the cover of
the brush.

It was heavy and toilsome going, boulders and rocks
alternating with soft ground where Porch Climber's feet
went through; gravel, coarse sand, or piled rocks in the
washes; tedious twisting in the brush and wearisome wind-
ings where a bay of open country forced a detour. He
passed by the mouths of Good Fortune, Antelope, and Cot-

tonwood cañons, struggling through their dry deltas; he drew abreast of the northern corner of the White Sands. The reflection of it was blinding, yet he found it hard to hold his eyes away. The sun rode high and hot. McEwen consulted his canteen.

More than once or twice came the unwelcome thought that he might take to the hill country, discard Porch Climber and hide by some inaccessible seep or pothole until pursuit died down. But he was a stubborn man, and his heart was set upon Guadalupe; he had an inborn distaste for a diet of chance rabbit and tuna fruit—or, perhaps, slow deer without salt. A stronger factor in his decision—although he hardly realized it—was the horseman's hatred for being set afoot. He could hole up safely; there was little doubt of that. But when he came out of the hole, how then? A man from nowhere, on foot, with no past and no name and a long red beard—that would excite remark. He fingered the stubble on his cheeks with that reflection. Yes, such a man would be put to it to account for himself—and he would have to show up sometime, somewhere. The green cottonwood of Independent Spring showed high on the hill to his right. He held on to the south.

And now he came to the mouth of Sulphur Springs Cañon. Beyond here a great bay of open plain flowed into the hill foot under Kaylor Mountain; and midmost of that bay was another windmill, a long low house, spacious corrals. McEwen was sick of windmills. But this one was close under the mountain, far west of the line of the other ranches and of the El Paso road; McEwen saw with lively interest that his pursuers left the road and angled across the open to this ranch. That meant dinner.

"Honesty," said McEwen with conviction, "is the best policy. Dinner-time for some people, but only noon for me. . . . And how can these enterprisin' chaps be pursuin' me when they're in front? That isn't reasonable. Who ever heard of deputies goin' ahead and the bandit taggin' along behind? That's not right. It's not moral. I'm goin' around.

Besides, if I don't this thing is liable to go on always, just windmills and windmills—to Mexico City—Peru—Chile. I'm plumb tired of windmills. Porch Climber," said McEwen, "have you got any gift of speed? Because, just as soon as these two sheriff men get to that ranch and have time to go in the house, you and me are going to drift out quiet and unostentatious across the open country till we hit the banks of the Salt Marsh. And if these fellows look out and see us you've just got to run for it. They can maybe get fresh horses too. But if they don't see us we'll be right. We'll drift south under cover of the bank and get ahead of 'em while they stuff their paunches."

Half an hour later he turned Porch Climber's head to the east, and rode sedately across the smooth plain, desiring to raise no dust. Some three miles away, near where he crossed the El Paso road, grew a vigorous motte of mesquite trees. Once beyond that motte, he kept it lined up between him and the ranch; and so came unseen to where the plain broke away to the great marsh which rimmed the basin of the White Sands.

In the east the White Sands billowed in great dry dunes above the level of the plain, but the western half was far below that level, and waterbound. This was the home of mirages; they spread now all their pomp of palm and crystal lake and fairy hill. McEwen turned south along the margin. Here, just under the bank, the ground was moist, almost wet, and yet firm footing, like a road of hard rubber. He brought Porch Climber to a long-reaching trot, steady and smooth; he leaned forward in his stirrups and an old song came to his lips, unsummoned. He sang it with loving mockery, in a nasal but not unpleasing baritone:

> *They gave him his orders at Monroe, Virginia,*
> *Sayin', "Pete, you're way behind ti-time"*—

"Gosh, it does seem natural to sing when a good horse is putting the miles behind him," said McEwen. "This little

old brown pony is holding' up right well, too, after all that
grief in the roughs this mawnin'.

He looked 'raound then to his black, greasy
*   fireman,*
"Just shovel in a little more co-o-al,
And when we cross that wide old maounting,
You can watch old Ninety-Seven roll!"

"Hey, Porch Climber! You ain't hardly keepin' time.
Peart up a little! Now, lemme see. Must be about twenty
mile to the old Wildy Well. Wonder if I'll find any more new
ranches between here and there? Likely. Hell of a country,
all cluttered up like this!

It's a mighty rough road from Lynchburg to
*   Danville,*
And a line on a three-mile gra-ade,
It was on that grade that he lo-ost his av'rage,
And you see what a jump he made!

He rejoined the wagon road where the White Sands
thrust a long and narrow arm far to the west. The old road
crossed this arm at the shoulder, a three-mile speedway. Out
on the sands magic islands came and went and rose and sunk
in a misty sea. But in the south, where the road climbed
again to the plain, was the inevitable windmill—reality and
no mirage.

McEwen followed the road in the posture of a man who
had nothing to fear. He had outridden the rumor of his
flight; he could come to this ranch with a good face. But
he reined down to a comfortable jog. Those behind might
overtake him close enough to spy him in this naked place.
Jaunting easily, nearing the ranch where he belonged, a
horseman was no object of suspicion; but a man in haste was
a different matter.

There was no one at the ranch. The water was brackish

and flat, but the two wayfarers drank thankfully. He could see no signs that any horses were watering there; he made a shrewd guess that the boys had taken the horses and gone up into the mountains for better grass and sweet water, or perhaps to get out of sight of the White Sands, leaving the flats to the cattle.

"Probably they just ride down every so often to oil the windmill," he said. "Leastways, I would. Four hundred square miles of lookin'-glass, three hundred and sixty-four days a year—no, thank you! My eyes are 'most out now."

JB was branded on the gateposts of the corral; JB was branded on the door. He found canned stuff on a shelf and a few baking-powder biscuits, old and dry. He took a can of salmon and filed it for future reference.

"No time for gormandizin' now," he said. He stuffed the stale biscuits into his pocket to eat on the road. "There's this much about bread," said McEwen; "I can take it or I can leave it alone. And I've been leaving it alone for some several days now."

A pencil and a tablet lay on the table. His gray eyes went suddenly adance with impish light. He tore out a page and wrote a few words of counsel and advice:

Hey, you JB waddies: Look out for a fellow
with red hair and gray eyes. Medium-sized man.
He robbed the bank at Belen, and they think
he came this way. Big reward offered for him.
Two thousand, I hear. But I don't know for
certain. Send word to the ranches up north. I
will tell them as far south as Organ.

JIM HUNTLEY

He hung this newsletter on a nail above the stove.

"There!" he said. "If them gay jaspers that are after me had any sense a-tall, they'd see it was no use to go any further, and they'd stay right here and rest up. But they won't. They'll say, 'Hey, this is the way he went—here's some more of the same old guff! But how ever did that feller get down here without us findin' any tracks? You can see what a jump he made.' I don't want to be ugly," said McEwen, "but I've got to cipher up some way to shake loose from these fellows. I want to go to sleep. . . . Now who in hell is Jim Huntley?"

Time for concealment was past. From now on he must set his hope on speed. He rode down the big road boldly and, for a time, at a brisk pace; he munched the dry biscuits and washed them down with warm and salty water from his canteen.

There was hardly room for another ranch between here and Wildy's Well. Wildy's was an old established ranch. It was among the possibilities that he might hit here upon some old acquaintance whose failing sight would not note his passing, and who would give him a fresh horse. He was now needing urge of voice and spur for Porch Climber's lagging feet. It sat in his mind that Wildy was dead. His brows knitted with the effort to remember. Yes, Wildy had been killed by a falling horse. Most likely, though, he would find no one living at the well. Not too bad, the water of Wildy's Well—but they would be in the hills with the good grass.

The brown horse was streaked with salt and sweat; he dragged in the slow sand. Here was a narrow, broken country of rushing slopes, pinched between the White Sands and the mountains. The road wound up and down in the crowding brush; the footing was a coarse pebbly sand of broken granite from the crumbling hills. Heat waves rose quivering, the White Sands lifted and shuddered to a blinding shimmer, the dream islands were wavering, shifting, and indistinct, astir with rumor. McEwen's eyes were dull for sleep, red-rimmed and swollen from glare and alkali dust. The salt water was bitter in his belly. The stubble on his face was gray with powdered dust and furrowed with sweat stains; dust was in his nostrils and his ears, and the taste of dust was in his mouth. Porch Climber ploughed heavily. And all at once McEwen felt a sudden distaste for his affair.

He had a searching mind and it was not long before he found a cause. That damn song! Dance music. There were places where people danced, where they would dance tonight. There was a garden in Rutherford—

V

There was no one at Wildy's Well, no horses there and no sign that any horses were using there. McEwen drank deep of the cool sweet water. When Porch Climber had his fill, McEwen plunged arms and head into the trough. Horse and man sighed together; their eyes met in comfortable understanding.

"Feller," said McEwen, "it was that salt water, much as anything else, that slowed yuh up, I reckon. Yuh was sure sluggish. And yuh just ought to see yourself now! Nemmine, that's over." He took down his rope and cut off a length, the spread of his arms. He untwisted this length to three strands, soaked these strands in the trough, wrung them out and knotted them around his waist. He eyed the cattle that had been watering here. They had retreated to the far side at his coming and were now waiting impatiently. "Been many a long year since I've seen any Durham cattle," said McEwen. "Everybody's got white-face stuff now. Reckon they raise these for El Paso market. No feeder will buy 'em, unless with a heavy cut in the price."

He hobbled over and closed the corral gate. Every bone of him was a separate ache. A faint breeze stirred; the mill sails turned lazily; the gears squeaked a protest. Ross looked up with interest.

"That was right good water," he said. "Guess you've earned a greasing." He climbed the tall tower. Wildy's Well dated from before the steel windmill; this was massive and cumbersome, a wooden tower, and the wheel itself was of wood. After his oiling Ross scanned the north with an anxious eye. There was no dust. South by east, far in the central plain, dim hills swam indeterminate through the heat haze

—Las Cornudas and Hueco. South by west, gold and rose, the peaks of the Organs peered from behind the last corner of the San Andrés. He searched the north again. He could see no dust—but he could almost see a dust. He shook his head. "Them guys are real intelligent," he said. "I'm losin' my av'rage." He clambered down with some celerity, and set about what he had to do.

He tied the severed end of his rope to the saddle horn, tightened the cinches, swung into the saddle, and shook out a loop. Hugging the fence, the cattle tore madly around the corral in a wild cloud of dust. McEwen rode with them on an inner circle, his eye on a big roan steer, his rope whirling in slow and measured rhythms. For a moment the roan steer darted to the lead; the loop shot out, curled over, and tightened on both forefeet; Porch Climber whirled smartly to the left; the steer fell heavily. Ross swung off; as he ran, he tugged at the hogging string around his waist. Porch Climber dragged valiantly, Ross ran down the rope, pounced on the struggling steer, gathered three feet together and tied them with the hogging string. These events were practically simultaneous.

McEwen unsaddled the horse. "I guess you can call it a day," he said. He opened the gate and let the frightened cattle run out. "Here," he said, "is where I make a spoon or spoil a horn." He cut a thong from a saddle string and tied his old plough-handle forty-five so that it should not jolt from the scabbard. He made a tight roll of the folded bridle, that lonely can of salmon, and his coat, with his saddle blanket wrapped around all; he tied these worldly goods securely behind the cantle. He uncoupled the cinches and let out the quarter straps to the last hole.

The tied steer threshed his head madly, bellowing wild threats of vengeance. McEwen carried the saddle and placed it at the steer's back, where he lay. He found a short and narrow strip of board, like a batten, under the tower; and with this, as the frantic roan steer heaved and threshed in vain efforts to rise, he poked the front cinch under the struggling body, inches at a time, until at last he could reach over and hook his fingers into the cinch ring. Before he could do this he was forced to tie the free foot to the three that were first tied; it had been kicking with so much fury and determination that the task could not be accomplished. Into the cinch ring he tied the free end of his rope, bringing it up between body and tied feet; he took a double of loose rope around his hips, dug his heels into the sand and pulled manfully every time the steer floundered; and so, at last and painfully, drew the cinch under until the saddle was on the steer's back and approximately where it should be. Then he put in the latigo strap, taking two turns, and tugged at the latigo till the saddle was pulled to its rightful place. At every tug the roan steer let out an agonized bawl. Then he passed the hind cinch behind the steer's hips and under the tail, drawing it up tightly so that the saddle could not slip over the steer's withers during the subsequent proceedings.

McEwen stood up and mopped the muddy sweat from his face; he rubbed his aching back. He filled his canteen at the trough, drank again, and washed himself. He rolled a smoke; he lashed the canteen firmly to the saddle forks. Porch Climber was rolling in the sand. McEwen took him by the forelock and led him through the open gate.

"If you should ask me," he said, "this corral is a spot where there is going to be trouble, and no place at all for you." He looked up the north road. Nothing in sight.

He went back to the steer. He hitched up his faded blue overalls, tightened his belt, and squinted at the sun; he loosened the last-tied foot and coiled the rope at the saddle horn. Then he eased gingerly into the saddle. The steer made lamentable outcry, twisting his neck in a creditable attempt to hook his tormentor; the free foot lashed out madly. But McEwen flattened himself and crouched safely, with a full inch of margin; the steer was near to hooking his own leg and kicking his own face, and he subsided with a groan. McEwen settled himself in the saddle.

"Are ye ready?" said McEwen.

"Oi am!" said McEwen.

"Thin go!" said McEwen, and pulled the hogging string.

The steer lurched sideways to his feet, paused for one second of amazement, and left the ground. He pitched, he plunged, he kicked at the stirrups, he hooked at the rider's legs, he leaped, he ran, bawling his terror and fury to the sky; weaving, lunging, twisting, he crashed sidelong into the fence, fell, scrambled up in an instant. The shimmy was not yet invented. But the roan steer shimmied, and he did it nobly; man and saddle rocked and reeled. Then, for the first time, he saw the open gate and thundered through it, abandoning all thought except flight.

Shaken and battered, McEwen was master. The man was a rider. To use the words of a later day, he was "a little warm, but not at all astonished." Yet he had not come off scot-free. When they crashed into the fence he had pulled up his leg, but had taken an ugly bruise on the hip. The whole performance, and more particularly the shimmy feature, had been a poor poultice for aching bones. Worse than all, the canteen had been crushed between fence and saddle. The priceless water was lost.

His hand still clutched the hogging string; he had no wish to leave that behind for curious minds to ponder upon. Until his mount slowed from a run to a pounding trot, he made no effort to guide him, the more because the steer's chosen course was not far from the direction in which McEwen wished to go. Wildy's Well lay at the extreme southwestern corner of the White Sands, and McEwen's thought was to turn eastward. He meant to try for Luna's Wells, the old stage station in the middle of the desert, on the road which ran obliquely from Organ to Tularosa. When time was ripe McEwen leaned over and slapped his hat into the steer's face, on the right side, to turn him to the left and to the east.

The first attempt at guidance, and the fourth attempt, brought on new bucking spells. McEwen gave him time between lessons; what he most feared was that the roan would "sull," or balk, refusing to go farther. When the steer stopped, McEwen waited until he went on of his own accord; when his progress led approximately toward McEwen's goal, he was allowed to go his own way unmolested. McEwen was bethorned, dragged through mesquite bushes, raked under branches; his shirt was ribboned and torn. But he had his way at last. With danger, with infinite patience, and with good judgment, he forced his refractory mount to the left and ever to the left, and so came at last into a deep trail which led due east. Muttering and grumbling, the steer followed the trail.

All this had taken time, but speed had also been a factor. When McEwen felt free to turn his head, only a half-circle of the windmill fans showed above the brush. Wildy's Well was miles behind them.

"Boys," said McEwen, "if you follow me this time, I'll say you're good!"

The steer scuffed and shambled, taking his own gait; he stopped often to rest, his tongue hung out, foam dripped from his mouth. McEwen did not urge him. The way led now through rotten ground and alkali, now through chalk that powdered and billowed in dust; deep trails, channeled by winds at war. As old trails grew too deep for comfort, the stock had made new ones to parallel the old; a hundred paths lay side by side.

McEwen was a hard case. A smother of dust was about him, thirst tormented him, his lips were cracked and bleeding, his eyes sunken, his face fallen in; and weariness folded him like a garment.

"Slate water is the best water," said McEwen.

They came from chalk and brush into a better country; poor, indeed, and starved, but the air of it was breathable. The sun was low and the long shadows of the hills reached out into the plain. And now he saw, dead in front, the gleaming vane and sails of a windmill. Only the top—the fans seemed to touch the ground—and yet it was clear to see. McEwen plucked up heart. This was not Luna's. Luna's was far beyond. This was a new one. If it stood in a hollow place—And it did!—It could not be far away. Water!

For the first time McEwen urged his mount, gently, and only with the loose and raveled tie string. Once was enough. The roan steer stopped, pawed the ground, and proclaimed flat rebellion. For ten minutes, perhaps, McEwen sought to overrule him. It was of no use. The roan steer was done. He took down his rope. With a little loop he snared a pawing and rebellious forefoot. He pulled up rope and foot with all his failing strength, and took a quick turn on the saddle horn. The roan made one hop and fell flat-long. McEwen tied three feet, though there was scant need for it. He took off the saddle, carried it to the nearest thicket and raised it, with pain, into the forks of a high soapweed, tucking up latigos and cinches. With pain; McEwen, also, was nearly done.

"My horse gave out on me. I toted my saddle a ways, but it was too heavy, and I hung it up so the cows couldn't eat it," he said, in the tone of one who recites a lesson.

He untied the steer then and came back hotfoot to his soapweed, thinking that the roan might be in fighting humor. But the roan was done. He got unsteadily to his feet, with hanging head and slavering jaws; he waited for a little and moved slowly away.

"Glad he didn't get on the prod," said McEwen. "I sure expected it. That was one tired steer. He sure done me a good turn. Guess I'll be strollin' into camp."

It was a sorry strolling. A hundred yards—a quarter— a half—a mile. The windmill grew taller; the first night breeze was stirring; he could see the fans whirl in the sun. A hundred yards—a quarter—a mile! An hour was gone. The shadows overtook him, passed him; the hills behind were suddenly very close and near, notched black against a crimson sky. Thirst tortured him, the windmill beckoned, sunset winds urged him on. He came to the brow of the shallow dip in which the ranch lay; he saw a little corral, a water pen, a long dark house beyond; he climbed into the water pen and plunged his face into the trough.

The windmill groaned and whined with a dismal clank

and grinding of dry gears. Yet there was a low smoke over
the chimney. How was this? The door stood open. Except
for the creaking plaint of the windmill, a dead quiet hung
about the place, a hint of something ominous and sinister.
Stumbling, bruised, and outworn, McEwen came to that low
dark door. He heard a choking cough, a child's wailing cry.
His foot was on the threshold.

"What's wrong? *Qué es?*" he called.

A cracked and feeble voice made an answer that he
could not hear. Then a man appeared at the inner door; an
old man, a Mexican, clutching at the wall for support.

"*El garrotillo,*" said the cracked voice. "The strangler
—diphtheria."

"I'm here to help you," said McEwen.

VI

Of what took place that night McEwen had never afterward
any clear remembrance, except of the first hour or two. The
drone of bees was in his ears, and a whir of wings. He moved
in a thin, unreal mist, giddy and light-headed, undone by
thirst, weariness, loss of sleep—most of all by alkaline and
poisonous dust, deep in his lungs. In the weary time that
followed, though he daily fell more and more behind on
sleep and rest, he was never so near to utter collapse as on
this first interminable night. It remained for him a blurred
and distorted vision of the dreadful offices of the sick-room;
of sickening odors; of stumbling from bed to bed as one
sufferer or another shook with paroxysms of choking.

Of a voice, now far off and now clear, insistent with
counsel and question, direction and appeal; of lamplight
that waned and flared and dwindled again; of creak and
clang and pounding of iron on iron in horrible rhythm, endless, slow, intolerable. That would be the windmill. Yes, but
where? And what windmill?

Of terror, and weeping, and a young child that
screamed. That woman—why, they had always told him

grown people didn't take diphtheria. But she had it, all right.
Had it as bad as the two youngsters, too. She was the mother,
it seemed. Yes, Florencio had told him that. Too bad for the
children to die. . . . But who the devil was Florencio? The
windmill turned dismally—clank and rattle and groan.

That was the least one choking now—Felix. Swab out
his throat again. Hold the light. Careful. That's it. Burn it up.
More cloth, old man. Hold the light this way. There, there,
pobrecito! All right now. . . . Something was lurking in the
corners, in the shadows. Must go see. Drive it away. What's
that? What say? Make coffee? Sure. Coffee. Good idea. Salty
coffee. Windmill pumpin' salt water. Batter and pound and
squeal. Round and round. Round and round. Round and
round. . . . Tell you what. Goin' to grease that damn windmill. Right now. . . . Huh? What's that? Wait till morning?
All right. All ri'. Sure.

His feet were leaden. His arms minded well enough,
but his hands were simply wonderful. Surprisin' skillful,
those hands. How steady they were to clean membranes
from little throats. Clever hands! They could bring water to
these people, too, lift them up and hold the cup and not spill
a drop. They could sponge off hot little bodies when the
children cried out in delirium. Wring out rag, too! Wonderful hands! Mus' call people's 'tention to these hands sometime. There, there, let me wash you some more with the
nice cool water. Now, now—nothing will hurt you. Uncle
Happy's goin' to be right here, takin' care of you. Now, now
—go to sleep—go-o to sleep!

But his feet were so big, so heavy and so clumsy, and his
legs were insubordinate. 'Specially the calves. The calf of
each leg, where there had once been good muscles of
braided steel, was now filled with sluggish water of inferior
quality. That wasn't the worst, either. There was a distinct
blank place, a vacuum, something like the bead in a spirit
level, and it shifted here and there as the water sloshed
about. Wonder nobody had ever noticed that.

Must be edgin' on toward morning. Sick people are

worst between two and four, they say. And they're all easier now, every one. Both kids asleep—tossin' about! And now the mother was droppin' off. Yes, sir—she's goin' to sleep. What did the old man call her? Estefanía. Yes—Est'fa'—

He woke with sunlight in his eyes. His arm sprawled before him on a pine table and his head lay on his arm. He raised up, blinking, and looked around. This was the kitchen, a sorry spectacle. The sick-room lay beyond an open door. He sat by that door, where he could see into the sick-room. They were all asleep. The woman stirred uneasily and threw out an arm. The old man lay huddled on a couch beyond the table.

McEwen stared. The fever had passed and his head was reasonably clear. He frowned, piecing together remembered scraps from the night before. The old man was Florencio Telles, the woman was the wife of his dead son, these were his grandchildren. Felix was one. Forget the other name. They had come back from a trip to El Paso a week ago, on some such matter, and must have brought the contagion with them. First one came down with the strangler, then another. Well poisoned with it, likely. Have to boil the drinking-water. This was called Rancho Perdido—the Lost Ranch. Well named. The old fellow spoke good English. McEwen was at home in Spanish, and, from what he remembered of last night, the talk had been carried on in either tongue indifferently. What a night!

He rose and tiptoed out with infinite precaution. The wind was dead. He went to the well and found the oil; he climbed up and drenched the bearings and gears. He was surprised to see how weak he was and how sore; and for the first time in his life he knew the feeling of giddiness and was forced to keep one hand clutched tightly to some support as he moved around the platform—he, Ross McEwen.

When he came back the old man met him with finger on lip. They sat on the warm ground, where they could keep watch upon the sick-room, obliquely, through two doors; just far enough away for quiet speech to be unheard.

"Let them sleep. Every minute is so much of coined gold. We won't make a move to wake them. And how is it with you, my son?"

"Fine and fancy. When I came here last night I had a thousand aches, and now I've got only one."

"And that one is all over?"

"That's the place. Never mind me. I'll be all right. How long has this been going on?"

"This is the fifth day for the oldest boy, I think. He came down with it first, Demetrio. We thought it was only a sore throat at first. Maybe six days. I am a little mixed up."

"Should think you would be. Now listen. I know something about diphtheria. Not much, but this for certain. Here's what you've got to do, old man: Quick as they wake up in there, you go to bed and stay in bed. You totter around much more and you're going to die. There's your fortune told, and no charge for it."

"Oh, I'm not bad. I do not cough hard. The strangler never hurts old people much." So he said, but every word was an effort.

"Hell, no, you're not bad. Just a walkin' corpse, that's all. You get to bed and save your strength. When any two of 'em are chokin' to death at once, that'll be time enough for you to hobble out and take one of them off my hands. Do they sleep this long, often?"

"Oh, no. This is the first time. They are always better when morning comes, but they have not all slept at the same time, never before. My daughter, you might say, has not slept at all. It has been grief and anxiety with her as much as the sickness. They will all feel encouraged now, since you've come. If it please God, we'll pull them all through."

"Look here!" said McEwen. "It can't be far to Luna's Well. Can't I catch up a horse and lope over there after while—bring help and send for a doctor?"

"There's no one there. Francisco Luna and Casimiro both have driven their stock to the Guadalupe Mountains, weeks ago. It has been too dry. And no one one uses the old road now. All travel goes by the new way, beyond the new railroad."

"I found no one at the western ranches yesterday," said McEwen.

"No. Every one is in the hills. The drought is too bad. There is no one but you. The nearest help is Alamogordo—thirty-five miles. And if you go there some will surely die before you get back. I have no more strength. I will be flat on my back this day."

"That's where you belong. I'll be nurse and cook for this family. Got anything to cook?"

"Not much. *Frijoles*, jerky, bacon, flour, a little canned stuff, and dried peaches."

McEwen frowned. "It is in my mind they ought to have eggs and milk."

"When the cattle come to water, you can shut up a cow and a calf—or two of them—and we can have a little milk to-night. I'll show you which ones. As I told you last night, I turned out the cow I was keeping up, for fear I'd get down and she would die here in the pen."

"Don Florencio, I'm afraid I didn't get all you told me last night," said McEwen thoughtfully. "I was wild as a hawk, I reckon. Thought that windmill would certainly drive me crazy. Fever."

The old man nodded. "I knew, my son. It galled my heart to make demands on you, but there was no remedy. It had to be done. I was at the end of my strength. Little Felix, if not the other, would surely have been dead by now, except for the mercy of God which sent you here."

McEwen seemed much struck by this last remark. He cocked his head a little to one side painfully, for his neck was stiff; he pursed his lip and held it between finger and thumb for a moment of meditation.

"So that was it!" he said. "I see! Always heard tell that God moves in a mysterious way His wonders to perform. I'll tell a man He does!"

A scanty breakfast, not without gratitude; a pitiful attempt at redding up the hopeless confusion and disorder. The sick woman's eyes followed McEwen as he worked. A good strangling spell all around, including the old man, then a period of respite. McEwen buckled on his gun and brought a hammer and a lard pail to Florencio's bed.

"If you need me, hammer on this, and I'll come a running. I'm going out to the corral and shoot some beef tea. You tell me about what milk cows to shut up."

Don Florencio described several milk cows. "Any of them. Not all are in to water any one day. Stock generally come in every other day, because they get better grass at a distance. And my brand is TT—for my son Timoteo, who is dead. You will find the cattle in poor shape, but if you wait awhile you may get a smooth one."

McEwen nodded. "I was thinking that," he said. "I want some flour sacks. I'll hang some of the best up under the platform on the windmill tower, where the flies won't bother it."

They heard a shot later. A long time afterward he came in with a good chunk of meat, and set about preparing beef tea. "I shut up a cow to milk," he said. "A lot of saddle horses came in and I shut them up. Not any too much water in the tank. After while the cattle will begin bawling and milling around, if the water's low. That will distress our family. Can't have that. So I'll just harness one on to the sweep of the horse power, slip on a blindfold, and let him pump. You tell me which ones will work."

The old man described several horses.

"That's O.K.," said McEwen. "I've got two of them in the pen. Your woodpile is played out. Had to chop down some of your back pen for firewood."

He departed to start the horse power. Later, when beef tea had been served all around, he came over and sat by Florencio's bed.

"You have no drop or grain of medicine of any kind," he said, "and our milk won't be very good when we get it,

from the looks of the cows—not for sick people. So, everything being just as it is, I didn't look for brands. I beefed the
best one I could find, and hung the hide on the fence. Beef
tea, right this very now, may make all the difference with
our family. Me, I don't believe there's a man in New Mexico
mean enough to make a fuss about it under the circumstances. But if there's any kick, there's the hide and I stand
back of it. So that'll be all right. The brand was DW."

"It is my very good friend, Dave Woods, at San Nicolas.
That will be all right. Don David is *muy simpático.* Sleep
now, my son, sleep a little while you may. It will not be long.
You have a hard night before you."

"I'm going up on the rising ground and set a couple of
soapweeds afire," said McEwen at dark. "They'll make a big
blaze and somebody might take notice. I'll hurry right back.
Then I'll light some more about ten o'clock and do it again
tomorrow night. Someone will be sure to see it. Just once,
they might not think anything. But if they see a light in the
same place three or four times, they might look down their
nose and scratch their old hard head—a smart man might.
Don't you think so?"

"Why, yes," said Florencio, "it's worth trying."

"Those boys are not a bit better than they was. And your
daughter is worse. We don't want to miss a bet. Yes, and I'll
hold a blanket before the fire and take it away and put it
back, over and over. That ought to help people guess that
it is a signal. Only—they may guess that it was meant for
someone else."

"Try it," said Florencio. "It may work. But I am not sure
that our sick people are not holding their own. They are no
better, certainly, even with our beef-tea medicine. But we
can't expect to see a gain, if there is a gain, for days yet. And
so far, they seem worse every night and then better every
morning. The sunlight cheers them up at first, and then the
day gets hot and they seem worse again. Try your signals, by
all means. We need all the help there is. But if you could only

guess how much less alone I feel now than before you came, good friend!"

"It must have been plain hell!" said the good friend.

"Isn't there any other one thing we can do?" demanded McEwen the next day, cudgeling his brains. It had been a terrible night. The little lives fluttered up and down; Estefanía was certainly worse; Florencio, though he had but few strangling spells, was very weak—the aftermath of his earlier labors.

"Not one thing. My poor ghost, no man could have done more. There is no more to do."

"But there is!" McEwen fairly sprang up, wearied as he was. "We have every handicap in the world, and only one advantage. And we don't use that one advantage. The sun has a feud with all the damn germs there is; your house is built for shade in this hot country. I'm going to tote all of you out in the sun with your bedding, and keep you there a spell. And while you're there I'll tear out a hole in the south end of your little old adobe wall and let more sunlight in. After the dust settles enough, I'll bring you back. Then we'll shovel on a little more coal, and study up something else. And tonight we'll light up our signal fires again. Surely someone will be just fool enough to come out and see what the hell it's all about."

Hours later, after this program had been carried out, McEwen roused from a ten-minute sleep and rubbed his fists in his eyes.

"Are you awake, Don Florencio?" he called softly.

"Yes, my son. What is it?"

"It runs in my mind," said McEwen, "that they burn sulphur in diphtheria cases. Now, if I was to take the powder out of my cartridges and wet it down, let it get partly dry and make a smudge with it—a little at a time—There's sulphur in gunpowder. We'll try that little thing." He was already at work with horseshoe pinchers, twisting out the bullet. He looked up eagerly. "Haven't any tar, have you? To stop holes in your water troughs."

"*Hijo,* you shame me. There is a can of piñon pitch, that I use for my troughs, under the second trough at the upper end. I never once thought of that."

"We're getting better every day," said McEwen joyfully. "We'll make a smoke with some of that piñon wax, and we'll steep some of it in boiling water and breathe the steam of it; we'll burn my wet powder, and when that's done, we'll think of something else; and we'll make old bones yet, every damn one of us! By gollies, tomorrow between times I'm goin' to take your little old rifle and shoot some quail."

"Between times? Oh, Happy!"

"Oh, well, you know what I mean—just shovel on a little more coal—better brag than whine. Hi, Estefanía—hear that? We've dug up some medicine. Yes, we have. Ask Don Florencio if we haven't. I'm going after it."

As he limped past the window on his way to the corral he heard the sound of a sob. He paused midstep, thinking it was little Felix. But it was Estefanía.

"Madre de Dios, ayudale su enviado!"

He tiptoed away, shamefaced.

VII

Sleeping on a very thin bed behind a very large boulder, two men camped at the pass of San Agustin; a tall young man and a taller man who was not so young. The very tall man was Pat Garrett, sheriff of Doña Ana, sometime sheriff of other counties. The younger man was Clint Llewellyn, his deputy, and their camp was official in character. They were keeping an eye out for that Belen bandit, after prolonged search elsewhere.

"Not but what he's got away long ago," said Pat, in his quiet, drawling speech, "but just in case he might possibly double back this way."

It was near ten at night when Pat saw the light on the desert. He pointed it out to Clint. "See that fire out there?

Your eyes are younger than mine. Isn't it sinking down and then flaring up again?"

"Looks like it is," said Clint. "I saw a fire there—or two of 'em, rather—just about dark, while you took the horses down to water."

"Did you?" said Pat. He stroked his mustache with a large slow hand. "Looks to me like someone was trying to attract attention."

"It does, at that," said Clint. "Don't suppose somebody's had a horse fall with him and got smashed, do you?"

"Do you know," said Pat slowly, "that idea makes me ache, sort of? One thing pretty clear. Somebody wants someone to do something for somebody. Reckon that's us. Looks like a long ride, and maybe for nothing. Yes. But then we're two long men. Where do you place that fire, Clint?"

"Hard to tell. Close to Luna's Wells, maybe."

"Too far west for that," said Garrett. "I'd say it was Lost Ranch. We'll go ask questions, anyway. If we was layin' out there with our ribs caved in or our leg broke—Let's go!"

That is how they came to Lost Ranch between three and four the next morning. A feeble light shone in the window. Clint took the horses to water, while Garrett went on to the house. He stopped at the outer door. A man lay on a couch within, a man Garrett knew—old Florencio. Folded quilts made a pallet on the floor, and on the quilts lay another man, a man with red hair and a red stubble of beard. Both were asleep. Florencio's hand hung over the couch, and the stranger's hand held to it in a tight straining clasp. Garrett stroked his chin, frowning.

Sudden and startling, a burst of strangled coughing came from the room beyond and a woman's sharp call.

"*Hijo!*" cried Florencio feebly, and pulled the hand he held. "Happy! Wake up!" The stranger lurched to his feet and staggered through the door. "Yes, Felix, I'm coming. All right, boy! All right now! Let me see. It won't hurt. Just a minute, now."

Garrett went into the house.

* * *

"Clint," said Pat Garrett, "there's folks dyin' in there, and a dead man doin' for them. You take both horses and light a rag for the Alamogordo Hospital. Diphtheria. Get a doctor and nurses out here just as quick as God will let them come." Garrett was pulling the saddle from his horse as he spoke. "Have 'em bring grub and everything. Ridin' turn about, you ought to make it tolerable quick. I'm stayin' here, but there's no use of your comin' back. You might take a look around Jarilla if you want to, but use your own judgment. Drag it, now. Every minute counts."

A specter came to the doorway. "Better send a wagon-load of water," it said as Clint turned to go. "This well is maybe poisoned. Germs and such."

"Yes, and bedding, too," said Clint. "I'll get everything and tobacco. So long!"

"Friend," said Pat, "you get yourself to bed. I'm takin' on your job. Your part is to sleep."

"Yes, son," Florencio's thin voice quavered joyously. *"Duerme y descansa.* Sleep and rest. Don Patricio will do everything."

McEwen swayed uncertainly. He looked at Garrett with stupid and heavy eyes. "He called you Patricio. You're not Pat Nunn, by any chance?"

"Why not?" said Garrett.

McEwen's voice was lifeless. "My father used to know you," he said drowsily. He slumped over on his bed.

"Who was your father?" said Garrett.

McEwen's dull and glassy eyes opened to look up at his questioner. "I'm no credit to him," he said. His eyes closed again. "Boil the water!" said McEwen.

"He's asleep already!" said Pat Garrett. "The man's dead on his feet."

"Oh, Pat, there was never one like him!" said Florencio. He struggled to his elbow, and looked down with pride and affection at the sprawling shape on the pallet.

"Don Patricio, I have a son in my old age, like Abrahán!"

"I'll pull off his boots," said Pat Garrett.

Garrett knelt over McEwen and shook him vigorously. "Hey, fellow, wake up! You, Happy—come alive! Snap out of it! Most sundown, and time you undressed and went to bed."

McEwen sat up at last, rubbing his eyes. He looked at the big, kindly face for a little in some puzzlement. Then he nodded.

"I remember you now. You sent your pardner for the doctor. How's the sick folks?"

"I do believe," said Pat, "that we're going to pull 'em through—every one. You sure had a tough lay."

"Yes. Doctor come?"

"He's in sight now—him and the nurses. That's how come me to rouse you up. Feller, I hated to wake you when you was going so good. But with the ladies comin', you want to spruce yourself up a bit. You look like the wrath of God!"

McEwen got painfully to his feet and wriggled his arms experimentally.

"I'm just one big ache," he admitted. "Who's them fellows?" he demanded. Two men were industriously cleaning up the house; two men that he had never seen.

"Them boys? Monte, the Mexican, he's old Florencio's nephew. Heard the news this mawnin', and comes boilin' out here hell-for-leather. Been here for hours. The other young fellow came with him. Eastern lad. Don't know him, or why he came. Say, Mr. Happy, you want to bathe those two eyes of yours with cold water, or hot water, or both. They look like two holes burned in a blanket. Doc will have to give you a good jolt of whiskey, too. Man, you're pretty nigh ruined!"

"I knew there was something," said Mr. Happy. "Got to get me a name. And gosh, I'm tired! I'm a good plausible liar, most times, but I'll have to ask you to help me out. Andy Hightower—how'd that do? Knew a man named Alan Hightower once, over on the Mangas."

"Does he run cattle over there now somewhere about Quemado?"

"Yes," said McEwen.

"I wouldn't advise Hightower," said Garrett.

"My name," said McEwen, "is Henry Clay."

Dr. Lamb, himself the driver of the covered spring wagon, reached Lost Ranch at sundown. He brought with him two nurses, Miss Mason and Miss Hollister, with Lida Hopper, who was to be cook; also, many hampers and much bedding. Dad Lucas was coming behind, the doctor explained, with a heavy wagon, loaded with water and necessaries. Garrett led the way to the sick-room.

Monte helped Garrett unload the wagon and care for the team; Lida Hopper prepared supper in the kitchen.

Mr. Clay had discreetly withdrawn, together with the other man. They were out in the corral now, getting acquainted. The other man, it may be mentioned, was none other than Ben Griggs; and his discretion was such that Miss Hollister knew nothing of his presence until the next morning.

Mr. Clay, still wearied, bedded down under the stars, Monte rustling the credentials for him. When Dad Lucas rolled in, the men made camp by the wagon.

"Well, doctor," said Garrett, "how about the sick? They are going to make it?"

"I think the chances are excellent," said the doctor. "Barring relapse, we should save every one. But it was a narrow squeak. That young man who nursed them through —why, Mr. Garrett, no one on earth could have done better, considering what he had to do with. Nothing, practically, but his two hands."

"You're all wrong there, doc. He had a backbone all the way from his neck to the seat of his pants. That man," said Garrett, "will do to take along."

"Where is he, Mr. Garrett? And what's his name? The old man calls him 'son,' and the boys call him 'Uncle Happy.' What's his right name?"

"Clay," said Garrett, "Henry Clay. He's dead to the world. You won't see much of him. A week of sleep is what he needs. But you remind me of something. If you will let me, I would like to speak to all of you together. Just a second. Would you mind asking the nurses to step in for a minute or two, while I bring the cook?"

"Certainly," said Dr. Lamb.

"I want to ask a favor of all of you," said Garrett, when the doctor had ushered in the nurses. "I won't keep you. I just want to declare myself. Some of you know me, and some don't. My name is Pat Garrett, and I am sheriff of Doña Ana County, over west. But for reasons that are entirely satisfactory to myself, I would like to be known as Pat Nunn, for the present. That's all. I thank you."

"Of course," said Dr. Lamb, "if it is to serve the purpose of the law—"

"I would not go so far," said Garrett. "If you put it that my purpose is served, you will be quite within the truth. Besides, this is not official. I am not sheriff here. This ranch is just cleverly over the line and in Otero County. Old Florencio pays taxes in Otero. I am asking this as a personal favor, and only for a few days. Perfectly simple. That's all. Thank you."

"Did you ask the men outside?"

"No. I just told them," said Mr. Pat Nunn. "It would be dishonorable for a lady to tip my hand; for a man it would be plumb indiscreet."

"Dad Lucas," said the doctor, "is a cynical old scoundrel, and a man without principle, and swivel-tongued besides."

"He is all that you say, and a lot more that you would never guess," said Garrett. "But if I claimed to be Humpty Dumpty, Dad Lucas would swear that he saw me fall off of the wall." He held up his two index fingers, side by side. "Dad and me, we're like that. We've seen trouble together —and there is no bond so close. Again, one and all, I thank you. Meetin's adjourned."

* * *

Lost Ranch was a busy scene on the following day. A cheerful scene, too, despite the blazing sun, the parched desert, and the scarred old house. Reports from the sickroom were hopeful. The men had spread a tarpaulin by the wagon, electing Dad Lucas for cook. They had salvaged a razor of Florencio's and were now doing mightily with it. Monte and Ben Griggs, after dinner, were to take Dad's team and Florencio's wagon to draw up a jag of mesquite roots; in the meantime Monte dragged up stop-gap firewood by the saddle horn, and Ben kept the horse power running in the water pen. Keeping him company, Pat Garrett washed Henry Clay's clothes. More accurately, it was Pat Nunn who did this needed work with grave and conscientious thoroughness.

"Henry Clay and me, after bein' in the house so long," said Mr. Nunn, "why, we'll have to boil up our clothes before we leave, or we might go scattering diphtheria hither and yonder and elsewhere."

"But how if you take it yourselves?"

"Then we'll either die or get well," said Mr. Nunn slowly. "In either case, things will keep juneing along just the same. Henry Clay ain't going to take it, or he'd have it now. It takes three days after you're exposed. Something like that. We'll stick around a little before we go, just in case."

"Which way are you going, Mr. Nunn?" asked Ben.

"Well, I'm going to Tularosa. Old Florencio will have to loan me a horse. Clay too. He's afoot. Don't know where he's going. Haven't asked him. He's too worn out to talk much. His horse played out on him out on the flat somewheres and he had to hang up his saddle and walk in. So Florencio told me. He's goin' back and get his saddle tomorrow."

Miss Mason being on duty, Jay Hollister, having picked up a bite of breakfast, was minded to get a breath of fresh air; and at this juncture she tripped into the water pen where Mr. Nunn and Ben plied their labors.

"And how is the workingman's bride this morning?" asked Ben brightly.

"Great Caesar's ghost! Ben Griggs, what in the world are you doing here?" demanded Jay with a heightened color.

"Workin'," said Ben, and fingered his blue overalls proudly. "Told you I was goin' to work. Right here is where I'm needed. Why, there are only four of us, not counting you three girls and the doctor, to do what this man Clay was doing. You should have seen Monte and me cleaning house yesterday."

"Yes?" Jay smiled sweetly. "What house was that?"

"Woman!" said Ben, touched in his workman's pride. "If you feel that way now, you should have seen this house when we got here."

"You're part fool. You'll catch diphtheria."

"Well, what about you? The diphtheria part, I mean. What's the matter with your gettin' diphtheria?"

"That's different. That's a trade risk. That's my business."

"You're my business," said Ben.

Jay shot a startled glance at Mr. Nunn, and shook her head.

"Oh, yes!" said Ben. "Young woman, have you met Mr. Nunn?"

Soap in hand, Mr. Nunn looked up from his task. "Good morning, miss. Don't mind me," he said. "Go right on with the butchery."

"Good morning, Mr. Nunn. Please excuse us. I was startled at finding this poor simpleton out here where he has no business to be. Have I met Mr. Nunn? Oh, yes, I've met him twice. The doctor introduced him once, and he introduced himself once."

Mr. Nunn acknowledged this gibe with twinkling eye. Miss Hollister looked around her, and shivered in the sun. "What a ghastly place!" she cried. "I can't for the life of me understand why anybody should live here. We came through some horrible country yesterday, but this is the worst yet. Honestly, Mr. Nunn, isn't this absolutely the most God-forsaken spot on earth?"

Mr. Nunn abandoned his work for the moment and stood up, smiling. So this was Pat Garrett of whom she had heard so much; the man who killed Billy the Kid. Well, he had a way with him. Jay could not but admire the big square head, the broad spread of his shoulders, and a certain untroubled serenity in his quiet face.

"Oh, I don't know," said Mr. Nunn. "Look there!"

"Where? I don't see anything," said Jay. "Look at what?"

"Why, the bees," said Pat. "The wild bees. They make honey here. Little family of 'em in every *sotol* stalk; and that old house up there with the end broken in—No, Miss Hollister, I've seen worse places than this."

VIII

The patients were improving. Old Florencio, who had been but lightly touched, mended apace. He had suffered from exhaustion and distress quite as much as from disease itself. Demetrio and little Felix gained more slowly, and Estefanía was weakest of all. The last was contrary to expectation. As a usual thing, diphtheria goes hardest with the young. But all were in a fair way to recover. Dr. Lamb and Dad Lucas had gone back to town. Dad had returned with certain comforts and luxuries for the convalescents.

Jay Hollister, on the morning watch, was slightly annoyed. Mr. Pat Garrett and the man Clay were leaving, it seemed, and nothing would do but that Clay must come to the sick-room for leave-taking. Quite naturally, Jay had not wished her charges disturbed. Peace and quiet were what they needed. But Garrett had been insistent, and he had a way with him. Oh, well! The farewell was quiet enough and brief enough on Clay's part, goodness knows, but rather fervent from old Florencio and his daughter-in-law. That was the Spanish of it, Jay supposed. Anyhow, that was all over and the disturbers were on their way to Tularosa.

Relieved by Miss Mason, Jay went in search of Ben

Griggs to impart her grievance, conscious that she would get no sympathy there, and queerly unresentful of that lack. He was not to be seen. She went to the kitchen.

"Where's that trifling Ben, Lida?"

"Him? I'm sure I don't know, Miss Jay. That Mexican went up on top of the house just now. He'll know, likely."

Jay climbed the rickety ladder, stepped on the adobe parapet and so down to the flat roof. Monte sat on the farther wall looking out across the plain so intently that he did not hear her coming.

"Do you know where Ben is?" said Jay.

Monte came to his feet. "Oh, yais! He is weeth the Señor Lucas to haul wood, Mees Hollister. Is there what I can do?"

"What are we going to do about water?" said Jay. "There's only one barrel left. Of course, we can boil the well water, but it's horrible stuff."

"*Prontamente*—queeckly. All set. Ben weel be soon back, and here we go, Ben and me, to the spreeng of San Nicolás." He pointed to a granite peak of the San Andrés. "There at thees peenk hill yonder."

"What, from way over there?"

"Eet ees closest, an ver' sweet water, ver' good."

Jay looked and wondered, tried to estimate the void that lay between, and could not even guess. "What a dreadful country! How far is it?"

"Oh, twent-ee miles. *Es nada.* We feel up by sundown and come back in the cool stars."

"Oh, do sit down," said Jay, "and put on your hat. You're so polite you make me nervous. I shouldn't think you'd care much about the cool," said Jay, "the way you sit up here, for pleasure, in the broiling sun."

"Plezzer? Oh, no!" said Monte. "Look!" He turned and pointed. "No, not here, not close by. Mebbe four, three miles. Look across thees bare spot an' thees streep of mesquite to thees long chalk reedge; and now, beyond thees row and bunches of yuccas. You see them now?"

Jay followed his hand and saw, small and remote, two

horsemen creeping black and small against the infinite recession of desert. She nodded.

"Eet ees with no joy," said Monte, "that I am to see the las' of *un caballero valiente*—how do you say heem?—of a gallan' gentlemen—thees redhead."

"You are not very complimentary to Mr. Garrett," said Jay.

"Oh, no, no, no—you do not understand!" Monte's eyes narrowed with both pity and puzzlement. He groped visibly for words. "*Seguramente, siempre,* een all ways Pat Garrett ees a man complete. Eet is known. But thees young fellow —he ees play out the streeng—*pobrecito!* Oh, Mees Jay, eet ees a bad spread! Es-scusame, please, Mees Hollister. I have not the good words—onlee the man talk."

"Oh, he did well enough—but why not?" said Jay. "What else could he do? There has been something all the time that I don't understand. Danger from diphtheria? Nonsense. I am not a bit partial to you people out here. Perhaps you know that. But I must admit that danger doesn't turn you from anything you have set your silly heads to do. Of course Mr. Clay had to work uncommonly hard, all alone here. But he had no choice. No; it's something else, something you have kept hidden from me all along. Why all the conspiracy and the pussyfoot mystery?"

"Eet was not jus' lak that, mees. Not *conjuración* exactlee. But everee man feel for heemself eet ees ver' good to mek no talk of thees theeng." For once Monte's hands were still. He looked off silently at the great bare plain and the little horsemen dwindling in the distance. "I weel tell you, then," he said at last. "Thees *cosa* are bes' not spoken, and yet eet ees right for you shall know. Onlee I have not those right words. Ben, he shall tell you when he come."

Again he held silence for a little space, considering. "Eet ees lak thees, Mees Jay. Ver' long ago—yais, before not any of your people is cross over the Atlantic Ocean—my people they are here een thees country and they go up and down to all places—yais, to *las playas del mar,* to the shores of the sea by California. And when they go by Zuñi and by thees rock El Morro, wheech your people call—I have forget that name. You have heard heem?"

"Yes," said Jay. "Inscription Rock. I've read about it."

"*Si, si!* That ees the name. Well, eet ees good camp ground, El Morro, wood and water, and thees gr-reat cleef for shade and for shelter een estr-rong winds. And here some fellow he come and he cry out, *"Adiós, el mundo!* What lar-rge weelderness ees thees! And me, I go now eento thees beeg lonesome, and perhaps I shall not to r-return! *Bueno, pues,* I mek now for me a gravestone!" and so he mek on that beeg rock weeth hees dagger, *"Pasó por aquí, Don Fulano de Tal"*—passed by here, Meester So-and-So—weeth the year of eet.

"And after heem come others to El Morro—so few, so far from Spain. They see what he ees write there, and they say, *'Con razón!'*—eet ees weeth reason to do thees. An' they also mek eenscreepción, *'Pasó por aquí'*—and their names, and the year of eet."

His hand carved slow letters in the air. His eye was proud.

"I would not push my leetleness upon thees so lar-rge world, but one of thees, Mees Hollister—oh, not of the great, not of the first—he was of mine, my ver' great, great papa. So long ago! And he mek also, *'Pasó por aquí,* Salvador Holguin.' I hear thees een the firelight when I am small fellow. And when I am man-high I mek veesit to thees place and see heem."

His eye followed the far horsemen, now barely to be seen, a faint moving blur along the north.

"And thees fellow, too, thees redhead, he pass this way, *Pasó por aquí'* "—again the brown hand wrote in the air— "and he mek here good and not weeked. But, before that— I am not God!" Lips, shoulders, hands, every line of his face disclaimed that responsibility. "But he is thief, I theenk," said Monte. "Yais, he ees thees one—Mack-Yune?—who rob the bank of Numa Frenger las' week at Belen. I theenk so."

Jay's eyes grew round with horror, her hand went to her throat. "Not arrested?"

For once Monte's serene composure was shaken. His eyes narrowed, his words came headlong.

"Oh, no-no-no! You do not unnerstan'. Ees eemposevilly, what you say! Pat Garrett ees know nozzing, he ees fir-rum r-resolve to know nozzing. An' thees Mack-Yune, he ees theenk *por verdad* eet ees Pat Nunn who ride weeth heem to Tularosa. He guess not one theeng that eet ees the sheriff. Pat Garrett he go that none may deesturb or moless' heem. Becows, thees young fellow ees tek eshame for thees bad life, an' he say to heemself, 'I weel arize and go to my papa.'"

She began to understand. She looked out across the desert and the thorn, the white chalk and the sand. Sun dazzle was in her eyes. These people! Peasant, gambler, killer, thief—She felt the pulse pound in her throat.

"And een Tularosa, all old-timers, everee man he know Pat Garrett. Not lak thees Alamogordo, new peoples. And when thees old ones een Tularosa see Meester Pat Garrett mek good-bye weeth hees friend at the tr-rain, they will theenk nozzing, say nozzing. *Adiós!*"

He sat sidewise upon the crumbling parapet and waved his hand to the nothingness where the two horsemen had been swallowed up at last.

"And him the sheriff!" said Jay. "Why, they could impeach him for that. They could throw him out of office."

He looked up smiling, "But who weel tell?" said Monte. His outspread hands were triumphant. "We are all decent people."